HUNTER KILLER

HUNTER KILLER

THE WAR WITH CHINA—
THE BATTLE FOR
THE CENTRAL PACIFIC

DAVID POYER

ST. MARTIN'S PRESS
New York

HUNTER KILLER. Copyright © 2017 by David Poyer. All rights reserved. Printed in the United States of America. For information, address St. Martin's Press, 175 Fifth Avenue, New York, N.Y. 10010.

www.stmartins.com

The Library of Congress Cataloging-in-Publication Data is available upon request.

ISBN 978-1-250-09795-8 (hardcover)
ISBN 978-1-250-09796-5 (ebook)

Our books may be purchased in bulk for promotional, educational, or business use. Please contact your local bookseller or the Macmillan Corporate and Premium Sales Department at 1-800-221-7945, extension 5442, or by email at MacmillanSpecialMarkets@macmillan.com.

First Edition: November 2017

10 9 8 7 6 5 4 3 2 1

(Here is a mountain range at last, old man, across
your easy path;

No mole-hills, these!—bare cliffs, sharp ledges,
frowning chasms, overhanging steeps;

No valley, no way through—only the pass, high up
and far.

Now gird your loins—face ancient facts—take stock
of what is in you;

You are brave enough—you do not hesitate;

No fear!—you will scale a higher mountain than
 you climb—you will surmount yourself;

You will be glad and amazed to find your old true
self returning to you.)

—LINCOLN COLCORD, *VISION OF WAR*

I

WAR

1

Joint Base Pearl Harbor–Hickam, Hawaii

HIS ride showed up at the Navy Lodge that morning, as promised. "Captain Lenson?" The driver peered up, bulky in flak vest, sidearm, and helmet. He had a black carbine bracketed by the Humvee's wheel. "Needed a lift, up to Camp Smith?"

"That's me."

"Don this vest, sir."

Dan started to protest—they were only going from one base area to another, and the temperature was already in the low nineties—but pulled the Kevlar over his khakis. Then wriggled in, jamming his briefcase by his feet and settling his combination cap in his lap. The motor roared and he settled back, trying to get comfortable in a seat obviously designed for someone much shorter.

Hastily erected barbed-wire-and-concrete barriers, as well as bright orange plastic road barriers—confiscated, no doubt, from the Hawaii roads department—walled off the base area. Dan shaded his eyes as the morning sun flashed off the Southeast Loch. Off Ford Island, the *Arizona* Memorial bridged white against the glowing water. Beyond loomed the gray bulk of USS *Missouri*. A war had ended on her decks, with the surrender of an empire.

Now a new war had come, and with it new horrors.

The driver muttered, "What they got you doing in this fucked-up war, Captain?"

"Uh, saw some action off Taiwan . . . but right now, I'm sort of up in the air."

The marine's glance snagged. He squinted at the road, then back at Dan's chest. "Is that the . . . ? Sir?"

The blue-and-white ribbon often got that reaction. "Yeah."

"The Congressional? Sir?"

"Correct."

"Jeez. I mean . . . now I know who you are. Um, what I said, about the war being fucked up, I meant . . ."

He trailed off, and Dan didn't ask him to elaborate. Because he was exactly right.

They skirted the pier area, tires humming. Deserted, except for one littoral combat ship and the gray upperworks of a Burke-class: USS *Mitscher*, at the naval shipyard. The destroyer had absorbed three missiles in the Taiwan Strait action. He should stop in and see her CO. . . . Two weeks of medical leave had caught him up on sleep, restoring him somewhat from the *Savo* crud, and he'd gotten his neck and shoulder looked at. He'd written an after-action report, and put his people in for decorations. But he still had outstanding issues. Such as the investigation into his actions aboard USS *Savo Island*, the Ticonderoga-class cruiser he'd commanded.

Dan twisted a heavy gold Annapolis ring. He was on his way in to meet with Barry "Nick" Niles. Once Dan's patron, then nemesis, then reluctant rabbi again, Niles had just taken over as chief of naval operations. Now, apparently, he'd come out to consult with the theater commander about the direction of the war.

The driver halted at a barriered gate. Diesels snorted. A crane-arm rotated in slow jerks, dangling another concrete barrier into place. Armed sentries examined their IDs, then waved them through, returning their scrutiny to the road in.

Dan cleared his throat. "What's the Corps take? We expect Hawaii to be attacked?"

"Happened before," the sergeant observed laconically.

Dan raised his eyebrows, but couldn't think of a comeback.

The war had begun with a nuclear exchange between Pakistan and India. China's attack on India, to support its ally, had broadened the conflict. The U.S. and India had imposed a blockade. Escalating in turn, the People's Republic had knocked out American communications and reconnaissance satellites.

When the Allies countered, Premier Zhang Zurong had upped the ante again. He'd suppressed Taiwanese defenses with ballistic missiles and air attacks, then launched a cross-strait invasion. And when USS *Franklin D. Roosevelt* had sailed to assist the Taiwanese, he'd done the unthinkable. Destroyed the entire battle group with a nuclear-tipped missile . . . killing almost ten thousand U.S. servicemen and -women.

Meanwhile, war had resumed between South and North Korea, and U.S. bases in Okinawa had been taken down with missile strikes, then seaborne invasion.

Now battles raged in India and Vietnam, on Taiwan and Okinawa. And so far, the Chinese seemed to be winning them all.

The driver murmured, "Said you saw action, Captain?"

"At sea."

"Fighting the slants, right?"

Dan hadn't heard this term before, but it was easy to guess what it meant. The marine said, "So, they tough, or what? We gonna come back out there, right?"

"They're definitely tough," Dan said. "We're going to have to put our shoulders to the wheel to win this one."

They left the expressway for a winding two-laner, climbing through a residential area. Many of the homes were boarded up, as if for a typhoon. The driver noticed him noticing. "A lot of the folks up here packed up and left town. Went back to the mainland."

A wooded hill rose. They passed a football field, a baseball field, parking, a pool. At another sentry post, a machine gun overwatched sandbagged barriers. Dan's ID got a more thorough inspection here, and his briefcase was searched. Sweat trickled under his Kevlar.

Finally they were waved through this one too. The engine labored as the Humvee climbed. At last it coasted to a halt beneath nodding nipa palms, between two huge new buildings. "In that side door, not the front," his escort advised as they got out. So the guy was there to take him in personally. "You can leave the ballistic protection in the vehicle, sir," he added.

Building 700, the Nimitz-MacArthur Pacific Command Center, overlooked the harbor and the shipyard. To the north rose ridges of hills, the nearest crowned with homes, the farthest still green with palms and tropical hardwoods, laced with pearlescent mist. To the east rolled more forest, more hills. To the west, the city. The palm fronds clashed in a sudden breeze, like the rattle of swordplay. He stood for a moment looking down toward the sea, letting the wind dry his sweat. Then followed his escort into a concrete entranceway.

HE'D figured to meet Niles in some office, but his escort led him down a back corridor to an unmarked steel door. After another ID check, the driver racked his rifle in a wall mount, getting a metal tag like a coat check in exchange.

The four-person elevator started slow. Dan looked for a control panel, but there wasn't any. Then it dropped *very* fast. He grabbed his nose and cleared his ears. He grunted, "How far down are we . . . ?" Then comprehension arrived.

The Sanctum.

The Bunker.

The Navy had determined never to be taken by surprise again.

He stepped out into an icy-cold, compact, hospital-stark, LED-lit passageway.

The marine led the way. Obviously he'd been here before. Dan nodded to Army personnel—they tended to sulk if ignored in passageways—but didn't to Navy or Air Force unless they greeted him first. Which most, looking harried or intent on their own tasks, didn't. Meeting rooms, situation rooms, intelligence spaces, opened off the central passageway. They turned one corner, then another. Dan's nape prickled as he recognized the right-angle designs, the slanted-away walls at the corners. It looked like feng shui, but it was to limit blast damage, in case a bunker-penetrator made it this deep.

Admiral Barry "Nick" Niles stood before a large-screen display, his back to the door. With his arms crossed, his shoulders looked even broader than they were. The screen glowed with the Pacific Command logo, an eagle with wings spread over a globe oriented to display the Western Ocean. Niles seemed to be studying the Chinese coast. It was the first time Dan had ever seen him in a civilian suit. It didn't make the new CNO look any smaller.

"Admiral? Captain Lenson's here." The marine eased the heavy door shut behind himself. So the guy wasn't just any old pool driver. He must be one of the CNO's aides.

"'We'll be back,'" Niles said to the screen, not turning.

He was quoting what Dan had told a pool reporter after *Savo Island* had limped home damaged from the battle in the strait. "They're making you into a hero. CNN, Fox, they showcased your attack. Bankey Talmadge quoted you on the Senate floor."

"I'm no hero, Admiral."

"Hey, I'm not objecting. Right now, we can use some positive news. They've kicked us back to Guam. The Marianas. Hawaii. Still believe it? That we can win this thing?"

Dan tried to fight his Academy reflexes, in terms of coming to attention, but didn't do all that well. "Yes, sir. If we can scrape our shit together."

Still speaking to the screen, like the Dark Queen to her magic mirror, Niles rumbled, "There are those who don't. Who think we're finished, as a country."

Dan coughed into a fist. "The Germans thought that about us, twice. The Japanese. And the Russians. Zhang's just the latest to make that mistake."

Silence, as if his answer were being weighed. Then Niles said reluctantly. "I hope you're right. How's your ship?"

"*Savo*'s getting a new bow. Also, the ALIS software upgrade. Sonar's degraded—"

"Rearm?"

"A hard point. We get excuses, but no rounds. There's adequate gun ammo, but very few missile reloads."

"I'm working that. Who did you leave in charge?"

"My exec. Cheryl Staurulakis."

"She good?"

"Good as they come."

"Combat proven?"

"Yes, sir. I put her in for the Bronze Star. And maybe we could discuss the other decorations I put in for, for my people—"

"Later, okay? Maybe we'll leave her there. How's the wife . . . Blair? Did she win her election?"

"Not sure yet, sir."

"Not *sure*? What's that mean?"

"They're in a recount, sir. Less than two hundred votes difference."

"Well, if she loses, could be for the best." Niles turned away from the screen, and Dan blinked with shock at a ravaged visage. Reddened, swollen lids above sleepless eyes. Vein-shot, puffy cheeks.

Maybe we'll leave her there . . . could be for the best. He contemplated both equivocal statements as Niles lumbered to a side table, bent over a notebook, and began typing, the huge fingers darting with incongruous delicacy.

Equivocation wasn't Niles's style. But Dan Lenson wouldn't be here if the new CNO didn't have something in mind. Most likely, something he wouldn't like.

Niles cleared his throat. "I've been getting unpleasant questions about you from a certain European country. And from Congress."

Congress . . . he knew who was behind that. "Yes, sir. May I address any of them?"

"Yeah, you *may*. First, about your hasty retreat after a Chinese sub sank your tanker in the East China Sea."

"True, sir. I left the torpedo danger area after GNS *Stuttgart* was attacked. You can tell Berlin we were the only ballistic-missile-defense-capable unit left in theater. I withdrew to protect that asset. I left USS *Mitscher* to prosecute the datum and rescue survivors."

"I see. What about your unauthorized attack on the invasion force as it crossed the Taiwan Strait?"

Dan took a deeper breath. "I kept Fleet and PaCom informed as the situation developed, to the extent compromised communications permitted. I requested guidance, but received none. I judged that if we degraded the invasion fleet, it might be enough to let the ROC kick the mainlanders off the beach. As it turned out, we sank most of their heavy armor."

"Actually, we think now one of our subs got those transports. But it's murky." Niles shrugged. "Let's say half credit. Finally, about your killing a Joint Missile Program scientist."

"Dr. Noblos was NCIS's prime suspect in a series of sexual assaults, rape, and attempted murder aboard *Savo Island*. He stole a pistol and hijacked a boat. He was headed for Chinese-held territory. He knew everything about our missile defenses. My choices were to let him go, or blow him out of the water."

"And as usual, you took the extreme solution."

Dan clenched his fists. "With all due respect, sir, that's uncalled for."

Niles sagged into a chair like a collapsing warehouse. He blinked at the bulkhead. "Maybe so . . . I also know about your yanking Min Jun Jung back by the scruff of the neck when he was trying to pull off a new Charge of the Light Brigade. You probably saved us the Korean Fleet there."

A tap on the door. "Yeah," Niles barked. A commander stuck her head in, looking apprehensive. She tilted her wrist to display a watch. "Coming," Niles rasped. To Dan, "I'm still making my mind up about you." He got up like a Wellsian Martian heaving himself out of the pit. "Meanwhile, why don't you tag along to this. You're the only one here who's actually fought these people. Maybe you can contribute something useful for a change."

THIS room was larger than the one he'd met Niles in. The briefer had a familiar tanned, too-handsome face. Jack Byrne, now in a gray suit and tie instead of the trop khaki or blues of a Naval Intelligence captain. They exchanged lifted eyebrows, but there was no time for more. Too many stars were settling into the front row, looking tense, impatient. Looking angry.

Byrne opened. "Admiral, Generals, CNO: a quick overview, leading to discussion of a limited set of immediate options," he said into a sudden eerie quiet. "Most of you know this, but we have to start from the same page. Our security position in the Pacific lies in ruins. Our job is to stabilize the situation.

"Premier Zhang Zurong has threatened the continental U.S. with a secretly amassed arsenal of over a thousand nuclear warheads. His position: Beijing is now a superpower. Washington must acknowledge that by withdrawing from the Asian Rim. There are reports of food shortages in mainland China, but also of savage repression. In Hong Kong a hundred thousand people have been imprisoned or deported to the interior, and many shot in the streets. On land, massive armies are invading Vietnam, India, Mongolia, and north Burma. All, quote, to 'restore China's historic borders.'"

A four-star admiral leaned to confer with Niles. Dan recognized the twisted, almost deformed face of Justin "Jim" Yangerhans, the commander in chief, Pacific. The viceroy for half the globe. In charge, now, of fighting the most populous country, and the largest economy, on earth.

Which was whipping the United States soundly on every front.

Byrnes said, "Zhang's consolidating his hold on western Taiwan. Six divisions there now, nearly half a million troops total. He's imprisoned thousands in makeshift camps. This morning mainland troops blew up Chiang Kai-shek's tomb. But some loyal forces are still holding out in the mountains."

"For how long?" an Army general whispered.

Byrne continued. "The Philippines has neutralized itself, acknowledging Chinese hegemony and renouncing all claims in the China Sea. Japan's called its navy home, and is mulling the proffered cease-fire. India, Vietnam, Australia, and South Korea are still aligned with us. Indonesia may be coming in. They can add little in the way of forces, but—location, location, location. Canada and Britain are cheering us, but from the sidelines.

"We're still fighting. The Koreans and the U.S. Second Division are holding, but isolated and reduced to in-place logistics." Byrne looked at Dan. "The South Korean Navy, led by Admiral Min Jun Jung, retreated shoulder to shoulder with the United States Navy, after a daring raid into the strait led by Captain Daniel V. Lenson. Who is with us here today." Men and women craned to look in Dan's direction. "They plan to fight on alongside us, and someday soon, return."

Byrne lifted a finger, and a wall screen lit. A heavyset Asian in a military uniform and black plastic-rimmed glasses stared out at them. "Captain Lenson, I believe you know this man."

Dan stared into Zhang Zurong's expressionless, chilling gaze. The sensation was like pressing his eyeballs against cold, polished steel.

He'd met the smooth-faced, pudgy Zhang decades before, in a Chinatown restaurant, at what had seemed at the time like a family party. But "Uncle Xinhu" had turned out to be a senior colonel in the Second Department, China's equivalent of Defense Intelligence. Dan had turned over fake Tomahawk schematics in Operation Snapdragon. But by the time the FBI had showed up on Zhang's doorstep, he'd decamped for his homeland. Leaving a dead girl on a towpath in Georgetown . . . an innocent, idealistic woman Dan had loved.

He dragged himself back to the present as Byrne said, "Zhang's executed his rivals and consolidated his position as both Party general secretary and state president. He now holds all leading titles in the state.

"On the diplomatic front, he proposes peace on the basis of 'union and demilitarization' of the two Chinas and the two Koreas. He offers to return Okinawa to Japan. But in exchange, all remaining U.S. bases in Japanese territory must be vacated, and alliance ties dissolved.

"He also warns that anyone who offers America basing rights is the enemy of what he calls the 'Associated' or 'United' Powers—China, Iran, North Korea, Pakistan, Laos, and 'Miandan,' their puppet state in northern Myanmar.

"Finally, Russia has announced major aircraft and ordnance sales to China." Byrne paused. "Any questions?"

One of the generals lifted a hand. "Energy supplies?"

Byrne flicked slides and briefed on stockpiles, consumption, and imports. "Seaborne imports are essentially zero, but roughly two hundred thousand tons a day of oil and liquefied natural gas are flowing in via a pipeline across Xinjiang from Pakistan."

"Can we cut that?"

Yangerhans twisted in his chair to say over one shoulder, "It's deep in Chinese territory, and well protected . . . but it's a possible target."

Dan felt reluctant to speak up, but finally did. "We have weak points too. Iran's threatened to close Hormuz before. If they do—?"

Byrne said, "CentCom has plans against that contingency. If they try to close the strait again, we land an armored regiment to occupy Qeshm Island, on the eastern side of Hormuz, and cut off all Iranian exports by sea. We'll see how they like that." He waited a moment, then stepped back.

Yangerhans pulled his feet in, got up, and paced back and forth. He tucked his elbows like a boxer. "One thing Jack didn't brief is the domestic reaction. They're still suffering from power and network outages back home. The financial markets have reopened, but most folks have lost half or more of their net worth. And Zhang's threats are having an effect, especially on the West Coast. The civil defense program's been reactivated. People are stockpiling. Defense industries are reporting difficulties keeping labor forces in place. We're taking steps to fix that, but they'll take time.

"That and the focused cyberattacks on defense industries mean production is not going well. Missiles and torpedoes, especially, are in short supply. I've called the Canadians, Australians, British. They've promised to ramp up production, but their capacities have always been limited compared to ours."

A lifted hand. "The Europeans?"

A grim look. A negative headshake. "They've got their own problems, with the Russians."

Another hand; an Air Force uniform. "Admiral, the *Franklin Roosevelt* battle group was wiped out with a nuclear missile. Can you enlighten us on the rationale for not retaliating in kind?"

Yangerhans paced again, fingers twining behind his back. "I won't go into my exchanges with national command authority on that issue. Suffice it to say they were . . . frank. The bottom line, I guess, is that as long as we don't respond, we hold the escalatory advantage. Zhang won't know where, or how hard, we'll counterpunch. Only that we owe him one."

"He won't see it as a sign of weakness? That we took ten thousand casualties, lost six ships? And didn't hit back?"

Dan twisted in his seat, but didn't see who'd asked that. Yangerhans grimaced. "Like I said, that's above even the theater commander's pay grade. A lot of people don't believe retaking the western Pacific is worth risking Los Angeles. The pundits thought the elections would give us a clear signal. They didn't. If we want leadership, we're not going to see it from Washington."

The four-star turned brisk. "All right . . . outlining my intent." Instead of a new slide, the display went to bluescreen. Yangerhans gazed off above his audience's heads. "We're digging in on the line Honshu-Saipan-Guam, the second island chain. We've bought, or been granted, a breathing space while Zhang, and his naval staff chief, Admiral Lianfeng, consolidate their gains. Taiwan, Korea, Okinawa, Vietnam—those battles will determine whether this so-called People's Empire pulses outward again." Yangerhans eyed Dan. "One of our officers has said, 'We'll be back.' But to do that, we have to keep our logistics open, and concentrate on building up our warfighting capability.

"We face a lot of negatives. Ordnance is short. We have high ship and airframe losses. The enemy's on a roll. But we can't simply hold. If we do, that solidifies into the new status quo. Somehow, we have to push back. Even if we come a cropper, it keeps the Allies in the fight."

Nods from the audience, but also doubtful looks.

Yangerhans nodded, and the next screen showed the South China Sea. "We already have a left hook started. On hold at the moment, but it can resume once we beef up our shipping numbers, and reassure the Australians and Indonesians they can release some of their covering forces. Next, please."

A kidney-shaped island. "Let's look more closely at Taiwan. An idea a think tank in DC's pitching. How solid is the mainland's grip? Granted, they hold the west coast, the plain, and the northern metropolis—Taipei, and its industrial and residential suburbs. But that's not the whole island. And everything they fight with has to come across the strait.

"Like every struggle in the Pacific, this will be conducted across vast distances, dependent on access, production, reinforcement rates, and logistics pipelines. The good news is, we can make life hell for the enemy too. We're redeploying from Europe and the Atlantic. As our sub numbers in the strait and the south ramp up, we'll be able to reduce his shipping, start starving his deployed forces.

"Meanwhile, significant elements of the Republic of China Army have fallen back into Taiwan's eastern mountains. The Chingyan Shan is unpopulated, ravined, forested. In other words, ideal for a guerrilla campaign. We've established contact with Luong Shucheng, deputy chief of the general staff. As far as we can tell, he's the senior general still at large. If we can supply him with weapons, ammunition, and food, we can keep Zhang fighting, while we bleed him at the end of his supply lines.

"It might be possible to strand half a million troops on Taiwan. Cut them off, and force them to surrender. An island Stalingrad. If our other allies hold, that may give us a chance at war termination on reasonable terms."

The group seemed to take a collective inhale. Yangerhans paused as if gauging the reaction, twisted face screwed up as if in pain. "We'll see if the enemy cooperates . . . and whether Washington supports us. Any further questions? . . . That'll be all for now, then."

They got to their feet, not with the alacrity of a group of junior officers, but PaCom didn't wait. Just waited for Niles to lumber up, and gestured him aside.

The meeting broke in an undertone of murmurs. Dan glanced at Niles, but the four-stars had their heads together. He strolled over to Byrne. "Jack. What're you doing here? I thought you retired."

"Civilian policy adviser. Triple the salary."

"Nice. How's Rosemary? The kids?"

Byrne lowered his voice. "Got 'em out to the country. Blair, I guess she's—where? Still parked square on the bull's-eye?"

"Uh, still in DC, if that's what you mean."

"Your daughter?"

"Seattle. A good job, microbiology."

"Good Lord. *Seattle?* Get her out of there. Or at least, ready to evacuate."

"Lenson? *Lenson?*" Niles's rumble, over the mutter of side conversations.

"His master's voice," Byrne cracked.

Dan bit back an angry response. Turning away, he located the CNO in the far corner, by a GCCS terminal. Niles and Yangerhans were contemplating a ground terrain display. The northern border of Vietnam. Yangerhans shook Dan's hand, grip bony and dry. "Nick here says you're a fighter."

"We've had our differences," Niles put in. "And right now, he's suspended from command pending an investigation. But I kept him in my back pocket, just in case."

"We need bruisers." PaCom nodded curtly. "That was a good question about Hormuz, by the way. You're thinking ahead. Any amphib experience?"

"A PHIBRON staff, in the Med. During the Syrian crisis," Dan said.

Yangerhans half smiled. Close up he looked even uglier. "And you led the attack in the Taiwan Strait?"

"That was him," Niles said.

"I've been looking for a street fighter. Somebody with balls and brains, both. You can stonewall these investigations, right, Nick?"

"Lenson's your guy," Niles rumbled. "Only problem will be keepin' him on the leash."

"If you vouch for him, Fireball, that's good enough for me," Yangerhans said equably.

With surprising grace for such a huge man, the CNO executed a wheeling movement, opening the distance between him and Yangerhans. A beefy hand plumbed a pocket. Fat fingers tore open a plastic packet. "Sorry Blair couldn't be here for this," Niles grunted.

Dan stood bewildered as the two admirals manipulated his lapels, as a camera flashed. Applause battered his ears. He looked down at his palm. His old captain's eagles glittered there.

"It's not a permanent commission." Yangerhans leaned in, still holding the handshake as he grimaced into another camera-flash. "Only Congress can give you that. Which, as I understand it, isn't going to happen in your case. This is just a fleet-up, understand? A temporary wartime rank."

Dan touched his new insignia. The hard outline of a five-pointed star. "Um, yessir. I get that. But still. Thank you."

"Don't thank me. You haven't heard the job description yet."

"You'll love this, Lenson," Niles said. "Right up your alley."

Yangerhans said, "I mentioned a pushback. I want you to lead it."

Dan nodded cautiously.

"It'll be like sticking your face in a blast furnace. But we can't sit on our thumbs. Nick and I envisioned TF 76 as a combined U.S.–Japanese force. But Japan's accepting Zhang's cease-fire. We'll plug the Koreans in instead. That'll give you a robust force level. Concur?"

"I'd be happy to fight alongside Min Jun Jung," Dan said. "But wouldn't he be senior to me?"

Niles said, "Why d'you think you got the promotion? Your first task will be to clear the sea lanes between Guam and the fighting on Okinawa. Then, land an element of the Second Marine Division in a location to be designated. Also, be ready to position as a blocking force to protect Guam and the Marianas, if the enemy moves faster than we expect."

"I personally don't think Zhang will make the mistake Tojo did, and overextend," PaCom said somberly. "But he's kicked our asses so damn hard already, Lianfeng might just persuade him to keep it up. So be wary. They've got more surprises for us, I'm sure."

"Your next question will be about carrier support," Niles rumbled. "For obvious reasons, there won't be any. Not after what happened to *FDR*."

Yangerhans said, "We're holding the remaining battle groups out of missile range. *Nimitz*, *Vinson*, and *Reagan* east of Hawaii. *Abraham Lincoln*, off Australia. The good news: we have more decks on the way.

Not attack carriers, but ESBs and containership or tanker hulls with modular decking. And we should have microsatellite recon and at least limited chat up again before too long."

"Report to USS *Hornet*, and take command of your force," Niles concluded. "Your orders will be there this afternoon."

WHEN they emerged from the building a siren was screaming. Dan was looking around for a shelter when a passing trooper called, "It's a drill, sir. Testing a new missile-attack warning." The wind freshened, blew harder. The palms clashed above their heads, and rain danced across the asphalt, bringing coolness and the smell of the never-far-off sea.

Niles was lumbering toward the Humvee that had brought Dan up the hill. The driver stood holding the door. Dan double-timed after him. "Admiral," he called.

The massive head half turned. "Yeah—Admiral?"

"I'm not ready."

"Nobody's ready for a war, Lenson. I think you know what's at stake. Otherwise I wouldn't have pinned those stars on you."

A second siren joined the first, then a third. They dropped an octave, then rose again, and began to keen in earnest: a spine-chilling, off-key note that sawed at some primitive chord of the back-brain. Niles frowned. "Or did you mean the *rank*?"

"I didn't ask for it. I don't want it."

"I don't remember asking for your fucking *preferences*, Lenson. The Navy needs somebody we can afford to lose. You fit the requirement. Clear?" Niles slammed a beefy hand on the frame of the vehicle. Half-ducked into the door, then paused. "I'm gonna data-dump you everything you need to know about wearing those stars. Listening?"

The sirens rose another octave, screaming like attacking velociraptors, like plunging Stukas. The rain prodded Dan's face like the icy fingertips of hungry zombies. Humid air was supposed to be easier to breathe, but his airways, scarred from sucking smoke on 9/11, were starting to constrict. He said with difficulty, "I'm all ears."

Niles squinted toward the mist-glitter of squall-shrouded sea. "Lead your people. They want to see who's taking them into harm's way.

"Tell them what you want done, then let 'em do their jobs."

He paused, scowled. "Stay out of the fucking press! Yeah, I know, you've already fucked the dog on that one. But try harder, got it?

"Read Nimitz's memo to Spruance on calculated risk. Right now we have inferior forces. So we engage only when we can count on the attrition rates being on our side. But if you decide to gamble, don't go halfway. Shove all your chips in.

"Be ready to pick up that red phone and answer a call from the president.

"And remember, those stars don't belong to you. Be ready to take 'em off whenever we ask for 'em back."

Niles eyed him as the sirens quavered, dropped, then lifted again to a skull-splitting scream. Dan fought the impulse to cover his ears. The driver, too, was eyeing him curiously. As if waiting for some response, comment, or reaction. But he didn't have one. He just felt numb.

Lifting his face to the falling rain, closing his eyes, he concentrated on taking one breath after another.

2

Camp 576, Western China

THE POWs slept in a corrugated iron lean-to built against one wall of the gigantic pit. Behind the hut a cave went back into the rock. The ceiling was just high enough that Teddy could sit upright, but not stand. Dried turds littered the ground between this hut and the next. More hut-caves stretched around the jut of the bluff. All night long lights shone down from the guard towers. Dried grass was the prisoners' only bedding. Teddy slept nestled with Pritchard and the Vietnamese, and was glad of the warmth.

There were seven POWs in the cave. Teddy Oberg, captured in the raid on Woody Island. "Magpie" Pritchard, the Australian, shot down in the South China Sea. The three Vietnamese, Trinh, Phung, and Vu, whose ship had gone down in the same action. And two U.S. airmen, Fierros and Shepard, shot down over the Taiwan Strait. The space was cramped, but it wasn't important where you crawled to sleep.

What mattered was more basic.

There was no clock. Only the whistle. No calendar, so Master Chief Teddy Oberg, SEAL Team Eight, U.S. Navy, didn't know what day it was. Or even what month.

Only that the wind kept getting colder, and now and then crystals drifted down. The air was too dry to snow. But their piss froze in the plastic buckets, and they shivered all day long. The camp's only concession to winter was to issue a thin flannel-lined jacket and one too-short, weary-looking quilted cotton blanket per man. The prisoners scavenged anything that would burn. Paper, trash, broken shovel handles. One of the Vietnamese stole a discarded tire, but when they burned it in the cave, the smoke drove them out like sprayed hornets.

Lice spread among the prisoners, then fever. The guards sniffled and blew their noses into their fingers, then slapped the POWs. This sickness spread. One by one, prisoners began to vanish.

At night, wolves howled. And now and then machine-gun fire clattered from the towers.

Their Australian messmate raved and shook in a corner. His cough grew worse. Once Teddy caught Pritchard studying what he'd expectorated. Bright blood blossomed in his palm.

One day one of the trusty mechanics left a screwdriver near Teddy's tray, at the breaker where they processed the ore. When the trusty came back later, Obie said he hadn't seen it, didn't know where it was.

Some days there wasn't any soup, only rice gruel. Then for two days there was no gruel either. After that they were served slops of some grain he didn't recognize. The hulls were sharp and scratched his throat as he swallowed. He had to force himself to eat it.

He mostly stopped shitting. When he did manage to squeeze a turd out, it was small and hard and licorice-black, with bits of the undigested grain sticking out.

For several days, Phung complained his legs hurt. Soon he screamed softly, talked to himself, and crawled back to the darkest part of the cave, raving and twisting under his blanket. He stank like rotting meat. Vu smuggled back his own corn gruel for him, but Phung wouldn't touch it.

The next morning Phung was dead. They dragged him outside, and when they came back from work, his body was gone.

THEN one day the truck didn't show up. Instead one of the guards came hiking along, rifle slung. She was about five feet high, and her uniform might have fitted her father. She looked to be about fifteen.

Over the last month, the military-age guards had disappeared, leaving only kids and old men. Also, Teddy had stopped hearing the distant thuds he'd always figured were dynamite, excavating explosives, down in the pits. "Prisoners, come with me," she snapped.

They fell in slowly, picking their way down the rockfall to the road like arthritic centenarians. She scolded and pushed them into raggedy columns, wailing insults in a high, comical singsong.

For a moment Teddy felt an urge to take charge, get them formed up, but it faded. He realized then that he'd understood her insults without having to translate in his head. He shuffled into the rearmost rank, set his teeth, and tried to match the pace. They didn't move fast, only at a sort of starvation shuffle.

His interrogators had torn the ligaments in his foot, stamped on it when they'd realized that it hurt, and laughed when he'd asked for medical attention. He had it strapped up now so it didn't hang, and had carved a makeshift wooden brace for ankle support. With it cinched tight he could limp, but it hurt like a sonofabitch. From time to time the guard would look back and shout at the laggards, or unsling her rifle and point it at Teddy. Finally, she squeezed the trigger.

But it didn't fire. Only clicked. The kid laughed.

But Teddy narrowed his eyes. So the guards carried their old AKs with chambers empty. That would give him a second's grace, if he ever had the chance to grab one.

He might even, still, be stronger than a fifteen-year-old girl. If he could take her by surprise, plunge a stone-whetted screwdriver into her throat . . .

Hobbling along, he bared rotting gums in a ghastly grin. Once he'd have looked at her and fantasized about sex. Now he wondered how her tits would taste roasted. Probably like fatty ham . . . The best parts would be thighs and buttocks. But he wouldn't turn down a tasty morsel of liver, or a kidney.

Teddy pointed up to his breaker as they neared, and she nodded. He fell out and slowly climbed the ladder. At the top, his trusty boss was pacing back and forth, looking worried. When he saw Oberg, old Lew spouted a long explanation, out of which Teddy could get only *"bo"*—none, nothing. They were missing something, but who knew what.

At last their prime mover started up, chugging black sulfurous smoke. The gears groaned as the roller mills clanked into motion, grinding the last fifteen- or twenty-ton load of ore from the day before. A few minutes later, through a gap in the corrugated iron that sheathed the breaker, he glimpsed a gray tide cresting the rise between him and the pit. This tide lifted erratically, spilling between outcrops and hollows in the ground, but rolling steadily toward him. The resemblance to an advance of army ants was creepy.

"Shangban, shangban," Lew grumbled, flicking him with the stick he carried more to lean on than for anything else. Get to work. He put a finger to his nose and blew snot onto the ladder. Teddy bent to his broom again, clinking nodules into the hole, which led down to a bin at the bottom of the breaker that got emptied every couple days. He still didn't know what they were mining. His only clue had been a weathered signboard atop the bluff that still bore traces of paint. After many examinations, he'd deciphered the faded letters as CHINA WESTERN RARE EARTH

GROUP COMPANY. From the whitish growths on old Lew's hands, he suspected it might be radioactive.

THEY worked through the day, but even with hundreds of prisoners
dumping their baskets, Teddy worried his breaker would shut down. If
he was in charge, that's what he'd do. Instead of running all these breakers at half capacity, pull the manning out, and put those hands to carrying baskets of ore too. Old Lew looked anxious. He kept scurrying up
and down, scolding and chattering at them to hurry, though the convey-
ors themselves were running at half speed.

At noon, instead of one droning note, the whistle hooted staccato
bursts. A jeeplike vehicle dropped off the guards. The prisoners downed
tools and mustered in marching order. Teddy hung back, but the guards
hustled him into line too.

They filed down into a deeper pit lined with crumbling red rock, as if
whatever had been here had been mined out down to the floor. Now it
made a natural amphitheater. They were shouted and buttstroked into
squatting ranks. Teddy settled in with Pritchard, Trinh, Shepard, and
Fierros. Then nothing happened for about an hour, except that the cold
wind shuddered through him.

Finally, with a snort and rumble from the direction of the town lights,
a menacing shape clanked and squealed into view. Shading his eyes,
Oberg made it as an old Soviet-era T-55. The tank crawled down the
gravel road, rocks spitting from beneath iron treads. It halted, venting
black smoke. The engine revved, then shut down.

Two guards brought a ladder, and a middle-aged man in a green uniform climbed onto the back deck of the tank. A guard handed up a loud
hailer. As he spoke, the prisoners in front of Teddy and Pritchard turned
and glared at them, hissing through their teeth.

Major Trinh translated in a mutter. "He is Colonel Xiu, commander
of Camp 576 Production Cooperative. He says: The war is going well.
China army is advancing on all fronts. Enemy dogs, Japan, Vietnam, are
running with tails between legs. However, the U.S. has grown desperate. It has begun criminal biological warfare. Many, many are dying."

Teddy hung his head, understanding now why the other prisoners had
hissed and shot them murderous looks. The officer tried to whip the prisoners into a cheer, but it sounded more like the weak bleating of under-
fed lambs.

"He says . . . the Party announces a generous release program. Convicted criminals, even political prisoners, can demonstrate love for country. Those between twenty and fifty with less than five years on sentence can join army. They will get large meal of rice, fried pork, and hot tea. A new, warm uniform. They will leave camp now, today."

Teddy couldn't help it; his mouth watered. Here and there, men began standing. They shouted and yelled, shaking fists. Then a rock lofted. It hit Pritchard in the chest. More followed, raining down, and the Chinese around them scrambled away, clearing the field of fire. Teddy shielded his face with both arms but took a stone to the skull from behind. Stunned, he slumped over.

A staccato crack echoed. Blue smoke drifted from one of the T-55's machine guns. The Chinese prisoners subsided. They turned away from the Caucasians, and joined a queue. Officials were setting up the same folding tables at which they'd checked Teddy's transport in, months before.

Obie stood with arms dangling, looking into the sky. He couldn't shake the images. Warm uniform. Hearty meal. Hell, he could *taste* it. Sweet and sour pork, fluffy steamed rice . . . he took one sliding step toward the desks before reality hit and he halted, hammering a fist on his thigh and grunting like an angry camel. Get control, Oberg! That would be ringing the brass bell the loudest any SEAL ever had. Not to mention that with this strapped-up, useless fucking foot, he wouldn't be accepted into any army on the fucking planet.

Another rock came flying. This time he didn't bother ducking. His hand came away from his cheek smeared with red. Shit, even his fucking blood looked darker, felt stickier than it used to.

No. He couldn't stay here any longer. Or he'd die.

Maggie Pritchard, beside him, tugged at his sleeve. "Come on, Teddy. Let's get the fook out of here."

THE next morning, on the road, mustering the prisoners who remained, their brigade commander announced in a singsong that Breaker Twenty-Three was closed. All hands employed there would report to Pit Three.

"I am sorry, Ted-ti," he added. "I tried to get you place in kitchen. But no joy."

At least that was what Teddy thought he said. "That's okay," he told him.

The girl guard formed them up, joking in her lilting tones. The column was more than decimated. Most of the Chinese had volunteered, leaving the too-old, the too-sick, and the foreign devils. They huddled shivering in thin jackets and ragged blankets, hands under their armpits. When they shuffled into motion, Obie found himself in the middle of the column for the first time. The girl trailed them, singing something gay as they marched a mile and a half to Pit Number Three.

In all the time he'd been here, he'd never seen where the ore came from. Even when he peered from atop the breaker, piles of waste had hidden whatever lay beyond. The path twisted through culm hills, acres of loose rock and shale, then began to drop.

They marched down, and down, along sloped ramps into a sort of reversed ziggurat. He couldn't make out the bottom. The cold wind was stirring up a haze of grit that coated their lips and made everyone cough. Teddy kept peering around, half expecting something with teeth and claws to emerge out of the haze.

Gradually, from the dust-fog, the floor emerged. A mile-wide yawning in the earth, at the bottom of which lay containers, stacks of tools, scattered puddles of dully reflecting, dirty water, tar paper-roofed shacks. And parked to the side, well-used power diggers, graders, augurs, dump trucks. They were motionless. The dust-haze was thinner down here, the wind less fierce. As they reached the pit floor, he saw the ore. It writhed in twisted veins across the rock, amid dun-colored, softer-looking slate. Trusties waited by each excavation point. Sidling in among the new arrivals, they broke the column into six-man work units. With peremptory gestures and pidgin Han, they explained the quota. Ten cubic meters a day.

"You got to be shitting me," he muttered to Maggie. He'd watched this stuff go past on the belt. It took forty-ton hardened-steel rollers to crush it. But the unit leader was handing out picks and shovels, pointing to dump barrows with bicycle wheels and stacks of woven plastic baskets. Teddy grabbed a pick. With his leg, he wasn't going to be any use on a wheelbarrow.

His first blow struck sparks from the rock, but didn't loosen a grain. The leader shouted something at him. To hit harder, apparently. He re-shouldered the tool grimly.

Ten cubic meters.

It didn't *sound* like all that much.

THAT night, back in the cave, he and Maggie and Toby Fierros, the pilot, huddled over the hot water that was all they had to brew. Even two feet from the little smoking fire, the cold was numbing bitter. "They wouldn't even fucking feed us," Pritchard marveled. "Wouldn't even fooking . . ."

"*Méiyou pèi'é, méiyou shíwù,*" Trinh said, coming over.

"And that means?"

"No quota, no food." The Vietnamese looked grim. A twist of grass stuck out of his mouth. It gave you racking gut-aches, but it was something. Vu, the other Viet, squatted behind him, silent.

"We got to get out of here," Fierros said.

No one spoke again for some time. Until the pilot added, "Doesn't matter where we go. Probably, just out there to die. But we're gonna get bagged here, anyway."

Teddy slumped against the cave wall, massaging his leg. He'd kept falling down, passing out, all afternoon. Each time the unit leader had kicked him back to his feet. Fourteen hours straight. And since they hadn't made quota, they'd been sent back to the cave hungry, pushed away from the chow line. Just corn gruel, tasteless, stale, and icy cold, but he and one of the guards had locked gazes for a long time before Teddy had lowered his head and shambled off.

This wasn't the first time they'd discussed escape. He and Pritchard had talked it over on and off since they'd arrived. Each time, they'd concluded it might be possible to get up the bluff and over the wire. Or, alternatively, that they could make their way along the bluff at night, and attempt an escape via the town side, although they didn't know what was down there. Teddy had hobbled a mile in that direction when it was warmer, and he hadn't felt so weak. But he hadn't seen a way out, just passed more culm piles, pits, and huts. And what lay outside the wire? At SERE, the Escape phase had emphasized two points to plan for: cooperation of the locals, and food supplies en route. Neither seemed promising here.

The other airman, Bill Shepard, said, "We can't live without the ration."

Fierros said, "But they're not feeding us."

"You heard the wolves," Pritchard observed. "We leave the wire, mytes, *we're* the fooking food."

"Those aren't real wolves," said the pilot.

Teddy did a double take. "Fuck you talking about? I've heard wolves howl before. In the White Mountains. Those are fucking wolves, dude."

"They're *recordings* of wolves," Fierros said. "You haven't figured that yet? To scare us off escaping."

Teddy hoped he was joking. "No, those are real *wolves*, swim buddy.

Ever seen a grave around here? I haven't. I figure, they just put the dead up on the bluff. That's what's attracting them."

Trinh looked disturbed. "You say . . . animals eat them? That is where they took Phung?"

"That a problem, Major?"

"No, no, not a *problem* . . . I am a Communist. No matter, what happens to the body. After one is dead." But he still looked disturbed, and muttered something in an undertone to Vu.

They debated this, Fierros stubbornly maintaining his point, but Teddy thought the guy was getting lightheaded. So was he, for that matter. Fantasizing about roasting that guard's breasts. Jesus. She was probably on the Camp 576 People's Itty-Bitty Titty Committee. But nobody knew they were here. No one had ever seen anyone from the Red Cross. The Geneva Convention said you couldn't make prisoners work. But here they were being worked to death. And now, not even being fed.

They had to either escape, or just die one by one.

"If we did, where would we go?" Teddy said.

Fierros shrugged. "Only one way from here, Scarface. West."

"Into Tibet?" Pritchard said.

"No, amigo. Tibet's actually to the south of us." Fierros's dark eyes glittered as the fire flared up. "We head for Kyrgyzstan. Tajikistan. Possibly, northern Pakistan, but I don't think we're that far south. I flew missions in Afghanistan. From the sun height at noon, I think we're about four hundred miles north of the latitude of Kabul. That'd put us somewhere in the Tien Shan mountains."

Magpie said, "Where you say we'd be headed. They friendly?"

The pilot shrugged. "Who knows. When we were flying out of Bishkek, they were neutral. Manas Airfield. But even if they interned us, wouldn't we be better off?"

"At least they'd feed us." Pritchard smacked his lips, as if the words themselves could be sucked for nutrients.

Teddy nodded. "Yeah. And probably, eventually, turn us over to the nearest allied forces. How far would we have to go, across the mountains?"

Fierros said, "I figure two hundred and fifty, three hundred miles."

They all stared into the fire. "On foot?" Magpie said at last.

"No, we take the train," Teddy said. "Of course, on foot. Ragger, how sure are you about those distances? And the direction? We can steer by the stars. But we don't know where we're starting from."

"I'm pretty sure about it," the pilot said, but Teddy, remembering that the guy didn't think those howls at night were from real wolves, figured they'd better build in a Jesus factor. At SERE they told you that traveling at night and laying up during the day, you could make fifteen to twenty miles in twenty-four hours. Even at the low end of Fierros's estimate, and the high end of miles per night, that would hang them out in hostile territory for two weeks. From the looks of the hills around the camp, it would be slim pickings along the way. And they weren't in good shape to start with.

"I see what you're all thinking," Fierros added. "But I'm at the point where I'm gonna say, fuck it. They shoot me on the wire, I'm not hungry anymore. Who's with me? Teddy? You're probably the fittest here, except for that foot."

"Uh-huh," Teddy said, feeling like he was stepping over a cliff into deep water. "Yeah . . . all right. So, when do we leave?"

"Sooner the better. Two days? Three?"

"The longer we wait, the weaker we get." Teddy leaned and spat. "Maggie and I did some exploring, before you got here. There's a spot three-quarters of a mile down, where a ravine cuts. It's narrow, steep, but there's a power cable leading up."

Shepard said, "You serious? Climb that bluff?"

"Anything can be climbed. If you take your time, and have the balls. What we find at the top could be another story. We could pop our heads up and be looking into an IR-sighted machine gun."

Trinh tossed the grass chew into the fire. It flared up, illuminating haggard visages. "But are you saying, Americans only? Because we want to go too." He tilted his head at the silent Vu.

"I'm not an American," Pritchard said. He coughed hard into his hand, and hid it under his haunch. "But I'm going."

"You can barely drag your dick out to piss," Fierros said.

"Nevertheless, I'm going."

"He's going, all right," Teddy said. "Major, we're not leaving you guys here either. Okay, it's Ragger, Magpie, Vu, the Major, and me." He looked at the other airman. "Bill, you in?"

"Somebody has to stay," Shepard said.

"What?"

"To buy time. You're going at night, right? In the morning, I'll say everyone's sick in our cave. They're too scared of whatever everybody's dying of to come in and look. That'll give you a day, maybe more, head start. Until they figure you're gone."

"You sure, amigo?" Teddy asked him.

"No," the airman said. "But I'm gonna stick it out here. I wish you guys all the luck."

The fire flared up once more, and they sat silently around it. Then, one by one, each drew a thin blanket over himself, and nestled against the others, drawing warmth from the rest.

THE next day Magpie stayed in the cave. He said he was too weak to walk. The rest mustered at the road, but Trinh stepped out from the ranks when the guard arrived. Not the girl, this time, but a hard-faced oldster whose iron visage gave away nothing as the Vietnamese explained they had to have some food. They couldn't work without eating, and there'd been nothing the day before. He kept bowing. The guard fingered his rifle. Teddy, gripping the screwdriver under his jacket, tensed to jump the guy if he took the safety off. Instead, at last, he only nodded. "He says there is not much for the troops, either," Trinh said, shuffling back in line. "But he will ask. Pass our concerns up."

Their work unit pecked away at the seams all morning. Teddy was getting better with the pick. He could swing hard, and hit at an angle that chipped off several flakes of the quartz-heavy, sparkling ore. When he'd knocked free a couple of cubic feet, Ragger or Trinh or Shepard or Vu would rake it into a basket, hoist it, then set off on the trek back up to the breakers.

But he had to rest for minutes in between swings, and it took the carriers forever to reach the surface. They weren't going to make quota. Hell, that was for healthy, well-fed prisoners. The guards shambled among them. They didn't look all that great either. Their uniforms hung on them, scarecrow-style. They coughed and blew their noses constantly, and perched shivering on rocks. Teddy kept eyeing their rifles. A snatch, when they were nodding off, would be easy. But then what? Down here in the pit, the other troops would mow them down like weed-whackers clearing a highway divider.

The sun came out and hung pale and cold as a frozen opal. He blinked up at it between swings, savoring the faint warmth on his skin. The dust-haze was clearing. Before, he hadn't been able to see the sun at all.

Around noon a truck coasted down the ramp, silently, engine off. Teddy had a bad turn seeing this, but was reassured when the guards started handing down the familiar tureens. Only three, though, and the prisoners who'd worked in the pit before murmured that there would not be enough.

And it wasn't corn mush, but the brown soup, the kind that made his turds prickle like he'd been eating briars. A soggy leaf was threaded through the grains, and one tiny slice of what might have been an actual vegetable—turnip, or parsnip. As the whistle droned, Teddy fished it out with his fingers and wolfed it, then inspected the rest like a finicky cat. Squatting on his haunches, he stared into the bowl. Hungry as he was, he didn't want to eat this crap. It hurt too much when it came out the other end.

He lifted his eyes to the sky. Was that blue? He'd never seen blue here before. Maybe it was a good omen.

Or maybe, just the last blue sky he'd ever see.

They got a break to eat. No more than fifteen minutes, but it was always observed. If nothing else, he understood now why eating was sacramental. When they had their bowls in hand, the prisoners drifted to the shade of the parked equipment. His unit settled against one of the trucks. He examined his ration again, and almost threw it on the dirt. But, finally, forced himself to lick the last grains off the cold metal. If they went tonight, he'd need every erg of energy.

Getting up to return the bowl, he caught a flash of movement above him and cringed. Then hesitantly glanced up, arm lifted to protect himself.

He was staring into red-rimmed, terrified eyes set in a black-smeared, hair-covered face. It was gaunt. Filthy. Only the radiating scars under the grime informed him, after a shocked second, that this was his own visage, reflected in the truck's side-view mirror. He dropped his gaze.

Then raised it again, struck by a thought.

He looked around. The guards were on lunch break too. The only one visible was across the quarry, facing away.

He reached up. Pressed the button on the driver's-side door handle, and eased it open. Then, swiftly as a snake, glided up and into the cab, greasing the door closed behind him. Crouching, so his head wouldn't show.

The cab smelled of diesel and old sweat. He plundered through the glove compartment, then pawed behind the seats. A white metal box: a first-aid kit. But when he unlatched it, it was empty. Next: a tool roll. He unrolled it, hoping for something weapony. Crank rods, a rusty socket wrench set. "Fuck," he muttered.

Then he saw what lay beneath it.

A nylon towing strap, neatly made up with zip ties.

"Ted-ti?" A familiar croak. He flinched and rolled out of the cab, stuffing the bundle hastily down his pants.

Old Lew was in what looked like gray pajamas. He nodded to Teddy in an avuncular way, and held out a small package wrapped in brown paper.

"*Tíngzhi! Nà shì shénme?*" shouted the hard-faced guard, strolling over. Lew flinched but stood his ground, chattering so rapidly that Teddy couldn't follow. He unfolded the paper, displaying the contents. The guard smiled and took some. The old man grinned and bobbed. The guard nodded, spat on the ground, and turned his back to them.

"*Ted-ti,*" the old man said again, "*zhè shì gei nín de. Yigè liwù. Wo bù chouyan de yancao.*"

Which he didn't get, but the way the codger held it out in both hands, bowing, made his intent clear. Teddy bowed too, unfolded it, and sucked air. His astonishment must have been clear, because the old man chuckled as he tottered away.

Leaving Teddy staring down at two slightly bent, obviously well handled, but perfectly genuine Winston cigarettes.

THAT night he laid out his gear. Just like before a mission. Only this time, instead of Knight's Armament SR-25 and magazines of M118 heavy-bullet sniper rounds, suppressor, and cleaning kit, a screwdriver sharpened on a shard of flint. Instead of his thin-blade, a stone axe cobbled from a piece of bone and a chunk of black quartz he'd hand-flaked to a point. Instead of battle dressings and a bugout kit, a faded quilt rolled and tied with string woven of braided grass. A discarded plastic bottle filled with water. And the towstrap. Instead of MREs and Power Bars . . .

For breakfasts, before a mission, he'd liked to eat heavy. Ribeye steaks, or thick slabs of pink fried ham. Fried potatoes, ice cream. Protein and fat you could burn for fuel while humping overland, or up a cliff, or busting down doors clearing a compound.

Fuck that, Oberg. Fuck it. It was probably a lie, but he told himself, *Get up that cliff, and you'll be eating roasted goat.* He twisted grass into a plug and tucked it into a cheek. Next to the left upper bicuspid, which was dying, loose in its socket. He scooped ash from the firepit, spat into it, and worked the paste into his skin. Not camo paint, but it would work.

Ragger, at his elbow. "Ready?"

"All set. Maggie?"

Pritchard was gagging in the far corner, where they pissed when they were too sick to stagger outside. Teddy rolled over. "Up for this, Digger?"

"Just lemme cough. . . . I'm game. I'm game." He wiped his face and pushed up to hands and knees.

Outside, for the first time in days, the stars were visible. Light to steer by. On the other hand, better for any guards at the top of the bluff to pick them out. He'd never seen any night vision equipment here, but if there was, it would be in the towers. Teddy muttered that he'd take point, to maintain a five-yard interval, and to stay low and hug the cliff.

They went slow, which his foot appreciated. He'd wrapped the prosthesis even tighter than usual, and it quickly numbed. That worked. He slid along the bluff, trying not to turn his good ankle on the scree littering its base. That tuff, or whatever it was, was going to make it hard to climb, but he thought he could make it. Maybe by cutting in steps with the axe. Once he got to the top, the others could haul themselves up by the towing strap.

The stars glittered down. The wind was cold, but not as sharp as before. Spring was on the way, all right.

Would he be here to see it?

He figured the odds were about fifty-fifty.

AN hour later, the stars had wheeled on. They passed fire-flickers, but most huts were dark, untenanted. From these blew a cold stink like rotting meat.

At last, his leg aching, they reached the ravine. Here the bluff curved in and steepened, but in such a way that they were screened from overhead view. Here, too, a line of poles ended. Which meant either power or communication. From the size of the wires, carefully observed day after day from where he'd been entowered, like a hungry, ugly Rapunzel, atop the breaker, he guessed power. This was confirmed by a sixty-cycle hum.

"Transformer," Ragger whispered, close to Teddy's ear. "Which means—"

Teddy put his lips to the pilot's ear in turn. Mouthed, so low he couldn't hear it himself over the wind, "Shut the fuck up."

Fierros fell back. Teddy leaned in and eyed the wire. Then froze, motionless as coal, at an almost nonexistent wash of ruby light somewhere above. So faint that if he hadn't been in the dark for an hour, he'd never have detected it.

Someone was above them where the cables crossed the wire, drooped, then lifted again to scale the cliff. With a perfect field of view to observe their route up.

He gestured the others down. He wasn't sure he was fit for this. But he'd taken down sentries before. Killed with a knife. He had the best chance.

Thinking this, he'd already slid into the eroded-out gully under the wire. Had a bad moment when he thought: *Mines.* But probably erosion would expose them. If he was lucky, he'd hit an edge before he contacted the detonator.

Just take it slow, then . . . and the stars above his upturned face had wheeled fifteen minutes farther before he hoisted himself by slow degrees to hands and knees.

The shack was above him. The cliff, a black absence above that. From this angle, he doubted that whoever was in there could see him. In sniper lingo, he was in a dead zone. Still, he crept like a tortoise, breathing through his mouth. Extending one hand at a time, then oozing his body up the loose scree after it. Not disturbing a pebble until he reached the rough cold poured-concrete supports of the guard box.

He kept going under it, until he came out the other side.

The back of the shed was open. The light, he saw now, came from a shaded lamp down near a pair of boots. Its upper half painted over, the pilot lamp topped a box he guessed was an intercom linking the posts. The boots belonged to a small soldier perched on a stool high enough to give a view over the wire and up the ravine. A set of black binoculars hung from a nail. The unmistakable shadow of a Kalashnikov leaned against the wall.

Teddy debated. Chert axe, screwdriver, bare hands? He finally slipped out the screwdriver. Six inches of shiv, stone-honed to a needle point.

One more step.

The trooper stared out into the darkness.

Teddy closed, rotating in, jammed his knee into the guy's back, and wrapped a hand over his face. He jerked the head back with all the rage he'd pent up for months, and with his right plunged the screwdriver in. The guard shuddered, and started to cry out before Teddy's palm corked her breath.

Startled, Teddy loosened his grip. It was the girl guard, who'd sung and joked with them.

The next moment he was jolted back by a vicious elbow strike that caught him in the solar plexus. He choked, folding, only just managing to hold on. *Control the head. The body follows.* Warmth drenched his hand as he reoriented the screwdriver and drove it down, through the angle between neck and shoulder, probing for the heart.

She writhed in his arms. Her boot flicked back to hook his ankle. She was small but strong, and he was weak. His only advantage had been surprise, and now that was gone. If she broke free, there had to be an alert button in here. Or she could simply grab the AK. With four puncture wounds in the neck, she'd bleed out, but even after your heart stopped, you had a good thirty seconds before you lost consciousness.

Another elbow strike, but weaker. He kept forcing her head back, palm sealing her mouth and nose. *No breath, no fight.* He jammed the pick in again, deeper, like a harpooner feeling for the whale's life.

She fell back, limp, into his arms. *Finish your opponent. . . .* He did it, then let her slump to the floor. Slowly, without unnecessary noise.

He sank too, upper body propped against the wall, red and black curtains eddying and flaring before his eyes, like one of his grandmother's Hollywood openings. His whole body shuddered. The reeks of blood and shit filled the wooden box.

When he had his breath back, he bent to the corpse. It was still warm. Wet. He unbuttoned her shirt, and thrust his hand in. Yeah. Itty-bitty. He pulled out the sharp chert. Positioned it, like a prehistoric hunter preparing to skin his kill.

A hiss jerked him around. "Teddy!"

It was Pritchard. The Aussie dragged himself up the steps and halted, staring. In the faint light Teddy saw his jaw drop. "What the *fook* are you doing?"

"I took the guard out."

"I can see that, mate, but what the . . . never mind. We taking this?" He touched the rifle.

"Bet your ass." Teddy let the girl's blouse fall closed and stuck the axe back in his pants. Had he really intended to cut them off? And then do what? His head swam. "Grab it. Let's go. Somebody's gonna be calling to check in." He bent again, searching the body, but found only a metal belt buckle and, in the pockets, a scrap of handkerchief and a small plastic billfold. Leaving the wallet, he rebuttoned her blouse and propped her against the wall. Then, after a moment, covered her face with the cloth.

THEY climbed in single file, stooped to the ground. When his feet slipped he fell to his knees, which grew warm and wet with blood. His jacket was growing stiff. Caked with more blood, no doubt. Hey, at least it wasn't his.

He avoided thinking about what he'd been about to do when Maggie had come in.

At the sheer cliff he halted abruptly, bewildered. How had he planned on scaling this? He stood scratching his beard, brain vacant.

At last he remembered, and bent, and slipped off his ragged cloth POW-issue shoes. He dug bare toes into rough rotting stone, getting the feel of it. Knotted the laces, and hung them over his neck. Unlashed the grass rope on his bindle.

He'd cut the steel fittings off the tow line back at the cave, leaving only braided nylon. He doubled it and rewrapped it around his waist and shoulder in the familiar configuration of a climbing rope. Let four yards dangle free, then rethought that and tucked them into his pants. The fewer Irish pennants, the less likely it would snag.

He looked up, hesitated, then reached out. And looped the line around the heavy metal cable that led up the bluff.

The thick wire hummed like a hornet's nest. Enough volts were coming through it, from some faraway hydroelectric plant or reactor, to run the whole camp. It didn't even seem to be insulated, from the way the nylon slicked along it when he leaned back. Just smooth, bare copper.

Touch it with his toes dug into the ground, and that would be all she wrote. Actually, if a body part got close enough, high voltage could jump a gap.

Okay, enough *thinking* . . . he leaned back even farther, keeping tension on the strap. Planted his feet, and bounced his upper body to slide the nylon up ten or twelve inches. Then, searched again with bare toes for the next gritty foothold.

The bad foot folded on him. He slipped, caught himself, but his sweat-coated face hovered within inches of the bare wire. The soil was crumbling away beneath his clawed right toes. He cocked his head, looking into the face of Death.

Deep slow breaths. Imagine looking through a gunsight at a distant target. Heartbeat. Another breath.

He lifted his leg again, feeling with his toes for the barest crack in the crumbling rock.

HALF an hour later he lay full length at the top of the cliff, shaking. Patterns chased themselves like flocks of starlings over his retinas.

Their black wings throbbed. He gasped for air. Then lifted his head, and peered around.

As he'd expected, it was wired. Jagged coils of concertina outlined themselves against the starlight. It was staked in with what looked like four-inch I beams. Thinner wires within it looked ominous, might be live. He couldn't tell if there was another belt beyond that, but he'd have put one there. Trap any would-be escapees between the two, pin them with lights, and machine-gun them. He lifted his head higher and picked up the tower, dark against the sky, thirty feet up. That was where the searchlight had come from, the one they'd watched from the cave. Every few minutes, all night long, it roved the pit below, and presumably the wire here too. He clawed up crumbly dirt and rubbed a fresh layer into face and hands. It wouldn't be enough if the guard was alert, but if he wasn't, he might not see a motionless shape the color of everything around it.

He thought about neutralizing the guard up here too, but dismissed it. He was too weak to go hand to hand again.

If only he had some way to divert their attention . . .

First, though, he had to get the rest of the team on deck. After ten frozen minutes, he began a low crawl toward the nearest I beam. Shook it, but it didn't move. Good.

In the dark, he put a bowline in the end of the nylon, making it fast to the beam. Waited another two minutes; then slid back and dropped the line over the cliff.

Ragger came up next. When he had his breath back, Teddy hissed at him, "Roll off to the right and find a way under the wire." For once the airman didn't argue, just crawled off. A smaller shadow next: Trinh. Obie whispered, "Go left and look for a gap." The shadow nodded.

"Where's Maggie?" Teddy hissed.

"He is not doing well."

Fuck. He crawled to the edge. Gradually he made out a darker blot ten feet below. "Magpie! That you? Get your ass up here!"

A cracked whisper-cough floated. "Not . . . quite sure I can, Teddy-boy."

"Stay clear of the cable. I'm gonna come in on this line." He began hauling it up, almost dragging his own flagging corpse over the edge. He gasped as the crumbling rock gave way, and scrabbled backward. But returned to whisper fiercely to the prisoner below, urging him up. At last he gripped outstretched fingers, and pulled him up and over to lie together.

The Australian's shoulders were shaking. Teddy realized he was coughing, silently, face pressed into the dirt. "Maggie, y'okay?"

"Taken a bit crook today, mate. Just . . . a bit crook."

"We've gotta get through this wire before that searchlight comes back on."

"Just . . . can't."

Something liquid bubbled in Pritchard's throat. Teddy could make out the dark gleam of blood in his beard. "Knackered here, mate. Done for. You . . . go on without."

"Don't give me that shit, Magpie. You're coming, if we have to drag you."

"No, oi . . . been thinking. Gotta cut that light off. No chance making it without." His cave mate was fumbling at his back, freeing what Teddy realized was the AK. Pushing it into his hands. "That cable . . . feeds the light, right?"

"Looks like it. Why?"

"Short it with something, breakers'll pop. No lights."

"We don't have anything to short it out with, Maggie. Or—oh—you mean the rifle?"

"No, you're going to need that." The Australian waved a hand. "Ready?"

"Magpie . . . Pritchard . . . what the fuck are you talking about?"

"I've got fooking galloping consumption. Not going to make it into those hills. But, you know what?" He coughed hard, and the bubbling sounded deeper. "Least, I'm dyin' free. Tell 'em that, if you make it." He writhed, and Teddy realized he was digging one arm into the friable soil. Spitting his own blood onto it, to make the short circuit complete. His other arm hammered Teddy's back. "O-roo, mate. Now get the fook going."

Major Trinh, in the dark. Vu, a smaller, silent shadow behind him. "Gap in the wire. Ten meters to our left."

Closer to the tower, but maybe that wasn't bad. Teddy wavered, grinding his teeth, about to argue. Then accepted it. He squeezed Pritchard's wrist. "We'll miss you."

"Half your luck, mate. Half your luck."

They were on the far side of the wire and crawling for the second belt when the searchlight came on above them. It swept up the bluff, then toward them. Teddy hugged the ground, face buried, but they were too close to be overlooked now. In the next second, a machine-gun bullet.

A sputter and hiss from the cliff edge. A cry, cut off almost instantly.

The searchlight flickered, and went out.

* * *

THERE were three wire belts, with a ditch between the first and second, but the outermost was only half finished; more a warning to outside trespassers than a serious barrier. Once past that, they rose warily to stand erect. Almost not believing they'd made it through. But despite shouting between the towers, no lights had come on. And when Teddy had brushed against a wire with his back, it had been dead, without power.

They began walking.

They trudged along all night, keeping to hard surfaces and then the tops of ridges, when ridges rose. Keeping rock under their feet so they'd leave no tracks. Teddy didn't have to drive them on. They knew they had to push it. He had to admit, Maggie had been right. No way he could have kept up. Not in his condition.

At dawn they lay concealed on a hill, lost in a chaotic jumble of immense rocks that made him think of the White Mountains. Far ahead the snowcapped peaks of the Tien Shan floated in the clear air.

He lay motionless, belly empty, staring up. Could they really cross them? It seemed impossible. But they had to, or die. He, and Trinh, and Vu, and Fierros.

Yet even death would be better than recapture, and the camp again.

3

Apra Harbor Repair Facility, Guam

WATCH yourself!" The supervisor pulled the slight officer in the white hard hat back as a silver-hot shower of sparks burst out high above them. The liquid steel fell in a crackling, coruscating waterfall exactly where she'd been about to step. Molten drops sizzled on wet iron like a fiery snowfall. Blue smoke rose, with the hot choking stink of burning metal.

Commander Cheryl Staurulakis, USN, hesitated, blinking through the data streaming in front of her eyes. Then, adjusting her smart glasses, she settled the hard hat more firmly over a black-and-olive shemagh and marched ahead, through the smoke and sparks.

A step behind her pale-haired, hard-cheekboned, steeltoe-booted, blue-coveralled figure, a foreman sighed and hitched a tool belt over a drooping paunch. The dry-dock supervisor punched numbers into a battered notebook.

Above them loomed a darkling presence so immense and curved that, like a planet, only a portion could be glimpsed. The cruiser's hull was spotted with the dull red and bright yellow and glistening black of fresh paint, the charred seams of fresh welds, the silvery patches where workers had ground them down to bare metal. As soon as the metal cooled, women in dust masks slapped paint over it, edging along platforms above the wetshining floor of the dry dock. Shouts and the clatter of pumps echoed in the cavernous space. The sun glittered through catwalks far above. A pump throbbed; water spattered down. A grinder shrieked, scattering sparks like gold coins thrown to paupers by a pope. The workers were finishing the new bow structure, and buttoning up the other repairs.

Through the augmented-reality lenses, Cheryl noted the blisters along the hull where the new Rimshot sensor/output modules had been welded in. She squinted at where fresh paint ended and barnacles started. If only they'd had time to strip and repaint the whole hull . . . The bright blue sky seemed far away as the supervisor explained, "We edge the dock out into the channel, then start flooding. Right before you float, we secure ballasting. Our fitters are down belowdecks inspecting your seals and sea valves for watertight integrity. Once you're satisfied your DC checks are set, you give the order, 'Float the ship.' I'm up at the head of the dock, watching trim and list. If you go off half a degree, I stop and we figure out what's wrong. Once you're fully afloat, we power you out with the trolleys and wire pendants up there"—he pointed up to where steel threads crisscrossed the blue—"and make you up to the tugs, take you over to Victor Wharf. Just make sure your engineering guys know—"

"Excuse me." Staurulakis halted again, shielding her gaze with a gray-gloved hand as she read the repair and readiness status of each object she looked at. "But can we pressure test that sonar dome one more time?"

"We already did that twice, Commander—"

The radio clipped to her web belt, her Hydra, clicked on. *"Commander? Comm here. Where exactly are you right now?"*

"XO here. Down in the dock. By the bow dome."

"Got a message for you. Running it down."

"Never mind, I'll be right up." She clicked off. Said to the super, "I'm not confident we found the weak point. Out there in some sub's torpedo danger area is not when I want to find out we have a reduced acoustic capability. Keep pushing, okay? We appreciate everyone's efforts."

"You got it, Commander. Fix yer battle damage, get you back out there to fight, that's why we're here."

Pompously put, but the shipyard people *were* coming through. Three shifts, working around the clock since USS *Savo Island* had pulled in. Despite the missile raid drills and the flights evacuating military dependents back to the States. Almost all the workers were locals anyway, Chamorros and Filipinos. The naval shipyard had been BRAC'd years before, but the wharves, cranes, and most of the other facilities—foundry, labs, motor rewind, industrial gases—had remained. Now hastily remanned, the facility's wharves were lined with damaged ships.

No one knew what was coming. Invasion, perhaps, or the bombardments that had preceded the landings on Taiwan and Okinawa. Worst of all, a nuclear strike like the one that had wiped out an entire battle group at sea. The Army had moved a THAAD battery here from Meck

Island, and the Air Force a squadron of F-22s, but they wouldn't be enough to stop a serious attack.

The story of the whole war so far. The Allies had been surprised, outmaneuvered, outthought, and overwhelmed. The only good news was that the carriers were still holding east of Hawaii. Which meant her husband, Ed, aboard *Vinson*, wouldn't see action for a while. So she could stop worrying about him. Short of the usual back-of-the-mind anxiety about flameouts or bad landings. But he was a solid flier. A squadron leader, now. And since the wedding, he'd promised to take fewer risks.

Thank God, at least they still had an operational dry dock out here. The huge, hollow mass of steel could be ballasted down, allowing a ship to be floated in. Then the ballast was pumped out, buoying the carefully propped-up vessel and exposing the hull for repairs.

The missile had come in from astern during a confused nighttime imbroglio in the Taiwan Strait. They'd known a sub was out there, but hadn't been able to localize it closely enough to neutralize. Though the missile could have been air-launched, too, programmed to loop around and approach from astern to maximize surprise.

At any rate, it had bored in so fast—transonic, or supersonic—and so low that their radar had picked it up only a second before impact. *Savo*'s electronic-countermeasures team had managed to spoof it away from the centroid, but not enough to miss entirely.

A hundred yards ahead and above, another coverall-clad figure, also female, waved and started down. Two men trailed her down the steel stairway that descended flight after flight into the dry dock's Stygian depths.

Hitting at an angle, the warhead had penetrated before explodings. The blast had blown off everything forward of the wildcats. Lifelines, bulwarks, bullnose, ground tackle, both anchors, and the upper part of the stem down to four feet above the waterline. The anchor chain had run out with a grating thunder. After they'd gotten the fire under control, Captain Lenson had ordered them to cut away what was left, leaving a gaping hole. "Have to call her Old Shovelnose from here on," the first lieutenant had cracked.

The damage-control teams had welded and shored bulkheads, but they'd had to avoid taking heavy seas head-on for the agonizingly slow twelve-hundred-mile creep back. During that passage, apparently, more of the forward stringers had cracked and separated from the shell plating. The Tiger Team engineers from Pearl Harbor Naval Shipyard had reviewed the damage documentation Cheryl and the chief engineer had prepared, and translated that into work orders. *Savo* had to wait her turn—she wasn't the only battle-damaged ship around—but eventually it had come.

Since then both the yard and ship's force had been cutting, fabricating, welding. Covering everything in the ship with dust, and tracking grinder grit over the decks. But cleanliness was the least of her worries now. Neither was aesthetics, though she hated that the new bow wasn't as graceful as the old. Where the original had been sharp, it was square, shorter, cruder, and carried only one anchor. A hasty wartime repair, for a ship needed back on the front line. The super had promised to have everything buttoned up before dawn tomorrow. Get her off the blocks, a quick engine test, then under way to load ammo at the magazine wharf.

Everyone expected the next phase in the Chinese offensive. Only what would it be? She murmured, "Glasses: power off," as the approaching woman angled to meet her, snagging the admiring gazes of the male workers. No wonder, the way she filled out her coveralls, that long dark hair flowing from under her hard hat . . .

"XO. Good morning."

"Good morning." Cheryl tucked the glasses away and returned Lieutenant Amarpeet Singhe's salute. "Amy? Dave? And Master Chief. What's this little party for? I said I'd be right up."

Singhe was *Savo Island*'s strike officer, in charge of the Tomahawk and Harpoon missiles, though she had other responsibilities too. The taller lieutenant behind Singhe was Dave Branscombe, *Savo*'s communications officer. The third, lagging them, was Master Chief "Sid" Tausengelt. The senior enlisted's receding hairline and grooved cheeks went with his being probably the oldest person aboard.

"Thought we'd bring this one down ourselves," the comm officer said, handing over an aluminum clipboard.

Cheryl carried it to where sunlight slanted. They stepped around water-soaked oaken blocks as big as buffaloes, picking their way between pools of dirty slime, over the uneven rusty steel. Other balks had been stacked into a makeshift shelter. She doubted they'd afford much protection. If the enemy hit this harbor, a ballistic-missile cruiser parked helplessly in the single floating dry dock west of Hawaii would be a prime target.

"As soon as we realized what it was, we printed it out and called your cabin," Branscombe said. "Then we got on the Hydra."

"Dave was going to bring it down, but I had to come too," Singhe said. "I grabbed the master chief on the way."

What the heck? Cheryl flipped the cover up.

TO: COMMANDER CHERYL STAURULAKIS USN
EFFECTIVE IMMEDIATELY ASSUME COMMAND USS SAVO ISLAND.

That was all. Other than the prosign *BT*, which just meant the end of the text proper.

Shouldn't there be more?

But maybe that was all there had to be.

And maybe it wasn't really a matter for congratulation.

As she stood blinking, her relationship to the mass of metal above her, to the other officers, to the crew, to the world, had changed.

"Cheryl?" Singhe was smiling radiantly. Even through the smells of scorched iron, paint, and fetid mud, her sandalwood perfume penetrated. "This is great. Really, really. We're going to make some changes. Make everything different. Right?"

Branscombe said nothing, just studied her. Of course, the comm officer knew what it said. As probably everybody in the ship above them did too, by now. Scuttlebutt traveled faster than light. The old master chief's weathered face was attentive, but unreadable as a catcher's mask.

Staurulakis pulled off a glove, took the proffered pen, and initialed the message. Scratched the itchy patch between her fingers, and handed back the clipboard. Singhe's expression changed, faltered, as Cheryl didn't respond to her enthusiasm. Altered, in some indefinable way, when the woman who was suddenly, now, to them all, the captain, gave her only a brief smile, and headed for the stairs.

THE work-progress meeting convened at 1300 in the wardroom. Cheryl ran it just as she would have if she were still the exec, but the oxygen content of the atmosphere had changed. As the chief engineering officer, Bart Danenhower, briefed on the checkoff list for flooding the dock and getting under way, she propped her chin on one fist. Remembering how often the previous skipper had looked abstracted, rubbing his face or massaging his eyes as they'd briefed him. Snatching a few seconds to multitask behind those opaque gray eyes.

Yeah, he was a hero. Medal of Honor. Silver Star. Been everywhere. Done everything. But he was so damned demanding. A perfectionist. She'd never felt she knew him, even as she'd worked like a dog to anticipate his next thought. He didn't shout when someone fell short, like other skippers she'd worked under. In a way, that silence was worse. Facing the disappointment, in those flat, cold, judgmental eyes. He never doubted. Saw everything in black and white. Expected too much, of himself, and then, of them.

Now *she* was in charge. Her chance to do things differently. And, she hoped, better.

At the same time, some of the things he'd done right, she hoped she could do half as well.

The first question was who was going to fill her billet as second in command. No clue in the message, which meant she'd have to select, or "fleet up," someone to fill her still-warm steeltoes.

But who? Danenhower was the obvious choice, as next senior lieutenant commander. Matt Mills, the handsome blond intent on his notebook next to him, was another option. The operations officer was usually next in the pecking order after the XO. But Mills was still a lieutenant, too junior even in wartime. Amy Singhe was smart, ambitious, a Wharton grad. But she wasn't senior enough either, plus she'd gone behind the chiefs' backs to stand up for the enlisted women too many times. Praiseworthy, but it didn't make her popular with middle management. Slotting her as XO, even as a temporary fill, would guarantee friction. And it was the chiefs who made the ship titivate, motivate, and navigate, as the saying went.

Scratching absentmindedly between her fingers, she looked from one to the next of her department heads. Better a guy backing her up than another woman. Danenhower . . . Mills . . . Ollie Uskavitch, the weapons officer? Physically, the biggest hunk aboard. But . . . kinda dumb. Her Supply Department head, Hermelinda Garfinkle-Henriques? Not a line officer. A woman. And only a lieutenant. Three strikes, she's out. Branscombe, the comm officer? Reasonably smart. A male. But again, too junior.

If only she could Frankenstein them together, Amy's Wharton degree, Ollie's size, Matt's Harlequin-cover looks, Bart's seniority, and Engine Room savvy—

Danenhower was winding up. "Dry-docking or not, we've been at sea way past our overhaul date. This was supposed to be just a Med cruise, remember. Then we got extended. To the Red Sea. The Indian Ocean. Then here. Machinery wears out. At some point . . . well, I've said it before. Sooner or later, we're asking for major equipment degradation."

He paused, looked to her, and she murmured, "Thank you, CHENG. What about the moisture issue in the CRP?"

"Um, Chief McMottie had them ultrasound the bottom all along the starboard shaft. They found a crack. Minor, but enough so that inaccessible void under the sump would fill up slowly. We cut that section out and rewelded it."

"The grounding issues in the engine control consoles?"

"They put that in the 'too hard' file. Said we needed rip-out, all new consoles. Just got to be careful, don't get ourselves in situations where we depend on instant engine response."

She nodded and leaned back, enjoying the way they eyed her. If only Eddie could see her now. "All right . . . Oh, the dock supe wanted me to remind you, make sure your shafts are locked out during the undocking. . . . Let's move on. Ollie, did you check on the Annex?"

"I went over there this morning with Chief Quincoches. Did you know, he's got family around here?"

"Really? Interesting . . . What have they got for us?"

The weapons officer said, "The flight got in from Australia, but with only four Advanced Standards. Which makes a light loadout." The weapons officer went over the tally, but since he was sending her the inventory on the LAN, she just checked that it was in her queue. She'd get all too familiar with those numbers. Provided no one was lurking offshore waiting for them. Fleet had warned that even with swept harbor exits, it was possible smart mines would be waking as days and weeks passed. Just to keep the pucker factor high, she reflected sourly.

Murmuring around the table; it ceased as she cleared her throat. "We need an acting XO. I'm going to call Squadron and request a permanent fill." She didn't look at Singhe, but noted her cheeks paling, the heavy black eyebrows contracting. "For now, CHENG will be acting XO as well as our resident Harry Potter expert." A dutiful chuckle; as ever, even a lame pleasantry from the skipper got a laugh. "But he really deserves a full-time exec billet. There are other folks we could promote from within"—she dispensed Singhe a glance—"but they're still too junior. I know, wartime, but years in grade still counts. If we don't get fills in a reasonable time, then I'll fleet people into the billets. We'll just have to deal case by case.

"For the time being, though, Bart will dual-hat as CHENG and XO."

She pulled up tomorrow's plan of the day on her notebook. "Bart, can we start this checklist at 04 vice 05? I want to be ready when the yard people start ballasting down, with fenders ready for the tugs. Both sides, in case the wind changes. Once there, single lines. We have to be ready to clear the channel quickly, once the engine tests are complete. If Apra is attacked, I'd rather have sea room. Lieutenant Singhe"—she deliberately didn't use Amarpeet's first name—"how's the software patch to ALIS? And, are we doing a combat systems battery alignment after the dry dock?"

ALIS—the acronym had originally stood for Aegis Light Exoatmospheric Projectile Intercept System—was the cruiser's antiballistic missile system. A major radar and combat upgrade, it had made USS *Savo Island* the first ship capable of shooting down incoming ballistic missiles. At least . . . part of the time. Singhe said, still pale, "I'd rather brief you offline on that. With the new bow, hog will change by the weight delta—"

"Bottom line, please, Amy." God, she even sounded like Lenson now.

"Um, yes. We should do a CS alignment, yes. If we have time."

"All right, I'll meet you in CIC."

SHE was breezing through the mess decks when Tausengelt snagged her. "XO . . . sorry, sir, ma'am, I mean, Skipper." He snapped his turtlelike beak shut, looking confused. "Basically, I . . . was used to . . ."

"Forget it, Master Chief." She pressed a surprisingly frail arm. "Gonna take everybody a little while to adjust. Me, too. What've you got?"

"New joins . . . indoc. Want to say a word?"

"Absolutely."

The replacements were seated with coffee and bug juice as the mess cranks swabbed down at the far end. Duncanna Ryan, one of the hospitalman seamen, was setting up a CPR dummy. "Attention on deck," the old chief bellowed, and everyone jolted up, looking startled, then apprehensive. Not as many as she'd hoped for. With the folks they'd lost, they were down five on the total head count. Which wasn't going to help on the GQ watchbill. "This is our CO. Commander Cheryl Staurulakis," Tausengelt told them.

"Take a seat," she said, motioning them down. Looking them over, and letting them take her in too. Girls and guys, most looking fresh out of high school. The majority seemed impressed, but two heavyset black men sitting together, older than the rest, eyed her up and down skeptically, lifting their chins and folding their arms. "How many of you just got out of Great Lakes? . . . Uh-huh. How was that? Challenging? . . . We'll be picking up from your graduation battle problem in your damage-control training once we get under way."

Facing them, she searched for words. What would Captain Lenson have said? "Um . . . *Savo Island*'s motto is 'Hard Blows.' The words come from a bitterly-fought battle during World War II.

"Now we're in another war. Right now, the situation looks . . . dark. But as our last captain said, we will come back. And you will be part of that history. Historically—" She caught herself. *Keep it short.* "I have time for one question."

One of the beefy men raised a hand. "There in back. Petty Officer— I can't quite read your name from here."

"Sergeant, ma'am. Alonzo Custis. I just wondered, if it's not out of place, about your warfighting philosophy. How aggressive your style is, as a CO."

Heads lifted. She noted now that Custis and several others wore Army-style BDUs. Which made them part of the California Guard unit that had joined. The rack for their short-range Stingers was set up on top of the hangar structure, to prevent another stab in the back when *Savo*'s attention was elsewhere. . . . How *aggressive*? Was he challenging her? She measured her words. "Human qualities such as aggressiveness aren't really the issues in modern warfare that they were years ago. At least, at sea. Our job is more technical in nature. We follow orders and execute doctrine. Strategy pushes us forward, supported by logistics.

"Where boldness is required, yes, I believe in showing initiative. But only after a careful risk analysis. I expect all of you to think before you act, as well."

She looked to Tausengelt. "I'd like to spend more time getting to know you all, but we're getting under way tomorrow. The master chief will steer you through indoc. Learn as much as you can, as fast as you can. His life, my life, and all your shipmates' lives will depend on you."

She nodded, once, then turned away. Behind her, they bolted to their feet again with a creaking of chairs, a thundering of boots on polished flooring.

IN the Damage Control Room, two decks below. Brightly lit, smelling of the diesel-like distillate, the turbine engines ran on. Diagrams of electrical circuits, firefighting lines, and fire-extinguishing systems lined the bulkheads. Computer screens reflected statuses. She was reviewing the closure log with the damage-control officer and the chief and petty officers who'd make sure *Savo* floated when the dry dock ballasted down. Basic, but sometimes ignoring the basics bit you in the ass.

"Undocking calculations?" she murmured.

The DCA said, "Here, Skipper, but we haven't been in long enough to have much in the way of weight changes. Ballast, fuel, fresh water—pretty much the same as when we came in, except for the steel we added with the new bow. And that's an easy calculation."

"All right. But I'd feel better if we got all our accesses to the sea closed early," she said. "Tonight, if the repairs are finished."

Chief McMottie murmured, "They're not planning on flooding until 0500, Captain."

"I know. But like I said before, this rustbucket dry dock's not only forty years old, it's the only one west of LA that can take a ship this size. If the enemy wants to take out our repair capabilities, I don't want to go down with it."

THE Combat Information Center stretched from port to starboard, two decks above the main deck. Enclosed, windowless, painted dead black, it smelled of electronics and old sweat. Just now, most of the consoles that funneled data to the four large-screen flat-panel displays, LSDs, were deserted. Only the combat systems controller and radar system controller consoles were manned. Doing systems tests, Cheryl assumed. On ship's power, with only one gas turbine generator online, there wasn't enough wattage to operate the SPY-1. Only two of the LSDs were lit. She folded her arms in front of them as the ventilation whooshed chills down the back of her neck.

One display—from the Global Command and Control System, she assumed, since the radar was down—showed the Mariana Islands. Only a few green lines—air activity, air patrols—laced the periphery. The other screen displayed dusk falling over Apra Harbor, video from one of the aft gun cameras.

Smaller text readouts above the screens presented statuses of the various combat systems, weapons inventories, daily call signs, and computer status summaries. The older displays were flickering green on black, or orange on black. The new full-color ones didn't shimmer.

She placed her gloved hands on the back of the padded leather chair she would occupy during general quarters. A cruiser's primary mission was to shield higher-value units in a task force. To knock down incoming weapons until its magazines were empty. Then, position itself between the carrier and the threat, and radiate electronically to look as much like that carrier as it could. Like a rook or a bishop sacrificing itself to protect the queen.

Fortunately, she'd had a thorough peacetime training on the system, and had fought under battle conditions, understudying Lenson. If everything worked, they could present a reasonable defense.

As long as they had rounds in the magazines. But even before the war, the experimental Standard antimissile rounds had been scarce. Now they were apparently worth their weight in rubies.

Off to the right of the command table, the Aegis team was manned up. Donnie Wenck was the leading chief. His mad blue eyes, cowlicked hair, and casual demeanor disguised a mastery of arcane software, some of which he'd written himself. Just now he was bent over the console with the leading petty officer. Bethany "the Terror" Terranova looked like a cream puff, soft-cheeked, meek-voiced, but she'd shown steel over the past few months. A civilian woman in a pantsuit was perched on a stool, code-scrolling the screen of her notebook. "How's the patch going?" Cheryl asked them.

"ALIS is being a bitch, as usual," Terranova huffed.

Cheryl nodded to the civilian, who looked Asian. As if reading her mind, the woman said, "I'm Thai, Captain. Not Chinese, in case you're wondering. From the Missile Defense Agency."

"Dr. Soongapurn installed the upgrade on *Hampton Roads*," Chief Wenck said. "They kicked her out of Kwajalein to do some actual work."

Cheryl shook her hand warily. Their previous tech adviser had been major trouble. *Hampton Roads* was one of their sister antiballistic missile cruisers, now on station off Australia. "How's it going?"

"Actually, not well," Soongapurn said.

"What's the problem? Can't we just patch, the way you did *Hampton Roads*?"

"*Hampton Roads* was a baseline nine. You're two generations behind."

"We can't update to baseline nine, then patch that?"

"Believe me, you don't want to crack that drum of snakes." Soongapurn grimaced.

"I see. Well, failing that, can we go back to the previous version?"

"Unfortunately," the adviser sighed, "the updates to 7.9 make that impossible. You can't go back. Only forward. We're trying to reverse engineer, get the first version of *Hampton Roads*' software running on your system. Then backtrack, to fix issues line by line. Including a new repertoire of clutter-cancellation waveformology, increased sensitivity for better low-flier detection . . . the lack of which probably explains why your skimmer punched through. Your chief here seems to be knowledgeable. As does the rest of your team."

"But can we get it up and any bugs worked out before we . . . actually need the system, real-world?"

"Your air-side capabilities will be fine. ALIS may be a different story. But I promise, if you aren't up by the time you have to go to sea, I'll come along."

Not exactly reassuring, but apparently all she was going to get. "Well, thanks, Doctor. Chief, Terror, we'll catch up later."

But even as she said this, their gazes were drifting back to their screens, as if a magnetic field had been turned on again.

AT the CO's at-sea cabin, one level down from the bridge. She fitted the key to the lock, then hesitated. Sucked a breath, and turned the knob.

It still smelled of him. One of his caps hung on a peg, the gold braid sea-tarnished green. Lenson had seldom used the more spacious inport cabin, on the main deck. He gave that to guests or riders, preferring to stay close to CIC and the bridge. This room, though it had a couch, a counter with drawers, and a desk, was only slightly larger than the junior officers' staterooms. Through a side door was a bunk, and a head with a stall shower.

Behind her a pimply, gangly messman coughed into a fist. " 'Want me ta get his shit outta here, XO? I mean, uh, Skipper?"

"Box it up. Get it down to ship's office. They'll send it on." She plopped her own bag and suitcase on the bunk.

"Know where to? Ma'am?"

"I have no idea," she snapped. Ship's commanders hadn't had stewards for years. When they needed help, they got assistance from a culinary specialist for housekeeping and delivering meals, since the cabin had no galley of its own. But she wasn't sure she wanted a male snooping around her personal space. Pawing her photos, makeup, tampons . . . "Um, can you ask Lieutenant—never mind, I'll ask her."

"Okay. Want me to strip this bunk? Get his nasty old sheets off?"

Yeah, she could see this creep sniffing her underwear. "Uh, yeah. Get it changed. The towels, too."

"You betcha. Want me to get you a sandwich? Some cookies? Anytime, just ask."

Hissing through his teeth, Longley began pulling off linens and stuffing them into a laundry bag. Avoiding looking at him, she went into the head, glanced around, and shuddered. Time for a scrubbing. She centered her notebook on the desk and plugged it in to charge. Longley let himself out, still hissing. She sank into the chair and pulled up the LAN.

The bandwidth wasn't good. Six of the eleven fiber-optic cables to Guam had been destroyed somehow, and satellite comms were still down. Which slowed everything to a crawl. Still, military took priority, and though graphics were scarce, text was coming through.

The news was as bad as it had been for weeks now. Another tanker sunk on its way out from Hawaii. The third, as far as she was aware. *George Washington* was officially interned in Japan, out of the war for good, it looked like. So much for steaming her all the way from the East Coast.

She massaged her temples wearily, then caught herself. How many times had she caught Lenson doing the same thing at the command desk, in the wardroom, here? It wasn't déjà vu, but it wasn't far from it. She needed sleep . . . tomorrow would be a full day. The float, then the engine test and fueling. If that went okay, shift berths and load ammo, always a nerve-racking evolution. Yeah. A busy day. She stifled a yawn.

A tap at the door. "Who is it?" she called.

"Amy." A moment, then, reluctantly, "Captain."

"Come in."

The darken-ship lights were on in the passageway, their glow a deep blood red. Singhe's silhouette seemed even more curvaceous than usual. *Was she gaining weight? While I'm losing it,* Cheryl thought. "What have you got?" she said, remembering how often she'd heard Lenson say just that, then growing annoyed at how often she was reminded of him.

Singhe raised an eyebrow. "A minute?"

"I was hoping to get my head down, but if it's important . . ."

"I wanted to clear something up."

"Sure. Go ahead." She didn't invite her to sit, though there was a chair. Hoping to get what promised to be a scene over with quickly.

The dark eyes were accusing. "I thought we had an understanding."

"Um, what understanding was that, Amy?"

"That we'd run things differently. If we ever got the chance."

Cheryl sucked a slow breath. Without Amarpeet Singhe and her strike team, *Savo Island* might look like a warship, but it was just junk metal. "Amy, some of those ideas were dreams. Some were ambitions. But they were all based on peacetime conditions. Equal opportunity, leveling management—those were great goals. *Are* great goals. But now we have to concentrate on combat readiness. If we can't stop the next incoming skimmer, none of that will matter. We're all going to burn alive."

"You're really disappointing me." She moved to the bed. Stood beside it.

Right, it was all about her. Cheryl put ice in her tone. "We'll discuss it later, Lieutenant. Good night."

When Singhe was gone, she pushed out a breath. Not as bad as she'd feared. Though she had the feeling this wasn't the end of the issue. How had Lenson handled Singhe? Good grief . . . had she visited him at night too? The spicy scent of sandalwood lingered. Then, gradually, faded, as she showered, brushed her teeth, her hair, and sank at last, with unutterable gratitude, into her rack.

Only to stare up at a photograph pinned just above where Lenson's head would have lain. Of a blonde. Oh dear. A rather . . . intimate snapshot. She recognized the woman, despite the seductive pose. Blair Titus had visited the ship in Crete. Cheryl smiled unwillingly. Slipped it out and placed it facedown on the desk, to mail out tomorrow. Or maybe, better, just to shred it?

She lay back again and closed her eyes. Her stomach rumbled. Lacing her fingers over it, she pressed. That seemed to help. Tomorrow she'd put a picture of Eddie "Afterburner" Staurulakis up there. Maybe leaning shirtless on his F-18. Yeah, right . . .

THE buzzer woke her, raucous, unending. She groped blindly, not grasping at first what the noise was, or where she was. . . . A red light flashed in the dark. She snatched a handset off the bulkhead. A covered remote. Oh, yeah . . . she was in the CO's at-sea cabin. The buzzer cut off. Thank God.

"Matador, Matador, this is Barbarian, Barbarian, over."

"This is Matador, over." Matador was *Savo Island*'s call sign. A petty officer was answering up, guarding the Navy Red circuit.

"This is Barbarian. Request Matador Actual, if available."

A moment of uncertainty. Then she realized that would be her. She pressed the button, waited for the sync. "This is Matador Actual. Over."

"Stand by. Over."

A new voice, one she recognized instantly. *"This is Barbarian Actual. Are you in my sea cabin, Commander? Over."*

"This is, um, Matador Actual. Now. That is correct. Sir. Over."

"Congratulations. A message is on its way. You're joining my task group."

"This is Matador. Um, congratulations to you, too. We heard about the promotion."

"For the duration only. Was the Q-89 upgrade completed? Are you ready for alfa sierra whiskey operations?"

"The sonar upgrade's done. Assuming we pass FAST and machinery tests, which I have no reason to assume we won't . . . yes, we'll be ready for ASW operations." A moment too late, she recalled the dome leaks. Well, the supervisor had said they were fixed. "Though we don't have a great loadout for antisubmarine work. Details via reporting-in message. Over."

"Do that, but we're all short-stroked on logistics. You know about the glitches with the production lines back in the States. . . . I did get a couple extra fish broken out for you tomorrow. And some of the new hypervelocity projectiles for the five-inchers. Make sure you have full food and fuel loadout. Commandeer any bagged rice, cabbage, cigarettes, and seven six two and fifty cal you can lay your hands on. Over."

Rice? Cabbage? Oh, for the Korean units. "Um, roger. Bagged rice, cabbage, cigarettes, small-arms ammo. I'll get Hermelinda and Ollie on that, over."

"There's fighting ahead. TF 76 will be in the thick of it. Oh, and I sent you some Army point defense. For that keyhole problem. But . . . can I depend on you? Are you ready for sea? Over."

For just the fraction of a moment she considered telling him they were undermanned. They needed a bottom strip and repaint. Their combat systems software was half-done and untested. Now she was taking the risks, not he.

"Yes, Admiral," she said firmly, pressing the button with a suddenly desperately itchy finger. "We are ready for sea."

4

Marine Corps Recruit Depot, Parris Island, South Carolina

THE Booger Squad had been marching all night. Up and down the rolling hills, through dead, crackling marsh grass. Splashing through cold water. Under icy clouds, buffeted by gusts of rain and bitter wind. Breaking into a staggering, lurching double time whenever they emerged onto the beach, to the crash of Atlantic waves. The shortest man, at the end, kept staggering, then catching himself just before he fell. Occasionally one of the others would drop back and pull him forward. Shouting into his ear, "Keep going, Ramos! You gotta keep up, man. Grab the drum if you have to. Let us drag you."

Hector Ramos shook himself back into consciousness. Tried to remember where he was. What he was. To keep his rifle pointed toward the threat. But he kept sliding off into sleep. Staggering, losing his grip on the ropes that lashed him to their shared misery, their black, unendurable, hellish burden.

Back to the Line.

THE long low building is set back from the highway behind chain link topped by sparkling concertina wire. This early the mist from the bay lies over it, softening the angles of blue-and-white-painted concrete block, cooling towers, and boiler smokestacks in the main plant and the by-products plant. The morning light plays in bronze and rose and lavender through the white plumes of smoke and steam the exhaust fans expel, rising toward a light blue sky where seagulls soar and wheel.

But a disquieting stench of burnt feathers, manure, and ammonia breathes through the old Kia's heater as seventeen-year-old Hector nears the plant. A whine begins under the hood. When he turns the wheel to swing into the lot, a vicious knocking throbs. The guard ducks to peer in, then waves him on. A sparkly rosary and a laminated picture of a dark-haired, sloe-eyed girl sway from Hector's rearview. He heads for the corner that gets shade from one of the few trees. He doesn't have the money to fix the car, or the credit to buy a better one, so he just parks, and hoists the rusty door back into place so it can latch, if not actually lock.

He follows the other arriving shift employees through the front guard shack and out back to receiving. He stalks tensely up the ramp into the rear loading area, past the idling line of trucks, nodding to Sazi and Fernando. Checking out of the corners of his eyes for Mahmou', but the Arab isn't in yet. Relieved, Hector sighs and punches in with his employee card.

The Line starts here, though it's still early, so it isn't moving yet. Dozens of trucks wait grille to tailgate, engines rumbling, diesel-smoke drifting up to join the mist. The drivers slouch by the ramp, jeans sagging on their hips, smoking and talking. They're Peruvian, Salvadoran, Mexican. There were Haitians here when Hector hired on, but they made trouble over wages and one day were all gone. Desaparecido, *though probably not in the way the Salvadorans mean. Yellow plastic modules flecked with curling down are stacked on the tractor trailers, twenty to twenty-five birds to a cell. A forklift will slide them off onto the conveyor. Hector walks past the door to his own cage, past José, his foreman, who's studying a seagull with a broken wing, which is watching him hopefully from below on the loading dock.*

But Hector doesn't go in yet. Instead he heads back to the break room and puts the bag lunch his mother packed into the fridge. He fidgets in front of the drink machine, studying prices, then the buttons. Numbers puzzle him. He can add, but it takes time. If someone interrupts, he has to start over. The TV's on. A fat white man with a comb-over is talking about Mexicans. They sneak over the border and anchor themselves with babies. They draw relief and don't work. They sell drugs, rape, and kill. The camera pans to his audience. They're chanting something Ramos can't make out, shaking placards. The television shows a wall in a desert. Hector recalls that desert, but he doesn't remember a wall.

The news changes to the war. Hector watches explosions, aircraft. He pushes sleeves up on thin arms. Dark, raised scars, like vines of poison ivy on a tree, run from the backs of his hands to above the elbows.

He's pushing coins into the machine one at a time, counting aloud, when another teen bounces in, bony, wiry, dark, with high cheekbones and a tattoo on the side of his neck. "Ay, Hector!" Mahmou' calls. "How is that hot little Mirielle? You get in her sweet pants yet?"

Hector flinches. The machine whirs, thunks, and disgorges a can. Almost too fast to see, the other boy snatches it. Hector lunges, but the other holds it away teasingly. He takes a long swallow, then upends it over a plastic-lined trash bin and lets it gurgle away. Flips him the empty, and slaps his back. "Got to be faster next time, 'migo. That is what I am training you for, the speed. You are not fast, you will not last. Not in the Cage."

Outside a bell clangs long and loud, echoing. Motors begin powering up. A metallic crashing begins, underlain by an electric hum. When Hector steps out of the break room he has to jump back to avoid the polished prongs of a forklift. He hurries across gray-painted concrete, following Mahmou', who pulls a pair of nylons from his back pocket and draws them up over his hands.

In the Hanging Room a long chain of stainless hooks sways, tinkling faintly, almost like music. Dozens of upside-down U's of heavy, polished stainless metal, each just long enough to trap a man's hand within. The chain passes through a vertical slot in the concrete wall to their right. Slot, wall, and floor are spattered with a brownish-black crust inches thick. The kill lines run faster than the eviscerating lines, two lines diverging into four, with the kill lines at 180 units a minute and the eviscerating lines at 90 or so. Hector stamps heavy steeltoes, testing his footing. The men fit goggles over their eyes. They pull on thin gloves, or, like Mahmou', women's nylons over their lower arms.

"Ready?" José, the production foreman growls, his single hand on the light switch. He lost the other in an ice-grinding machine. Without waiting for an answer from the men ranged tensely along the line of glittering hooks, like runners poised for the gun, he jerks down the heavy knife switch. The lights douse, then reignite a deep carmine red.

With a prolonged, grinding rattle, then a clashing metallic clanging, the Line surges into motion.

HECTOR came back sputtering, choking, cold seawater splashing his face, light dazzling his eyes. He blinked up into the Hat's flashlight.

"Get the *hell up*, yoohoo!" the drill instructor screamed into his face.

"*Now*, chickenhead. Get him on his feet. Get that rifle *alert to the dirt!* You point that thing at me again, I'm gonna personally kick you to Korea!"

They jerked him up on his boots. Sand grated in his MARPATs. For two hours that night they'd carried logs through the surf, trying to build a bridge out to an island. Burdened the entire time with the unendurable weight DI Brady had saddled them with. The DI thought them *too weak* to be in his Corps. Because they were *pansies* and *good Army material* and *not trying hard enough*, he'd torn up their stress cards and decided that wherever they went, even during the Crucible, the final hours of hell that marked the climax of boot camp, the Booger Squad would carry, in addition to their combat gear, a full fifty-five-gallon drum of water. A clumsy, four-hundred-pound, impossible-to-grip burden that after the first hour they would have traded instantly for a cross and a crown of thorns.

Boot camp in peacetime, the DIs told them, had been twelve weeks. In World War II, Korea I, Vietnam, and now this war, it had been shortened. A special Corps good deal, so they could get to the best part of being a Marine: killing the enemy. The Booger Squad got everyone who bilged from other platoons. The men and women with ankle injuries, or who were too fat, not aggressive enough with the pugil sticks, who couldn't get over the obstacles. Hector's problem, aside from slow arithmetic, was that he couldn't swim. Whenever his head went under, he panicked. He flailed around, choking, and had to be hauled out by the scruff.

Which Bleckford was doing now, hauling him along by the scruff. His fellow recruit had to be far beyond the peacetime body-fat standards, Bleckford was stupid, Bleckford never could come up with the right answer when the Hat started in on him. Yet his yard-wide ass was usually ahead of Hector on the confidence courses, balance beams, log runs. Squirming through muddy ditches with barbed wire hanging slack over them, waiting to snag their rifle barrels, helmets, their uniforms, coated with slick Carolina mud like the chocolate shell on an ice-cream bar.

"*Ramos!*" The Hat, right next to him, double-timing like he always did while the recruits were dragging one boot after the other. The man was inexhaustible. Relentless. Could see in the dark like a cat. Knew everything. Could curse in Spanish, Chinese, and Arabic. Had fought in Iraq, been wounded in Afghanistan. "That rifle points at a forty-five-degree angle to the direction of movement. It does not point at the back of the trooper ahead of you. It does not point at the ground. It does not do any good pointing at the ground, like your dick! *Ramos!* What are the characteristics of the Chinese standard rifle round?"

Hector stumbled over his boots, searching a fatigue-erased brain.

Words reached his tongue by reflex, without any thought process. "Sir! The DB 95 cartridge has a 64-grain bullet with a muzzle velocity of three thousand feet per second. Sir!"

"When fired from what?"

"Sir! When fired from a Type 95 rifle with a rate of 650 rounds per minute in full automatic fire. Sir!"

"Bleckford! What is the cost of the standard Chinese rifle round?"

A hoarse, tired bark. "Sir! Uh . . . This . . . recruit . . . does not know the cost of the Chinese, uh, whatever you said. Sir."

"You dumbass Detroit bullet stopper . . . the Chinese rifle round costs a yuan and a half. A yuan is worth ten cents. So that's fifteen cents. Evans! How much does it cost the Corps to train you?"

"Sir, this recruit—"

"Louder, goddamn it. *I can't hear you!*"

"Sir, *this recruit does not know—*"

"*Shut the fuck up!* It costs the United States Marine Corps a million dollars to train each of you meatheads. It costs the People's Liberation Army fifteen cents to kill you. How in the name of Christ are we going to win this fucking war? Ramos, tell me."

"Sir, this recruit is going to have to kill a shitload of Chinese, sir!"

"At last, he makes sense. Are you a fucking Christian, Ramos?"

"No, sir. I'm a Catholic, sir!"

Brady screamed into his right ear, "What is this 'I'? *There is no fucking 'I' in my Marine Corps, chickenhead!*"

"Sir, this recruit is a Catholic!" Ramos screamed back, stripping his throat raw. *"Sir!"*

"Do you *love all men, Ramos*?"

"Sir, this recruit tries to, sir!"

"Do you love *me*, Ramos?"

"Sir, this recruit loves the drill instructor as a sinful piece of human shit, sir!"

Brady put his face close in the dark and snarled, "Barely acceptable, Ramos. Just *barely*. But do you love the *Chinese*, Recruit? That's what you sad little motherfuckers are going to have to figure out. Or do you hate them, like, enough to blow their fucking guts all over the dirt and stamp on them?"

"I hate the—"

His helmet rang so hard he reeled in his boots. He bit back a gasp. "Sir, *this recruit* hates the fucking Chinese, Drill Instructor."

Brady lifted his arms and howled, "I am here to bring clarity into your benighted universe, fools! To force you to gaze into the abyss of your fucking empty souls!" The howl faded to a mad chuckle, ominous in the dark against the dull thudding of boots, the dull clink of gear, the dull slosh of water in the drum, the dull exhausted gasps of the recruits, the dull crash of waves on sand. "There'll be no stress cards and no safe words in Korea. Triple the size of the Corps, they said. So we get sand-blowers, transdragons, shitforbrains, chickenplucking yardbirds. The bitched-up scrape of every fucked-up abortion. Every waddling, slow-paced, lefthanded, non-English-speaking, obese, wrong-eye-dominant Cat Five . . . pick up the pace, assholes! Tide's a-comin' in, gotta beat it before we drown. Ramos! Bleckford! Breuer! Conlin! Schultz! Evans! Vincent! Let's hear it back there, ladies! *Titcomb!* Count, cadence, *count!*"

A deep Alabama voice foghorned,

"When ah slid out of mah mama's womb,
Ah foun' mahself in a delivery room.
All bloody an' wet ah rappelled to the floor,
Cut mah umbilical an' crawled to the doah."

Wheezing, panting, struggling up sand hills and down, Hector Ramos blacked out and on again like a faulty computer. Sometimes he regained consciousness on his feet, sometimes on his knees. Sometimes carrying the drum, sometimes being dragged along. Even being dragged, his eyelids drooped closed.

Taking him back to the Line.

WITH a prolonged, grinding rattle, the chain of stainless hooks surges into motion. They sway back, then forward as they accelerate. They precess along without end, one every second.

An aluminum door folds open with a grating rattle, revealing one of the yellow plastic modules. Shoulder to shoulder, the men reach deep into it for the birds, which mill around furiously, squawking and flapping clipped wings. Hector flips one upside down, facing him, so it can't shit on him. Inverted, the bird suddenly goes quiet. Hector spins. As one of the U's approaches, he hooks the bird's claws dexterously into the wire loops. Hanging upside down in the shackles, struggling only a little, the bird is carried out of sight through the slot in the wall. Another follows it, hooked in by Mahmou', then another by Joju.

Then comes a seagull, struggling wildly upside down in the shack-

les, its broken wing hanging down to drag on the dirty floor. José barks a mad laugh and holds up his right arm, wagging his stump at the boys. Then come two more chickens, hooked in by Fernando and Sazi.

Then an unfaltering, unbroken stream of upside-down birds leaves the Hanging Room as the team settles into a rhythm, bending, grabbing, straightening, in a flurry of feathers, cursing, cackling, scratching, the hum and clash of steel in the deep red light. Hector gets a deep scratch from a poorly clipped beak, and blood streams down his arm, mixing with the shit from the birds. He keeps his fingers clear of the shackle as he hooks each chicken. The Line does not stop. If he gets caught, he'll go through the wall along with the poultry. Into the Kill Room, where the pre-stunner stiffens them with direct current so they don't move as a hydraulic blade snicks through their throats. Then the post-stunner, where a different current keeps their hearts beating, the blood pumping out, as they circle over vats. Then on to the scalding area, the picker, eviscerating line, unloader.

After chilling for seventy-five minutes they slide down stainless chutes polished to a mirror-finish by the carcasses. Only a few drops of pinkish fluid now ooze from the pimpled skin. Women pull the units off the ramp and impale them on tapered stainless stakes. Holding her knife tightly, so it doesn't slip, each slices off the ribbon of fat that circles the back of the unit. Seizes it with her left hand, tears it free, and without looking drops it on the conveyor to go to another area of the plant. Then turns, to face the next unit, and the next.

There are many lines and processes, deboning, whole bird, grading, cut up. All the lines run at different speeds, but no one can stop. Five minutes' break every hour. Half an hour for lunch.

Around them, the drone and snarl of machinery, shouts, the pulsing whir of exhaust fans, the mutter of propane-driven forklifts bustling cartons of flensed flesh to the freezers. Brown faces, black, now and then the wrinkled visage of an older white. Above, looking down from their offices, the bosses. Walking between the machines, the supers and foremen. And the clattering endless whine of the Line echoes from the high ceiling, stainless, reinforced with steel mesh, greased with fat and blood. But the chicken is cheap in the bright red packages with cheerful, friendly Farmer Seth, lanky and white-bearded, smiling from the plastic wrapping.

Hector always thought he looked not all that different, really, from Uncle Sam.

* * *

THE Hats weren't supposed to kick recruits, but somebody was kicking him. Hector came to clutching his gut and retching. He was curled at the bottom of a dune. The drum lay on top of him, and Brady was talking into the radio he wore on his belt. "Follow here. Got a casualty."

"Get 'em all back here, ASAP," the radio buzzed. Hector recognized the gravelly voice. It was the Heavy Hat, the second-to-senior drill instructor, who gave the junior Hats their orders. There were others above him, the officers, but only distantly glimpsed, unimaginable. *"Shortest route, double time. They got a load, ditch it. Get 'em back to the Grinder. Out."*

Shouting above him. Hands, hoisting. The grating of the drum lifting from his legs, then the crackling hiss of it rolling off over the brittle grass. He kicked and feeling returned to his legs. Bleckford's big soft mitts set him gently upright. Without the burden of the drum he felt ready to float up into the night. Like Jesus, ascending into the clouds in the holy pictures. They broke into double time, toward yellowish lights that suddenly winked on. Back to the Grinder.

THEY'D glimpsed the Senior only a few times during training. Usually standing off to one side, observing silently, his swagger stick locked behind him. Tall, thin, rugged. His dark face both severe and somehow compassionate, he looked across the heaving sea of recruits and DIs like God himself brooding over the sufferings of mortal men. From time to time his gaze sought one or another of the instructors, and a lifted chin or beckon of the stick would gesture him or her over. He'd called Brady over more than once. No one had heard what passed between them, but their DI had seemed subdued when he returned. Though unfortunately never for long.

The platoons formed up swiftly in the dark, on the yellow footprints they'd oriented on the first day they'd arrived. Their uniforms were stained with sand and mud, dark with wet. Some faces were bloody, some running with tears and snot. The Booger Squad formed up on the starboard side, toward the rear. The recruits stood trembling. The mustard-yellow lights glared down as a cold rain fell out of the dark, the wind blowing it across their ranks, stinging their faces.

A marine ran up, lugging a varnished platform with the eagle-and-globe insignia. Without glancing at it, the Senior stepped up. A woman brought a wireless microphone, while others positioned speakers. When the Senior flicked the mike with a finger, the snap echoed across the Grinder and off the barracks like the crack of a whip.

The rain blew harder as he lifted his head to stare out over them. "As you know, we are at war."

Absolute silence reigned. Here and there a recruit wavered, sagged, then collapsed, and got dragged out of formation by a corpsman. But no one broke ranks.

"Many of you are undocumented immigrants. The Corps offered citizenship to anyone who joined the service, and completed a full term of enlistment.

"Congress has just passed an amendment to that legislation. Those who joined under that proviso are American citizens now, effective as of 0800 today."

A couple of the other recruits glanced at him sideways. Hector panted, blinking rain and sand from his eyes. Shouldn't he feel different? He was legal now. But he didn't feel different.

"The Crucible is over," the Senior went on. "Your recruit training is officially completed. You are now, all, Marines. Congratulations."

He drew himself up to attention and came to a full salute.

"Atten-hut," the DIs bellowed. "Pree-sent . . . *harms.*"

Hundreds of rifles snapped into position, compensators pointed up into the beginnings of a charcoal dawn. The Senior held his salute for three seconds, then broke it off like an icicle.

The DIs' voices floated high in the misty dawn. "Orrr-der . . . *harms.*"

"Parrr-ade . . . *rest.*"

In a less formal tone, the Senior resumed: "The usual final parade and celebration are canceled. With the exception of those turned back for medical reasons, recruit training is over. You will proceed from here to the mess hall for the Warriors' Breakfast. In two hours you will ship out for advanced training, or direct to units. You will have your seabags packed and be ready to embark by 0800.

"Dismissed." Without looking, he handed the microphone off, stepped down, and strode away.

But "Booger Squad, stand fast," Brady's tenor sang out, before any of them could move a muscle. Around Hector, men and women froze. "*Stand fast*, boneheads! Before I see assholes and elbows. Single line!"

The rain started again as the DI stalked back and forth in front of them. "All right, you're Marines. The Senior says so. So I guess that makes it true.

"But I'll tell you a secret. A lot of you baa-baas wouldn't have made it through in peacetime. We'd have flushed you, day one. You're good enough to hold down a seat in the head. And that's about all. A lot of you weak, slow, trusting fuckheads are gonna die out there."

Ramos swayed. The words seemed to travel around his brain without making contact with anything, like a bullet circling the inside of his skull.

Brady snarled, "Look at fucking Bleckford here. He's not smart. But you don't need a degree in rocket science to be a combat Marine. It just takes two things. Discipline, and hate. So . . . Bleckford. You hate me, *retard?*"

The fat marine hesitated. Then growled, "Sir, yes, sir. I hate you, sir."

Brady nodded and clapped his shoulder. "Good man." Then moved on, to stop again in front of Hector. "But you know what? Ramos here, he's different. He doesn't hate Chinese. He doesn't hate *anybody.*

"I don't want to see you simple assholes coming home in body bags." When Brady put a hand to his eyes it seemed to tremble slightly. Hector frowned, squinting, not believing what he was seeing. No. It had to be the rain.

"Forget your fucking religion," Brady grated. "Forget your fucking families. Forget your fucking girlfriends, or boyfriends, or whatever you gay fuckers call your sweeties. Learn to hate. That don't mean contempt. Don't think the other guy's stupid. Respect your fucking enemy, or he'll win. Blind hate blinds you. But you're gonna have to learn to kill.

"And you're gonna stick together. Bring your buddies back. Don't worry about anything else. Make sense of it later." He raised his voice, to a scream. "Do you assholes understand? Excuse me: Do you *Marines UNDERSTAND ME?*"

"*Yes, Drill Instructor!*" they shouted, together, confused, cold, hungry, scared.

"Now *get the fuck out of here!*" Brady screamed.

Hector looked back over his shoulder as they scattered. The DI had turned away and was bent over, hands on his knees. Shuddering. Sucking slow deep breaths. Staring down as if at something beyond this world entirely. Maybe, at the rain, carving its endless rivers into the all-encompassing mud.

5

The White House

STRIDING across West Executive Drive on a cool windy day, trying her best not to limp, Blair Titus tapped her phone to take a call. "Titus."

"Blair, Jessica. Got a sec?"

Jessica Kirschorn was her campaign manager. She was punk, pierced, and twentyish, her hair color changed by the week, but she understood the social media that drove campaigning these days. Especially when you were trying to win while holding down a job and a half advising on a war. Swerving to miss a cart laden with cleaning supplies, Blair caught an admiring glance from the man pushing it. "Yeah, whatcha got? Any news on the recount?"

"I'm in Annapolis, talking to the people about the state code, election law. The benchmark's one-tenth of one percent of the turnout, to demand a recount. We're within that. But there's a question about the counting methods on optical scanners, if we're the initiator."

Blair clutched her coat against a gust that blew trash across the asphalt. Above her, elms whipped in the wind. The sky was an unfriendly gray. "Any advantage to getting Beiderbaum's people to demand the recount?"

"Unfortunately, he's the one who's that inch ahead. If anybody's going to request one, it's got to be us. Are you—?"

"Hell yeah." She headed for a white awning flanked by creepy dwarfed pines and blasted-looking, shriveled flowers in cast concrete planters. The West Wing entrance. "Um . . . what's the tab? We're getting pretty deep into my credit line here."

"There's a small enough margin you won't have to pay. But there's something else we'd better—"

"You think we can pick up enough votes to—?"

"Oh, there's a chance, Blair. Just be aware, even if you come out ahead, there might be a legal challenge. But there's also a—"

"Okay, whatever, we'll deal with that down the road. Get on it."

"Blair, wait. You have to—"

"What *is* it, Jessica? Please be quick. We've got a major crisis. I'm going into a meeting in the West Wing."

Her manager seemed to be nerving herself. *"Actually, Blair, you have to make a decision, pretty soon, about . . . when to concede."*

"About when to—? Why would I want to do that?"

"I mean, at some point, you'll just look desperate. You know? And that could hurt you two years down the road, when this guy gets caught with his male intern or something, and it's time to run again."

"You're saying I need to concede now, Jessica?"

"No! No, not right this minute. But"—the girl sounded close to weeping—*"like, if the recount's a fail—"*

"Fuck," Blair muttered. She tapped End Call, slipped the phone into her purse, and flashed her old Department of Defense ID to a Secret Service woman at the entrance. The card was out of date, but matched against the admission list for that morning, it got her in.

"We'll need you to leave that phone at the desk, ma'am," the agent called after her, and she turned back, cursing herself for forgetting protocol.

Inside the carpeted, low-ceilinged, quiet corridors, she hung her wrap and scarf, submitted to a briefcase check, and found a restroom. She reapplied powder and lipstick, then brushed her hair, pinning it to make sure the left side covered her ruined ear.

The woman in the mirror looked chalky. Worn. No longer as stunning as at thirty. But still, all in all, presentable enough.

She bent closer, staring into her own eyes. If she wasn't going to be Congresswoman Titus . . . who the hell was she going to be?

Mrs. Admiral Dan Lenson?

"Concede, hell," she told her reflection. "Fuck that."

They'd have to drag her out of this race kicking and screaming.

THE meeting convened in the windowless, too-small Situation Room. There were six other principals, with their seconds seated along the walls, hugging briefcases. The chairman of the Joint Chiefs, General Ricardo Petrarca Vincenzo, gave her a warm smile; they knew each other from her undersecretary days in the previous administration. Actually, she knew everyone around the table. A professor from Stanford, Dr. Dean Glancey. The current undersecretary of defense for plans and policy; another polite nod. A three-star general, Randall Faulcon: Ashaara, Afghanistan, Iraq, now deputy Pacific Command under Jim Yangerhans. And the new president's press secretary.

And at the top of the rosewood table, inclining his head with a slight ingratiating smile: *Blair, we meet again.* The national security adviser was in a light gray suit and pale lavender tie. His hair was going platinum at the temples now. An American flag pin decorated his lapel, as usual. Behind professorial horn-rims his eyes were keen as a soaring osprey's.

She'd faced off with Dr. Edward Szerenci before the war went hot, in the parking garage of the Russell Senate Office Building. He'd advocated a nuclear strike on China while the force balance was still favorable. But Blair had felt the time was past for preemptive nuclear war.

A rep from Central Intelligence opened. Blair had heard the worst news back at SAIC: the unanticipated North Korean breakthrough of the main line of resistance in Korea. They were facing not just a crisis, but possibly a disaster. A watch officer added an update on the fighting withdrawal of the U.S. Second Division and associated forces. "There's no doubt the situation's serious. However, the command hopes they can restabilize and hold farther south, as long as the Chinese don't intervene. Thus far, Beijing's limited themselves to supplying weapons, likely because Pyongyang wants to win on their own this time."

"We're discussing that at the highest level," Szerenci put in. "So far, Tokyo's letting us continue logistic support across the Korea Strait. But no telling for how much longer. And we have to be able to conduct a fighting withdrawal if Japan goes neutral. But there may be significant costs, trade-offs . . . well, we'll get to that later."

She shifted in the too-soft reclining chair. Her hip ached. She herself was representing neither her party nor Congress, but SAIC, where she was a vice president, Strategic Plans and Policy Division. The think tank had been tasked with gaming possible responses to aggression in the Far East. More quickly than anyone had dreamed, their worst imaginings had become dire realities.

The watch officer finished with casualty figures from Okinawa and Korea, and was dismissed with a flick of Szerenci's manicured fingers. "I guess . . . we'll hear from Ms. Titus next. What our civilian whizzes have brainstormed for a comeback strategy."

She hoisted herself, careful not to wince as her hip poniarded her. "Dr. Szerenci, a pleasure to be here. General, Major General, Professor, the honorable Mr. Undersecretary. First slide, please."

This showed comparative population statistics for the Opposed Powers versus the Allies. "As Dr. Szerenci said, we were tasked with looking one to three years out. Unfortunately, our options are limited. Obviously, we're never going to conquer mainland China. Zhang has a huge demographic advantage. Specifically, almost two million more young men than young women—probably one driver for his expansionism. With his current beef-up of land forces, we'll probably face an army of approximately fifteen million within a year."

She paused to gauge their suddenly frozen expressions, then went on. "This second slide shows gross domestic product in dollar equivalents, with the red pie sections graphed to show defense sectors in the out years."

Grimaces ringed the table. The chairman shook his head. "Can these numbers be right? *Forty trillion dollars?*"

"The numbers are from a Congressional Research Service study commissioned by the Senate Armed Services Committee. If it makes you feel better, think of it as buying back half the planet."

Szerenci looked displeased. "This isn't strategy. You were tasked to—"

"Resources drive strategy, Doctor. Otherwise, you're talking hallucination. Overreach. And finally, catastrophe. Strat Plans focused on where and how we could seize the initiative again, and sustain that effort to end the conflict on acceptable terms."

The professor bobbled his head. "Acceptable to us, or to both sides?"

She said, "Excellent question, Dr. Glancey. To both, I would hope."

"Because this has never been done before. War termination between nuclear states—this is unexplored territory," Glancey observed.

"Then we've got a chance to draw the maps." She smiled professionally and strolled back and forth, trying not to limp. Unwise, in a room full of wolves. "Given those facts, how do we come back?

"What Zhang is calling the People's Empire has significant disadvantages. Limited energy supplies, internal stresses, restive minorities, and the fact that it's essentially a racially based hegemony, like Nazism. Unlike democracy or communism, it offers little ideologically to attract outside adherents. Thus, as it expands, it must expend more and more energy to prevent revolts among captive populations.

"Zhang also has to police his own people as shortages grow, casualties mount, fear builds, and food supplies drop. The Hong Kong shootings are a warning to the rest of the country. Geography forces China to expand radially, but each outward step doubles its problems.

"This early in the war, then, perhaps we should even let them expand, especially into areas which require supply by sea, while we work to weaken China from within. Our submarine forces are still superior technologically. General, any reports from SubPac on exchange ratios?"

"Early reports are three to one," Faulcon said. "Our force levels are still building as we rebalance. But mines are taking a heavier toll than we expected. On the bright side, we've destroyed half their submarine-launched deterrent. The rest have returned to port."

"Those are the missiles we reported being offloaded onto mobile transporter-erector-launchers," the intelligence officer put in. "Basically, they're giving up on the sea-based leg of the triad."

"And despite his threats against the continental United States, Zhang hasn't launched one warhead against U.S. territory," Szerenci observed. "Of course, we took out the two subs he had deployed to the Arctic, hours after he hit the *Roosevelt* battle group."

The first she'd heard of that. She filed it to think about later. "All right, let's say they succeed in occupying most of the inner island ring. Perhaps we can retain toeholds in Korea and Okinawa, if the Japanese let us reinforce and resupply.

"But we begin the bleeding process. We maintain the blockade, and begin fracking at every fissure point we can find or create within China. Next slide." She nodded and it came up. This should please Szerenci. "The graph compares our estimates of wartime production of the two alliances, based on energy and raw materials availability. As you can see, production by the Opposed Powers peaks six months from now. Then it falls as their stockpiles of metals, oil, and foodstuffs dwindle. Meanwhile, allied production ramps up. The year after, our production doubles theirs. The year after, quadruples it.

"A strike at the mainland would remind Zhang he has to keep most of his forces at home. The way Doolittle did, attacking Tokyo. Then, we penetrate the inner ring at one of several possible points. Finally, we threaten the homeland. At that juncture, in all likelihood, we can expect Zhang to fall."

Silence around the table. "And if he doesn't?" the press secretary said at last.

"We locate a broker, offer terms, arrive at some face-saving modus vivendi," Dr. Glancey said tentatively, glancing at Blair. "Was that your thinking?"

"That lies down the road, Professor. Most likely, the army will overthrow him before then."

The intelligence director smiled. "Perhaps we can find a Colonel Stauffenberg somewhere." The staffers tittered. One bent to peer under the table.

Blair strolled back toward her chair, but didn't sit. She debated how to present her next point. Finally said, "There's something else we need to be aware of. A significant element, both in the American public and in Congress, may be open to some form of negotiated peace, rather than fighting on."

Faulcon frowned. "After the loss of a battle group? I don't think so."

She said soberly, "You might be surprised, General."

"Not in our party," Szerenci drawled. His lifted eyebrows intimated volumes. "In yours, perhaps?"

She shrugged. "The source doesn't matter. But whatever strategy we adopt, we have to keep this war contained. Above all, keep it from escalating."

"No. What matters is victory," the national security adviser observed.

"There can't be a victor in a nuclear war," Blair shot back.

"I'll settle for not being the loser," Szerenci said calmly.

They were staring each other down when the press secretary lifted a finger. "Corey," Blair said, only reluctantly unlocking her gaze from that of the small man at the head of the table.

"Uh, we're here debating ultimate strategy, while the immediate question should probably be our response to Zhang's recent offer of terms. Is there wiggle room? Space for a deal?"

She said briskly, "An excellent question. This could become a long conflict, with huge risks along the way. How might we achieve peace short of mutual exhaustion, like World War I? It's worth asking."

Faulcon squinted. "Where do you stand on his offer, Blair?"

She shrugged. "That's easy. I stand for prosecution of the war. Not surrender, which is what Zhang's proposing. But not nuclear Armageddon, either."

Szerenci closed his eyes. For that moment, the facade of confidence cracked, revealing the fatigue. When he opened them again, the groove between his eyes remained. "CIA says that even without the sub-based leg, they have megatons targeted on every one of our major cities. Our antimissile batteries can take out maybe a tenth. We'll obliterate them if they attack us. But they can still destroy us, as a country.

"We could have stamped out this threat without any danger ten years ago. Even five. As I and a few others pointed out then. With minimal collateral damage." He spread his hands like a magician at the reveal. "Now, somehow, I've got to pull a rabbit out of the hat. Find a way to destroy them, without us suffering millions of dead."

"If we'd followed your advice then, we'd have been destroyed too," she couldn't help pointing out. "Zhang had missiles in reserve."

"There are still those who think they're fictional."

She inclined her head at the intel officer. "Is there hard data yet?"

He looked away. Shuffled papers. "Um, we . . . we're still arguing that."

Szerenci said, "Zhang's a master bluffer. If you mean to suggest I'm some kind of Doctor Strangelove, the way I'm portrayed in the mainstream press . . . I simply rid myself of illusion, my dear Blair. I try to see the world as it is, and act accordingly."

She said evenly, "I judge you by what you say, Edward."

They regarded each other for a second more. Then she passed out a summary of her briefing. "In accordance with the Dawn Gold protocol, you will not find this on your classified e-mail servers. Paper only. Lock and key. Make no copies. Do not refer to our discussion on cell, landline, e-mail, or other electronic communications. Assume all conversations in public areas are being overheard."

OUTSIDE, in the corridor, it was hard not to sag into the wall. Her hip flamed. Her back ached. She needed coffee. Could there be coffee here? And three or four Aleves?

Beside her Randall Faulcon cleared his throat. The major general said, "We need to get you out to Camp Smith, Ms. Titus. I want you to brief our J3 shop. We've got to start thinking long term, like you're doing."

"Any time, General. But I understand, you have to put out the fires."

"Am I mistaken, or is your husband Daniel Lenson?"

"That's correct."

"We met in Hawaii. Congratulations on his promotion."

"Thank you." She hesitated. "Do you happen . . . I haven't heard from him for some days now."

Was that a puzzled glance? "You mean, where he is . . . ? Probably, getting his task force ready to sail."

She wanted to ask for details, but stifled the urge. "Thank you. I'm sure he's very busy." She turned away, and almost collided with Szerenci, just behind her. His bodyguards waited down the hall, regarding her with impassive expressions.

"Edward," she muttered unwillingly.

"A word." He led her into an alcove. "I understand the election didn't turn out well."

She forced a tight smile. "It's in recount. We're going to win."

"Well, I certainly hope so. But what happens if you don't?"

"I'm not following." She folded her arms, frowning. Szerenci wasn't just from the opposing party; they were on the opposite sides of other divides as well. The way he calculated trade-offs in terms of megadeaths made her suspect he didn't actually identify with human beings at all. Years ago, she understood, he'd been Dan's professor in his postgraduate work. Now and then Szerenci had offered him a helping hand. But her own relationship with him had been that of competing pro boxers.

Though Szerenci was the headliner, while she was far down on the event card.

He murmured, "Do you read Doris Kearns Goodwin?"

"The historian? Sometimes. Why?"

"*Team of Rivals?*"

"Abe Lincoln, right?" she said warily. Where was he going with this? God, she'd kill for a latte right now. Grande. With peppermint.

"I'll refresh your memory. Lincoln knew the nation faced the greatest test in its history. Instead of forming a cabinet of mediocrities, he asked his most capable rivals to join him."

She muttered impatiently, "And?"

"The president's thinking about forming a national administration. As Lincoln did. And Roosevelt, in World War II. To unite the country. I think you'd be a good addition to our team."

She glanced down the corridor. But through her astonishment, remembered to maintain a poker face. "How about Madam Clayton? You could invite her back—"

"Never. Can't have two national security advisers in the West Wing. Anyway, I like the way you think. We've butted heads, but I respect your brainpower."

She sucked air, but maintained a bored expression. What would it do to her dynamic within her party, how would it alter her relationships with peers and backers? "It's . . . unorthodox, Edward. But as you say, these aren't normal times."

"Think about it. But don't take too long."

"I'll have to, of course. But, as I said—"

"I know, you're in recount. You're going to win. But just in case you don't."

"And if I was to consider it, I wouldn't work *for* you. Perhaps *with* you, but—"

"I wouldn't have it any other way. But events are moving. *History's* moving. We have to get ahead of it." A glance around, a crimped smile, and a nod to the two temple dogs hulking down the hall.

He moved off, and she looked after him, eyes narrowed. Then sighed, and went to gather her things.

II

THE HUNT

6

Guam

THE bells echoed out, resounding through the hangar bay. The ship's gray-painted steel sides towered eighty feet into the air. On the wharf engines clattered, cranes snorted, lines of men and women ant-marched boxes out of tractor-trailers. An arched gangway led to a side port. A canvas banner read USS HORNET. A HERITAGE OF EXCELLENCE.

"*Expeditionary Strike Group Seven, arriving,*" the 1MC announced. Dan marched up the gangway, followed by his driver, and halted. Facing aft, he saluted the ensign, then the officer of the deck. Six other sailors and marines stood at attention, perfectly aligned. Dan nodded and said, "Carry on, please." They broke ranks, scattering.

A four-striper stepped forward, and a Marine colonel. They introduced themselves as his deputy commander, Captain Jeremy Dudley, and Colonel Bob Eller. Dan took stock as they shook hands. Dudley was tall and black, Eller white, broader, and stockier. Both had goodly racks of decorations, with Eller's Bronze Star edging out anything the naval officer's chest displayed.

"How about we go by your quarters, Admiral? Give you a break, if you need one," Dudley said.

Dan almost turned around to look for this "admiral." It sounded weird. It would be nice to put his feet up, but Niles and Yangerhans had made it clear that they wanted his strike group to sea as soon as possible. "Not necessary. Just have someone take my luggage." He nodded to the driver, who'd met him at the airfield. "Thanks for your help. I'll keep the briefcase, thanks."

The hangar was even more crowded than the pier. Helicopters with folded blades were crammed cheek by jowl. To the clang of a warning bell, an overhead crane was lifting an engine from an F-35 Lightning fighter/attack. Stacks of palleted soft drinks, food, dry stores, and ammunition were being driven about. It looked like only partially organized chaos.

Hornet, ninth U.S. Navy warship of the name, was an America-class amphibious assault helicopter carrier. A landsman would just have called her an aircraft carrier, but she lacked the slanted deck and catapults that let strike carriers launch fighters and attack jets. Still, at forty-five thousand tons and 850 feet long, she dwarfed the frigates and destroyers he was used to. He tried to stay oriented as his subordinates led him aft and upward. "Familiar with this class?" Dudley said.

"Been aboard a couple. Not for long, though."

"She's based on the later LHDs, but without a well deck. More aircraft stowage. The hangar deck's wider. We've got an onboard hospital, more fuel capacity, better maintenance support. And you'll see, the command spaces are a lot bigger."

Dan wanted to ask about the self-defense loadout, but realized one critical player wasn't here. "Where's the CO? Captain Graciadei?"

"Some kind of ballast tank problem came up. Sent her respects. She'll join us as soon as she breaks free." Dudley cleared his throat. "About staff. You know we're basically an amphib squadron setup, out of Sasebo."

"Any Japanese pressure on you to leave?"

"Let's just say there were no obstacles placed on our departure. But we're only partially manned. Thirty-one bodies aboard, billets for forty-two."

"I plan to augment them," Dan said. "One of the things I want to discuss."

"Just be aware we already have an air-centric marine for the F-35s. Also a Marine Embark guy who works for you, not the colonel here."

Dan ducked through several doorways, with Eller opening watertight doors and Dudley dogging them behind. They climbed two steep ladderways, stepping into an air-conditioned, quieter layout of blue-terrazzo'd passageways flanked by staterooms. Dudley pointed out the wardroom and two lounges. A blue curtain screened off a thwartships passageway at frame 59. "Your cabin's down there, opposite the CO's. Sure you don't need a moment?"

"Let's blast the JIC first."

Sixty feet forward, two heavy steel button-locked doors barred their way. The port one was haze gray and marked CIC. The starboard one was painted a dull green. An ON THE AIR sign glowed above it.

Eller hit the buzzer, and a lieutenant opened the door to a roomy white-overheaded space with briefing displays, terminals, and a conference table with a dozen seats. The Joint Intelligence Center. The lieutenant's "Attention on deck!" brought everyone to his or her feet. Dan waved them down and took the head of the table. He let the silence dwell a moment, to let his new staff take him in. The faces were surprisingly young. Half wore Marine greens, the rest shipboard working uniforms: BDUs, blue coveralls, or khakis for the middle-grade officers.

DAN'S J3, or operations officer, started with the building blocks. Expeditionary Strike Group Seven, centered on *Hornet*, consisted of six U.S. ships, twelve South Koreans, and an Australian conventional submarine, HMAS *Farncomb*, currently en route to join up. The U.S. units included *Savo Island*, *Green Bay*, two later-flight Burke-class destroyers, *McClung* and *Kristensen*, and a T-AKE, USNS *Amelia Earhart*, with ammo, stores, and limited fueling capability. The 13th Marine Expeditionary Unit, or 13 MEU, was embarked aboard *Hornet* and *Green Bay*, with Eller commanding.

The ops officer paused. Dan took the cue and got to his feet. "Good morning. And good to meet you all. . . . Our initial mission is to clear the sea lanes between Guam and the fighting on Okinawa and Taiwan. Then, land one-three MEU on Okinawa to reinforce our troops in contact there. Also, we're to be ready to shield Guam and the Marianas, if anything goes wrong.

"PaCom doesn't think the Chinese plan further offensive operations after Taiwan. But Admiral Lianfeng, Zhang's naval chief, might persuade him to test the second chain. Regardless, it's going to be up to us to hold the line, and kick the first dent into their fenders."

A raised hand. "What about the carriers?"

"Not until closer to the landing," Dan said. "After what happened to the *Roosevelt* battle group, PaCom's holding them east of Pearl."

He waited, then went on. "Our eventual target, as I said, is Okinawa. I have the specifics in my briefcase. But nothing goes on the LAN, even SIPRNET, and I won't discuss it in more detail until we're under way. OPSEC must be paramount. I depend on all of you to bear that in mind.

"Our assault, along with demonstrations at other points along the coast, will draw off Beijing's attention from Second Division, Third Marine Expeditionary, and associated forces now fighting in South Korea. Our submarines are taking a toll on cross-strait shipping, but a major undersea force got by our blocking before hostilities began. They, as well as a sizable and powerful surface action group, are so far unaccounted for."

A broad-shouldered, tired-looking woman with a lank ponytail let herself in. Dudley leaned to mutter, "Captain Graciadei." Dan pointed to a seat beside him.

"Sorry, material issue," she whispered.

"Not a problem. Brief me on it later. Now I'd like to hear from the Intel side."

A Middle Eastern–looking lieutenant commander with a mustache got to his feet. "Qazi Jamail, sir. The admiral is correct that both sides will largely be maneuvering without satellite surveillance or over-the-horizon targeting. However, we do have some insight into Chinese intentions due to a compartmented source called 'Night Light.' I can't say more about that, but it points to reinforcements, airstrip improvements, and antiair and antiship missile emplacements at each occupied point in the South and East China Seas. That's why the timetable's so short. The longer we delay reinforcing Okinawa, the tougher resistance Colonel Eller's troops can expect on landing.

"But sub activity to the east is growing more worrisome. As you said, sir. Air patrols have been increased between Pearl and the Marianas, but there aren't enough airframes for adequate coverage. And we can't commit attack boats to the hunter-killer role, since they're fully tasked for near-shore interdiction. We're also moving into the typhoon season."

Murmurs around the table. Dan raised his voice over them. "Thank you, Commander. Is that all?"

"Maybe a little more one on one, sir—"

"Hold that for later. Colonel, your R2P2 process has started, I'm sure. Let's have a concept of ops briefing as soon as possible after we get under way.

"But I'm going to shut this down for now. I'd like all the skippers aboard at 1400. Invite Admiral Jung. Colonel Eller, I'd like you there too. Captain, where would be a good place for a COs' meeting?"

Graciadei said, "That would be Secure VTC, Admiral. Right next door."

The deputy said he'd pass the word. "Some of them are at the ammo wharf, though, or satellite anchorages outside Apra Harbor. How about 1500, sir?"

"Make it so." Dan glanced at his Seiko. "Here's my briefcase. Run off ten copies. Number them. Then lock them up, under two-key control. I'm going over to the shipyard. No need to bong me off."

SAVO wasn't far away. In fact, the whole basin was tight at the moment, packed with ships. A marine escort, rifle slung, fell in behind Dan as he loped over the brow. A huge guy with a massive chest. The rock-solid face seemed somehow familiar. It wasn't a long walk, but they had to thread mountains of supplies and be alert for forklifts and trucks hustling last-minute items aboard.

Savo Island's familiar upperworks lifted ahead. He ran an eye over the bow, where the missile had blown off or mangled everything forward of the wildcats. The hastily welded steel gave her a broken-nosed look, like an old boxer.

"*Admiral, United States Navy . . . correction . . . Strike Group Seven, arriving,*" the 1MC announced as he swung up the brow. Familiar faces on the quarterdeck. Smiles. Staurulakis stepped forward. "Cheryl," he said, returning her salute, then taking her hand.

"Good to have you back, sir. Even if only for a visit. Wardroom?"

"Can't stay long. Did the Army team arrive, with the point defense?"

He followed her diminutive form through familiar passageways. She threw back over one shoulder, "They're aboard. Tying to shoehorn them in."

"How'd dry-docking go?"

"You saw the bow, I assume. We're operational. But there's some indication of strain on the hull girder. Maybe from the tsunami wave."

"Is there a speed restriction? How's the sonar look?"

"On the speed issue, no restriction. Haven't tested the sonar."

"Keep me informed. Ordnance?"

"They promised us the new SMXs, but we only got Block 4. And not as many as we need. The rest of our cells are full, but more what we could get our hands on than an optimal mission loadout. We're topped off on fish, chow, fuel, and bullets, though."

Dan nodded. Shortages of the antimissile rounds had dogged them through the deployment, and with the "accidents," fires, and cyber attacks on the defense industry . . . "Can you have the personnel chief meet us?"

Staurulakis glanced away, lips going taut. "Aye, sir."

The wardroom was familiar territory too. He'd captained *Savo* most of the way around the world. Fought in the East Med, at Hormuz, and in the Taiwan Strait. Now, unfortunately, he had to stab her in the heart.

Settled at the table with coffee and a Danish, Staurulakis said with her customary directness, "Who do you want? And how can I persuade you not to take them?"

"Ahead of me as usual, Cheryl." He covered his unease with a cough into a fist. "My staff's short eleven bodies. And there are folks here I've come to trust. Chief Wenck came from TAG with me. So did Rit Carpenter. I want them, of course."

"Carpenter, good riddance. But losing Donnie will hurt."

"I need Garfinkle-Henriques, too."

Staurulakis raised pale eyebrows. "Hermelinda? Why?"

"I'm going to need a resourceful N4. I mean, J4. I also want Amy Singhe and Bart Danenhower."

The eyebrows climbed even higher. "I know he was with you on *Horn*. But Bart's my acting exec now. *And* dual-hatted as CHENG. Losing him shorts me two. Amarpeet? I never thought the two of you got along."

"It's not a question of likes or dislikes. I've got to have someone who knows strike ops."

"Strike's one of our missions, Admiral. Taking her will degrade our capabilities."

"You've got a deep bench. The Terror, she's excellent. Kick Terranova up a grade. Ginnie Redmond, Eastwood, they're strong. Jiminiz can step up to Engineering. Promote from within. You can do wartime commissions now."

His former XO dropped her gaze. "I'd rather not lose Amy. Sir. Plus . . . maybe I shouldn't mention this . . . but your wife didn't seem to like her being around."

Okay, so that was how it was. It was true; Blair had mentioned Singhe before. And sometimes the lieutenant could be a distraction. But this was business. He couldn't keep irritation from his voice. "Afraid you don't have a choice, Cheryl."

"You're ripping our guts out, sir. Isn't this kind of, I don't know . . . disloyal? Maybe that's too strong a word. But I need them to keep this ship running."

Dan shook his head. "I'm sorry, Captain. But I have to get this operation all in one sock, with people I can depend on. Have Donnie, Rit, Hermelinda, Bart, and Amy on *Hornet* before we sail tomorrow. I'll do a by-name request to Fleet. If it's any consolation, I'd love to take you along too. But I won't pull you from a command." He gave it a beat, then added, "I need an Aegis ship I can depend on to ride shotgun on me, and run the air picture for the task group. I want you in the driver's seat here."

"Aye aye, sir." Staurulakis sighed, surrendering to the inevitable. "But I'll need replacements. We started this deployment short-handed."

"I'll pull you a fresh TAO and senior enlisted from CONUS."

"Can you take Longley, too?"

Dan blinked. "Can I . . . uh, all right, sure. If you want to bottom-blow him, I'll take him off your hands. And did you get the word, presail meeting, *Hornet*, 1500?"

A discreet tap at the door; the personnel chief let himself in. Dan leaned back and let Cheryl give him the bad news.

STAURULAKIS offered him the 1MC to address his former crew. He was tempted, but declined. She was the Skipper now. He hiked back up the pier, the big marine dogging his steps, rifle at port arms. "You don't need to do that," Dan snapped, then relented. "I mean, I don't think we'll be attacked here."

"There've been assaults on senior military stateside, sir," the guy said. "Colonel Eller assigned me as your personal protection."

Dan really looked at him for the first time. An impressive physique, massive arms, a Western accent. And he still looked familiar. "I see. And you are?"

"Staff Sergeant Gault, sir."

Dan halted beside a roaring generator. He hadn't looked at the guy's name tag. *"Gault?"* he shouted.

"I'm his little brother, sir. Ronson Gault. Why I stepped up when the colonel wanted a body."

Dan touched his ear, remembering the doomed Signal Mirror mission into Baghdad with Gunnery Sergeant Marcus Gault. "Your brother was the bravest guy I ever knew."

"You were with him, sir, when he died?"

"Not exactly. He fell in a rearguard action. So we could get out." Dan exhaled. "I was honored to serve with him. We'll talk about that later, okay?"

HE met with his new staff in the flag spaces. Dudley introduced them, while Dan made mental notes. The operations officer, Fred Enzweiler, seemed colorless but savvy. The Intel guy, with the affected little mustache, was Jamail. The others were still just faces.

They'd have to short-circuit all three phases of pre-deployment planning en route to the objective. Fortunately, the Marines had a Joint Rapid Response planning process. It began with a concept of ops brief, then a course of action selection brief, and a final sit-down with Dan and the landing force commander, Eller, to bless it.

Enzweiler presented a sortie plan and initial formation stations. Dan approved it, but with changes. With enemy subs unlocated, he had to take precautions. *George Washington* had hit a mine in the first days of the war, damaging her so badly she was still in port. *McClung* would go out that night to sanitize the channel. She'd had a sonar upgrade to detect minelike objects. The ROK ships would go next, spaced through the dark hours, so everybody wouldn't bunch up in the excruciatingly narrow harbor exit. At dawn the remaining units, *Kristensen*, *Green Bay*, *Earhart*, and *Hornet*, would leave, in that order.

He excused himself and spent a few minutes with his feet up. The Flag Cabin's main room was the size of a studio apartment's living room. It held a round conference table with blue-plastic-covered chairs, a sitting area with a coffee mess, and a desk with computer, J–phone, and 21MC. His sleeping area was behind it, with a small head and shower behind that. Someone had left a fresh set of blue ship's coveralls, a gold-encrusted USS *Hornet* ball cap, and a brand-new pair of flight-deck boots on his bunk. He shaved, changed, and headed for the VTC, Gault trailing him through the passageway. He'd been waiting outside his door. Was the guy going to shadow him wherever he went?

"Attention on deck," Dudley called as he entered.

"Carry on, everyone," Dan said.

The videoteleconferencing center held the largest table yet. He smelled coffee. About a dozen faces, some familiar, others not, turned from the sideboard. None of the skippers looked particularly happy to be there. Cheryl was in khakis. Eller and Dudley were present.

So was a compact, older, hard-faced Asian. Dan took a stride forward, extending a hand. "Admiral. Hate to meet like this, but I'm glad you made it out."

"I'm pleased to see you again too. Congratulations, Admiral." Min Jun Jung's two-fisted handshake was iron hard, and he held it for extra seconds. They'd faced North Korean submarines together in the Eastern Sea, and fought shoulder to shoulder again in the Taiwan Strait battle.

But Dan felt awkward. Now *he* was the task force commander, with the Korean commanding only his ROKN screen elements.

"I look forward to serving under you." Jung added in a low voice, "Don't worry about ranks."

Dan murmured, "Let's make it *with* me, instead of under me."

Jung just smiled, and waved another Korean forward. "Perhaps you remember Captain Hwang. A commander when you saw him last. I'd like to make him my liaison, on your staff."

It was really getting to be Old Home Week. "I was going to ask for one." Dan shook Hwang's hand too. No longer quite as young, but still willowy, pale, and languid-looking. And his grip was as flaccid as ever. "Min Su, right?"

"That is correct. A long time since we were shipmates, sir."

"I remember our time on *Chung Nam* together."

"I am pleased to see you again, Admiral."

Dan turned to the others. "Let's get seated, then we can go around the table."

They kicked off. Not all the COs had been able to make it, but Dudley had set up those who couldn't on videoteleconference screens. After introductions Dan laid out the sortie plan, including the early exit of the Korean units. "I want to say again how glad I am to have our allies with us. I have no worries about your crews' professionalism, Admiral Jung. I've served with them, and respect them."

Jung inclined his head. Dan went on, "This operation will be the first landing of reinforcements on territory under attack by the People's Empire. Supported by a carrier task force to our rear, and with the Chinese diverted by other demonstrations, our Expeditionary Strike Group will land Colonel Eller's 13th MEU on an island in the Ryukyu chain."

The lieutenant returned, burdened with heavy sealed manila packages. A few skippers started to open them, but Dan stopped them. "Not until you're at sea. These are the op plans. Memorize them. Required reading for your ops types and execs too."

He took a breath, glancing at the overhead. Now was the time to say something inspiring. To channel Nelson gathering his lieutenants before Trafalgar.

"So far we haven't been terrifically successful in this war. The enemy's surprised us. Hurt us. The loss of the *Roosevelt* strike group . . . we all had friends on those ships.

"But I promised the country we would be back. That we would not abandon our allies, who are being bullied and invaded. Zhang will fall. But to start that process, we have to show that China isn't invincible. Our forces are still relatively weak, but that doesn't mean we cower and wait to be attacked."

They were listening, but they didn't look inspired. He was so damned tired. . . . "Any questions?"

Jung held up a hand, and Dan nodded. "I have twelve ships," the Korean said.

"Um . . . yes?"

"It is a good sign. In 1597 Admiral Yi Sun-shin had only twelve, and he was victorious. When you call on us, we will attack. Without mercy and without restraint."

Dan reflected wryly that Niles had worried about leashing Dan Lenson. Now was he going to have to worry about restraining Jung? He hoped not. Not only was he junior to the guy, but there would be political ramifications if he was offended somehow or, even worse, lost in battle. Min Jun Jung was the senior military officer escaped from the debacle on the peninsula. As such, he might eventually head a government in exile.

A tap at the door. Dudley brought back a red-striped Secret clipboard. Dan scanned the message. Another logistics ship had reported a torpedo attack four hundred miles south of Gardner Island. Damaged, but proceeding. Dan rubbed his mouth. Well, someone else would have to deal with that. His force was headed west, not east. "No more questions? Very well, then. Remember to keep those packages under lock and key until you're under way."

HE was back in his office-cum-stateroom, wearily paging through his own copy of the three-ring-bindered op order, when the J-dial beeped. He unhooked it without rising. "Captain. I mean, Commodore. I mean, *Admiral*." Damn, he'd better get this straight.

"Sir, flash message on its way."

The rap at his door came before he socketed the phone. What fresh hell . . . "Come in," he called.

Gault entered behind the messenger and stood to one side. Dan flipped open the clipboard.

The landing was postponed.

He read rapidly, skipping paragraphs. A wolf pack of Chinese nuclear submarines was confirmed loose in the mid-Pacific. They were sinking westbound containerships and tankers vital to the war effort. They were also sinking Japanese shipping, contrary to the cease-fire agreement.

3. (S) IF ENEMY FORCES REMAIN AT LARGE, COALITION FORCES WILL HAVE TO ABANDON THE SECOND ISLAND CHAIN. THE NEXT FALLBACK POSITION IS WAKE-MIDWAY-HAWAII.

4. (S) CTG 76 IS DIRECTED TO POSTPONE OKINAWAN LANDING OPERATIONS AND DEBARK 13 MEU ON GUAM. CONVERT TASK FORCE TO COMBINED US/ROKN/AUS HUNTER-KILLER GROUP. PROCEED EAST TO POSITION 20 DEGREES NORTH, 170 DEGREES EAST AND AWAIT ORDERS.

Further orders . . . he could guess what they'd be. Track down and destroy the wolf pack. Clear the shipping lanes, so an offensive had some chance.

His strike group was being retitled and repurposed, and his axis of advance turned 180 degrees.

And his first elements were sortieing tonight.

A knock. Gault peered in. "Captain Dudley, Admiral."

"Always let Dudley in, Sergeant. —You got the message?"

The deputy commander looked stricken. He wrung his hands. "They can't be serious. We're combat loaded. Leaving tomorrow."

"Welcome to wartime, Jeremy. Get used to having new plays called on short notice." Dan waved the clipboard. "Lianfeng's backstabbed us. Got his boats out before the war started, laid low until we forgot about them, then started the slaughter. We may not like it, but PaCom's right. If we lose our logistic train, we're helpless. We can have the latest equipment and the biggest fleet, but without beans, bullets, and black oil, we're toast."

Dudley put a hand to his brow. "The marines—"

"Will have to offload. Like it says." Dan jotted initials, handed the board back to the messenger. The J-phone beeped. "That'll be Eller."

The colonel sounded disturbed, but not flummoxed. "Can we get your guys ashore?" Dan asked. "How soon? By tomorrow morning?"

"Um, that's pushing it, sir. It'll require an all-out effort to debark the MEU overnight."

"I understand. But can we? Leaving most of your supplies behind, mainly getting the troops off and clearing the hangar deck and deep storage? If we're going to operate in an ASW role, we're going to need the rolling gear off, to embark more aircraft. "

He could hear Eller gulping. "It'll take working all night, and some luck. But I think we probably can."

"What are the bottlenecks?"

"Um, mainly, craning the high-profile stuff off the flight deck. The seven-ton trucks, the highback Humvees, the MRAPS, and tanks."

"We can't use the ramps?"

"Not for everything."

"How can we work around it?" There would be hundreds of problems to solve tonight. But then again, if they'd gone west they'd have had to offload all the equipment anyway. Just in a different way, for a different destination. "Can we use the flight deck elevators?"

"That might work. Drive stuff up onto the hangar deck. Lower them on the aircraft elevator. Then drive off onto the pier? I'll need to huddle with Graciadei—"

"Get started." He hung up and rubbed his face, trying to reorient. "What ASW assets do we hold, Jeremy?"

Dudley cast his gaze overheadward. "The destroyers. The Koreans. The Aussie sub, when she joins. And a small search-and-rescue det, with a secondary antisubmarine capability."

"Good, but we need more helos. SH-60Ss and Rs. An ASW/surface attack squadron."

"Actually, there's one available," Dudley said.

Dan blinked. "On Guam?"

"I mean the one on *George Washington.* Remember? She's immobilized in Japan."

"Draft a message. Figure out some way to lily-pad them aboard. Next, air cover. We're going to be sitting ducks out in the central Pacific. Especially if PaCom continues holding the carriers east of Pearl." He remembered the Lightnings in the hangar bay. Vertical takeoff fighters. Not terrific at the interceptor role, but adequate. "Who owns the F-35s? Those are Marine, right?"

"Correct, Marine Air. Six of them, with five currently operational."

"I'll get with Eller and see if he can leave them with us. What else?"

"*Green Bay.* Leave her in port, or take her along?"

They debated the pros and cons. Dan finally decided the LPD would be safer with the main body, rather than in Guam. "Take her. Gives us an extra helo deck, extends our radar detection, and so forth."

Dudley punched his PDA. Dan said, "Get the warning order out. Eller's already working his offload. Give the staff two hours to blitz this, then reconvene. Midnight. Flag plot."

Looking shaken, the deputy left. Dan massaged his stockinged feet, only now having time for doubt. How was he going to localize submarines in the vastness of the Pacific, without satellite recon? In World War II, hunter-killer groups had been guided to U-boats by Ultra decrypts. But as far as he knew, they had no such insight into Chinese movements. Even with "Night Light," whatever it was; if they had, the subs' presence wouldn't be such a surprise.

What other ugly treats did their enemy have in store? So far they'd bulldozed, overwhelmed, outmaneuvered, and outsmarted the Allies at every turn.

He sighed and bent to zip on his boots again. One thing was certain, at least.

He wasn't going to get any sleep tonight.

7

DAN leaned back in his bridge chair as predawn bleached the eastern horizon. They'd busted balls all night, both the marines and *Hornet*'s crew. They hadn't quite gotten everything ashore. But most of the heavy equipment was offloaded, the vehicles and tanks. Enough to clear the hangar and stowage areas for the helicopters.

Helicopters . . . The task force's initial course would be north, to close Japan. If he maintained twenty-five knots, in thirty-two hours he'd be within range . . . assuming the pilots were cool with no return ticket if anything went wrong. Once they were safely aboard, he'd turn east.

His brick crackled. *"Ready to execute, Admiral,"* Dudley transmitted.

"All right, Jer. Let's move 'em out." The execute message would be sent from Flag Plot, on the 02 level. He'd be down there soon. But just now, he wanted to oversee this with the naked eye.

Messages had been flying thick and fast during the night, clarifying things a bit. The sinkings were concentrated in the immense empty bowl of ocean southwest of Midway, north of the Marshalls and Micronesia, and east of the Marianas and Guam. Premier Zhang's, or Admiral Lianfeng's, intent was clear. The shortest line between Hawaii and California to the western Pacific led through this central sea. Cut off, even the few allied forces currently in action would wither like tourniqueted limbs.

Given that reality, postponing Operation Mandible was the only possible response.

But sending his task force after subs signaled a sobering reality. The U.S. Navy was spread so thinly that it couldn't both control the sea lanes and cover an amphibious landing.

On the other hand, a second ASW task force was assembling at Pearl. He and they together might be able to vise the wolf pack between them.

"Now make all preparations for getting under way," the 1MC announced.

From the slanted-out windows of the bridge he looked down on his high-value units moored along Romeo and Sierra wharves. The ROK destroyers and frigates had cast off from their mooring buoys in the basin and steamed out one by one. From an unfamiliar harbor, darkened, radars off, but without so much as a scrape or a single radioed order. Jung ran a tight organization. . . . Getting under way now, the larger U.S. ships would pass the sub piers, empty except for the moored bulk of the tender—the only remaining submarine tender in the Pacific, now—and transit the northern exit, which was barely three hundred yards wide. A hard port turn would take them out of the basin into the outer harbor. They'd still be sheltered then, barriered by a jetty to the north and the peninsula to the south. The harbor security team had a sonar watch set there, to guard against any special forces swimmers, SDVs, or autonomous penetrators.

The next bottleneck was the harbor exit itself, to the west. Once past that they'd be in open sea. An ideal spot for an attacker to lurk, so he'd asked Jung to detail two of the more sonar-capable frigates to scrub the area down. He hoped this, along with *McClung*'s sweeping the channel out last night and drones extending persistent surveillance out a hundred miles, could get them clear without much danger.

Once out there, though, it would be an open question who would be the hunter and who the hunted.

Captain Graciadei materialized at his elbow. She was in blue coveralls, with the cowl-like flash hood pushed back. "Admiral. Good morning, and we're ready for sea."

Dan tapped a salute back. "Morning, Sandy. What's the latest on that elevator?"

"Up and operating." Accompanied by a wink. "Too bad we couldn't get the F-35s offloaded."

"Yeah, that was unfortunate." A complicated game played around 0300, when Dan's request to leave the fighters aboard had come back approved by Fleet but denied by MARFORPAC. PaCom could have resolved the issue but hadn't responded, and Colonel Eller had been caught in the middle. The solution was a "transient electrical casualty" to the single elevator capable of moving the fighters to pier level for debark. With it out of action, Dan had had no choice but to "reluctantly" order them left aboard. The colonel was off the hook, and they had organic air cover.

"Yes, unfortunate," she echoed, then got businesslike again. "We'll go to general quarters shortly. Will you be here or in Flag?"

"I'll start the transit up here."

"Would you like flash gear, Admiral?"

"Uh, I guess so," he said, grimacing. The hot, heavy cowl, thick gloves, and flak vest were de rigueur for bridge personnel at GQ. But scuttlebutt traveled fast. If he held himself above the rules, it gave everyone else an excuse too. "If you'll hand me that helmet?"

OVER the next half hour they cast off, one by one, to avoid mutual interference. *Kristensen* left first, followed by *Green Bay*, then *Earhart*. ESM reported low-power radars. Dan had no problem with that. Commercial fishing boats used them, and so did pleasure craft. Although, from the empty piers at the marina, most of those had left for points east. He leaned on the starboard wing, glassing each ship as it passed. Each rendered honors, and he saluted back, though he wasn't actually sure they could see him.

The officer of the deck stepped up to Graciadei. "Ma'am, ready to get under way." He followed it with a litany: engine status, steering, radars.

The CO turned to Dan. "Admiral—"

"Copy all, Captain. Cast off when you're ready."

A boatswain bent to the 1MC, setting his pipe to his lips. *"Under way. Shift colors."* Graciadei stood centerline as the OOD twisted *Hornet* away from the pier against a pinning wind. Light stanchions began to walk past them on the port side.

"Cap'n," said a familiar voice. An acned face presented a covered dish. "Thought you'd be down in that Plot Room. So it might be cold. Bacon, eggs, coffee."

"Thanks, Longley." Dan took the plate more out of duty than hunger, but got down some toast and eggs before setting it on an angle iron below the window.

He joined the navigator beside the nav plot. *Green Bay* was exiting the outer harbor. *Earhart*, their loggie ship, was dead ahead, beginning her turn. A bell jangled and *Hornet* gathered speed. The pilothouse was silent, other than murmured commands as the OOD centered her on the narrow exit ahead. *Earhart*'s gray bulky profile lengthened as she turned, presenting her port side and putting on speed as she entered the outer harbor and lined up to transit the Apra entrance.

The bridge-to-bridge crackled abruptly. *"Matador, this is War Drums. Suggest you search bearing two-nine-five true. Over."*

Dan stopped his hand in midgrab. Cheryl was "Matador," *Savo Island*, now. His own call sign was "Barbarian." "War Drums" was Min Jun Jung, reporting something one of his screen units had observed. But what? He crossed to the piloting radar, but it showed nothing amiss.

"This is Matador. Searching that bearing. Over." Beth Terranova's voice; she was one of the petty officers Dan had recommended for promotion.

Savo was five miles outside the harbor exit and slightly to the south, set to tuck in as shotgun when *Hornet* emerged. From there she would open the range to seventy-five miles, close by modern standards, up-axis toward the threat. The cruiser would be at general quarters with umbilicals in, ready to turn keys and engage.

He wished he was back aboard her. A ship that could strike back, not the slow, fat target USS *Hornet* presented at the moment.

The 21MC console lit. *"Bridge, Combat: we have* Savo Island *going out to Guam airfield, to us, to all force units and the THAAD battery: Multiple incomers, bearing 290 to 297, correlates with intermediate-range ballistic missiles entering terminal phase descent."*

Dan jerked the binoculars to his face. *Green Bay* was exiting the outer harbor, but only just. Pinned between jetty and peninsula, she had zero maneuvering room. *Earhart* was in a slightly better position. But just at this moment *Hornet*, her stem just entering the three-hundred-yard-wide passage from the inner basin, had the least maneuverability of all. He gripped the binoculars more tightly, searching for something, anything, he could do . . . but came up with nothing.

He'd made his plan, and set his pieces on the board as effectively as he could.

Now it was the other side's move.

As if detecting his thoughts, the VHF radio sparked to life. *"Vampire, Vampire, Vampire. Multiple incomers. Two gaggles, gaggle one bearing two-eight-five, range three-seven miles, gaggle two bearing roughly two-five-five to two-six zero, twenty miles."*

Vampires were sub-launched cruise missiles.

It was a coordinated attack.

His first responsibility: Keep Higher informed. He seized the red phone and reported the incomers to Fleet. Type, numbers, and suspected targets, which were of course both the task group and the base. Fleet rogered tersely.

He signed off, resocketed the phone, and looked around, feeling helpless. Yes, he commanded the task group, but *Savo*, as his air warfare commander, controlled its defense. He grunted, cursing the lack of over-the-horizon reconnaissance. He'd been hoping to vanish in the vast Pacific, but the enemy had somehow known to strike *precisely when* the highest-value unit would be least able to defend itself. Which had to mean either better recon than the Allies possessed, or a spy ashore.

Still, he had a few cards left. *McClung, Kristensen, Sejong the Great,* Jung's flagship, and *Savo* were all capable antiair units. They should be able to knock down most of the incomers. At least if everything worked, and until their magazines went empty . . . He snapped to the Air Control circuit but only heard a couple of transmissions. *"This is Matador. Going hot."*

"This is Turtleship. All units, batteries released." Then rapid, peremptory Korean as the ROKN units pulled in, interlocking defenses like a phalanx's shields.

Graciadei pressed the key on the 21MC. "Weps, CO: RAM, Sea Whiz, batteries released." *Hornet*'s weapons were relatively short-range: the rolling-airframe missiles first, then, as a last resort, the radar-guided, self-laid 20mm guns forward and aft. In terms of self-defense, that was all she had.

Dan took a last look around, then pivoted. The boatswain slammed the door open, and Dan slid down two ladders, spun, and pelted aft.

Flag Plot was manned, but not with many folks he recognized. His new staff, and there'd been no time to get to know them. The space was Spartan, with dated-looking comms except for two huge vertical displays, nearly deck to overhead, positioned to his left. Their fused picture integrated the Aegis inputs of the entire task force with geo and some intel information. The near-complete absence of weapon control or sensor consoles was disturbing. He swung up into his elevated command chair as a dark-haired lieutenant and a blond chief turned in their seats. "Admiral," Amarpeet Singhe said.

"Amy. Donnie. What've we got?"

The radio remote overhead spoke in Cheryl Staurulakis's flat tones: *"All stations command net, this is Matador. Taking tracks 0001, 0002, 0003 with Standard."*

Wenck said rapidly, holding a headset to his ears, "Three incoming DF-4s or -5s. The Terror says impact point overlay dead on the central harbor."

DF-4s and -5s were ballistic missiles. "Nuclear, Chief?"

"No way to tell, Dan."

"Chief, you need to—"

"Sorry, I meant *Admiral*." Wenck shoved a blond forelock out of his eyes. "They're nuclear *capable*. What they put on there, we got no way of knowing. Oh, wait . . . second wave. Three more. No, four more. No, hell, *five*. May be others behind them."

Dan's heart sank. *Savo* had only five rounds capable of intercepting something coming in from that altitude, at that speed. He felt even less confident as Singhe added, "Following them in: two groups of high-speed skimmers. Correlates with CM-708, C-801 seeker heads."

"Can you spoof them . . ."

She frowned. "Sir?"

"Shit, never mind. I keep thinking we're aboard *Savo*."

And there they were on the display, the red carets of hostile cruise missiles. Over a dozen, along two axes of attack. The ballistic warheads were only seconds out now. Lagging them, but more numerous, were the CM-708s, Tomahawk clones, and the shorter-range C-801s. He leaned in his chair as the tracks jumped forward, hesitated, jumped again. Aimed, so far as he could judge, directly for where *Green Bay*'s and *Hornet*'s screws churned green water, desperately but all too slowly thrusting them toward the open sea.

Singhe said, "More pop-ups. Another eight 801s, one minute behind the first salvo."

He took one deep slow breath, then another, trying to ignore the cold sweat that broke over his back. Panicking wouldn't help.

"*Savo* reports Standard launch," one of the other staffers said.

Christ, he felt so damned helpless. . . . He sucked air, watching the blue carets of the Standard Block 4s separate from the cruiser and accelerate outward. The space leaned. A pencil rolled, dove off a table, rolled away down the deck. He glanced at the rudder-angle indicator and gyrocompass repeater. The rudder was hard left. A vibration tremored through the massive hull around them. Graciadei was pushing them through the turn. Cramming on power, trying to get them hauled around and out to sea before the warheads arrived.

The carets, jumping ahead every half second, told him they weren't going to make it. "All hands, flash gear," he called. Though most of the staff were already in it, sleeves rolled down, socks over pant legs, with flash hoods and gloves. They didn't have flak jackets down here, apparently.

"We're still in TF-wide EMCON," Singhe reminded him.

"Thanks, Amy. Get all our radars up," Dan snapped. "They obviously know we're here. And pass to *Savo*—never mind." He reached for the red phone. "All units Horde, this is Barbarian. EMCON lifted for entire force. Stay alert for more attacks in the ten- to twenty-mile range." If those low gaggles were from subs, there could be yet another salvo from even closer in. The Chinese had a capsulized, shorter-range missile, not really equivalent to the U.S. Harpoon, but closer to it than anything else in the inventory.

Okay, Lenson, try to think. . . . This was a carefully planned attack. All three waves of missiles—ballistic, turbojet cruise, and short-range rockets—had been fired on schedule for a simultaneous TOT, time on target. Arriving too close together to shoot down, fox, chaff, spoof, or jam them all.

Thus overwhelming his defenses with a massive bludgeoning. Exactly the way that in 1942, Admiral Mikawa's cruisers had overwhelmed *Quincy*, *Astoria*, and *Vincennes*—timing their attack so that torpedoes and shells arrived at the same moment—in the Battle of Savo Island.

"Barbarian, this is Vandal. I have targeting on archers." Simultaneously with the voice report, a contact bloomed to the northwest. The red semicircle of a submarine.

Dudley called from a desk just below him, "Admiral, we want to counterfire?"

Dan studied the display. He'd positioned *Sejong*, Jung's flagship, to the north, with her supporting destroyers. *Savo* was closest to the harbor exit, with the Burkes out to the west. "Affirmative. Move both DDGs out to the northwest. Get their helos in the air, if they're not already. Proceed with caution. Counterfire Harpoon and get the helos out there with torpedoes as soon as firing platforms are detected. Break up their fire control solutions, at least. Pull *Savo* back—no, wait—better leave her free to maneuver to optimize intercept geometry."

"Stand by for intercept, Meteor Alfa," Wenck announced. He was hunched into headphones, intent on what Dan presumed was the Aegis coordination net. The stream of digital data over the net, computer to computer, was driving the battle now. No longer did the brawn of burly ammunition loaders and the sharp eyes of gunnery officers determine victory or defeat. Networked algorithms would fight this battle at speeds no human could match.

It was a war of microseconds, fought by millions of lines of code.

He yearned after the second-by-second updates he'd gotten on *Savo*. God, he hated being a spectator. Which more and more, apparently, one became as one ascended in rank. Now, the only indication of victory or defeat was when a contact winked out on the display, silently as a dying firefly

Just then, one did. "Meteor Alfa, successful intercept," Wenck called. "Stand by for Meteor Bravo, Meteor Charlie, Meteor Delta."

Over the next few seconds, though, Bravo and Charlie penetrated successfully. Dan pounded his seat rest, cursing. The Block 4 had tested at only a 50 percent kill rate, true. But to actually see it happening . . . to watch the blinking red symbols emerge from their near collisions with their blue interceptors . . . and arrow in, toward the blue cross-in-circle that meant Own Ship . . .

The command space fell silent as the leading warhead, pulsing brightly, flashed down the final miles to impact.

FIVE minutes later, the battle was half over.

Savo had taken down three out of ten ballistic missiles. Two of those remaining had been intercepted by the shorter-range endoatmospheric interceptors of the Army THAAD battery at the airfield. Of the five left, two had detonated cratering munitions across the main runway. The other three hit hangars, maintenance buildings, and fuel storage with heavy warheads. The feed from *Hornet*'s flight-deck cameras showed heavy, slow columns of black smoke boiling the blue air, and the black specks of helicopters airlifting the wounded out to hospitals elsewhere on the island. On the western horizon lighter smoke, mixing to a faint brownish tinge, marked the residua of high explosives, rocket boosters, and chaff mortars. A streak of fire bored toward *Earhart*. The ship heeled, attempting to evade, but the flying flame curved to follow. At the last second it climbed, pitched over, and plunged into her side like a dagger. Half a second later, a red-orange lily of fire and smoke bloomed.

"*McClung* reports hit by debris," Dudley called.

"Damage report, ASAP," Dan said. "How are the Koreans doing?"

"Stand by . . . one hit on a frigate. Set it on fire. But they report most of the missiles passed them by. Seem to be targeted on the main body."

Hornet, Green Bay, and *Earhart.* The carrier was leaning into another hard turn. A drumming thud carried through the steel. Fired in clusters, the decoy mortars would present the incoming cruises with thousands of radar-confusing dipoles and infrared-bright flares.

Singhe called, "Admiral, I'm tracking these missiles passing south of us. They're heading for . . . stand by . . . looks like, for the THAAD battery and base radar. Targeting air warning, suppressing air defenses."

Dan and Dudley exchanged glances. "Let's get the F-35s up." Dan picked up the phone to the bridge. A short discussion with Graciadei ended with her telling him she'd already given that order. He said, "Good, you're thinking ahead. Only question is, what's the threat axis?"

"We don't have anything from our air search . . . nothing from screen units."

"*Savo*'s going to be keyholed, looking for more ballistic incomers." He checked the screen. *McClung* was farthest out, but she'd been hit. So it was *Kristensen*'s ball. "Birkenstock, this is Barbarian, over."

"Birkenstock, over."

"Keep your eyes peeled for hostile air. Maybe from . . . shit, could be from any point of the compass. Can you get your helo up at angels ten? See if there's anything coming over the horizon." Lacking air surveillance or satellites, a helo with a decent radar at high altitude would give the best coverage he could expect. He squeegeed sweat off his forehead. Once the F-35s were up, he'd have only an hour before they bingoed. If he sent them the wrong way, the force could end up without cover in the face of a major strike.

The kind of wrong guess that had cost the Japanese four carriers at Midway.

A deep bass thrum overhead. The 20mm CIWS, firing a storm of depleted-uranium projectiles to tear apart an incoming weapon.

Kristensen rogered. Dan socketed a sweat-dampened handset and checked the large-screen fusion again. The waves of cruise missiles were passing. Yeah, continuing on to Guam, now behind and south of *Hornet.*

"Barbarian, this is Birkenstock, over."

Singhe got to the handset before he did. He resisted the impulse to step in. Stay above the fray, he reminded himself. Think ahead. "Barbarian, over," she said.

"Many bogeys headed in. Putting 'em on the net now."

"This is Barbarian, roger—"

"Tuck his helo back under his envelope," Dan said. "Before they pick him up—"

Wenck was typing madly at his console. The downlinked radar picture came up on the leftmost screen.

And there they were. Hard to count, but at least a dozen. Speed, six hundred knots, and hugging the wavetops. He fought astonishment. Where the fuck had *they* come from? Bearings and ranges would be from the helo . . . convert for the ship, then for the task group—

"Roger," Singhe said into the handset. "Drop your bird below the radar horizon and backpedal him under your defensive envelope. —Flash, flash, flash! All units Horde, all units Horde. Incoming air strike, threat axis two-five-five from Fullbore. Barbarian, out."

"Bearing and range from us, two-five-five, eighty-two miles," Dudley put in. Dan nodded thanks, setting it up in his head as he clicked to the air control net. The missiles had come in from a different bearing. Obviously, to disguise the location of the enemy air strike. He clicked Transmit on the red phone and advised Cheryl of the incoming planes. "I know you're our ABM shield. But you need to go to antiair mode now, and pull in to cover us."

The intel officer called, "*McClung*'s ESM reports incoming strike correlates with Shenyang J-15. Fighters. Short-range. Most likely, from *Liaoning* and *Shandong*." He turned a monitor so Dan could see. "Ski-ramp carriers."

Dan knew them. *Liaoning:* bought from Ukraine, rebuilt and put into service as the first Chinese carrier; *Shandong*, built from scratch as the second. But no one had warned him a carrier battle group might be out here. The enemy had achieved total surprise.

From *Savo Island: "We're headed your way, but we're already out of the ABM business, Admiral. My shot lockers are empty of Block 4s."*

Crap. The next salvo of ballistic missiles, now that the Army battery was down too, would find them all defenseless.

But they weren't defenseless against aircraft, and the F-35s *Hornet* had launched were on their way too. The enemy fleet commander, whoever he was, had scored surprise. But he'd left too many minutes between his cruise strike and the arrival of his aerial punch. Just long enough for his targets to recover, take a breath, and reorient to the new threat.

Fortunately, this was one the Navy was ready for. The J-15s were coming in low, but the radars on *McClung* and *Kristensen*, out to the west, were holding a solid lock-on, with plenty of antiair missiles in their capacious magazines. Launch reports crackled over the air command net. Blue carets, U.S. weapons, began marching toward the incoming red contacts.

Dan was glad he wasn't in one of those cockpits. The only worry he had now was blue on blue. A call to *Hornet*'s air boss relieved him on that score. The Lightnings were assigned and deconflicted. They would take the oncomers between the outer ranges of the Standards and that of the shorter-range point defense systems.

If the enemy got in that far . . . already red symbols were winking out and splash reports were coming over the air.

He tried to detach, stay on the big picture . . . he grabbed the red phone again. "Turtleship, Barbarian actual. Over."

Jung answered as if waiting for the call. *"Turtleship actual, over. Hello, Dan. I see you have located their carriers."*

"Hello, Min. I guess you could say that. We're heavily engaged south of you."

"I have the battle picture on my screens. Want me to join up?"

"Negative, we have this under control. Look, you're already half a degree west of us. Go to flank speed with your fastest units. Leave the slow movers behind. Vector north twenty miles, then west again. With the short legs on J-15s, these guys didn't launch from far away. And if they want any of their pilots back on deck, the carrier's going to have to linger there. I want you to hook out and try to get behind them. Or at least, take them on the flank. I'm going to try to get localization on their main body, get you targeted on the carriers."

"This is Turtleship. Copy all. I'll spin up my Hyunmoos."

Those were a long-range cruise, not too different from the old surface-attack Tomahawk. If the J-15s were short ranged, so unfortunately were his Lightnings. But if he could get Jung within two hundred miles of the enemy group, maybe he could clobber them. Get a little revenge for the columns of black smoke rising over Guam.

"Uh-oh," Wenck said, hands clamped over earphones.

"What, Donnie?"

"ESM's picking up datalinks for C-803s."

This was bad news. The 803 was an antiship missile that cruised in, then accelerated to supersonic for its final dash. Combined with a wave-skimming profile, that left most close-in defense systems out in left field. "Can you fox them?"

"Savo's trying to. But they're coming in fast . . . stand by . . . there's a launch report."

The large-screen display showed the missiles coming off five fighters left after running the gauntlet of Standards and Lightnings. Each turned away after its drop. They were still outside the range of the closer-in systems. But as everyone in the space stared, gazes magnetized by the screen, the incoming symbols suddenly leaped ahead with each sweep of the digital refresh.

Three were headed directly for *Hornet.*

The seconds blurred as the ship heeled, and the 1MC said something that was blotted out halfway through by a howl from forward. In the flight-deck cameras brilliant flashes signaled the rolling-airframe missiles departing their tubed mounts forward of the bridge. Short-ranged but fast off the dime, they were the last line of defense before the Phalanx. The 1MC spoke again in sepulchral tones. *"Missiles incoming, port side. Port side personnnel, take cover."*

A perfectly straight pillar of solid violet-white flame, perhaps three feet wide, suddenly transected Flag Plot, extending from the port bulkhead across to the starboard one.

The air turned instantly into fire. The noise was a vise squeezing his head. Sparks filled the compartment as the casual flick of a panther's paw flung Dan from the chair and whiplashed him into the bulkhead, nearly impaling him on the corner of a vertical plot.

Dazed, deafened, he found himself on hands and knees, crawling blindly amid whirling smoke. His throat closed against a cloud of stinging, choking white that tasted of summer fireworks and burnt plastic.

For a moment he crouched, confused. Was that the E Ring ahead? The glow of fire, the drip of melting wiring? His head rang like a shell casing kicked out of a hot breech. This *was* the Pentagon, wasn't it? He was crawling over bodies. Some moved, others didn't. One lay face upward. *Dudley . . .*

He wasn't in the Pentagon, and this wasn't 2001. He was aboard USS *Hornet,* and his chief of staff lay convulsing, eyes wide but blank, the back of his skull torn away. His arm and shoulder gushed pumping blood, his coveralls were blazing, and his right arm twitched as if trying to grip something unseen. Dan crawled toward him. He had to help. Stanch the blood. But before he could reach him the pulsing spurt from his second in command's torn shoulder weakened, then ceased.

Sound returned, accompanied by a hammering headache and the keen of sirens. He couldn't tell if it was tinnitus or the ship's alarms. Shouts and screaming came from the far, smoke-invisible side of the compartment. Everybody on his side seemed to be dead. He still hadn't taken in a breath, nor did he plan to, in this superheated air and white acrid smoke. He couldn't recall exactly who he was, but he remembered being in places like this before. If you didn't keep your head, you were

toast. If you concentrated you might survive, and maybe even help someone else get out.

A dark-mustached face bent over him, and yanked his head back to
cut his throat. Dan fought him off, panicking, before he understood. Lieutenant Commander Jamail was snapping the elastic hem of an emergency escape breathing device around his neck. Dan blinked through
fogged plastic as gas hissed, and inhaled a tentative breath. "Thanks,"
he gasped, but Jamail had already moved on to someone else.

Clear air. He sucked it deep, panting. Then levered himself up, and
squinted around.

Flag Plot was a smoking wreck. The only illumination was a smear
of daylight penetrating via holes in the port bulkhead. Sailors played
the cottony cone-plumes of extinguishers on smoking, burning repeaters
and consoles that lay tumbled, torn apart, sparking with shorted wires,
pierced by that violet-hot lance. One of the large-screen displays had
been plastered into the overhead. Most gruesome, the fiery jet had passed
directly above three watchstanders at their stations. Their lower torsos
remained seated, cauterized bloodlessly black at pectoral level. Above
that, everything else had been vaporized.

He flinched as the ship shivered beneath him. Facts slowly reassembled
in a clanging skull. Air attack. J-15s. Their warheads packed a hundred
pounds of semi-armor-piercing explosive. Not enough to sink you, but
enough to penetrate most ships' sides and trash several compartments
in the line of their impact. Which this one apparently had, coming
through the port side around frame 49, then detonating in the stateroom
areas outboard of CIC and Flag Plot and the Intel spaces. Blasting fire
and fragments from some kind of shaped charge into and through the
control spaces.

"*Missile hit aft,*" the 1MC announced. "*Vicinity frame 250. Repair
three, provide.*" So, other hits as well.

Hands helped him up. Gault, blood streaming down his cheek. And
behind the marine, Rit Carpenter. The old submariner looked calm behind
the plastic of his own EEBD. His lips writhed, but Dan couldn't make out
what he'd said through the gongs. He shook his head, pointed to his
ears. Gault steadied him on his feet and patted him down for other
wounds. Gave a tentative thumbs-up and led him toward the exit.

The conference table in the Joint Intelligence Center was a battle-
dressing station now. Wounded lay sprawled about. Corpsmen were administering injections and bandaging wounds. Gault and Carpenter led
him to the table and pulled the EEBD off. Dan rubbed something wet

off his face. His fingers felt wooden, but there was no blood on them, just snot and tears. The medic gave him a quick once-over and aimed a penlight into his eyes. "Sir. *Sir?* Can you hear me?"

"Barely."

"How many fingers?"

"Four."

"What's your name?"

"Lenson. Dan Lenson."

"Admiral, you look shaken up. I'd like to administer a mild sedative, then get you to lie down."

"I can't. I have to go to the bridge."

Gault and Carpenter had to argue on his behalf, but finally the corpsman relented. Gault supported him on one side, the old sonarman on the other. Dan staggered down a passageway foggy with smoke, stumbling over laid-out fire hoses, to the ladderway. He had to step over the exhaust ducting from desmoking blowers, but clambered steadily upward, helped along by Gault's hands boosting his ass. From time to time the deck canted again, but he didn't hear any more hits being announced.

When he reached the bridge it went silent. He glanced around, wondering if his hearing had gone out again. Then noted Graciadei in her CO's chair. On the red phone. He lurched over to hear her saying, "That's negative. He's critically wounded and definitely out of action. Making me next in line. Over."

"Captain," Dan said. Almost enjoying how her eyes widened as they slid over to meet his. "May I have that?"

When she wordlessly passed the handset, he pressed the button and waited for the sync. Then said, as calmly as he could, "This is Admiral Lenson. Over."

"Dan. Jim Yangerhans. You okay?"

Dan told PaCom, "Shaken up. Inhaled a little smoke. We took an 803 in Flag Plot."

"Graciadei said you were wounded."

"First reports are always exaggerated, Admiral." Dan shot a glance at *Hornet*'s skipper. Her cheeks were flushed; she avoided his gaze. "No doubt that's what the captain heard."

"Well, good. If you're sure. I know you've got to be busy, but is there a damage report yet?"

Something was being pressed into his hand. A clipboard, presented by Fred Enzweiler, his so-far-unimpressive operations officer. Dan cleared his throat. "Uh, damage report. *Hornet*, three medium-weight missile hits, seventeen dead, forty-seven wounded or incapacitated, mainly smoke and burns. One F-35 lost through engine flameout during launch. Pilot recovered. *McClung* hit by debris, three wounded. *Green Bay*, one heavy missile hit forward of the bridge, on fire, ten dead, many wounded, fires not yet under control. *Earhart*, two medium missile hits, on fire, two dead, six wounded, fires aft, being contained. One Ulsan-class frigate, *Kyeongbuk*, sunk by two heavy missile hits, crew being recovered, no KIA numbers yet. Looks like heavy damage to the base, airfield, and shipyard, but we haven't been able to raise anyone there. Heavy expenditure of defensive ordnance. Several units report Winchester on defensive loadout." "Winchester" was the proword for all ordnance expended. "Uh . . . over."

A moment of silence. Then, *"Copy all. Keep reporting to that level of detail. And try to find out if the tender's been damaged; SubPac can't raise them. What about the enemy? Did you lay a glove on him?"*

Dan explained how they'd splashed most of the attacking fighters, and that Jung was executing a runaround to localize and attack the carriers.

The four-star seemed doubtful, but approved it. Yangerhans added, *"I have four B-2s from Hickam airborne en route your estimated posit for the* Liaoning-Shandong *strike group. We knew they'd left port, but they surprised us this far east. If they break radar silence when Jung's cruises hit, we'll take them off the board with JDAMs. Can you continue mission?"*

Dan thought fast. "Assuming *Earhart* can get her fires under control and continue loggie support, affirmative. But we still need flyout by the helo group and soonest possible resupply of defensive ordnance—SM-3, 4A, RAM, Sea Sparrow, and twenty millimeter. Total requirements to follow by message."

"Let me know. But that wolf pack's clobbering our resupply. Clear the route and you'll get everything you need. Otherwise, we're not going to have an offensive." A moment of blank hissing ether. Then, *"This is PaCom actual. Out."*

THE battle fever ebbed, leaving vacant stares, smoky passageways, and subdued voices. Dan pulled the main body in tight and set base course north at twenty-five knots. Occupying the port chair on the bridge, he monitored as the damage reports, and the KIA/WIA numbers, kept coming in.

The task force had survived. But they'd been shaken. Deaths and injuries dislocated a crew's confidence. Especially when they'd never had a chance to punch back. And with most of the self-defense ordnance expended, if they got hit again the chances of avoiding major losses were bleak.

So . . . should he change his mind? Take counsel of his fears, and turn back?

No. The time for that had passed, when he'd stepped up to the plate with Yangerhans.

Someone had to clear the mid-Pacific. It looked like it was up to him, and to the other task force, out of Pearl. Somehow they had to lure a slippery, silent enemy to battle. Pincer him between them. And crush him.

Just before evening meal, Jamail came up with a report on the wolf pack. Dan perused it, head down, as the sun sank along with his spirits. The enemy order of battle included ten Song-class diesel-electric attack submarines and ten more advanced Yuan-classes with air-independent propulsion. Also, up to five nukes, types not yet known, but presumed to be Hans and Shangs. The Hans were old boats, freight-train noisy at top speed, but still dangerous. The Shangs were rated equivalent to Russian Victors, quiet, fast, and deadly. All were presumed to carry both torpedoes and missiles, but so far only torpedoes had been used on the tankers and freighters they'd been preying on.

The report's terseness meant no one knew much more. The Chinese had played submarine development close to their vest, and whatever allied submariners were finding out about their opposite numbers now wasn't getting passed to the rest of the fleet. How good were his opponents? How aggressive? Unanswerable questions. But in terms of mass alone, it was a huge pack, bigger than anything Nazi Germany had fielded in the Battle of the Atlantic.

Huge, yes. But compared to the millions of square miles it had to hide in, a needle in Kansas. If they had any battle sense, they'd flow around his hunter killers like water around a shark. Hiding like mice until the cat was gone. He rubbed bristly cheeks violently with both hands. How could he even localize, much less engage such a force?

Graciadei came over to stand by his chair. "Admiral."

"Captain."

"About that voice message—"

"Don't worry about it, Sandy. A misunderstanding." The words had to be said, to keep working together. But now they both knew her ambition loomed naked between them.

"Ah, yessir. Admiral, we have a temporarily locked shaft. We'll have to slow to twenty knots for a couple of hours."

"Battle damage?"

"Uh, not exactly. The top snipe was moving fuel from storage to service tanks. One of the guys got stuck on stupid and overfilled a service tank. The fuel ran down the penetrations to the deck below. It's raining down out of the cableways, onto a power panel."

"Ouch."

"Yes, sir. Short squirt, it's six inches deep down there. We had to gas flood the space. Meanwhile we lost power to the lube oil service pumps. We're getting the fuel pumped out."

Jamail fidgeted behind her. Dan crook-fingered him forward. "Something hot, Qazi?"

"Admiral, message from the Aussie boat, *Farncomb*."

"Give me some good news."

"Admiral, I can do that. They put two torpedoes into a Varyag-class ski-jump carrier headed west. Ship has slowed to steerageway. Three destroyers standing by her."

"Outstanding!" Dan pounded the arm of his chair. The dice of war had finally rolled their way. The submarine standing east to join him had intercepted his withdrawing foe. "That's one of the bastards who bushwhacked us. Did they by any chance include a posit report? Yes? Great! Forward that to PaCom, right now. He's got B-2s armed to the teeth out searching for these guys."

Graciadei brightened too. "Okay if I put that out to the crew?"

Dan nodded. As the 1MC spoke, cheers resounded from the repair parties on the hangar deck.

He leaned back, fingering his chin. Trying to grab the lizard-tail of an idea as it flicked around a corner of his mind.

The enemy carrier.

Wounded, trying to withdraw . . .

Focusing all their attention on it . . .

"Come here," he told Jamail, and beckoned Graciadei back as well. He lowered his voice. "Just between the three of us . . . let me try an idea out on you."

8

In the Tien Shan Mountains

ALL that day it came down in the same fine crystals they'd seen back in the POW camp. Not in a way Teddy had ever seen it, even in the White Mountains, what he'd thought of as high-altitude powder. But this air was even drier than Afghanistan's, apparently. It just didn't snow in any way he thought snow should be.

Lying up, they spent the daylight hours huddled close as maggots in a cleft between massive jagged rocks. The cavern was freezing, but it sheltered them from the wind. They could have managed a fire, between his stone and steel and the twisted grass Major Trinh collected at every opportunity, but aside from that scant tinder there was nothing else to burn. They hadn't seen a tree since the escape.

Teddy lay shuddering in his rags, staring up at the blue-black sky as hour after hour oozed past. Only seldom did his eyelids drift closed. But one of the men on either side of him always chose just that moment to turn over.

Then, somehow, they dragged themselves out from the rocks, and began climbing again.

Since leaving the prison camp days before, they'd walked by night single file, navigating by the stars, which were brilliant and close, more than bright enough to hike by, even across this rough ground. Obie let Fierros lead, since the pilot seemed to have a clear idea where he was going. Keeping the North Star on his right, he'd pick out a peak or an escarpment ahead, then line up on it until the lay of the land concealed it, or they got lost in one of the gullies they mostly followed. Then he'd halt them and crawl up to where he could catch the guiding star again.

They straggled on all night this way, trying to ignore the howls of wolves, now far away, now closer. Toward dawn they started looking for another cave, or a narrow enough ravine that they didn't have to worry about overhead cover.

Which worried Teddy more and more as he dragged along. Now and then the whine of a distant motor echoed among the precipices in such a way they couldn't actually tell where it was coming from. The Chinese had drones too. Would they use them for tracking escaped POWs? He had his doubts, but it was possible. Better not to take chances. At least not for the first few days.

Now, as dawn approached once more, they hugged the dark side of a rugged, twisting valley, clambering awkwardly among huge black boulders that lay tumbled from the heights far above like dice thrown by titans. The slabs were shattered into slanting prisms of dark rock. He staggered as he climbed, slid, climbed again. At each step pain jarred up from his ruined leg. A bedroll was lashed over one shoulder. Over the other, the nylon tow strap. A rope belt carried the screwdriver, the chert axe, and a cloth bag that had once held food.

They climbed past the point where their legs died to all sensation, past where the cloths binding their feet were soaked with blood and pus. Past when their hands were scraped raw from grasping at sharp flint to avoid falling. Long past when they'd staggered and fallen time after time, until the sensation of falling was as familiar as that of walking, and they simply let go and collapsed, buckling into the rough gravel and lying for long seconds until one of the others cajoled them up with weary, angry curses.

And then came the gray shaking radiance before the sun. Vu, in the lead just then, beckoned from beneath a fallen monolith. Under which they crawled, and fitted themselves together, and passed nearly instantaneously from numb exhaustion into the unconsciousness which lives next door to death from starvation.

THE lobby of the old Team building, at Dam Neck. Blue tile. Folding chairs. Teddy was standing in front of the sandwich machine, trying to decide between egg salad and tuna. "Sumo" Kaulukukui, his old swim buddy, was there with him. "Got change for a five?"

The Hawaiian thumbed through his billfold. "What, it won't take a five?"

"Tried that. Fucking machine rejects it."

"Stick it in the other way. Sometimes they like that."

The feed sucked the bill in and considered, humming to itself, then unreeled the bill like an outthrust tongue. "Shit," Kaulukukui said. "Your money's no good here, Obie."

Teddy eyed the sandwiches through the glass. One butt-stroke of the pistol on his hip would break it. He licked his lips. "God, that fucking egg salad looks good." He could taste the eggs, glistening and chilled. Taste the cool rich mayo. The nice fresh thick bread. But the tuna looked good too. Made with chunky white albacore, not the cheap stuff.

"Huh. That's on whole wheat," the other SEAL observed.

"You ain't helpin' me here, fatass." He stared into the machine, unable to make the choice.

But was there really a choice to be made?

And who, exactly, was making the choice?

THEN somehow he was in the White Mountains. Back in the Parachinars, sprawled in the snow, with a rifle butt in his shoulder. The Dragunov was too long and too heavy, the angles on it all wrong. The snow was coming hard and every time a gust whipped it up he couldn't see anything, just milling glitter like stirring dark green paint mixed with chrome sparkles. "Got the four guys in front? And the flank guards?"

"Yeah. I saw 'em," muttered Sumo, beside him. "We gonna take 'em?"

"No. Just foot soldiers. Who's behind 'em? Anybody back there?"

"Don't think so. I don't see any . . . wait." Then the big soft hand tightened on his shoulder. Squeezed once. Again. A third time.

Three targets. Teddy swung the scope left. The soft whine of the infrared scope died. He jiggled the rifle. The scope buzzed, powering back up, and the mountainside came on again in green and black but fizzy, like licorice-and-pickle soda. He eased left again.

He crawled deep into the scope and there they were. Three centaurs, horses' bodies and men's torsos and heads, wavery as if sealed away under murky green glass.

"Turbans," Kaulukukui whispered. "Capes. Shorty AKs. That's his bodyguard."

"Check. On the lead?"

"Check."

"See these guys behind them?"

"Roger. On horses."

Teddy scoped them. The one in the middle, shoulders slumped as if tired, still sat taller in the saddle. Then more snow blew in, but he didn't think he was wrong. If he hadn't dropped and broken the fucking

SR-25 . . . the night sight on it had imaged clear as crystal, laser-ranged out to a thousand yards.

The scope he *did* have was buzzing and cutting off, and he was close to losing consciousness.

He could just let them go by. Trade their lives for his own.

Only . . . the mission wasn't to lie here and let the bad guys walk past.

If it were just him, he'd make the shot. It would be fun. The way he wanted to go out.

Trouble was, he wasn't alone up here. Somehow it was different, when you were telling others to lay down their lives.

Of course he'd seen guys die before. Good guys, like Sumo.

Wait a minute.

He groped out a hand. No one lay to his left. He stared, trying to force a jagged piece into his mind that somehow, no matter which way he turned it, would not fit.

When he got his eye back to the scope, there they were. There *he* was, nodding along on a horse that looked dead on its feet as one of the bodyguards flailed at its flanks with a stick.

The bearded man who'd killed so many. Who'd happily kill even more.

Unless Teddy Oberg nailed him, here and now.

A burst of snow left him with only a seething speckle like boiling oatmeal. He grunted, maintaining pressure on the trigger, not breathing.

Then the snow parted and there he was again, haloed for an instant as the beams of his guardians swept back and forth. Teddy exhaled a little more and the crosshairs rose to quarter the chest. The last ounce came out of the trigger. He corrected left for the wind as the snow-veil closed again.

The rifle slammed into his shoulder.

But he'd *missed*.

What did that mean?

His action hadn't been a choice. It had been a chance.

What was the difference between a choice and a chance?

Was there a difference?

TEDDY'S eyes snapped open.

He stared into the fading light without hope, without thought. Grabbing after something he'd understood just for a moment, then had lost.

When the shadows grew long, the valley dim, Trinh finally crept out. Stone scraped steel. After many minutes the scraping stopped, and he blew on the crimped grass. The smell of burning and a faint blue smoke filled the gap in the rock.

They shared a steel bowl of warm water. "White tea," the Viets called it. Melted from the snow that collected in the depressions. Teddy swallowed it hungrily, wishing there were more. It trickled into a hollow place under his breastbone, and sank as if into desert sand.

Then they rose and stretched, buckled on their meager possessions, and lurched once more, groaning, into the march.

Fierros led. Stocky once, lean now, with his quilted blanket torn into a makeshift poncho and another piece of ragged cloth formed into a hood. He carried the AK they'd taken from the girl guard.

Next walked Major Trinh. Shorter than the American pilot, and older, but he kept up. He'd torn his blanket into long strips, wound puttee-fashion around legs and body. He carried a heavy stick strapped across his back by a braid of the tough grass he seemed to be able to fashion into anything he liked.

Ten yards behind came his slight shadow, little Vu. The dark-faced Viet enlisted had imitated his senior with strips of blanket, but had found another blanket as well. Teddy suspected, but wasn't sure, it had been the dead Phung's. This seemed risky, who knew what the little fucker had been sick with, but then, they'd all slept huddled together back at 576. So what the hell. Whatever Phung and the other inmates and guards had died of, he hadn't gotten it. Not yet, anyway.

The last red streaks slit the sky, succeeded by purple, lavender, then velvet gray. A salt-sprinkle of stars appeared. Gradually the ragged band emerged from the rocky valley into a more open land. As they left the sheltering mountains Teddy felt naked. He limped faster. Then faster still, forcing his legs into painful motion. The wooden brace slipped and slid on sand and loose rock. He almost pitched over, but caught himself with an agonizing twist of the hip. Vu flinched away and grabbed the hilt of his bayonet as Teddy hobbled furiously past. Trinh blinked, raising an eyebrow. Teddy panted, limping ever faster. "Toby," he muttered. "Ragger. *Fierro!*"

The figure ahead halted in its tracks. Turned its head. "Fuck you want, Obie?" it hissed.

"Where the hell're you going?"

Fierros pointed. "Down there. West. Like we said."

Teddy squinted. Downhill. Undulating slightly, but falling away in what looked like miles of sand hills. In the far, far distance, orange lights twinkled. A long line, sparkling and wavering. Above them small blue lights were moving. Circling, it looked like. The black bowl of starry sky curved down over them. A road? A barrier? They crouched and studied the lights, motionless, for some time, Trinh considering them through the binoculars they'd taken from the guard shack.

"What are those moving lights?" Teddy asked him. "Can you make 'em out?"

"No. I don't know."

"Birds? Drones? Planes?"

He lowered the glasses. "Too far away."

"Hell of a lot of activity down there," Teddy muttered. "For the middle of fucking nowhere."

Fierros said tentatively, "Where there are lights . . . there are people."

Teddy frowned. "I thought we were sticking to the mountains."

"No, we were headed west." The airman jerked a thumb over his shoulder. "But we done ran out of mountains, unless you want to go north now. And where there are people, there's going to be food."

"We can't move in the open, Toby. They'll spot us in a second, come daylight. Maybe at night, too, if they have anything up with IR scanning. That's why we were sticking to rough terrain."

"It's been a week. We're at least a hundred miles away. They've got better things to do than look for four escaped POWs. And we're out of food." The airman glanced at the Viets, who'd caught up. "Right, guys? We gotta put something in our bellies besides white tea. Or just lie down and not get up one morning."

They stood debating it. Teddy thought it was too soon to figure the authorities had stopped looking for them. In wartime, special units were assigned to track down escapees. "Also, we aren't just 'escaped POWs.' We killed a guard. If we're captured, they'll line us up and shoot us. While they video it, as a warning, to the other POWs."

Vu muttered something in Vietnamese. "What did he say?" Fierros demanded.

"He said, 'Perhaps they will give us hot rice before they shoot us,'" Trinh translated.

Fierros yelled, "Look, fucker! The way these valleys run, if we go back in it might be thirty, fifty miles before we see another breakout to the south. We'll starve before we get out!"

"We could shoot something," Teddy said. "Besides, we've got to hit a village sooner or later."

"Shoot? Shoot what? There's nothing out there! We haven't even spotted a road, much less a village."

"Okay, Okay—impasse." Teddy turned to Trinh. "Major? You guys get a vote here. The desert or the mountains? We gotta decide. And we gotta do it now."

The two Viets conferred in an undertone. At last Vu spread his hands, apparently leaving it up to the officer. Trinh grimaced. Looked at the desert. Then bowed his head. "If it's up to me . . . the mountains."

Fierros's face fell. He fingered the stock of the AK. Then nodded heavily. "Majority rules, I guess. Maybe we'll get lucky."

As they turned away, Teddy threw a glance over his shoulder at the dancing lights. Remembering, vaguely, something from his dream. Something about a choice not being a choice . . . no, that wasn't it.

He hoped they were making the right decision.

THEY backtracked uphill again and followed the next valley north. Very slowly.

Teddy figured he was starting to get the layout. All these streams were dry now because it was winter. But in spring they must be torrents. You could see that from the way the sand, even rocks, lay tumbled and shoaled. Snowmelt must rage down out of those huge snowcapped peaks that walked with them. The Tien Shans. They had to find another valley headed west, the way they'd done before.

They followed the dry stream bed, flanked by rising, dry, dun-colored banks of what looked like hardened sand sculpted into weird formations. Here and there toppled and twisted gray trees were seemingly frozen into the hardened soil. They could have been centuries old, or thousands of years. The sand the men scuffed through was grayish black, grainy, and heavy. It didn't feel as if anything had ever lived in it. When they buried themselves in it for a day, at the base of a bluff, it felt to Teddy as if he were already dead.

The next night the valley of the dry river curved back and forth, and for a while he was afraid they were heading east again, but at last it did seem to curve more westerly than not. The mountains rose, towering to blot out the stars ahead.

But the tiny figures barely moved now.

Their legs dragged. Their feet barely scuffed over the ground.

They staggered, propped on sticks broken from the entombed and mummified trees.

That night they found bushes, and risked building a fire. Teddy felt exposed, but they huddled around the flames and then the glowing coals all that day, sucking the heat as if it were food. Picking through their rags for the last few lice, and eating them greedily. Vu dug into the stream bed and found dirty water a foot down, which they strained through cloths and sucked up.

Picking the lice, exploring his body, Teddy was appalled. His swollen stomach protruded as if he were eight months pregnant. His once-muscular arms and legs were shriveled; he could trace the bones under the skin. His penis and balls had all but disappeared, sucked back into his groin as if to nourish more essential organs. The damaged leg was withered, shrunken, the foot curled in on itself. Clearly, he was never going to walk on it again.

HE woke that night to absolute silence, save for the low crackle of the dying fire. And a hoarse panting somewhere out in the dark.

When he threw a dead bush on the fire and it blazed up, eyes glowed back like live coals.

He shook the others awake. They snatched up bayonets, knives, the single rifle, and stared back from their blanket cocoons.

The wolves lay just outside the circle of firelight, tongues lolling, watching the men unblinkingly, muzzles resting patiently on their extended forepaws.

When the dawn came, the wolves were gone.

THE next morning they rose while it was still dark, and began walking.

Picking their way during the day felt dangerous at first, but it was easier on their feet and legs, and took much less energy. They were able to see better paths. Gradually, as they continued to climb, more rocks littered the gorge they followed west. Now and then what might have been old trails led up the banks. They saw cloven tracks, goats or sheep, and wolf tracks. But they didn't see any actual goats or sheep. Nor any villages. Once they stumbled on what might have been a road, ruts from wheels, but it led due north. Which wasn't where they wanted to go . . . not to Siberia.

Dropping back to trudge beside Teddy, Trinh muttered, "I didn't know the world was so empty."

Teddy dragged his useless foot forward for the millionth time, but said nothing.

"It is obvious we are going to die out here." The once-husky Viet was mere parchment over coat-hanger wire. Sores covered his face. His eyes were glazed as if with cataracts. A wispy Ho beard hung from his chin.

Teddy whispered hoarsely, "Guess I got to agree with you, Major. For what it's worth."

"They will find our bodies centuries from now. Preserved, like these trees. And wonder who we were. How we got here. Two Asians, two Europeans. A mystery."

"I guess the AK's gonna be the only clue. That and the fucking POW clothes."

Trinh eyed his foot. "How can you keep on, like that?"

"If you don't mind, it doesn't matter," Teddy said. "How can you see, with your eyes like that?"

"It is true, I can't make much out anymore. Vu guides me."

"How's he doing?"

"We are all of us dying, Teddy. What more can I say?" Trinh waited, head cocked; then, when he got no answer, trudged on.

THEY were in a region of fissures and crags late that same afternoon when they lost Vu.

The stream bed they followed had climbed a series of what in flood had apparently been rapids, but were now just stepping-stones of grayblack boulders, rounded on their upper sides by millennia of rushing water. This rose hundreds of feet in ladder after ladder, interspersed with scooped-out areas that would become pools in the melt season.

The ravine was a sheer, vertical cut in a granite face. The rock fell sharp as blades on either side. The four escapees gathered at the foot of the climb, staring up. It was easily fifty feet, and straight up.

Teddy shrugged the strapping off. Its weight had dug a bleeding hole into his shoulder. He'd almost left it behind a hundred times. If they hoped to negotiate mountains, though, he'd figured they'd need it sooner or later. He lashed it around his waist and started up.

Footholds and handholds . . . But after ten feet it was clear he wasn't strong enough. He hung there panting as the world spun. But hunger brought patience, too. When the rock finally steadied he felt for another handhold.

Bit by bit, fitting bleeding fingers into niches and callused toes into nearly invisible knobs, he went up. Finally he could hook an elbow over a lip of rock and slowly, slowly lever himself to roll over.

He glimpsed, just for a moment, something dark high above them on the mountain. His head was still pounding, specks swimming before his eyes, so he couldn't be sure. He'd thought for a moment it was a horseman. But when he squinted again, the shelf was empty. Except for a seam in the rock, which he might just have taken for the outline of a man on horseback, with a raised rifle.

He secured the strapping to a boulder and dropped it over the edge. Then backed off, searching the cliffs above as the others worked their way up hand over hand. Vu seemed to be having the hardest time of it, which was odd, since he was both the slightest and the youngest. Not for the first time, Teddy wondered if he was sicker than he looked.

But they all reached the top at last, and after a rest set off along the new, higher course. This valley led almost straight west, which was good. But it was fissured and seamed, the gray-purple stone torn as if by some recent quake.

It was slow going, but better than trying to negotiate terrain like this in the dark.

Toward late afternoon, as they toiled around a seemingly bottomless pit, Trinh beckoned Teddy up beside him. Handing over the binoculars, he pointed to a patch of snow a mile above them on the mountainside.

"What am I looking at?" Oberg muttered, trying to set the focus. How could Trinh see anything at all with those clouded corneas?

"That snowy spot."

"Okay . . . I see . . . ski trails?"

"I don't think so, Obie."

"No, course not." He blinked and looked again. "What the hell are they, then?"

"I believe, some kind of grazing area."

"In the snow?"

"Animals have to eat, even in winter."

He looked again, more carefully. Elk, goats, sheep? He couldn't see any, but if Trinh was right, something had been up there, ruminating. "It's too far to climb. And whatever it is, we'd never get a shot. Not with a fucking worn-out fucking AK."

"But if there are, either game animals or livestock, someone's going to be around. Either herders or hunters."

Teddy thought about it. "We could fire the Kalash. See who shows up."

"That puts us at their mercy."

"Okay, your suggestion?"

"I don't have any. Just pointing out the first animal life we've seen."

Teddy nodded. He was turning away, handing the glasses back, when a thin scream echoed from off to their right.

WHEN they looked down they could barely see him. Just a corner of a gray blanket-strip, flirted out from around an outthrust of rock.

"Did anyone see him go?" Trinh was crouched so far over the edge of the precipice that Teddy reached for him involuntarily, anchoring the Vietnamese with a fistful of collar. "He slipped, right? And fell? He did not jump."

No one had seen him go. Fierros had been a few steps ahead, while the senior Viet had been talking to Teddy. Who, of course, had been looking up at the mountain. While Vu apparently had been skirting just close enough to the pit that a weak place had given way, dropping him so fast and with so little warning that he'd only been able to scream. Teddy rubbed his rag-bound foot along the edge. Fresh, crumbly rock.

"I can see him better from over here," Fierros said, edging to a vantage point farther out. "Better toss me your strap, there . . . in case this gives too . . . thanks, Oberg. Okay, I can see him."

"Is he moving?"

"A lot of blood around his head . . . He's not moving. His neck's twisted like it's broken."

Trinh squatted next to him, peering through the glasses for a few seconds before he stood, looking grim.

"Dead?" Teddy asked him.

"I'm . . . afraid so." He stood as if irresolute for a few moments, then came to attention. He snapped into a salute. Teddy lifted his chin and faced in the same direction, bringing up his hand in a bareheaded salute. Finally, as if reluctantly, the airman did too. They stood solemnly in the sighing wind until their arms began to quiver and sag.

When they dropped the salute, Fierros stalked back and forth along the cliff edge, peering. "That's gotta be a hundred yards down. No way we could get down there," he muttered. He rubbed his chin. "I mean, too bad we . . ."

He didn't finish the sentence, and both Teddy and Trinh cut him sharp glances. He scowled back. "*What?* Don't tell me you're not thinking the same thing."

"I don't know, Ragger. What *are* you thinking?"

The pilot showed yellowed teeth, what remained of them. "That we made the wrong choice back there."

"There aren't any choices," Teddy said.

"What?" Fierros's brows drew together. "What's that supposed to mean? Yeah, we got choices. We got to go down, where it'll be warmer. There'll be people. We have a rifle, don't we? We can steal food, take a hostage. Do *something*."

"This valley will lead us out of China," Teddy said. "If there's nobody up here, that's good. We're on the run, remember? Wanted men. It can't be that much farther to the border. All we have to do is keep going. We'll never get out your way."

"It's freezing. It's winter. All this wandering around, until we starve . . . or fall into a crevasse, like Vu . . . it isn't going to work."

Teddy looked at Trinh. Slowly, the major's shoulders lifted. Then sagged.

"All right," Teddy said. "Which way, then?"

The pilot grinned. "I saw a draw back there. Looked like it might go the way we want."

Teddy turned away, without wasting another word, and began to lead them down.

9

USS *Savo Island*
25°00.38′N, 159°42.37′W
500 Miles NW of Wake Island

CHERYL leaned back on the bridge chair. The sun warmed her face as she tried not to scratch the itchy patches between her fingers. The red, aggrieved spots were spreading. Doc Grissett had given her a steroid cream, but it wasn't helping.

The cruiser's truncated prow sliced through two-foot seas as every few seconds the singsong whine of her sonar pinged out into the deep. Scattered clouds chased their shadows over a sea so deep blue it hurt the heart. A balmy breeze coursed through the wing doors. Aloft, flags snapped. A breechblock rattled as a gunner's mate checked one of the machine guns. Down on the forecastle, cross-legged around portable computers, fire-control techs were carrying out the daily systems-operability tests, quizzing the missiles beneath the gray hatches set nearly flush to the deck.

The Ticonderoga-class cruisers had been designed around those weapons and the radars that guided them. Within a radius of three hundred miles, an Aegis ship could detect, track, identify, and knock down anything that threatened. Ahead, a black speck hurtled outward: a just-launched Blackjack, one of the drones that searched ahead of the advancing force with synthetic-aperture radar and a hyperspectral imager.

A week had passed since the near-disastrous exit battle from Guam. After forming up and completing a damage assessment, the task force had headed north. The Japanese had interned *George Washington*, still crippled from a mine strike, but had let her aircraft go. MH-60s from Helicopter Sea Combat Squadron 12 had flown out hundreds of miles over the open sea, well beyond their point of no return. *McClung* had hot-refueled them, hopscotching them the rest of the way to *Hornet*. One had to ditch en route, but *Kristensen* had picked up its crew.

Ollie Uskavitch cleared his throat beside her. She'd moved the Weapons Department head up to acting XO until the filler from stateside arrived. They went over the day's schedule. Helicopter and ordnance fire drills, mainly. Evolutions they could do with personnel already on station, without moving them around the ship. Things they could put a lid on instantly, if operational requirements dictated.

When he left she viciously scratched her fingers, musing. Wondering.

CTF 76 had passed intel that opposing forces comprised ten Song-class diesel-electric attack submarines, along with another nine to ten more advanced Yuan-class subs with air-independent propulsion. There might be an older boat, too, converted to carry fuel and torpedoes so the force could extend its stay, perhaps for months. . . . Also, there were up to five nuclear boats. This huge pack might be subdivided into attack groups, but Intel placed them all within a square bounded by 5 degrees north to 25 degrees north, and between 180 and 160 degrees west.

Unfortunately, that covered roughly a million miles of ocean.

She had no idea what Lenson's plan was for finding their enemy.

To take them on, he had helicopters, two U.S. destroyers, and *Savo*, *Hornet*, *Farncomb*, and the Koreans. The eastern jaw of the vise, out of Pearl, consisted of another LPH, four destroyers, an Independence-class frigate, and one U.S. sub. They were supported by land-based air out of Hawaii, while TF 76 was supposed to get flights out of Wake.

Meanwhile, logistic transits through the mid-Pacific had been called off. Even escorted convoys would be torn apart by a pack that large. Fuel, supplies, weapons, and parts had to come either by air or the long way round, through the far South Pacific to Australia, then routed north.

Which meant the task force couldn't expect much, and none of it on time. And the carriers were still holding east of Pearl. Safer for her husband, aboard *Vinson*, but not so good for her.

"Captain?"

She returned the salute. Lieutenant (junior grade) Todd MacAllister had moved up to head Supply since Hermelinda had left for Lenson's staff. Tall, heavy-jawed, and low-browed, he seemed to have a handle on the department, though he hadn't made the extra effort to qualify as OOD that Garfinkle-Henriques had. "Todd. How're we set for chow?"

"Numbers don't look good, Captain. That missile hit *Earhart* in the forward hold, where they stowed dry stores. Between fire and flooding they lost most of it."

"Which means we don't get resupplied?"

"'Fraid not." The Supp (O) looked regretful. "We got some fresh stores in Apra, but not a full allowance. Gonna be eating out of cans. Dehydrated stuff, powdered milk."

"Excuse me. Captain?" Past MacAllister, Lieutenant (jg) Mytsalo was angling for her attention.

"Yeah, Max, what have you got?—Excuse me, Todd."

"Lookout reports: *Hornet*'s showing a list."

She frowned. "Hand me those binoculars."

Through the glasses the gray slab of the carrier jumped close across ten thousand yards of sea. A slight list to port? Maybe. Something to fret about? She decided not. "How many days' chow do we have, Todd?"

"On normal rations maybe two weeks. If you give me permission to go to half rations . . . cut back on meat, provide more starches . . . a month."

She looked away to cover her dismay. But berating him wouldn't produce more. "Very well," she said reluctantly. "Our guys in Korea're probably not getting much to eat these days either. And we have no idea how long we'll be out here. Go to reduced servings. Do I need to make an announcement? Have the exec put it in the plan of the day?"

MacAllister grimaced. "Why bother, Skipper? The minute the word goes down in the Supply Office, it's gonna be all over the ship."

She checked her watch and swung down out of the chair. She gave the boatswain, at the 1MC panel, the nod. Took deep breaths, scratching her fingers, as he blew "attention" on his silver pipe. Then accepted the microphone.

"This is the captain speaking. Good morning.

"From today on we will be hunting a sizable submarine pack that we know is somewhere in this sea area. We may be attacked at any time, by missile or torpedo. We will continue steaming in Condition Three. Keep flash gear and breathing apparatus close at hand at all times.

"Now set Material Condition Zebra, modified for flight operations, throughout the ship. Make all reports to the bridge."

Steel slammed, doors and hatches dogging as *Savo* subdivided herself. Her captain passed a hand over her face, looking out again to where *Hornet* rode the horizon. Centerpiece of a task force flung across fifty miles of sea.

She hoped its commander knew what he was doing.

* * *

THAT afternoon in CIC she hunched in the padded command chair, absorbed in the displays. The space was darkened save for the screens. At Condition Three, wartime steaming, all consoles were manned except Strike. Voices murmured over tactical circuits. Keyboards clattered. The air was icy cold, but she was comfortable in a nylon flight jacket, though her sinuses hurt.

Propping her jaw on a fist, she studied the central screen.

Task Force 76, alone in an unislanded sea, headed east at twenty knots in a circular formation. *Hornet*, *Green Bay*, and *Earhart* steamed at formation center. *Savo* rode shotgun ten thousand yards southwest of the carrier. She was air guard, though the farther east they went, the less likely missile or air strikes became. Ahead, and to the north and south, were spread wings of destroyers and frigates, U.S. and Korean. *Farncomb*, the Australian sub, was out ahead, supposedly sanitizing their track, but running on diesels, snorkeling, at the moment.

The missile deck videos showed empty ocean. She studied the weapons inventory once more, dismayed. Then turned to the TAO, next to her at the desk. "What d'you think of this formation?"

Matt Mills reminded her of her husband. The same blond good looks, but without the fighter-jock attitude. He'd come from squadron staff in the Med as a temporary fill, and been with them since. "It's . . . not really optimal?"

"Is that all? No shit, Matt. It's weak."

He looked as if he wanted to agree, but didn't. "Okay, what?" she asked.

"Just that . . . Lenson's no dummy. If he set it up, there's something we're not seeing."

She studied the screen again. What was she missing? Lenson had reoriented the formation late the night before. The ROKN screen units were clustered on the northern and southern flanks, thirty miles out from the main body. Three frigates centerlined the leading edge of the formation, ten miles ahead. *Savo* was ten thousand yards to starboard of *Hornet*. *McClung* was ten thousand yards to port. *Kristensen* brought up the rear, protecting them from end-arounds.

Ship dispositions weren't the whole story, of course. Icons glimmered on the screen as recon drones and helos roved, busy as bees in clover. Every twelve miles HSC-12 dropped staggered rows of sonobuoys across the advance. The buoys hit the water, cut their chutes, and deployed microphones on wires a hundred yards long. They didn't ping unless ordered. Just hung passive, alert for the heartlike *whish-whish* of submarine propellers,the throb of pumps, the whine of air-conditioning, the clank as torpedoes were handled or watertight doors swung closed.

She scratched furiously, then made herself stop. Get more sleep, before things started popping again? But a motion on the after hangar deck camera caught her eye.

The California Guard was doing a slew check. The gyrostabilized turret, craned aboard in Apra, had two launcher pods, each with four Stingers. There was no direct link to the cruiser's combat system. Instead they had a watchstander on sound-powered phones. If they got an incomer, all they had to do was slew to the bearing and pickle off rounds in ripple fire. The missiles did the rest, streaking out at incredible pace.

She found herself scratching again, and cursed. Stingers were short-range, but one thing this war had demonstrated was that once action started, threats had to be dealt with faster than in any previous conflict. They could expect saturation attacks. A short-range backup was more than welcome, as far as she was concerned.

"What's wrong with this formation?" Mills mumbled, squinting into the screenlight. His fingers drummed the desk. Then he grabbed a red-backed publication, flipped pages. "Huh. See who he's got right in the middle, in the lead? *Seoul.* FF-952. Seems like a weak sister to you?"

"It's an older class," she agreed. "Definitely less capable than Jung's other units."

"The other van units are Ulsans too." Mills frowned, massaging his eyelids. "I don't get it."

The CIC officer clutched his headset. "Forward lookout reports smoke from *Hornet.*"

Cheryl grabbed the joystick on the command desk, slewed the missile deck camera, and zoomed in. Mills rattled his keyboard, and video popped on the left display.

A black cloud billowed from the flight deck.

"I don't see flames," Mills said. "But that's a hell of a lot of smoke."

She hit the key of the 21MC. "Sonar, CO. Anything from about zero-one-zero relative? Torpedo noises, explosions?"

Chief Zotcher's voice. *"Negative, Skipper. Why do you—ah . . . oh . . . wait one."*

She jumped up and stalked across CIC, brushing past bent backs at consoles, and rattled the blue curtain aside. "We have smoke from *Hornet*," she told the sonarmen.

One muttered, staring at his screen, "She just shut down a shaft too."

"But no explosion?" Should she close, to help? Strange, there'd been nothing over the air.

"Skipper?" One of the air controlmen. "TAO's asking you to step over."

Back at the command desk, Mills pointed to text glowing on the LAN screen. "Command chat just came up."

"I thought it didn't work without satellites."

"Guess they figured some way to do it without. Short range. Line of sight."

"Or it's someone trying to phish us. Remember, we were warned about comm compromises."

The screen read:

BARBARIAN: All units Horde, this is Barbarian. Comm check.

"Answer up?"

"*CIC, bridge: flashing light from carrier. Stand by . . . breaks as . . . 'come up command chat ASAP.'*"

She slid into the chair and pulled her keyboard into her lap.

MATADOR: This is SVI.
TURTLESHIP: Turtleship here.
BIRKENSTOCK: Online.
MARATHONER: Online.
FULLBORE: Present.
HALFBACK: Halfback online.

Seconds ticked by.

BARBARIAN: Is Hammerhead online?

No answer. "*Earhart's* not answering up, either," Mills observed.

"They're USNS, not USS. May not have chat capability. And the sub may not want to transmit. Even to acknowledge," Cheryl murmured.

BARBARIAN: Commander's intent follows. Horde proceed base
   course one-one-zero speed twelve.

"Twelve knots?" Mills muttered. *"Twelve?"*

BARBARIAN: New screen stations as below. Execute to follow.
Hammerhead position ahead of main body at 50 meters depth.

As the station assignments followed, Mills called up a formation diagram on the screen, and began pointing and clicking to sketch in the sectors. Cheryl pinched her lips with her fingers. At first glance it resembled a typical bent-line screen. But Lenson was pulling his most capable units back behind the main body. Leaving only the thinnest of lines ahead . . . three Ulsan-class ROKN frigates, and older flights, at that.

She, Mills, and the CIC officer exchanged puzzled looks. Usually, a hunter-killer group commander didn't want to be in the thick of the ASW fight; the destroyers and frigates were specialized for that mission. But this was even bolder. *Hornet* was the highest-value unit out here. If the enemy got a mission kill on her, the whole task force was out of commission.

The 21MC clicked on. *"TAO, Radio."*

"Go, Comm."

"HF message in the clear from Hornet. *I read back: 'Fires under control. My port shaft is locked. Headed to Pearl for repairs. Can make no more than twelve knots.'"*

Cheryl leaned back, nodding as it all clicked into place. Then leaned in and typed swiftly:

MATADOR: Quack, quack?

A moment passed. Then characters appeared.

BARBARIAN: Quack.

Mills was blinking. The CIC officer looked uncomfortable. "What gives, Skipper?" the TAO murmured. "That some kind of inside joke?"

"I guess you could say that." She pushed back from the table, zipping the jacket up under her chin. She shivered, and not just with the air-conditioning. "He's pulling a lame duck."

"Explain?"

"We're out here in a million square miles of ocean, with no clue where the enemy is until he strikes. The Chinese must have some kind of surveillance, or direction-finding capability. Though we don't know what.

"Lenson's going to take advantage of that, by making himself look like a target. Broadcasting a damage report. Making smoke. Shutting down a shaft. Probably, ballasting to produce that list too. All to make it look like *Hornet* was damaged in the Guam strike, and is heading back for repairs."

Mills drew a deep breath. "And softening his front line to suck them in."

She wondered if she looked as worried as they did. The tactic might attract the enemy, true. Localize the wolf pack in a way they couldn't otherwise. But weakening the defenses at the critical point, directly ahead of the formation . . . the optimal axis for a determined submarine attack . . .

She pulled the Hydra from her belt. "XO, CO here."

"*XO here. What you need, Skipper?*"

"Ollie, do this low profile, no fuss. But have all life rafts checked. And schedule an abandon-ship drill for tomorrow."

"*Ma'am? We already drilled—*"

"Drill it again." She signed off.

It was incredibly dangerous. Incredibly risky. Bold. And totally unorthodox.

Exactly the kind of tactic the Dan Lenson she knew might come up with.

10

Camp Pendleton, California

"T HE King fucks the Queen!" Sergeant Abdulhamid shouted. His boots crunched in the tan, coarse, metal-littered sand as he stalked the berm along the firing line.

Hector Ramos swallowed dust and blinked grit out of his eyes. He was sweating hard in desert MARPATs and flak jacket, goggles, helmet, and gloves. California chafed in his shorts. Frowning, he noted it accumulating on the dust cover of his M240 too. The dust cover was plastic on the exposed side and metal underneath with just two small metal clips securing it to the barrel. Maybe he should have left it in the A bag. He started to wipe it with his sleeve, but was afraid to get dirt in the ventilation holes. Finally he bent and blew it off, but a moment later another layer sparkled on the black surface.

The trucks had arrived before dawn with the trainees and the weapons. They'd unloaded as the sun rose, handing down tons of ammo, then smashing off the thin white pine sheathing before setting up. The green metal boxes sat open ready to hand, hundreds of brass rounds gleaming like tired gold. Fine dust eddied past. Abdulhamid's sweat gleamed in the sun. "The fucking infantry is the fucking Queen of the battlefield. Right? Well, the machine gun, he is the King. And the King fucks the Queen. *Let's hear it!*"

"The King fucks the Queen." The ragged chorus rolled along the firing line, under the broiling sun.

Infantry Training Battalion, Camp Pendleton, California. The first two weeks had been twelve hours a day of the skills of the MOS 0300 infantryman. Marksmanship under fire, grenades, identifying and countering IEDs. Manning convoys, basic tactics, combat conditioning, physical training. Land navigation, with forced marches through the hilly terrain. Urban combat and room-clearing training, the instructors told them, had been dropped, in the interest of "saving time." To which Troy Whipkey, easily the most cynical human being Hector had ever met, had muttered, "So they can ship us to Korea faster."

Only now it sounded like they might not get there. The Navy was pulling out of WestPac, leaving the forces there surrounded. It looked like the Army would be killed or captured.

"Gonna be up to us Marines, retrieve the situation," one of the sergeants had told them. "Or die trying."

"Most likely, die trying," Whipkey had muttered, fidgeting beside Hector in the sunrotted training bleachers. Whipkey was a redneck from central Florida, but his attitude was anything but patriotic. He'd shot a kid who'd kept "mudding" his family's back ten in his ATV. Fortunately, the kid hadn't died, and the judge had given Whipkey a choice: jail or the Corps.

Hector had sweated the math and the map reading. But now they were in the MOS-specific training. Somehow, the Corps had decided he would be an 0331. A machine gunner, trained on the M240, the Mk-19 40mm grenade launcher, and the M-2 .50-cal machine gun. Or, as Sergeant Abdulhamid put it, "The most bad-boy high-speed muthafuckas to walk this fuckin' valley, and the fuckin' steel spine of this man's Marine Corps."

Now Abdulhamid yelled, "Remember, jundies, you ain' got but so much ammo. We had to buy this shit wherever we could. Israel. Argentina. Germany. Ain' no U.S. ammo till we get makin' powder again. It's gon' go bang, but you gon' get dispersion. Focus on your target reference point. Track in from that. Check your wind. Range is hot! *Yallah yallah!* Gun up."

Forget Mirielle's kisses in the dark, forget everything but the checklist in his head. Safety on F. Bolt to the rear. Hector slotted the charging handle to the forward position and flipped up the cover assembly. *Ensure the feed tray, receiver assembly, and chamber are clear.* He slapped it down. *While maintaining rearward pressure, pull the trigger and ease the bolt assembly forward.*

"Double link at the open end," Troy yelled beside him. "Free of dirt and corrosion."

Place the first round of the belt in the feed tray groove, double link leading, with open side of links face down. Hold the belt six rounds from the loading end. Ensure that the round remains in the feed tray groove, and close the cover assembly.

Yells began to proceed down toward them. "Gun one up!" "Gun two up!" "Ready," Hector said. Beside him Troy yelled, "Gun three up!"

AMMUNITION: 7.62mm × 51
WEIGHT with bipod: 24 pounds
LENGTH: 47.5 inches
MAXIMUM effective range with tripod: 1800 meters (1.1 miles)
MAXIMUM range: 3725 meters (2.31 miles)
MAXIMUM rate of fire: 100 rounds/minute (sustained), 200 rounds/minute (rapid), 650–950 rounds/minute (cyclic)

He was wiping sweat out of his eyes with the back of his hand when, without warning, the targets began popping up, from fifty yards out to eight hundred. Whipkey was manning the combo scope/laser rangefinder, but there wasn't time to cut ranges. Not for pop-ups. Sweating in the blazing sun, lying full length in the sand, Hector traversed, depressed, and pulled the trigger.

The M240 machine gun supports the rifleman in both offensive and defensive operations. The M240 provides the heavy volume of close and continuous fire needed to accomplish the mission. The M240 is used to engage targets beyond the range of individual weapons, with controlled and accurate fire. The long-range, close defensive, and final protective fires delivered by the M240 form an integral part of a unit's defensive fires.

His gun was ugly and black and heavy and looked exactly like what it was, a machine to kill people as quickly and cheaply as possible. Sergeant Abdulhamid had assured them they would love it. Hector did not. It still seemed wrong to kill, but Abdulhamid said knowing how to use it might save his life and those of his fellow Marines.

The butt hammered his shoulder. Hot brass and parkerized steel disintegrating links spewed out, brass from the bottom, links from the right side, tinkling and smoking and piling until he had to scoop them out of the way with his elbow. Once in a while a round would hang up, and they had to clear it. Blue smoke eddied down the line on a breeze too slight to cool them.

The sergeant had told them not to depend on tracers. "Draws a line to you for the hajji with the RPG." Abdulhamid referred to any enemy as a "hajji" and to Marines as "jundies." He wouldn't let them use just the optic sights either. "Fucking optics gonna go south on you. The internal components shift and you'll lose the zero. Grease-smear, blood on the lens, you're fucking toast. Learn the fucking irons. Fuck the Queen. You the King."

Sometimes Hector wasn't sure Abdulhamid was all there. Scuttlebutt was he'd been blown up too many times. He was Iraqi, a translator who'd joined the Marines. But he knew the Pig. That's what he called the gun, the "Pig." As in, "The Pig, that's what's gon' fuck up them Chink hajjis."

The officer came down the line and Abdulhamid went silent, glaring at them and making notes in his little green book. But the instant the captain was out of earshot in the hammering noise he was crouching again, shouting into their ears. "You boys rockin' it? Feelin' that seven-six-two love?"

"Feelin' the love, Sergeant. Oorah!" Whipkey yelled.

"Then *get on your fuckin' target, Ray-mose*! And keep your fuckin' *head down*! You think Chink hajjis ain' got snipers? You think Sar'n Abdul gon' be holdin' your pecker for you, in country? Think that punk-ass shooting get you through ITX? Well, we got special treat for you on Range 400 this time. Whippy!"

Whipkey howled, "Sergeant!"

"Hot barrel. *Hot barrel!* What is it, you don' talk fuckin' En-lish? What is a fuckin' hot barrel?"

"A hot barrel is two hundred rounds fired in two minutes or less."

"So when you gon' pull you fuckin' tongue out of my ass and *change that fuckin' barrel!*"

A whistle blew. "Cease fire, cease fire," someone called, and Hector and Troy rolled over and bellowed it too, passing it down the line. Hector panted, running perspiration. When he wiped his arm across his forehead his sleeve came down black. "The line is cold. Make all weapons Condition Four," Abdulhamid shouted, stalking the berm. "Ammo to the centa line. Saved ammo, to the centa line. Brass and trash, in the buckets. Duds an' misfires, in the live-round drum."

Clear and unload . . . safety to fire F position. With his right hand, palm carefully up in case of a cook-off, Hector yanked the charging handle to the rear. He put his face in the dirt, flipped open the cover assembly, and did the physical safety check with his fingers. Whipkey did the visual check, looking for leftover brass, steel links, or live rounds. "Feed pawl assembly, feed tray, chamber," he muttered. When he jerked his fingers out Hector racked the bolt again to jar anything in there out into view. They checked under the bolt and op rod assembly, then put it on F again and recocked. Hector pulled the trigger while he rode the bolt home on the empty chamber. He snapped down the ejection port cover and they both rolled onto their backs, holding up their arms. "Clear and safe!" they yelled in unison.

"Take a break," Abdulhamid said. "Bongos're on the way. We'll clean back at the weps bay." He added unenthusiastically, "Decent shootin'. But ain't nobody shootin' back, 'member. And down, down, *down*! Got to keep them fuckin' heads down, or the hajjis shoot 'em off. *Baroor*, I don't shit you."

BACK in the sheds, they tore the guns apart. The cloying stench of CLP filled the bays. As Hector scrubbed, he noted chewed-up metal on one of the feed pawls. "Might be what kept hangin' us up," Troy muttered. When Abdulhamid came by, the sergeant told them to turn the part in to the armorer, get a replacement.

By the time the weapons were cleaned, reassembled, inspected, and turned in, the sky was dark. They climbed wearily into trucks for the ride to the mess hall. Most of the Mexican guys sat together, so they could speak Spanish without being hassled. But tonight they ate in silence, too fatigued to talk.

They were in the barracks when a lance corporal stuck his head in. "Liberty tomorrow," he announced.

"Say what, man?"

"What'd he say?"

"Sunday liberty. Church services, them as wants 'em. The Shame Shuttle down to area 51 gate will run starting at oh-seven-hundred."

THE line was already snaking out near the San Onofre gate when Hector joined it the next morning. Palm trees waved invitingly. The wind smelled of the sea beyond. But the access was blocked with orange plastic barriers and concertina. Humvees with mounted .50s overlooked it, and armed sentries paced the barriers. Few of the liberty guys wore civvies. Most were in newly issued class charlies, olive drab trousers and tan open-collar shirts and soft garrison caps.

Just ahead of him in line was a woman with short dark hair sticking out from under her garrison cap. She was short but muscular and looked as if she could press a mortar baseplate a few times. When she glanced back he caught dark eyes, chiseled cheekbones, copper skin. Not Mexican, maybe south of there. More Indio in her blood. They didn't have many women in 0331. Some had dropped out during the marches, but this one looked like she never dropped out of anything.

When she glanced back again he blurted, "Hey."

"Hey." She squinted, shading her eyes.

"Hector Ramos. 0331."

"Coreguaje. Orietta Coreguaje. 0341."

"Yeah? I don't know why, when I looked at you I thought, mortars."

"Oh, the big tubes. That must be why we ain't seen you," said Whipkey, leering up from behind Hector. "You friends with Heck-tor here?"

"Just met the guy." She extended a hand coolly. "Orietta. And this here is my friend, Pruss."

Pruss was blond and more heavily built, sort of like a guy. Hector actually took her for one at the first glance, then looked again. At the third glance, he still wasn't sure. "Oorah, kill," said Whipkey by way of greeting, looking her up and down.

"But they are off-limits," Coreguaje added, apparently meaning Pruss. Whipkey's face fell.

Pruss was in mortars too. And she, or he, had a phone, nonreg but some of the guys had them, and was saying Lyft was up again. Hector felt awkward not knowing how to address him, or her. Or, wait, "them," Coreguaje had said. She could be gay. Or transgender—there'd been some transgender recruits at Parris Island. But they were all marines, and they got acquainted while they stood in line, and pretty soon it was understood they were going to be libo buddies. When they got up to the gate at last there were cars there along with the buses. A rowdy, shouting crowd of civilians, too, held at a distance by cops. Some seemed to be protesting the war. Others were clearly here to cheer it on, or at least to applaud the troops. Both sides were waving signs and shouting through bullhorns. Avoiding them all, the Marines found an Excursion with six seats open and somebody's grandma driving.

"Hi, I'm Doris. Where you kids going?" the older woman said brightly.

"We're not kids. We're Devil Dogs," Coreguaje corrected her. Not in a mean way, just matter-of-fact. Hector liked this girl. Firm, but you could tell she wasn't looking for trouble. He kind of suspected she was with Pruss, but that didn't matter, he had Mirielle to come back to. If he actually came back.

"I know, I know. I didn't mean anything, honey. So where'm I taking you?" Doris was in the acceleration lane, pulling out onto a highway. A sign flashed past: Route 5 South.

"Where we can have some fun," Pruss said. "You know, let go a little. We're in SOI."

"School of Infantry? Well, we could go to Oceanside. Or San Diego. But that's a long drive. When's liberty expire?"

Hector squinted at her. "My son was in," she said, glancing apologetically into the rearview. "That's why I wanted to come down and kind of help out."

"Oh yeah? Where's he now?"

"KIA. Ramadi II."

He sat back, wishing he hadn't gotten nosy. "So, where to?" Doris said again.

"Someplace with karaoke. Dancing. Music."

"Oh God. Not fucking karaoke," Whipkey moaned.

Pruss shrugged. "A hookah lounge, then. Ever do hookah? You can get so wasted. And you know they'll piss-test us when we get back."

Doris said, "Well, there's restaurants in Oceanside giving free dinners to deploying servicemen . . . I mean, servicepeople. And there's a concert at the Amphitheater. And the pier, or the beach . . . Rich used to go skateboarding on the Strand. . . . Does any of that sound good?"

Pruss patted the back of the driver's seat. "Sorry about your son. Is there a hookah lounge anywhere?"

Doris frowned. "A hookup lounge?"

"Hook*ah*!" Pruss leaned forward, chortling.

"Oh." Doris seemed to be concentrating harder on the road. "I think there's a big one down toward Carlsbad. No, wait. There's one closer. North Freeman, Seagaze? We can go look. If that's what you dogs want to do before you ship out, well, shit. I say go for it."

THEY had dinner at a Thai restaurant. It wasn't free, but it was half price and the first drink was half price too. So they had one each, then went out into a dusk studded with lights. The wind was cooler. People were out in the streets. They went with the flow, down toward the water. Toward the Strand, where Doris had said her son used to skateboard.

Hector shivered, and not just from the wind. Like they were hooked to the same chain, being driven on toward the Kill Room . . . no, don't think about that . . . look at the lights twinkling over the pier, drink the beer you just bought, cold in your hand. The girl beside you, who even if she isn't yours is drawing envious looks from the other guys on the boardwalk.

Pruss kept talking hookahs, but Whipkey insisted he wanted another drink first. They found a place with tables outside. The bar inside was filled with men and women, but they were all looking at their phones, not at one another. Pruss said, "Guess OKCupid's back up too."

Orietta snorted. "Yeah, look at all the poor Tinderellas, hoping they get picked before midnight."

"And the fuckboys, all hot to get it in."

Two hipster-looking guys wandered out, studying their screens and swiping. They had stylish rumpled hair and half-growths of blond beard. They glanced at the four at the table and started to go back in. Then the one in the checked shirt nudged the other and turned back. "Hey, you guys soldiers?" he called.

"No, Marines," Coreguaje said.

"Thought so. Outta Pendleton, right? Buy you a drink?"

"You want to buy us drinks?" Whipkey scowled, though Hector didn't see why.

Tall Farmer said patronizingly, "To support the troops. Show our appreciation. These your girls?"

"Are they girls?" muttered the shorter guy, whose black hoodie was flipped back.

"These women are Marines too," Hector said quickly, before either of them could respond. Then hoped he hadn't stepped in it, that Pruss didn't mind being called a woman.

"You want to show your fucking appreciation, asshole, then join the fuck up," Whipkey snarled.

"Yeah, join the fuck up," Pruss chimed in. "With the fucking *girls*." They and Whipkey exchanged high fives.

"No need to be rude," the tall guy said, trying to laugh it off. "Just wanted to be friendly."

"You can save the friendly for when the fucking Chinks land on your fucking beach here," Pruss said, pointing to the surf.

Hoodie swiped his phone. "That the line of shit they feed you inside the wire, butch? This isn't our war. Let the Koreans and Japs fight it."

"If we let them take Guam, they'll be in Hawaii next," Hector said.

"That what they're telling you? Well, that's what we pay you people for. —Hey, how about her? Check that out." He shoved his phone at the other guy. "What are you, anyway? Mexicans? My grandfather was in the army. That's how it works in this country, you know. First generation pays the dues. After that, people wise up."

"My folks fought in the Civil War." Whipkey shoved his chair back.

"Wail, there's always the crackers. Lahk yew," said the short guy, mimicking a Deep South accent. "Who b'lieve Gawd invented the bolt-action Remington, ta kill the dinosaurs and the ho-mo-sexuals."

Hector got Whipkey's arm and dragged him back. The short guy held out both hands, palms out. "Okay, okay—sorry, dude. Bad joke."

"Did you two even register?" Coreguaje wanted to know. "There's a draft, ya know. Did you register your sorry, self-indulgent asses?"

The two chuckled. Hoodie sneered, "You don't *register*. They build the database from the Cloud. Driver's licenses, birth records, passports, big data. But any doctor'll give you a deferral. Or you sign up for a MOC. An online course counts as university registration. No, it's the illegal aliens they're sweeping up. Either join the army, or go back across the border in a truck."

"Makes sense to me." The tall guy kept swiping. "Let 'em pay their way, or go back where the fuck they came from. We got better things to do." He whistled, turned on one heel, headed to the bar. Called back, "Hey, Kyle. This one likes it on all fours, and she'll take us both. Got an apartment, ten minutes' walk."

"Jesus." Pruss threw a Corps-issue chip card on the table. "Let's get the hell out of here. I need a smoke."

THE shop was brightly lit outside but dim and cozy within. A front area, more of a head shop, was lined with showcases of pipes, bubblers, hand pipes, water pipes, stash cans, ash catchers, detox kits, downstems, bowls, scales. Behind that was a lounge lit even more dimly, furnished with long deep sofas and a chessboard, with some kind of sitar music playing. It was fogged with a low-hanging haze rich with spices and tobaccos and other things too. People were chatting and smoking cigars or vaping or toking off softly bubbling devices. Some watched a huge curved-screen television, where images flitted almost too fast to follow.

A short woman with penetrating eyes and a squinting smile murmured, "Hi, I'm Rosa. You kids is of age, right? I don't need to check no

ID, do I? You know there is a back room. Twenty dollars, and you soldiers can have privacy. Nobody else back there now."

Hector expected Coreguaje to say again *We aren't soldiers, we're Marines*, but she just nodded. "That'd be good. Not so many *hijos de putas.*"

The back room lay down a hallway past a grimy shared bathroom, then through a clattering curtain of blue plastic beads. It was darker yet, but though the smell was still strong the smoke wasn't as thick. Sofas faced each other, with a rosewood coffee table between them. A carafe and a tissue dispenser stood on it. A fan circled near the ceiling. Rosa passed out menus, and she and Pruss discussed the shisha choices. Hector figured "shisha" meant the tobacco mix you smoked. Finally Pruss settled on one, and Rosa brought in the pipe, a gaudy brass urn with dangling octopus arms of bright green and blue plastic.

Pruss filled the glass bowl with water from the carafe, then checked the gaskets. They sealed the top with a licked palm, and then their cheeks hollowed as they sucked in through the hose. "Just like checking your gas mask for leaks." They tightened one gasket, tried it again, and pronounced it airtight. Loaded the tobacco, not too tight. Pruss lit it with a piece of hot charcoal and took quick drags. A thick white smoke filled the glass. They sucked again, eyes closed, and let smoke trickle out their nose. The scents of orange and vanilla filled the air.

Pruss sighed, wiped the mouthpiece with one of the tissues, and laid it on the table. After a moment Whipkey picked it up. He sucked deep and held it, obviously used to grass, then burst out coughing.

When it came Hector's turn the smoke tasted sweet at first. Then the top of his head pried off and hovered. His stomach flipped a crazy twist. His heart thumped and started to race, pushing against his chest. His eyes popped and water sprang into his mouth. Shit, this was fun?

In the bathroom, after he was done puking, he stared at himself in the mirror. The goggles had left a white band across his upper face. Burn marks from hot cartridges tattooed his cheeks. He looked older, *sí.* Would Mirielle even know him now? He should get someone with a phone to send her a picture. Maybe Pruss would, if he asked her. No, *them.* Before they went back tonight.

Out front he got energy drinks for everybody. When he brought them back to the room a dirty guy in ragged clothes was hunched in a corner, playing two spoons clickety-clack under his arm like hambones. He talked a mile a minute and his eyes darted every which way. "Cigarettes is alls I needs," he kept saying, over and over. *Clickety clack, clackety clackety clack.* "Five bucks for cigarettes is alls I needs."

"Get out of here, Spoon Man," Rosa said wearily from the curtain, as if she said it a dozen times a day. "Go on, get out. Let these kids have some privacy, goddamn it."

After he left, Orietta got up and turned the lights out. The red coal of the hookah glowed like a demon's eye in the dark. They passed the mouthpiece around, but Hector only took a sip now and then. He and Orietta sat together on the sofa, and after a while she turned to snuggle into him.

As they held each other in the dark, he wasn't sure just how, her hand was inside his shirt. Then it was sliding under his belt.

Soon his fingers were inside a wet squirming warmth, her breath panting in his ear. Something was happening on the other sofa too, but they weren't looking over here.

He was lying back, breathing hard, when the bead curtain clattered. Rosa peered in. "Sorry, but . . . you guys might want to come out here, see this."

Clothes hastily tucked back together, they gaped up at the television.

Korea had surrendered. No, "accepted terms." South Korea would capitulate to China, not North Korea. It would remain a separate country, with a capitalist system, but would dismantle its armed forces and acknowledge Beijing's leadership. American forces fighting there would be permitted one week to leave. If they did not, they would be destroyed without mercy.

"Guess we won't be deploying after all," Whipkey muttered. He leaned back, elbows propped on the bar, and announced to the whole place, "Hey, we ain't goin' to Korea. Guess they're gonna send us home now, war's fucking over. Guess what? We lost."

A big older guy got up from one of the front room chairs. Hector tensed. This man looked like one of the fat angry whites who concealed-carried back where he came from. But the old gringo just came over and shook their hands without saying a word; then bent his head, face sad, and left.

11

The Central Pacific

R EADY to give it a shot, Admiral?"
Dan rubbed his face, wondering if this was worth the risk. Still, Chief Wenck seemed to think he'd pulled everything together.

The strange, nearly invisible contacts had dogged them on and off for the last year. The pips moved slowly, over a hundred thousand feet up. They only seldom registered, even on *Savo*'s powerful radars, which meant their cross sections were tiny. At first Dan had dismissed them as discontinuities in the atmosphere, "sprites," lensing effects, or artifacts of poor tuning. But they'd appeared again and again, high in the upper stratosphere. Seeming at times to follow the ships below.

At last, Donnie had come up with a proposal. An experiment, to find out just what they were.

Hornet's CIC was darkened and fully manned, but the large-screen displays had less data than Dan was used to from *Savo Island*. He hoped it would be enough to run a battle. . . . The LHA herself wouldn't be radiating, of course. Her radars lacked the precise focus of the Aegis ships. But the chief had set this up over the last few days, as the formation slowly steamed east, then south, then east again. Poking along at twelve knots. Trailing the bait through a vast deep oceanic basin, which had, according to Rit Carpenter, "the acoustics of a gymnasium. They gotta know we're here."

All that time, *Hornet* had made smoke, from cans of waste and lube oil on the stern, and kept one screw locked. Dan hadn't repeated the distress transmissions. That seemed too obvious. But if the pack commander had any sort of scouting screen out, sooner or later he'd pick them up.

What happened after that . . . well, Dan only hoped he didn't stumble into all two dozen subs at the same time. A force like that would execute a massacre like the battle that had given his old cruiser her name.

Savo Island, north of Guadalcanal, had been a knife fight in the dark. Night-practiced Imperial Navy ships had all but wiped out a surprised, confused U.S. destroyer and cruiser force.

"Sir?" Wenck prompted him.

Dan cleared his throat. "Sure this is worth trying, Donnie?"

The chief spread his hands. "Hey. . . . We got enough radiating elements and phase shifters. Got the transmitting arrays and the power. It's whether we can link the drivers, to focus it. I wrote a steering program, running it off the UYK-43 in *McClung*, but these ain't microwave lasers."

"All right. Initiate when you're ready," Dan muttered.

Wenck's fingers clattered on keys, sending coordinates and elevations to the four Aegis units. Clustered as close as they dared, *Savo*, *McClung*, *Kristensen*, and *Sejong the Great* were aiming the pencil-beams of their phased arrays to intersect a hundred thousand feet up: pouring over ten megawatts into a ten-cubic-meter volume of space, twenty miles in the sky.

"Building up to peak power," Wenck said. "We're gonna synchronize pulses, ten hertz, then vary the PRR and see if we can set up a harmonic."

Dan wasn't sure what that meant, and didn't care. He was more worried over the fact that they were deep in the danger area, yet hadn't made a single contact, or glimpsed as much as a periscope.

Where the hell were the Chinese?

He left Wenck to his own devices, and climbed to the bridge.

Clear and sunny. The sea was flat as a tabletop, and too aching blue to look down into for long. Out on the port wing, overlooking the flight deck, he searched the horizon. Aside from *Earhart* and *Green Bay* three miles away to port, only distant specks pricked it. *McClung* was on his port quarter, and *Kristensen* far astern. He shaded his eyes into the sun-glare, and caught *Savo* fine on the southern horizon, a tiny, all but invisible pinpoint at over ten thousand yards.

Even pulled in close for the Wenck Experiment, the main body of the task force covered twenty miles of sea. Jung's wing elements were even farther away. Not only did he have to worry about DF-21s, but the latest intel speculated that along with antiship missiles, Chinese submarines carried the Shkval-K, a two-hundred-knot rocket torpedo that could evade acoustic decoys and jamming. A Russian export, Shkvals were designed to burn through hull armor with rods of incendiary depleted uranium. Also, they might be carrying a small antitorpedo torpedo.

These weapons, code-named "Nightshade," might be immune to the countermeasures built into U.S. torpedoes.

On the plus side, the standard Chinese submarine torpedo, the Yu-3, had an effective range of only about eight miles.

Given that, Dan had instructed his helos to carry out attacks as soon as they had a datum, and to double the usual salvo rate of one torpedo per attack. Facing two incomers, any antitorpedo system would have to work four times as hard to identify, track, and intercept. And the farther away he could hold his adversary, the less risk to his own forces.

Of course, that strategy meant he might run out of torpedoes before he ran out of targets. And given the supply situation, he wouldn't be getting any more.

In which case . . . the task force would become the target. And, given the depleted state of his self-defense ordnance, an all but helpless one.

The hunter-killar group out of Pearl was closing him from the east. Slowly, searching every cubic mile of sea as it swept forward. It was built around *Makin Island*, protected by three Burke-class destroyers and an older U.S. nuclear submarine. If they could join up, the united force should be capable of knocking down whatever the Chinese could throw at them.

Unless the concentration invited Zhang to expend another thermonuclear warhead. If that happened, they were doomed. The magazines of *Savo Island*, their only ABM-capable unit, were empty of Block 4s.

They'd buried the dead from the exit battle at sea. His deputy, four watchstanders, and sixteen ship's company, all burned, blasted apart, decapitated, or sliced into pieces. But there wouldn't be any need for canvas shrouds, bugle calls, and the Service for the Dead if one of Zhang's massive thermonukes came down on them. It would cremate every ship in a fifteen-mile radius.

Shaking off dread, he stretched until vertebrae popped. Above his head, the ship's call-sign flags snapped in the wind.

When he looked back into the pilothouse the officer of the deck, the junior officers, the enlisted watchstanders, all glanced quickly away.

He lifted his chin, blinked, and tried to look more confident than he felt.

THE thing, whatever it was, fell very slowly. Which Wenck said meant it was probably some kind of winged craft. It drifted down from altitude, painting more clearly on their screens with each thousand feet it lost.

When it reached ten thousand feet, Dan tasked *Kristensen* to recover. The destroyer sent its helo, and a rescue diver plunged into the sea. The helo lifted, circling, but kept its video feed going. In CIC, Dan and Singhe stood watching the diver approach the floating object. One wing was crumpled, the other outspread. They were all but transparent, a gossamer film stretched over a complex frame. It looked like a giant wasp, complete with stinger. The diver paused a few feet away and took pictures before swimming closer.

He put out a glove and touched a wing gingerly.

When he was back in the helo and the thing was being winched up, Wenck and Jamail, the intel officer, were huddled in a corner discussing the imagery. Dan checked the radar picture, then strolled over. "What'd we catch, Donnie?"

"It's a drone. Of sorts." The chief flattened his cowlick, looking impressed. "A hybrid LTA and HTA. And some of this stuff looks like cell phone components. Cheap. Expendable."

"In English?"

"Halfway between lighter than air and heavier than air. Those big, long wings—they're probably filled with hydrogen. The ribs are lightweight foam. The dark elements on the back are solar cells. This central pod contains the computer, camera, and control actuators, and the antenna streams out the back, like a stinger. They're probably linked, relaying data back." The chief shook his head, grinning. "A network! A hundred of these up there, at a hundred thousand feet . . . you'd cover the whole western Pacific."

Dan bent over the screen, where Wenck had sketched an outline diagram. "Okay, but . . . what the heck makes it go? I don't see any propellers, no engine—"

"Maybe it doesn't need it," Jamail said. "With a combination of floating and gliding, and enough smarts to seek out air currents, it could ride the wind . . . like an upper-atmosphere albatross."

"Good name," Dan said. "Call it the Albatross, Qazi. Send these photos to Fleet. Info PaCom, CNO, and everybody else you can think of. This is how China does ocean surveillance without satellites."

"And the radar section's negligible," Singhe said, next to him. "With all that plastic, all that film. We're probably only detecting one in every ten."

At that moment he realized, looking at the photos of the broken creature, that it had probably provided the enemy with their location, and no doubt pictures, too. Relaying exactly where his task force was, and what tempting prey limped along at its heart.

With the realization, he spun and hit the 21MC lever. "Combat, CTG. Signal all screen units: Return to Formation Golf." The dispersed pattern he'd set up to invite their attackers in. If they'd seen *Hornet*'s smoke plume—

A petty officer leaned from a console. "Sir! *Farncomb* reports passive sonar contact. Bearing zero-six-zero, depth two-zero-zero feet, forty-two thousand yards. Permission to engage."

"Negative," Dan said. "Do not engage. Continue on base course. Remain covert unless individually targeted. —Qazi! Add that to the report to Fleet."

He straightened, easing his back, then headed for his chair.

The battle had begun.

THE threat revealed itself gradually. One reason why ASW also stood for Awfully Slow Warfare. Over the first hours, the Australian submarine, submerged and running in close to total quiet, reported five distinct contacts. Dan relayed the detections to Fleet as they came in. The buoy line laid across his advance tracked them as they crept in. Dan asked Min Su Hwang, his liaison with the Koreans, to warn the admiral, but found he'd already sent Jung a heads-up on ASW chat.

Longley brought a covered tray in at noon. Dan forced himself to down half a ham-and-cheese sandwich, three sweet pickles, and some chips. His staff had taken over the left half of CIC, since Flag Plot had been wrecked. Wenck, Singhe, Danenhower, Hwang, and the intel officer, Jamail, and his J3, Ops, Enzweiler, were all within speaking distance. Sandy Graciadei was in the captain's chair, not six feet from Dan, but their exchanges were muted by a distinct chill.

She finally spoke when the first goblins—submerged hostiles— altered course to pass north and south of the lead South Korean frigate. "Admiral. Are we going to take them?"

"Not yet, Sandy."

"Once they're inside our defensive perimeter—"

"Then they're in our kill zone. I want as many there as we can suck in. Just make sure you have enough 60s on deck, armed and fueled."

"We could use some help. P-8s?"

"They're on the way. And there might be some Air Force help too. If we really get our backs against the wall out here."

She frowned. "*Air Force?* Against submarines?"

"I know, I know. But that's what PaCom said. They wouldn't give any more details."

Hornet's skipper looked doubtful but sat back, smoothing her hair.

At 1310 a P-8 from Wake reported in. Dan asked for sweeps to the north and south. With only five out of twenty-six enemy units accounted for, he wanted advance warning of any end-arounds. He slid out of his chair and stood behind the petty officer at the eavesdropping console. "Nothing out there? No sub radars, radio transmissions?"

"Just us, and the long-range radars on Wake."

He scratched his head. How was this pack coordinating? The Germans had used shortwave radio. TF 76 was using the just-activated MOUSE satcomm uplinks, to dozens of hastily launched microsatellites in low orbits.

Unless . . . unless the Albatrosses had a comm relay function as well.

He was about to ask Wenck about this when the patrol air reported multiple contacts from ten miles astern and to the south of the leading incomers. Four new datums winked up on the display, showing two distinct enemy groups now.

The ship's ASW air coordinator had perforce become Dan's. A short Puerto Rican, Commander Soler, held up a hand at his console. Carpenter sat beside him, headphones clamped to the old sonarman's ears. "Two elements, Admiral, angling in from the north and the south," Soler muttered.

"Where are they headed?" Graciadei asked.

"Looks like, right for us," Carpenter said. Soler's keyboard clicked, and lines of advance lit on the display. Both elements were headed past *Seoul*, at the center and lead of the formation. The lines crossed one mile ahead of the blue circle and cross that represented *Hornet*.

Graciadei asked Dan, "How far in do you intend to let them come, Admiral?"

He chewed his cheek, wondering himself. The enemy was already close enough to launch missiles. Why hadn't they? Probably, feared his close-in air defenses too much. He couldn't let them get inside torpedo range too. If he lost control, this battle could degenerate into a mad swirl of individual combats. In a melee, the side with more numbers usually won. He had to make the right call. Whites of their eyes? Or hold them at arm's length?

No, he couldn't risk a knife fight. But so far, they didn't seem to know he had them on his displays. The passive buoys, bobbing quietly on the surface, gave the enemy no warning. They couldn't hear the P-8, either, or detect it on radar unless they pushed a mast above the surface. Which they must know would instantly make them a target in a calm sea like this.

CIC was dead silent, except for the endless whisper of air-conditioning.

"All right," he said, praying that his timing was right and he hadn't overlooked anything. And that luck, plain old luck, would turn out to be on their side. "Let's drop some bad news on these guys."

THE first salvo, air-dropped from *Hornet*'s and *McClung*'s helos, took out two boats. Sonar reported breaking-up noises. The shrieks of rending steel, the pops of imploding compartments, slowly faded. The bottom of this abyssal basin was four miles down. Vectored in to the northern group, the P-8 parachute-dropped eight Mark 54s on Soler's vectors, plotted at the intersections of sonobuoy bearings. Only one seemed to connect, though. Dan was disappointed, but not surprised. The Mark 54 had gotten a poor rating from DOT&E before the war. *Sejong* picked up the engagement via a convergence zone, though she was far to the north, and reported indications of damage on the single enemy who'd been hit. But not a sinking.

Farncomb requested permisson once more to attack. Instead Dan ordered the Australian boat to open to the north, and made sure all screen units knew where she was, to avoid blue on blue. He needed her ears more than her torpedoes.

The helicopters roved back and forth, stitching the sea with more hydrophones as the task force and the incoming pack slowly interpenetrated like colliding galaxies.

Three down, six to go. But those half dozen came on inexorably, and he couldn't be sure they'd picked them all up. There were too many left unaccounted for.

The southern group abruptly went sinker, vanishing as completely as if they'd never been built. Carpenter called, "They bought a thermocline. Nice 'n' handy. But they can't hear us under there, either." The helos clustered above where they'd vanished, then spiraled outward in expanding-search patterns. Soler recommended that the formation turn away to the north. Dan shook his head grimly. Turning away wasn't going to win this battle.

The first torpedoes hit *Green Bay*, to the north of the main body, and

ROKN *Jeonnam*, to the southeast of *Savo*, nearly simultaneously. Both ships began slowing. Unfortunately, the enemy boats, most likely AIP-equipped Yuan-class units, stayed unlocatable. Dan gritted his teeth and asked for damage reports.

The boats still being tracked were closing on *Savo Island*, southeast of *Hornet* and fifteen thousand yards out. Dan figured they were almost within torpedo range too. He picked up the tactical voice. "Matador, this is Barbarian, over."

"*Matador, over.*" Dave Branscombe's familiar voice.

"Heads up on two goblins bearing approximately one-two-five true, range sixteen thousand yards from you. Do you hold them active sonar? Over."

"*This is Matador. We see the datums on the shared picture, but negative contact on anything along that bearing. Over.*"

This was worrisome. The cruiser'd had problems with its sonar before. Excessive self-noise, and reduced sensitivity figures.

He was pressing the Transmit button again when the ASW coordinator spoke up. "Rocket noise bearing one-two-five. Correlates with Shkval launch." Dan let up on the button, then pressed harder. Waiting ages until the circuit beeped and synced, scrambling the transmission to any listener who didn't hold the key.

"Cheryl, did you hear that?" he said urgently. "Shkval launch. On you. Get your ass out of there!"

FIFTEEN thousand yards distant, Cheryl Staurulakis went rigid in her chair. The shout from Sonar had swiveled every head in Combat. "Shkval in the water. Bearing one-two-zero!"

Beside her Matt Mills was typing rapidly. "Two hundred knots. Six thousand yards a minute . . . two minutes until impact."

She pressed the 21MC key. "Bridge, CO: Come to flank emergency. Course three-zero-zero. Sound the collision alarm." Even at flank the cruiser would be traveling much more slowly than the Shkval, but the rocket's burn time was limited. Making it a stern chase just might save them. She shouted across the compartment, which was already slanting into a hard turn, "Activate Rimshot." The collision alarm came on, a shrill *dit dit dit, dit dit dit*. Warning everyone to brace for shock.

According to the Tactical Analysis Group, the Russian weapon was magnetically guided. An internal generator, driven by steam tapped off the envelope of gas in which the torpedo traveled, generated a powerful field around the torpedo. Internal sensors monitored that field, alert for deformations by outside influences.

Such as large masses of steel.

Navy warships already carried degaussing equipment, to strip off their natural magnetic fields. That protected them from mines. But to fool the Shkval, something more had been needed. Activated, Rimshot's sensors searched for approaching magnetic fields. If they detected one, they drew on the ship's power to generate a pulse simulating a mass of iron thirteen times the size of the ship itself.

Causing, or so the Naval Research Laboratory claimed, an incoming warhead to detonate prematurely.

Unfortunately, no one had yet tested it against a live Shkval-K.

"CIC, bridge: All engines flank emergency, coming to course three-zero-zero."

"Very well," she snapped. "Is Rimshot on?"

"AN/UYK-98 activated," Chief Zotcher confirmed.

"One minute," said Mills, beside her.

"Bridge, CO: All hands aft of frame 150, lay forward of frame 150. Reset Condition Zebra behind you." Maybe save a few lives, when the thing hit. Though with a shaped charge, and depleted uranium behind it, there might not be much left of the ship afterward. Especially if it penetrated to the after magazine, still racked with Tomahawks and Harpoons, and the fuel bunkers. Thousands of pounds of high-energy explosive and rocket fuel, plus a hundred tons of Navy Standard Distillate . . . it would make a spectacular fireball.

The next item on the agenda: counterattack. In its initial phase, the Shkval was a straight-runner. Only at the end of its run did it switch to internal guidance. Which meant that right now it was leaving a trail of hot gas pointing straight to their attacker. She clicked to the ASW circuit to find Winston Farmer, her antisubmarine officer, already coaching Red Hawk into a drop. Good.

"Fish one away. Fish two away," sang the ASW console operator.

"Think of anything else?" she asked Mills. He was dead pale. The bulkheads shook as the ship strained every nerve, coming up to full power away from the incoming weapon. He shook his head wordlessly.

Then there was nothing to do but wait.

GREEN Bay reported shaft damage and heavy flooding port side. She was counterflooding to regain stability. Jeonnam was dead in the water, listing, fighting a main space fire. Unfortunately, Dan couldn't help either ship, not right now. Finish the battle, then assist the wounded. He stared at the display. He'd hoped to clobber the incomers before they got in among the main body. But this was becoming what he'd dreaded: knives in a dark alley.

"Admiral, I'd advise pulling in the screen."

He half-turned to glance at Amarpeet Singhe. "I'm thinking about it."

She said, "I know that increases our exposure to nuclear attack. But right now, the closer we circle the wagons, the less opportunity they have to get in among us. Plus, sooner or later, they're going to go to missiles."

He nodded. "All right. Pass to screen commander: Pull in to five thousand yards."

"And the outer one?"

"Pull them in too. Forty thousand yards, but keep them behind our beam when we're on formation course. I don't want them ahead of us."

The orders went out on chat, the voice channels silent now. The reports were coming in that way too. The microsatellites, passing swiftly above in nongeosynchronous orbits, were giving him UHF data uplink and downlink again. Unfortunately, they weren't very effective in the reconnaissance role. With the Albatross network, the enemy commander might have a better picture of this battle than he did. And if they were linked back to the mainland, this pack, and this battle, might actually be directed from Admiral Lianfeng's headquarters in Beijing.

"*Savo Island* reports: Torpedo detonation close astern. Lost sonar tail. Slowing to investigate prop vibration."

"Very well."

"*Green Bay* reports fire under control. Seven casualties, two dead. Able to make five knots."

They hadn't reported a fire, but having it under control was good. "Make formation speed five," he snapped to Enzweiler. "Individual ships, maneuver at will within assigned sectors. We'll fight it out here. Keep pulling the screen in." It was the only way he could keep his damaged units under what bubble of protection he could still provide.

"*Savo Island* reports multiple underwater explosions vicinity datum Goblin Juliet."

"Very well, excellent." Another enemy piece off the board. And if it'd been the Shkval archer, it was probably one of the newer, air-independent enemy boats. But that still left over half the attacking force still out there.

"P-8 reports bingo fuel, Winchester ordnance. Permission to return to Wake."

"Crap . . . Granted." He made a face. "Ask him if he has a relief on its way."

"Relief inbound, one-five minutes out."

Fifteen minutes, an eternity . . . "Pass to the new guy, I need sweeps close in to the main body, to the south and then to the north. Immediate drop on any detection. The only Blue submarine bears ten miles northeast of *Hornet*."

Dan passed both hands over his hair. The palms came away wet, and he wiped them surreptitiously on his coveralls. He got down and stood behind Soler, watching the ASW coordinator position the helicopters as they dropped sonobuoys, dipped, conducted magnetic runs.

A crunching shock tremored the deck, which flexed upward, then snapped down, catapulting him into the air. The lights flickered. The shock whanged away through the overhead. He grabbed at the back of a chair but was still knocked off his feet. His head hit something hard on the way down. He blinked dazzle off his eyeballs, catching himself on hands and knees.

Alarms were beeping. *"Torpedo hit, starboard side forward,"* the 1MC announced. *"Repair One provide."*

"Dropping on Goblin Hotel, range seven thousand yards, bearing one-four-zero."

He hoisted himself to a crouch, trying desperately to reboot a scrambled brain. Regain the tactical picture . . . hands on his arms, helping him up . . . sandalwood and stale sweat . . . Singhe on one side, Soler on the other. "You okay, Admiral? You're bleeding. Hit your head?"

"Just a scalp wound. Give me a tissue, somebody."

Goblin Hotel had been part of the northern group, but that torpedo had come from the south. Meaning that its firer, and possibly others, had transited the thermocline directly underneath the inner screen, then risen on the far side to reorient and attack.

Maybe making himself a sitting duck hadn't been such a good idea. He listened, nodding as Graciadei updated him on *Hornet*'s damage: a massive hole in the starboard bow, flooded compartments, reduced speed. Her words reverberated in his ears. He turned away when she stopped speaking, pressing the tissue to his temple. "Uh, ASW air, where's that fucking P-8? We need sonobuoys and helos to the south."

"Still ten minutes out, Admiral."

Carpenter called, "Sir, we should maybe pull *Farncomb* back in, slide her under the thermo—"

"Negative. Somebody's going to hammer him by mistake if we do. The one sure thing we know now is, if we have contact, it's a hostile." Unfortunately, the only ASW-capable surface unit he had to the southward was *Savo*, and she'd just had her most effective sensor, her sonar tail, blown off. "Captain"—Graciadei turned—"you have all our helos in the air?"

"Bringing the first ones in for hot refuel, or padding them in on *McClung*."

He swung to check the display. *Kristensen* was pulling closer. "How are we doing on ordnance? We have to—"

"Vampire, vampire, vampire," the ESM operator announced, voice slicing through the hubbub. "*Multiple* vampires, bearing three-five-four to three-five-zero. Correlates to Yingji-82 Saccade."

There it was: the second wave. Out to the northwest. Waiting until the first was in among the inner screen before launching missiles.

Against ships already crippled, constrained in their ability to maneuver, and bunched tight.

For a moment he couldn't breathe. Clung to the back of his command chair, supporting suddenly weak knees, as one after the other scarlet carets bloomed on the display. As the readouts winked into existence. As incoming missiles jumped ahead with each sweep of the radar.

After an agonizing couple of seconds, he saw it.

The opportunity.

The red phone in his hand. Wait for the beep. "War Drums, this is Barbarian."

"*War Drums. Over.*" Jung's voice. The left wing, twenty miles north of the main body. Nine superbly capable ASW frigates and destroyers, flagshipped by *Sejong the Great* and led by one of the most aggressive commanders he'd ever met.

"Sub pack southwest of you, twelve miles, just launched multiple vampires against main body. Reverse course, sweep west, close in behind them. Wipe 'em out, Min."

"*This is War Drums. Roger all. Out.*"

FIVE miles distant, the Hydra on Cheryl Staurulakis's belt beeped. "Air Control reports: Multiple vampires, incoming. Bearing spread on three-four-zero. Correlates with CSS-N-8 Saccade."

She'd been trotting aft, intending to check out the damage, since reports were confused, but was slowed by all the dogged hatches. She reversed course and pelted back forward. She arrived puffing in Combat, and plunked down in her chair, checking that her firing key was still locked in. Beside her Mills was finishing target designations. He said from the side of his mouth, "We're splitting them with *Kristensen*. They're taking the three to the east. We've got the ones to the west."

Terranova was bent over the Aegis console. "We have lock-on." On the display, four of the quickly advancing red carets began winking bright orange halos.

Mills said, "Ready to fire, SM-2s on Vampires Alfa, Bravo, Delta, Charlie. One-round engagements. Followed by another one-round engagement on any leakers."

"Kill 'em," Cheryl snapped.

A distant clunk as the vent dampers toggled shut. The ventilators dropped the scale. The rush of icy air stopped, and suddenly it was much quieter in Combat.

Mills flipped up a switch cover and hit a button.

The roar rattled the bullkheads. A star ignited in the forward hatch area camera field of view. Terranova chanted, "Bird one away . . . two away . . . bird three away . . . bird four away. Preparing for refire from after magazine."

On the center display bright symbols left the blue circle and cross. Cheryl pulled her mind off that and clicked on the Hydra. "Lieutenant Jiminiz? Have you got a report yet?"

"We're still hauling in on the tail. It looks intact, but we're not getting an output."

"I'm more worried about the screws right now." She pushed buttons on the 21MC and hit the lever. "Main Control, CO. Can you up the turn count on the remaining shaft? We need maneuverability bad, right now."

"Skipper, we're still seeing a lot of vibration. I'm not sure what's going on down there."

"Is this Chief McMottie? I can't hear you very well."

"I have an e-beedie on. Toxic gas dump here. Halon leak. Shock from the explosion popped a valve. I evacuated everybody."

"Okay . . . the vibration . . . is it a shaft issue, or a prop issue?"

"Offhand I'd say the prop."

"Stand fast, Chief. I'll get you degassed as soon as we get a break here."

"Damage Control's working it, Skipper. No worries. Let middle management handle it."

The ASW operator called, "Sonar reports contact . . . torpedo in the water! Torpedo launch, torpedo noise bearing two-five-zero. Bearing drift . . . rapid right."

The ESM operator yelled from the other side of Combat, "I don't have radar altimeters on these 802s. Trying to fox them, but I'm not getting a response."

She lifted a finger to them both, clicked onto the command net. "Birkenstock, this is Matador. Torpedo headed your way. Out." Clicked off without waiting for an acknowledgment. Then, to Mills, "Red Hawk is where?"

"Strafer's bingo fuel. We need to come to recovery course."

"Divert him to *Hornet*. We're firing on this guy. Stand by on Mark 46s."

"Not ASROC?"

"Too close range. Dump three Mark 46s and let them figure it out." She hit the button to the bridge. "Come to two-four-zero. No, belay that. Continue right to zero-zero-zero. ASW Control, stand by to drop as we swing through two-four-zero. —Sonar, Chief Zotcher, got a firm ping on this guy?"

"*No. Mushy. Drifting in and out.*"

"Bearing, range?"

"*Two-three-zero. Twelve thousand. Course, one-niner-zero. Increasing turn count. Hauling ass away.*"

Extreme range for the Mark 46s *Savo* carried. But hearing the eggbeater whine of torpedoes behind him, at least he'd keep clearing the battle zone. Anyhow, the way this was going, maybe she shouldn't worry about conserving ordnance. She breathed deep and held it, trying to slow her thinking. Her outgoing Standards had almost reached the rapidly streaking missiles, which were apparently targeted on *Hornet*. *Savo* was on the far side of the formation from her, unfortunately, making intercept time longer, but they might get there. The compartment leaned as the cruiser, increasing speed but slowly, careened into the turn. "Torpedo one away . . . two away . . . three away," the ASW controller chanted.

Seconds ticked past as *Savo* steadied on her northerly course. Wilker reported he was headed to *Hornet*. Cheryl hit the 21MC to Main Control again, but no one answered. Had McMottie been overcome? She called DC Central. They said a party was en route with blowers to vent the gas.

"Stand by . . . intercept," Terranova called.

The red carets winked out, except for one, which kept coming. Straight for them now . . . no, for the carrier . . . it seemed to be confused, switching its attention between the targets. Any second now, though, it would make up its mind. "Leaker, leaker," Mills said tensely. "Stand by to refire."

"Inside minimum range," Terranova murmured. "Warhead won't arm."

Mills froze, fingers suspended over the keys, stare clamped to the display. The enemy missile paused, then jumped forward. Paused, jumped again.

"ESM—still no joy on jamming?"

"Can't fox this dude," the petty officer called. "I've run the program three times, but he's not responding."

"*Hornet* coming to zero-nine-zero," the command net talker announced.

Cheryl selected the ruler tool and measured distances. Too close for Standard. Too far for Phalanx. *Savo* was closing the carrier, but she was just on the wrong side.

The single C-802 took a longer stride forward. "Going supersonic, into terminal run," Terranova announced.

"Homing where?"

"Looks like . . . on us."

"ESM?"

"No joy, no joy. Not responding to foxing."

Cheryl clicked her IC selector to Weapons, trying not to think about the fate moving inexorably down its world-line toward *Savo*. Only one card left to play. "Sergeant, you on the line?"

"Custis here, ma'am."

"Incoming missile bearing three-four-zero."

"We've been looking. Don't see anything—"

"You won't. Too low. Supersonic. Slew to three-four-zero and salvo four rounds. *Now!*"

A rippling thud resounded from above. In the camera display, whitish-yellow smoke blew across the screen. Custis's Stingers were on their way. Short-ranged, and with only seven-pound warheads, but the incomer was only ten feet above the wavetops. If they could knock it even slightly off course, it would plow harmlessly into the sea. Across the compartment the operator shouted, "Phalanx in automatic." The 25mm operator was hollering, "Mount 21, mount 22, incoming missile, bearing three-four-four."

A clamoring racket started outside, the *blam blam blam* of the contact-fuzed 25s underscored by the bass *brrrrrrr* of the CIWS, and, at intervals, the heavier *wham . . . wham* of the forward five-inch, pumping out the new hypervelocity projectiles. Her gaze welded itself to the pulsing caret of the incomer. For three long seconds the noise was continuous.

The red caret winked out. "Splash Vampire Charlie," Terranova announced.

Cheryl sighed. "Very well. —Bridge, right hard rudder, course zero-nine-zero." She hit the lever for DC Central. "Any word from the Engine Room?"

"About to call you, Captain. McMottie was passed out in there. We hauled him up and Dunk's administering oxygen. She thinks he'll be okay. Getting the blowers lined up. The watch section's standing by to go in . . . wait one . . . they say, ready to answer all bells."

Abruptly there seemed nothing left to do. She checked with Sonar. No detonations from that bearing, but the goblin they'd fired torpedoes on was still tracking outbound. The air controller reported Red Hawk still refueling and rearming aboard *Hornet*. Cheryl realized she was panting. But no one seemed to have noticed. They looked shaken too. She pushed wet hair from her face and smoothed it back into its ponytail.

IN *Hornet*'s CIC, the pace of battle slackened. Dan caught up on the reports. The wave of 802s from the northwest had been knocked down, but at a massive cost in ordnance. His inner-screen units were scraping the bottom of their magazines. Another attack like that, and they'd be reduced to slow targets.

His Korean wings had barely expended a round yet. But Jung was racing west. His van units had begun the hook-around, surrounding and cutting off the boats that had just launched the wave of missiles. He told Soler to refuel and rearm the HSL and get them out to help. The Koreans would swing the front doors shut, the helos would slam the back, and the slaughter would begin.

A clink at his elbow, a waft of cinnamon. "Brought'cha some joe, Admiral. And a sticky bun. Y'oughta eat something."

He wanted to say "Not hungry," but made himself take a bite. Drizzled with hard sauce, and still hot. Longley must have run up the ladders from the mess decks. "Uh, thanks." He blew on the coffee and tried a sip. Twice as strong as usual, exactly what he needed just now.

Unfortunately, the cup clattered on the saucer as he set it down. Hoping no one had heard, he pushed the saucer aside and finished in quick gulps. Longley whisked the china away and vanished.

All right, recapitulate . . . This did seem to be a lull. . . . They'd beaten off two submerged groups, from the northeast and southeast. The enemy had penetrated the screen and inflicted damage, but paid a high price: five boats, by his count. He had tracks on two that seemed to be fleeing, or at least retiring, perhaps for reload. The wave to the northwest was still too far off to attack, and would shortly have their hands full with Jung's ravenous wolves, eager to avenge *Seoul* and *Jeonnam*. He'd never gotten a firm count on how many attackers there were overall. But if Intel was right, he'd just engaged fully half the total Chinese forces in the mid-Pacific.

He told Soler to pull *Farncomb* back inside the main body, slip her under the thermocline, and eavesdrop for any lurkers. "But make sure all units roger up on her location, to avoid mistakes." He asked Enzweiler for damage reports, and listened with chin in one hand as the ops officer totted up a grim butcher's bill.

Graciadei came over. Avoiding his gaze. "Congratulations, Admiral."

"On what, Captain?"

"On your victory."

"Uh, thanks. I guess. Anyway, it's 'ours,' not 'mine.' What's your status? I asked Bart Danenhower to give your people a hand."

She told him Commander Danenhower was in DC Central, helping coordinate the repair-team response. *Hornet* was speed-limited by the hole in the bow, although the compromised compartments had been sealed off and bulkheads were being shored up. "I hope to resume at least twenty knots in a couple of hours, though we'll need dry-docking, inspection, and repair."

Dan sucked air through bared teeth. That would mean heading to Pearl Harbor or San Diego. After the attack during their sortie from Apra, he couldn't see PaCom risking another major combatant in the dry dock there. The Allies might still hold it, but Guam was in the battle zone now.

He was updating Fleet by covered satcomm when a stir rose over by the air control consoles. "Stand by one," he said into the red phone. He called to Singhe, "What's going on over there?"

Then he swiveled, and saw the answer on the displays.

A barrage had emerged from the empty sea to the southwest. Small, fast contacts marched north. The ESM operator yelled, "Vampire, vampire—multiple X-band radars."

Dan grabbed the arms of his chair when he realized where they were headed.

Straight for his helos.

"Correlates to—German?—IDAS antiair missile," the operator stammered.

"Break right, break right—flares, *now*," the air controller spat over the circuit. "They're coming straight up your ass."

The CIWS on *Hornet*'s superstructure burst into its bass *brrrr*, but almost immediately cut off. "Out of range," the controller called.

"What are they? Where'd they come from?" he shouted, mind racing.

"*Farncomb* reports convergence zone contacts bearing two-one-zero, twenty-eight thousand yards from formation center. Two contacts, possibly three. Stand by . . . possibly four contacts. Classify as Victor-class nuclear submarines."

Not Russian Victors, of course, but Chinese Shangs . . . the enemy's nuclear boats.

The first team was on the field. At last.

And their opening play was taking down his helicopters.

The chatter rose to a crescendo. "Falcon two-two-one down, in the water."

"On the deck . . . incoming . . . Falcon leader, say again, over."

The leading red carets met the blue of friendly helicopters. They blinked, and callouts began spinning downward. In the video from a mast-mounted camera, puffs of black smoke stippled the horizon. From them fell comets of flame.

Dan leaned in, staring at the screen as the ambush unfolded. He'd been well and truly had. Far from "taking the bait," the enemy commander had deliberately sacrificed his slower, older diesel boats to deplete the task force's magazines before sending in the first team. Now, with a weapon the Allies hadn't even known he owned, he'd crippled the helicopters, the biggest advantage surface ships held over submarines. His next move would be to launch another wave of 802s, exhausting the last of the task force's antiair ordnance. Then he would close, to finish them off with a mass torpedo attack.

Sick at heart, nails digging into the arms of his chair, Dan realized he'd been outmaneuvered from the start. Baited, switched, and suckerpunched.

Singhe, at his elbow. "Admiral? Fleet calling."

He accepted the red phone as if in a trance. "Barbarian Actual."

"This is Husky. Interrogative situation and intentions. Over."

He cleared his throat with an effort. "Husky, this is Barbarian. We are being attacked from southwest by multiple Shangs. Taking heavy casualties to helicopter force. Ordnance nearly exhausted. My intention . . . I guess . . . to fight to the end." Though really there was no choice. He couldn't outrun the nuke boats. Their top speed submerged was faster than a damaged *Hornet*'s. "Uh . . . Over."

A deliberation in the background, only part of which he caught. Then, *"This is Husky. Clear the area to the east. Over."*

He blinked, uncomprehending. At the same moment, two contacts winked on to the eastward. The callouts identified them as friendly air, fifty thousand feet up. "What the hell are those?" he asided to Enzweiler.

"Wait one . . . IFF as C-5s."

What were Air Force transports doing out here? He could use a re-supply, but Galaxies took miles of runway to land. Probably just more troops on their way to Guam. His brain realized he was still squeezing the phone in a sweaty hand. "Uh, Fleet, this is Barbarian. Request you say again. I have helos down west of me. Crews in the water. Torpedo damage. What exactly are you advising me to do? Over."

"This is an order, not an advisement. Clear your task force to the eastward at maximum possible speed. Recover aircraft still operational. Leave damaged units and casualties behind for now. P-8s will drop rafts to them. Acknowledge."

Totally in the dark, he reluctantly rogered. He told the ops officer, "Make to all units: come to course zero-nine-zero, flank speed. Vector remaining helos to recover before they bingo. Pick up as many survivors as possible while withdrawing. Make sure War Drums rogers."

Enzweiler looked as puzzled as Dan was. "Aye, sir. Signal's going out. But withdraw . . . to where? These guys will just follow us."

Hornet leaned into a radical turn, steel fabric creaking. Graciadei was bumping on additional RPM, five at a time. Danenhower stood beside her, looking worried. Dan licked dry lips. "I agree, but it's not phrased like we have an option, Fred."

"Admiral." Singhe's tone twisted him round in his seat. "Look. Those air contacts."

He squinted, then frowned. The tracks of the Galaxies had bent north-ward. The altitude readouts on both contacts were spinning rapidly downward. Losing altitude. Their course would take them directly over the oncoming Shangs. For a moment he wanted to warn them, then re-alized it wasn't necessary. The missiles the subs had just taken down his helos with were short-range. Low-altitude. More like Stingers than anything else.

"What the fuck," Wenck muttered beside him. "What the—"

"I'm not sure either, Donnie."

"They're losing altitude, but coming in hot. WTF, over?"

Dan cocked his head, a light snapping on. Could they be going in for a drop? But of what? The huge cargo birds weren't equipped with anything more dangerous than flares. They weren't bombers.

"What the fuck," Wenck breathed again.

Dan lifted the handset again. Waited for the sync. "Husky, Barbarian Actual, over."

"Fleet, over. Are you clearing the area as ordered?"

"This is Barbarian. Affirmative. Interrogative: What is going on with these Air Force big birds? Over."

A pause, a hesitation. Then, *"This is Fleet. Do not log or record what's happening behind you. Do not discuss with the crew. This is close hold within the command team. Acknowledge. Over."*

Still confused, Dan acknowledged. Then sat back rubbing his chin, frowning up at the screen. The Galaxies had completed their pass in front of the oncoming pack. Then, still low, began a clockwise sweep, as if for a second run in front of the advancing submarines.

Singhe stepped up to his chair. He caught a whiff of her perfume as her lips brushed his ear. "We're getting a hint on one of the chat rooms," she whispered. "It's called 'Spyglass.'"

He frowned. "What is?"

"Whatever they're dropping. The word is, something hush-hush out of Silicon Valley."

The ASW controller lifted his voice. *"Farncomb* reports: low-order detonation bearing two-two-zero. Hold on . . . there's another."

CIC was silent. Dan bent forward, waiting too, though he wasn't sure for what. Someone put audio from Sonar on a speaker. Two more distant, trivial-sounding thunks echoed through the deep, reverberating like dull bells. Not nearly as dramatic as a torpedo detonation.

Aside from that, they heard nothing more.

12

Washington, D.C.

BLAIR swung down the corridor, following the junior officer who trotted ahead. The sun gleamed on the blue floor tiles. The windows looked down on the central garden and white gazebo at the heart of the Pentagon.

The past week had been grim. She'd finally buckled and told her campaign manager to place the call. Beiderbaum had been almost friendly on the phone. Said he hoped they could work together someday. She'd bitten her lip, and lied about how much she looked forward to it. After making the official announcement, she and several friends had gone to the Monocle for martinis. She didn't want to think about how much money she owed, or how narrowly she'd lost.

But she had no time to be depressed. Not while trying to hold together a fragile consensus on their course of action in the Pacific. Which would be the topic of today's meeting.

She hadn't heard from Dan for a week. Comms were still spotty out there, even though the nanosatellites had gone up. But surely he could have found time for a call. An e-mail, at least.

Unless something had happened . . .

Her phone vibrated. She pulled it out as she walked, squinting, but didn't recognize the number. "Uh, hello? Who is this?"

"Blair? Beverly Maclay. How are you doing today, dear?"

Mrs. Beverly Maclay chaired the House Intelligence, Emerging Threats and Capabilities Subcommittee. A moderate from Kansas, she dressed for the part in dark suits, her gray hair in a schoolmarm bun. They were from different parties, but Blair had met with her when she'd worked on Armed Services. "I'm doing all right, ma'am. Good to hear from you."

"*I called to say I'm sorry you lost the recount. It would have been great having you on the subcommittee.*"

"I very much appreciate that, Beverly." She followed the JO down a narrower corridor toward a checkpoint.

"*And how is your husband doing out in the Pacific? I hope he's safe?*"

"I haven't heard much lately from him, I'm afraid." She handed her SAIC ID and briefcase to an MP. "I mean, not that I'm *afraid*, but . . . okay, I'm afraid. When you don't hear anything . . . never mind. How can I help you today?"

"*Maybe it's how I can help you, Blair. You've heard the president is shuffling his cabinet in response to the emergency.*"

"Yes." The motorized belt hummed, carrying her briefcase and purse through the X-ray. "I read that in the *Post*." Szerenci had also mentioned it when he'd invited her to join him in the security adviser directorate.

Which she'd never responded to . . . The congresswoman said, "*Well, he wants to expand our tent. Form what the British would call a national cabinet. He asked me for recommendations. People who supported the war, who had defense credentials. I have to confess, you were the only one I could think of.*"

Blair nodded to the MP as he handed her briefcase back. "Oh. Well, thanks, Beverly. I'm flattered, really, but I'm pretty much fully tasked at SAIC."

"*I know, but couldn't you make a bigger impact as part of the administration? That's a rhetorical question. Of course you could. And that handsome husband of yours, who knows what you could do for him from there.*"

"I don't know . . . I really don't like this New Freedoms Act the administration's pushing. What kind of position are we talking about? Advisory, policy?"

"*I'm not privy to the specifics, but they're thinking of you for DoD. Not the spot you had under De Bari, I don't think, but you'd have to discuss details with the SecDef. And the Freedoms Act . . . I have misgivings about that myself.*"

"Well, Bev . . . This would be something I'd probably better sleep on."

"*Of course, we don't expect an instant response. But could you give me a call back by tomorrow? Or call Mr. Strohm's office if you want to discuss it further?*"

Leif Strohm was the secretary of defense. Blair took a couple of breaths. "Uh, I'm in the Pentagon right now."

"Well, why not stop by his office?"

"I'd need more time than that to—"

Her escort was steering her toward a heavy door with two more guards outside. Both had carbines ready to hand. "I'm sorry, ma'am, I just can't say yes or no right this moment. I'd need to sound out my people first. See how the land lies."

Sounding disappointed, Maclay said, *"I understand. Let me know, then. Good-bye."*

The MP held out a hand; Blair presented her ID again. "That phone, too, ma'am. We'll keep an eye on it."

She handed it over, musing on the offer. Pluses and minuses. An undersecretary position, most likely. She'd held one before, but with her own party in power. By joining this administration, even under some kind of national banner, she'd be burning her boats. The antiwar wing would never forgive her.

But maybe, for the good of the country, she ought to do it.

She just hoped it *was* for the good of the country. . . .

THE Chiefs were gathering around the big table. Ricardo Vincenzo, chairman of the Joint Chiefs, presided in Air Force blue. Dan's alternate mentor and enemy, Nick Niles, was in service dress blue. General Glee, the Army chief of staff. The Marine commandant. A face she didn't recognize; probably the commander of the National Guard. Ranged behind them were staffers and advisers, many of whom she knew, including Dr. Denson Hui, director of the Missile Defense Agency. She nodded to two others from SAIC: Professor Glancey, the war-termination scholar from Stanford, and Haverford Tomlin, retired general. Plus an ugly, tall man she didn't know.

The first presenter, a congressional liaison, gave a ten-minute overview of legislation currently before both houses. She listened carefully, chin propped on her cupped hand. The *Post* had outlined the issue, but now she was hearing the uncensored version.

Belatedly, the U.S. was facing full mobilization and the draft. The "New Freedoms" Act had been moved by Congresswoman Sandy Treherne, a Republican from Kentucky, and by a Democratic member from Massachusetts. "Both parties are getting some of what they've always wanted, under guise of wartime needs," the briefer said. The slide read:

- social entitlements halved
- defense expenditures doubled
- all privately owned assault rifles confiscated
- undocumented aliens either report for military service or they and their families are deported
- all citizens between ages of 18 and 50 subject to conscription for military or industrial duties
- first amendment and habeas corpus rights suspended for the duration
- guaranteed minimum income and health care for those in defense-related employment
- 100% taxes on incomes over $500,000

The generals and admirals stirred, but didn't comment. The briefer continued. "The 'partyless administration' being formed is intended to unite the country behind the war. But as you can see, there are significant social policy changes here."

She shook her head. Maybe Beiderbaum hadn't been as paranoid as she'd thought. What had he said in their final debate . . . "It happens in every war: our freedoms erode, government prying and control increases."

Regardless of whether they won or not, the United States of America was going to feel very different.

The head of Strategic Command spoke next. "This war is more dangerous to the homeland than any other we've ever fought. Zhang's secretly deployed new ICBMs exceed our heaviest missiles in terms of throw weight, accuracy, and number of independently maneuverable warheads. We estimate now he has at least seventy in service. All presumably targeted against major cities in the continental United States.

"Facing this surprise breakout, our options are constrained. We can wage conventional war, against overwhelming numbers. We can escalate to theater nuclear war. Zhang already has, so in a sense we're there. But escalation from that point runs the risk of a strike on the continental U.S.

"We've asked Professor Glancey to prepare a white paper on war termination between nuclear powers."

The academic stood, but Vincenzo asked politely if he'd mind holding that report for a separate briefing. "We need to keep things short today, and make some essential decisions." Glancey nodded and sat again.

Vincenzo said, "The president has asked our advice as to how to respond to Zhang's offer of a cease-fire on the following basis: Union of the two Chinas and the two Koreas. Return of Okinawa to Japan. U.S.-Japanese alliance ties dissolved. Respect for China's leading role in those islands and sea areas historically Chinese. The United States to withdraw from the western Pacific and refrain from what he calls 'additional provocations.'

"To give us the background . . ."

The next presenter was the military liaison to State, who explained what agreement to Zhang's terms would mean politically and economically. Was there any way to achieve peace with honor, without further war? Was compromise still possible, with the ten thousand casualties from the *FDR* battle group, thousands missing from the Army and Marine elements being extracted from Korea, and ongoing casualties from the all-but-lost battle for Okinawa?

The Chiefs quickly took over this debate. Their sentiment seemed clear, and when Vincenzo asked for a show of hands, it was unanimous. The president should not respond to the Chinese offer.

"All right, now we've got all that out of the way—" Vincenzo began, then stopped.

Two men had slipped in. One went to the State rep, the other to the chairman. Handed each a paper. The two read, then exchanged glances. Vincenzo nodded, placed his copy on the table, and cleared his throat.

"The Japanese have accepted Zhang's offer," he said. "In exchange for his promise to evacuate Okinawa. But they're asking for time to help U.S. forces stage a phased withdrawal. No answer yet from Beijing."

Vincenzo raised his voice into a buzz of worried discussion. "Another setback. But bear in mind, we're already moving forces out of Japan, and evacuating the last troops from Korea."

"But there'll be second- and third-order effects," Niles put in. At the admiral's bass rumble the hubbub lessened. "We'll lose logistic support from Japanese ports and airfields. Their industrial base. Fleet support. Intelligence. Cybersecurity."

The State rep said, "It's unfortunate, I agree. Tokyo doesn't make decisions without balancing the outcomes . . . and they've obviously decided who's going to win."

"If so, they're wrong." Vincenzo frowned. "But it's going to be a handicap. Especially since Manila's bowed out too.

"All right, let's hear from the combatant commander. Commander, Pacific Command, Admiral Justin Yangerhans."

Blair remembered Dan mentioning this guy. The bones of Yanger-hans's face were misshapen. He *was* ugly. And awkward. He hoisted himself gangling like a Halloween skeleton. But when he spoke a shrewd intelligence gleamed through.

"Tokyo's decision is unfortunate. But we have some good news at last.

"I'm referring to yesterday's battle in the Central Pacific. Details of losses will not be released to the public for some time. Nor will the spe-cifics of the new weapons that enabled us to take a heavy toll of the enemy. Historians will argue over this engagement for decades. I will note that one of the programs from the Air Force's Rapid Capabilities Office played a part in the final stage of the battle.

"We paid a price for victory in casualties and damage. But it's fair to say the stranglehold has been broken. The western Pacific's still danger-ous. But the most modern elements of their denial-of-access blockade are at the bottom of the sea. Which means the way could be open for an offensive."

Niles lifted a fat finger. "Our own submarines?"

"Thanks for the reminder, Nick. They're fighting hard, deep in the enemy's end zone. I can't give details—the silent service, after all—but though we've had losses there, too, they're taking a toll." The CNO nodded, sitting back, and Yangerhans glanced next at Tomlin, Blair's boss. "My command has been, shall we say, too busy to look beyond the immediate threat. But pursuant to direction, an SAIC committee ex-plored possible initiatives. It was chaired by Hav Tomlin, whom I be-lieve you all know. General Tomlin."

Tomlin rose, but nodded in Blair's direction. "If it's all right, I'd like to yield to Dr. Blair Titus. Vice president, Strategic Plans and Policy Di-vision. We were tasked with gaming responses to Chinese aggression in the Far East. And coming up with a plan to strike back."

"I know Blair. Fine, but let's keep it short." Vincenzo glanced at his watch. "I have to brief the SecDef, then be at the White House in an hour."

She'd presented in many venues but still felt nervous as she stood. Started to finger her damaged ear, but stopped herself. There'd been nothing on the news about this battle. Had Dan been involved? Was he hurt, even dead? Perhaps that was why he hadn't called?

Drawing a breath, she pushed her fears aside. The country's future would depend on what the Chiefs decided today. The lives of so many sons and daughters and spouses, and, if they miscalculated, of the pop-ulations of whole cities.

In the face of all that, she had to set her personal concerns to one side.

"General Vincenzo, gentlemen," she began. "I agree not all the news today has been good. But this is no time to retreat.

"We have to show we haven't lost our resolve. To demonstrate to those allies still remaining that we are not a spent force.

"The main limitation, as usual, will be supplies—fuel, ordnance, food, and parts, transported halfway round the world. But now that the way's been cleared, it's time to take the war to Premier Zhang, rather than reacting to his moves."

Niles was nodding, but Vincenzo's eyes were hooded. The other generals leaned back. She read their body language. They were distancing themselves from whatever she was about to present. Withholding judgment.

Her first slide flashed on the screen. It read:

OPERATION RECOIL

III

THE WHETTING
OF THE SWORD

13

San Diego, California

TWO months later, Dan woke with a headache. It was there most days now, ebbing and waxing with the hours.

"Are you up yet?" Blair called from the hotel bathroom.

For a moment, he wondered if this was still a dream. Then remembered. One day and a night together, slotted in after her visits to the Lockheed plants in Alabama, the Archipelago campus in Seattle, and the Defense Innovation Unit in San Francisco. She wouldn't tell him what that was about. Though, knowing Archipelago's driverless cars and pilotless airliners, it probably had something to do with autonomous systems.

There was a lot he couldn't tell her either. Their reunion had been a mix of passion and something English didn't seem to have a word for. Perhaps . . . regret, in advance? Knowing he'd just come out of danger, and was most likely going back to it again.

And now, a wartime parting.

She emerged from the bathroom in a dark pantsuit, a windbreaker over one arm. A briefcase and carry-on, already packed, slumped near the door.

"Do we have time for breakfast?" he asked.

She checked her phone. "Just. If you get moving."

"Hey, all those uniform races paid off. That was just about the most useful thing we ever did at the Academy." He threw back the covers, and within three minutes they were out the door.

BLAIR studied him over the menu. The night before, in the dark, Dan hadn't seemed changed. In the daylight he looked terrible. More gray at the temples. His face gaunt, his morning stubble silver too. "You've lost weight," she observed.

"Fleet's short on chow," he muttered, flipping through the entrees. "But I see everybody's still eating high on the hog here."

She frowned. "Are you telling me our forces are going hungry?"

"I'm sure it's stockpiled somewhere, but our logistics ship got whacked coming out of Guam. By the time we got back, we were fishing off the fantail." He beckoned to the waitress, and they ordered.

"So, it's off to sea again," she opened.

"That's what they tell me."

"I won't ask where. Because actually, I think I know."

"That's more than I do." The coffee arrived, and he sucked it down greedily while she ordered an omelet. He asked for the same, kneading his brow. His headache again, probably. When the server left he muttered, "Can you give me any hints, not where we're headed, but . . . how all this is going . . . how it looks from the top."

She smiled wryly. "I'm nowhere near the *top*, Dan."

"They censor the news. You must hear *something*."

"Well . . . you probably know we've finished withdrawing from Korea. Actually, Tokyo's neutral status helped. Without them, we could have been trapped in Pusan. The Taiwanese . . . General Shucheng is still resisting, in the mountains. That's no secret."

"How long can he hold out? Can we help?"

She sighed. "That's the question, all right."

"How about the Koreans?"

"They ceased resistance, but there's still a South Korea. That was the trade-off. Surrender, and they get to maintain the fiction of sovereignty." She spread her hands. "Actually, looking at it from Beijing's point of view, that was Korea's status for centuries . . . paying tribute, acknowledging imperial suzerainty. Historically, it's not that weird."

He grunted. "So, back to the Middle Ages?"

She sighed. "In a way. And, unfortunately, Zhang gets to add their industrial capacity to China's now."

Dan said, "But we still have elements of their fleet with us. Admiral Jung's refused to recognize the deal."

"Min Jun Jung's status would be a State question. Maybe like de Gaulle, fighting on in some sort of Free Korea framework?" She shrugged and fiddled with her napkin. "Again, remember, Korea was occupied by Japan from 1910 to 1945. A lot of resistance, which the Japanese ruthlessly crushed. There was a government in exile then, too. This is all more complicated than a purely military equation, Dan."

A very young woman in Marine greens entered the restaurant, looked around, and homed in on Blair. "Dr. Titus?"

"Guilty."

"I'm your driver, ma'am. We're due at the airport in half an hour."

Dan blinked. Blair had her own car. A military driver. But all she would say about what she was doing was that she was back at DoD.

The server brought their omelets. Blair grimaced regretfully at hers, drained her coffee with one swallow, and stood, pulling on her jacket. "I gotta . . . If you're hungry, eat mine, too."

"You don't have another minute?"

"No . . . but." She glanced sharply at the woman, who caught the look and edged a few paces away. "Uh, there's something I meant to say last night. But we sort of tangled up in the shower and got too busy to talk. But I need to get it on the table."

Dan pushed his own plate away, suddenly not as hungry. "What?"

"Remember the last time we were together? In Crete. When I said something like . . . how we needed to think about where we're going. If we stayed together."

He remembered, all right. The near darkness in the ruins. The smell of ancient dust. Lost, like Ariadne and Theseus, in Minos's ancient Labyrinth. "I remember," he said slowly. "You mentioned coming up on some kind of decision point."

"I think then I was talking about the campaign. If it failed. And it has. So that's one decision made for me."

"All right," he said, preparing to be hurt. "Get it on the table. You want out?"

"Out?" She rubbed her mouth. Mirroring, no doubt, his own habitual gesture of uncertainty. Strange, seeing it on her. Her breasts rose and fell under the windbreaker. "No, I guess . . . war changes everything. When I realized you'd been in that battle, that I might have lost you, it clarified things.

"If we come through this, let's think about what comes after. We're both ambitious. Me maybe the most, but you've done more with your career."

He frowned. "Not sure I see that, hon."

"Well, you're an admiral. I'm still just a fucking staffer, when it comes down to it."

"Actually a very junior admiral, and only for the duration. And you're selling yourself short. I don't—"

"I'm a staffer, Dan. High level, but them's the facts. I'd like to be a principal someday. To do something right for a change. But, for us . . . for *us*, I want a life together. To not be so separate."

He nodded. Sometimes you just had to listen. "What exactly would you really like, Blair? What would make you the happiest?"

"To grow old with you." She looked away and dashed at her eyes angrily. "Fuck," she whispered furiously. *"Fuck."*

He tried to take her hand, but she backed away, glancing at the marine. "Anyway, that's all I had to say. Got to go. Military flight."

"I wish you didn't."

"I wish we weren't at war, Dan."

"God. I'll second that."

"And I wish you weren't going out again." She swallowed. "I can't tell you more. I just want to say—I know you won't listen, but . . . be careful."

They kissed. She started to leave, then turned back on her heel. "Almost forgot. I brought you something." She dug into her briefcase. Held out a package.

He turned it over. Book size. Book weight. "A book?"

She rolled her eyes. "Amazing. Like you have X-ray vision. Now I really gotta run." She bent, kissed him again. He put his arm up and locked her in an embrace ounces short of a choke hold.

"I can tell you this," she whispered, directly into his ear. "The Chinese are planning a second-phase offensive."

"Striking where? And we know this, how?"

"I can't say. Just . . . intel. Zhang plans to invade Guam. Suck in our carriers. And sink them. With those off the board, he'll threaten Hawaii. At that point, he expects us to sue for peace."

The marine cleared her throat. Past her, Dan noticed his own aide and driver, Sergeant Gault, with arms folded. The other customers in the restaurant glanced at them, then at Blair and Dan.

"And will we?" he whispered into his wife's ear. Not the damaged one, the withered red nub, but the lovely curved one she'd been born with.

"It's not going to come to that. We're going to spoil it all for him. And with that . . . Dan . . . let me go. Damn it, I've got to *go*."

He released her reluctantly, but their fingers clung. They stood for a moment regarding each other. Memorizing each other's faces.

As if it might be the last time.

Then he set her free, and stood watching until she was out of sight.

SECURITY was tight at the pier. As the guards examined his ID, then his briefcase, Dan eyed two Burkes and the smooth towering superstructure of a Zumwalt-class destroyer. *Douglas Zembiec* was assigned to his task force, along with two autonomous, unmanned semisubmersibles developed for the antisubmarine work and radar picket duty that frigates had traditionally done. If only he'd had them for the central Pacific battle . . .

The gray cliffs of two nuclear carriers loomed like thunderheads over at North Island. That made five in the Pacific, not counting *George Washington*, still in Yokosuka. The subject, now, of negotiations between Tokyo and Washington. *Nimitz*, *Vinson*, and *Reagan* were at sea, whereabouts unknown, at least to him. *Abraham Lincoln* was in Australia. *Eisenhower* was holding the line in the Middle East. *Theodore Roosevelt* was in overhaul, and *George H. W. Bush*, fresh out of the yard, was working up off the Virginia Capes. That made the pair he was looking at *Truman* and *Stennis*, though their numbers had been painted out for wartime.

But this huge of a surge couldn't be maintained. Once in theater, the carriers had to be used. A push had to be scheduled.

His new mission would be part of it.

Of course, he'd already known most of what Blair had whispered. But nothing had been passed by digital means. They had to assume anything that went out over the now partially restored Internet, no matter how tightly encrypted, would be read by one of America's ring of enemies.

That mission might trigger a violent response from the unpredictable dictator who dominated what he was styling the Peoples' Empire. After completing helicopter escape training at Miramar, Dan had rented a car and driven up to visit his daughter. Nan was a microbiologist, in Seattle. He'd warned her to be ready to leave town at short notice.

If the worst happened, her city would be a prime target.

The guards paused, discovering a bulky red-and-white-striped envelope marked top secret. They snapped the briefcase closed, saluted, and stepped back. A lieutenant (jg) murmured into a handheld.

Savo Island's topheavy-looking superstructure loomed as Dan and Gault hiked down the pier. *Hornet*, his previous flagship, was still in dry dock over at the BAE yard. After sea trials, Graciadei would be headed to Guam, leading Dan to suspect that an island assault was also in the works.

"Task Force 76, arriving," the 1MC announced. Six bells sounded. Dan strode up the brow, wheeled, and saluted the ensign. High on *Savo's* mast, a blue flag with one white star unfurled. He faced left and tapped off another to Cheryl Staurulakis and, behind her, Enzweiler, whom he'd fleeted up to take Dudley's place as chief of staff. "Hello, Cheryl. Fred."

"We meet again," Staurulakis murmured. "Welcome back aboard, Admiral."

"Good to be here, Captain." Her gloved hand clamped on his, but she looked deeply fatigued. Like everyone, this far into the war. He nodded to other familiar faces. It would be strange being back, but no longer as skipper. An embarked admiral was only a rider, as far as his flagship was concerned. He directed its movements, along with those of the rest of his task force; but he wasn't, strictly speaking, involved beyond that with the crew or wardroom.

Enzweiler had stripped down Dan's own staff. *Savo* couldn't accommodate the complement he'd had aboard *Hornet.* Nor did he want all those bodies around, to be honest. "How are we on underway time?" he asked Staurulakis.

"Casting off at 1600, Admiral. Finishing fueling now."

"How's the vibration aft? You had damage from that Shkval?"

"The shimmy smoothed out on our way back. We have a new sonar tail. Aside from the engine panel issue, we're ready for sea."

Staurulakis briefed on the loadout as he followed her to the wardroom. Along with Tomahawks, antiair Standards, two cells full of Sparrows, and a reload of Harpoons, the first SM-Xs were aboard. Not just uprated antiair missiles, but fully qualified midphase antimissile interceptors, with longer-thrust boosters, a higher and wider intercept envelope, and two-color infrared seeker heads that guided kinetic-only kill vehicles. "Instead of a fifty percent P-sub-K, we're looking at seventy percent, with a greater capability against crossing targets. Dr. Soongapurn says—"

Dan frowned, thought back, but couldn't recall the name. "Who's he, again?"

"It's a she, from the Missile Defense Agency."

He grimaced. "Better than Noblos, I hope."

"Absolutely. She's been a big help updating ALIS. Also, she essentially retrained the Aegis team. We're a lot smarter now." The captain opened the door to the embarked flag quarters and stood back. "Again, welcome aboard."

"Thank you, Cheryl." He turned to Enzweiler. "Signal the task force to get under way on schedule. Initial steaming formation as in the op plan. Staff meeting at 1400?"

"We'll make it happen, Admiral."

THIRTY miles out to sea, his staff convened on the mess decks. Screens had been placed to give the impression of privacy, but he already missed *Hornet*'s capacious conference spaces. This brief was going out to the other units in the force via secure videoteleconferencing, line of sight only, to forestall interception.

A tall, sallow Korean reached to shake Dan's hand. "Good afternoon, Admiral."

"Min Su Hwang. Good to see you again. How is Admiral Jung? He's not here?"

"He will be joining us by teleconference."

Dan felt guilty. "I wish our last battle together turned out better for you. The losses, I mean. Your crews were taken care of properly? The survivors?"

"Yes, sir. Also, we are bringing a new ship into service. A Freedom-class frigate named *New Jeonnam*. We will man it under the flag of Free Korea. I am to serve as your liaison again for this operation, if that is agreeable to you."

"Of course, very glad to have you." Dan waved to a chair beside him. Cheryl Staurulakis, as his flag captain, stood on the other side. "Seats, everyone," he said, and promptly slid down to a backbone-testing slouch.

The already-distributed half of the op order, on white paper, covered the sortie and the steaming formation, transiting to a point east of Guam. The red-edged top secret addendum Enzweiler was passing out now, though, gave their final destination. Dan shifted in his chair, not looking forward to yet another meeting. It had been death by briefing for the last week, at North Island and San Diego. Conference after conference to hammer out schedules and tables of loading, force commitments and logistic support with representatives from Air Forces Pacific, PacFleet, the Army component command, and the various foreign contingents.

The meteorological presentation led off. Spring in the western Pacific looked calm. They could expect moderate winds and moderate seas, though a system might develop later.

Qazi Jamail began the intel presentation. Signals intelligence pointed to a second phase of Chinese offensive operations. Targeting Saipan and Guam, this would present PaCom with a hard choice. If he responded in force to defend the islands, the carriers could be sunk the same way the *FDR* battle group had gone down. If they didn't respond, occupation forces would land, preparing for the next move across the Go board. Against Wake, Midway, or Hawaii itself. The expectation being that at that point, Washington would sue for peace, as Manila, Seoul, and Tokyo already had.

Dan tented his hands, not liking the way the dominoes were falling.

At some point, they had to glue one to the table.

Jamail want on. "We have some advantages this time. First, our nanosatellites are up, giving at least limited surveillance capability. We also have low-baud-rate satcomm. As an operating base and fallback position, Guam has been hardened over the past months. Uprated THAAD batteries provide antimissile coverage, which *Savo* will reinforce when we get into range.

"Adversary forces: Our submarines have taken a heavy toll, but Opposed shipyards are working at full capacity. Imagery shows them building and repairing amphibious ships and destroyers and bringing two more indigenously-constructed carriers online. The main threat, however, is submarine and air, and as we near the mainland, a robust suite of area-denial missiles. Batteries are emplaced in Taiwan, Okinawa, Itbayat in the northern Philippines, and in a ring to the southward, to Woody and Hainan Islands. Other enemy forces as per Annex B of the op order."

The N2 took his seat, and Enzweiler, Dan's new deputy, brought up a slide of the western Pacific. "Operation Recoil will be a major carrier strike on the Empire naval base at Ningbo, near Shanghai. Home of the Eastern Fleet and surrounded by a ring of air bases, Ningbo supports combat operations in the Ryukyus and Taiwan.

"If we take out that staging area, we disrupt the second-phase offensive Admiral Lianfeng is planning. This task force will be the advance element of the strike. We will sweep for subs and attract air and missile responses, so enemy assets can be identified and degraded before the carriers come within range. Then, our remaining elements will cover the carrier groups as they launch their strikes on the mainland.

"Operation Recoil constitutes the northern half of a two-pronged attack. Simultaneously with it, the Marines will land to take Itbayat Island, to the south of Taiwan. This invasion is code-named 'Operation Mandible.'"

As the briefing proceeded, Dan reflected on how Task Force 76 had grown from the stripped-down hunter-killer force he'd taken into the central Pacific. Along with *Savo* and a second ABM-capable cruiser, *Hampton Roads*, he had four destroyers, *Kristensen*, *McClung*, *Stockdale*, and the newest, *Zembiec*, along with with Jung's destroyers and frigates. He had two submarines now, *Farncomb*, the Australian boat, and USS *Montpelier*, newly redeployed from the Atlantic Fleet.

Since most of the Pacific Fleet's tankers and tenders had been lost, he would be meeting a Chilean replenishment ship, *Almirante Montt*. And in place of *Hornet*, USS *Gambier Bay* was transiting from Seattle to join up on the way west.

He'd toured the latter ship in the yard while the conversion was under way. The idea of converting merchant ships to makeshift carriers had been around for a long time. In fact, the very first carriers had been hastily altered merchants, and escort or "jeep" carriers had performed yeoman service in World War II.

Gambier Bay, named after an escort carrier sunk in 1944, had started life as CSCL *Jupiter*, a hundred-thousand-ton-plus Hong Kong–flagged containership seized in Long Beach. A hangar bay had been Lego'd out of forty-foot shipping containers. More containers constituted living and messing areas, repair facilities, and fuel and ammunition storage. The two-inch-thick steel flight deck could take both helicopters and MV-22s, though it wasn't rated for F-35s due to the fighter's exhaust temperature. Her current complement was AV-8B fighters, heavy-lift helicopters for replenishment, and a helicopter antisubmarine squadron from the Med. She also carried a crane for the vertical launchers, which meant force units wouldn't have to transit back to Guam or Hawaii to reload their cells.

Unfortunately, she was slower than the rest of his ships, twenty-two knots all-out, and less maneuverable. Dan wondered how securely the bolted-together containers would ride in heavy seas. But most worrisome, her self-defense was limited to Army Stingers and Israeli SPYDER missiles, with hastily trained crews. If the jeep ventured outside the protection of the task force, one torpedo would probably sink it . . . with massive casualties, considering its lack of compartmentation, poor damage control, and heavy load of fuel and ordnance.

He realized Enzweiler had just asked him something. "Sorry, I missed that," he mumbled. "Say again?"

"Admiral, any questions or remarks to add?"

"Uh, no. Good briefing, Fred. Let's see if anyone else wants to raise any issues before we close." He waited, then stood. "All right . . . let's get to work. Captain, if we could talk later this afternoon?"

"Around four?" Staurulakis checked her watch. "CIC, or your stateroom?"

"Let's make it my stateroom."

He didn't miss the glances that were exchanged. But frankly, didn't much care.

IN the little head, he changed out of khakis into coveralls. Musing as he pinned stars to his lapels. This would be a larger force than he'd taken into battle before, and he'd be facing a multithreat environment this time, not just submarines.

Yangerhans had promised air cover. He hoped it came through. Even with the jeep, they wouldn't have nearly enough organic air. Adding to the risk, they had no support structure left, west of Guam. "If we'd just held Okinawa," he whispered.

Weird; it seemed he had a few minutes alone. . . . He tested the bunk, then remembered Blair's present. He pulled it out of his briefcase and tore off the wrapping.

The title was *Neptune's Inferno*. He turned it over and read the back. About the World War II battles off Guadalcanal. He flipped to the front, skimmed the first page, and soon was immersed. He hadn't realized the Navy had lost almost three sailors at sea for every infantryman who'd fallen on the islands.

The tap at the door came too soon. Gault stuck his head in. "The captain."

"Expecting her. Thanks." Rolling out of the bunk and setting the book aside, Dan waved Staurulakis in.

She wore a tired smile. "Gotta stop meeting this way."

"Let 'em talk. How's your husband doing . . . Ted?"

"Eddie's transitioning to F-35s. It's a great aircraft, he says."

"Good to know. He's on *Vinson*?"

She nodded. "But can't tell me where. I understand you and Blair had a visit?"

"A short one. Grab a chair, Captain."

"She's good people." Staurulakis crossed her legs and looked expectant.

He cleared his throat. "About the brief: one thing I didn't mention. Maybe I should have."

"What was it, Admiral?"

"I asked PaCom and Fleet if the possibility of heavy losses to the leading elements of this operation had been gamed. I was told that risk had been accepted at the highest levels."

She looked concerned. Scratched between her fingers, which, he noticed, were raw and scabbed. "I see. So . . . What are you telling me?"

"Mainly just that. I know you've already gone over firefighting, lifeboat drills, abandon-ship procedures. I'd also like you to drill on nuclear detonation." He reached into his briefcase and came up with a manila envelope. "I got you a copy of this."

She glanced up from the bound pages. "Top secret. *Report on the Loss of USS* Horn . . . This was your ship?"

"My first command." He took a deep breath. "We were sent to intercept an al-Qaeda bombmaking expert. We didn't know he'd hijacked a Russian demolition nuke. He packed a ship's hold with a goat-feed supplement composed of almost pure strontium. Not just a dirty bomb. The dirtiest ever detonated. *Horn* is still radioactive. She's still on the Navy List, but without a crew. Moored at Norfolk Naval Shipyard, but with no gangways leading aboard."

He took another deep breath. "I thought then I was ready. I wasn't.

"I don't ever want to do that again, Cheryl. Not to sound defeatist, but our ships aren't designed to take hits and keep fighting, the way they used to be. I'm directing every CO to revisit basic damage control. Look at every space. Pitch everything that'll burn overboard. Test every hose and piece of equipment. And double the DC and firefighting drills you have planned."

He sucked a deep breath, realizing his voice had taken on a tremor. But he couldn't help visualizing, again, the lambent violet flame that had transected Flag Plot aboard *Hornet*. Decapitated corpses sitting upright at their battle stations. He massaged his throat, trying to calm his heartbeat.

She studied her notebook, expressionless, and for a moment he wondered if he'd crossed a line. Did she think he was frightened, after their retreat from the Miyako Strait, their near defeat north of Wake? What lurked behind that opaque glance? At this moment, he didn't really care. "Do I make myself clear?"

"Abundantly, Admiral. Will that be all?"

"I guess. Yeah," he mumbled.

She rose, and the door eased closed. Leaving him alone in the creaking quiet, the hush of ventilation hissing through the diffusers. The hum of motors. A distant *clank . . . clank* as *Savo* rolled. The reassuring noises that meant a ship was still alive.

While he pondered, sweating, forcing air through his damaged, constricting trachea.

This could be a real bloodbath if he screwed up again.

Yeah . . . just like Guadalcanal.

14

Western Xinjiang, China

P OWDERY snow lay inches deep on the slopes, not yet evaporated in the thin, arid atmosphere. The wind fluttered gauzy veils from gravelly ridges. Oberg toted the binoculars now that the Major had gone nearly blind.

Just now he was grateful for the gusts, cold as they were.

He'd spotted the sheep several kilometers off. Not the beasts themselves, but their curving paths in the snow, where they'd nosed through to the scanty grass beneath. The three escaped POWs had squatted in a sheltered spot, plotting strategy as carefully as Montgomery or Eisenhower ever had. Testing the wind. Reading the terrain. Then split up and began the encirclement.

Teddy, as the qualified sniper, got the AK.

Now, as he lay in a shallow depression in the snow, wrapped in his cocoon of fraying rags, hunger weighted his gut like a stone. Black and heavy, like basalt. A dense cube, rounded at the corners. Sunlight glistened off the snow. Far overhead, a hawk circled.

Teddy's prey moved slowly, conserving what little energy they could glean in this cold, high, vacant world. Ambling a few paces, then punching their way through the crust with sharp-looking hooves to the brown grass beneath. The sheep were bigger than he'd expected, the size of mule deer. Their light-colored flanks shaded to reddish-brown backs. Their faces and necks were cream-colored. They looked more alert than he liked. Fitter, too. Actually, more like some kind of goat than sheep, and he hadn't seen any shepherds. So . . . wild goats?

Who cared what they were. They were made out of meat. He worked the handle to eject the round Fierros had carried ready in the chamber.

For all he knew, the same one the girl guard had loaded it with before he'd plunged the screwdriver into her heart. But the action didn't open.

He hammered at the operating handle with a fist, concealing the motion under his blanket, and finally got the cartridge ejected into the snow. Chinese steel-cased ammo. Bent, corroded, rusted. Great. He thumbed the other cartridges out of the magazine. Rusty too, but at least not bent. He polished one on the webbing of the sling and set it aside on a rock. He repeated this with the others, then worked the action and pulled the trigger several times. A creepy, gritty, nine- or ten-pound pull that didn't break the same way twice. SEALs trained on Kalashes, of course, but they were mass-fire, hurrah-charge weapons. Shit ammo, shit barrels, and shit maintenance meant he'd have to get close enough to practically club the fucking sheep to death.

But if he didn't, they were all going to die out here. Sooner rather than later. He counted the cartridges again. Ten good ones. Two bursts. He snapped them into the magazine, loading the best-looking ones on top, to feed first. Kalashes climbed fast in full auto. He'd have to hold tight, aim low, and let it climb.

A click of rock, far off. Trinh, moving into position. A millimeter at a time, Obie raised his head. It was covered with a scrap of blanket with snow rubbed into it. The wind was steady on his cheeks. And he was still downwind of their prey.

Any idiot could shoot accurately, given a well-made rifle. The battle for a sniper was getting close without being seen. And with this piece of pus, he was going to have to get *real* close.

Gradually, over the next hour, he low-crawled in, staying in the torn-up tracks where the goats had already grazed. The cold penetrated his bones. Froze the stone cube in his gut. Stiffened his fingers, until he hoped he could still bend them to shoot. These animals seemed abnormally alert. The largest kept eyeing him from atop a mound. But the ram also kept looking off to the right. Dividing his attention.

Teddy noted that another hawk had joined the first. No, not a hawk. A vulture, the same carrion birds he'd seen in the Parachinars when they were hunting bin Laden. One mountain chain, after all. Thousands of miles long, from western China all the way to Anatolia. The scavengers made wide sweeps in the blue, but stayed centered on this hilltop. Maybe a good sign. A vote of confidence from the experts. He worked his hand surreptitiously, trying to fight off the stiffening, but shuddering so hard he couldn't stop it anymore.

A deep, hoarse shout broke the mountain silence. The ram jerked his head around. His horns were amazing, twisted like a corkscrew, swept back like a jet's wings, and as long as Teddy's arms. The rack, the nobly lifted head, the broad shoulders . . . Christ, the thing was as big as a horse. . . . Teddy admired him, but wished the bastard wasn't so fucking suspicious. On the other hand, with wolves roaming out here, he couldn't blame him. A lot of the females, ewes, had the swinging bellies that probably meant little lambs getting ready to pop out pretty soon.

The ram was getting hinky. With a toss of the head, he gave a high, snuffling bleat. The ewes looked to him. Shaking with cold, Teddy held his breath. "Come this way," he whispered. "This way, you big old son of a bitch."

Fierros burst over the crest, yipping madly and waving a strip of blanket. The goats flinched, as if all shocked simultaneously from the same high-tension source, and broke into a gallop away from the airman. From the third side of the hill, Trinh erupted from beneath the snow like a geyser. He shrieked and screamed, pointing his stick like a rifle. The ram, in the lead, tilted like a broken-field runner and changed direction. Toward Teddy. The herd thundered around to follow, flinging up divots of grass and snow and frozen earth that the wind caught and blew over their swaying backs.

For a moment Teddy lay astonished, then paralyzed as twenty to thirty tons of muscle and bone on knife-sharp hooves tore down the steep bank toward where he lay. His finger stacked the trigger, the front sight post finding the chest of the lead animal, the ram's beady eye suddenly locking on him, turning murderous. The belligerent head going down. Those spiky horns, aimed like bayonets—

Teddy started the burst at the hooves and let the recoil walk it up, finishing with the muzzle pointed into the clouds. He pulled the rifle down and rolled into a fat ewe swerving white-eyed away. A perfect broadside shot at no more than ten yards.

As the herd parted around him, thundering past to left and right, he fired single rounds, leading the beasts as they bolted past. Aiming for the center of mass, since he had no idea where his sights were set. Registering only immense quadruped forms losing their rhythm, faltering, crashing to earth.

Then they were past, in a welter of blowing snow and dirt and flying fur. He rolled over, panting, and levered painfully to his feet with the rifle as Trinh and Fierros floundered up through the torn-up, blood- and shit-streaked snow.

Two goats lay struggling and kicking downslope. He blinked. Only two? He should have put bullets into five. And a burst into the ram. But Big Daddy was untouched, unhit, and long gone over the ridgeline, probably in Tajikistan by now.

Shuddering, Teddy limped to where the beasts gave their last, expiring kicks. Gut-shot. None of the ones he'd aimed at. And he'd used every cartridge, knowing this was their last and only chance.

Chance?

What guided bullets, when you had no idea where your sights were set?

The men he'd fought in Afghanistan would have said, Allah.

"Great shooting," Trinh said reverently. Facing those shining eyes, Teddy didn't have the heart to enlighten him. Instead he just squatted, took out his chert knife, and began unzipping the sagging belly of the pregnant ewe.

THAT night, groaning-full around a roaring fire, they lay back watching the sparks swirl to the stars. "Enough meat for days," Fierros observed. "You done good, Tedster. You really were a SEAL, I guess."

Obie covered it with a meaty belch. No point telling them he hadn't hit a thing he'd aimed at. The airman went on, "So now what?"

"Keep heading west," Teddy said. "That's the plan, right?"

Fierros mumbled around hands full of a greasy thighbone, "West. Uh-huh. How long?"

"You figured three hundred miles to the border."

"We never saw a map," Trinh put in. His beard dripped with juices. "That was only Ragger's estimate. We never knew where the camp actually was."

"The only smart thing to do's to keep going. There aren't any border posts up here in the mountains. Worst case, we go too far, we end up in . . . ?"

"Iran," said Fierros.

"Oh. Well, we don't want that, I guess. But we can push on a while longer, now." Teddy belched again. "Question is, when we come down, who are we?"

They discussed this around the fire, in the lonely night, and settled on becoming ethnic Russians from Kazakhstan. Their gear, maps, weapons, gone in a rockslide. No matter who was on which side by this point in the war, hunters lost in the mountains should pass for noncombatants.

Fortunately, Trinh had studied Russian in school, and spoken it with advisers as a junior officer. Teddy knew enough to ask directions and interrogate prisoners. Fierros could pretend to be shy and keep to monosyllabic grunts.

"Best case, when we come down, the war's over," the pilot muttered.

"You just keep thinking that," Teddy told him. "Me? I'm gonna assume the worst."

THE meat sustained their shriveled guts and shrunken appetites for days. They feasted on it roasted, then cut it into strips and fire-dried it. Teddy learned a new appetite for the fatty oozing of liver, and how to crack heavy bones with rocks for salty marrow. The hides, scraped, turned inside out, and lashed with sinew, became mittens, chaps, and hoods against the wind, and overboots against the bite of rocks.

In the end, there wasn't much left for the vultures.

But after that, they had no hope of bagging anything else. They kept the empty rifle as a deterrent in case they met herdsmen. And went on trudging.

They finished the dried meat, then gnawed the scraps clinging to the hides.

Then endured the torments of starvation all over again, until their heads spun and the world reeled as they scrambled across ridges that towered into the clouds, picking their way across fields of scree balanced so precariously that one misstep would send them all to destruction in thousands of tons of thundering rock.

One fireless night, trying to sleep on a divide so high there were no more of the scraggly dry bushes they rooted up for fuel, Fierros had crawled over. Snuggled close. For warmth, Teddy had sleepily assumed. Then came awake as the airman hissed into his ear, "Got a proposition."

"What," he muttered. The asshole was going queer on him now?

"Two can travel faster than three."

"Not trackin' you, Rag-man."

"I'm saying we're starving. And we still got a long way to go."

"Okay."

"We lost Vu."

"Right."

"Couldn't get to his body. But if we could've, would you have—?"

"Would I have what, Toby?"

But he knew. It wasn't that he hadn't thought it himself. Killing the goats had pushed those thoughts away for a while. But now they were back.

"You know what I'm asking." Reproachful. "He's fucking blind. He's gonna go down one of these crevasses sooner or later, like Vu. Come on, Obie. You must have been in situations like this before."

"Not like this, guy. Not quite." He'd half rolled to face the shadow in the dark. "But if you're saying leave Nguyen behind, then, no. We don't leave anyone behind."

Fierros was silent for a time. Then he whispered, "I'm not exactly saying that we leave him behind."

"No. No way. Forget it, Toby."

They'd regarded each other in the dark. Then Fierros had flipped his hides over them and nestled close, and Teddy had heard only the wind.

IT took a long time to get back to sleep after that.

Actually, he wasn't sure he *was* asleep.

Because lying there, feeling Ragger's hunger-boner pressed against him, his eyes wide open, Teddy Harlett Oberg started to separate, delaminate, pass out of himself.

Oh, he was still there, on the mountainside. Still shaking with the cold.

He just didn't seem to *be* himself.

The mountains glowed with an inner light. They were folded out of rock, like origami. The way the world itself was . . . folded . . . out of . . . light and . . . time.

He looked down, and saw . . . himself. A tiny seed of flesh, a dying ember in the dark, nestled beside two other embers. A few sparks of electrical activity still danced in its brain. But that wasn't him.

And he wasn't it.

He fell through, to a place colder and harder than the mountains. Where a monstrous evil laughed, and he screamed as he was torn apart. Pain. Incredible pain.

Through endless centuries he suffered.

Then he hovered above the mountains again, bodiless, without thought.

An enormous voice spoke into his mind.

I MADE ALL OF THIS.

I have to be dying, Theodore Oberg thought. This must be what happens at the end.

THERE IS NO END. AND NO BEGINNING.

What are you telling me? he asked, or thought. Is there something you're telling me? Something you want me to know? To do?

But without speech, without words, whatever spoke made itself understood.

YOU HAVE ALWAYS DONE MY WILL.

His entire life unlocked in an instant, and he saw how that single bidding underlay it, more rigid than iron. It was all of a piece. The mountains. The world. Everything that happened, had happened, or ever would. It had all been created, foreordained, before Time itself had existed.

Which meant:

There was no choice.

There was no will, other than Its will.

All was one thought. One act. One creation.

The creation by . . . whatever was speaking to him.

But now it was leaving him. Lifting, like a slowly rising, incredibly immense saucer departing for a distant star. He reached out, groping, flailing, conscious of a withdrawal like the receding tide. Trying to call it back. To go with it, if he could. Even if that meant leaving himself behind.

But it was not to be. Released, he hurtled down, like a high-altitude, low-opening night jump. Yeah. He'd been here before. But on oxygen, with a heated mask to keep his face from freezing. The black mountains below like open mouths. He cried out. Not wanting to go back into the dying, starving, agonized body. The time-bound, ignorant mind, pinched as in a narrow coffin.

Then he was gasping, convulsing on the icy gravel, and Fierros was kneeling on him, forcing a piece of wood between his teeth. The haft of his walking stick. Trinh leaned in too, looking scared in the starlight. "Get a grip, man," the flier was muttering. "You were stroking out. Going into a seizure. Jesus! You hear me? Talk, fuckhole. Talk to me."

But Teddy Oberg could not speak the whole rest of that night, nor for long into the next day. He stared about as they walked, like a man possessed, or a child just born.

AT last, weakened to shambling corpses, they decided to head south. It was that or die.

The valley wound between rocky outcrops, dotted with patches of pasture. When they heard the distant tinkle of bells, the bark of shep-herds' dogs, they climbed again, up ridges, covering themselves with the hide capes. Once, descending, they stumbled across a cleverly hidden sliver of field, nestled just where the sun could slide in between the peaks. Innocent green plants nodded in raked brown soil. Each spindly stalk was tipped with a tiny ball of bud. Teddy steered them away, though he still felt, in the aftereffects of his dream, that it wasn't really his own action, but something foreordained. "The winter crop," he explained la-conically when Fierros protested at the detour. "Poppy. Like in Helmand."

"Which means . . . the government isn't in control anymore?"

Obie shrugged. "Or that the army's concentrating on the war, not in-terdiction. Whoever's doing the growing, we don't want to meet them."

As they tottered on, he scanned the ridgelines for sentries. Opium cul-tivation might be a sign they'd left China behind. On the other hand, the airman could be right. It had been that way in Afghanistan.

Poppies grew where government withered.

15

Kwajalein, Marshall Islands

H ECTOR flipped through the in-flight magazines from the seat pockets. But his flight attendants weren't the smiling Asian women in China Airlines red-on-blue uniforms pictured on the covers. Instead, Red Cross volunteers pushed carts of coffee and cookies up and down the aisles, forced smiles alternating with grimaces as pockets of rough air tremored the plane.

The officers sat up front behind the curtain, in the big curved business-class seats, each with its own reading light and worktable. The staff NCOs were grouped farther back, and the junior enlisted aft of that. Hector was over the big shining wing. He could look out, but aside from a triangle of far-off sea all he'd seen for hours was acres of polished aluminum.

Which left too long to think. About where they were going, which they didn't know, and what would happen when they got there . . . which they didn't know either. There'd been chatter at first, and a couple guys had tried to figure out how to work the in-flight entertainment in the backs of the seats. But except for a video on what to do in case of a water landing, the screens stayed empty.

After completing SOI, Hector and Troy had been assigned to Third Marines. Their orders said Hawaii, but they'd stayed on the ground there only long enough to refuel. No one was allowed off. And they had to put their blinds down, so they couldn't even look out.

Obviously their home unit, Second Battalion, was farther west.

Finally he got up, peed, and strolled the aisle, up to the first-class section, then back to the tail. Passing incurious glances, scared faces, slack sleeping ones. Hands cupping pocket computer games. Slowly moving jaws, hypnotically masticating gum or smokeless tobacco. The women flipped through the in-flight mags, looking bored. He stopped to talk to Pruss. They were dipping too, spitting brown juice into a paper cup. "Seen Orietta?" Hector asked.

"Coreguaje? She's up there by the partition."

"What, you ain't sitting together?"

Pruss muttered, "Fuck off, Ramos. We had a argument. That's all."

"What's the scuttlebutt? Hear anything about where we're going?"

"Australia, I heard. You?"

Hector said, "Japan. Guard the Imperial Palace. But I don't believe it."

"Where's your friend? Troy?"

"Eighty-seven B. Want to swap seats?"

"Maybe . . . No. Forget it." They draped an olive-drab issue towel over their eyes and reclined the seat until the guy behind them cursed and kicked the back. At which Pruss lowered it even more. "I'm gonna get some winks. See you in wherever."

Hector talked to Orietta for a while, but she seemed fidgety. She was reading a Danielle Steel paperback. Hector thought about asking her to go to the little in-flight bathroom with him, but it didn't seem like the right time. No, he'd better not. She didn't seem in the mood, either. Everybody seemed subdued.

"THERE'S a plane out there," one of the guys said now, peering out through the plastic. A note of worry in his voice.

The others crowded to their windows. "F-18?"

"Hope it's one of ours."

They squinted into the glare as the speck neared. It slowed, then dropped into position a mile off. Pacing them in. Something whirred in the wing, thumped and hissed. They surged forward in their seats.

"Ladies and gentlemen, U.S. Marines, we're beginning our descent. The aircraft to right and left are our fighter escort. We'll be on the ground at Bucholz Airfield in twenty minutes."

The world vanished, obliterated in gray cotton. They were dropping through that cloud layer toward the sea. A single glimpse of a far-off island, before it too was wiped out in the whiteness.

"From the plane commander: Draw shades on both sides of the plane. All shades must be drawn at this time." They pulled down the shields obediently and settled back, checking their seat belts, bringing seats and tray tables to the full upright position for landing.

* * *

THE Word came back mouth to mouth: they weren't getting off. This was just another refueling stop. They all groaned. But then the NCOs got up and started deplaning. The front rows got to their feet, then had to sit down again. A couple of guys slid their blinds up to peer out, and got yelled at to secure them again. Hector sank back and massaged his dead-numb rear end.

"From the plane commander: Center section, prepare to deplane. Leave all personal gear in your seats. No cameras, phones, or electronic equipment. No photographs on the ground. Stay in the terminal area. Smoking in front of the terminal area only. Soft drinks, water, and refreshments are available in the terminal area. Reboarding will commence with the center section, as soon as refueling is complete."

THEY deplaned into heat, pale coral dust, and exhaust. The sky was a blue mallet. The sea, only a few hundred yards distant, was hammered out flat. The sun glared off white coral sand and boiled the air off black tarmac. "Christ, it's a fucking furnace." Whipkey mopped his face. "I'm gonna get back on the plane." But when he tried, one of the sergeants told him to get the fuck back in line. So they turned around again and trudged through the searing air, over the scorching concrete, toward the concrete building that shimmered ahead.

Hector became aware of other activity around the field. Of dollies of ordnance. Of white long missile containers. Pallets of rations. Actually, mountains of rations. The sun gleamed off an eerily regular pyramid of silvery slabs. They looked beautiful. Futuristic. It took a few seconds before he realized what they were.

The silver-toned coffins, stacked beside the airstrip, baked quietly in the tropic sun.

The marines shuffled past an open shed to the wail of distant sirens. Hector tensed; some kind of attack warning? But none of the workers seemed to be headed for shelter.

Several grim-faced men in coveralls were sitting at a picnic bench, around a radio, listening to a sweet female voice. "Shanghai Sue," somebody said, near Hector.

"Who the fuck's—"

Whipkey grabbed his arm. "Hold up a minute. Listen up."

The marines halted as a dulcet alto soothed, *"You must know by now this is not your war. It was started at the behest of the ruling classes, to keep the peoples of the East in subjection. You know who they are. Your own wise men—Glenn, Rush, Donald, Howard, and George— have warned you about them for years. The Bilderberg Group. The Trilateral Commission. The Jews and the CEOs. The rich white men who own America.*

"Why die for them? General Zhang has offered peace. If you have the chance to meet a Chinese soldier, trust him. He will become your new best friend.

"Because, I am sad to say, the U.S. is headed for the greatest disaster in its history. We do not want to destroy Los Angeles, San Francisco, Houston, Boston, New York. But China will strike back if attacked. Make no mistake. We will turn your hometowns into piles of melted, radioactive bricks. We will turn your loved ones into carbonized shadows. The way America did to Asians at Hiroshima and Nagasaki.

"It saddens me to utter these words. I know you soldiers and sailors and marines are not the aggressors. I feel I know you all. You, my faithful listeners. But if American aggression continues, the beautiful land you know will be vaporized behind you. And you yourselves, brave men and women of the Second Battalion, Third Marines, listening to me now on the island of Kwajalein, will return home only in body bags."

The marines stirred, shot uneasy glances at one another. "How'd she know we were here?" one muttered.

"Fucking bitch."

"Turn her off."

"Play some goddamned music."

"But enough politics. And enough gloomy predictions from the fun- loving girl you call Shanghai Sue. So here's a treat, a golden oldie from indie rock band Florence and the Machine, 'Ship to Wreck.'"

The lyrics faded behind him but he couldn't help hearing them.

And good God, under starry skies we are lost,
And into the breach we got tossed. . . .

INSIDE the terminal they sighed in air-conditioned cool. There were Cokes and Mountain Dews and Tropicana juices in tubs of ice. Sun

Chips and sandwiches and wraps. Hector bit into one, but his teeth stopped halfway. Chicken salad.

The hydraulic blade. The post-stunner kept the blood pumping out. Then on to the scalding area, the picker, evisceration, unloading, chilling . . .

He eased his teeth apart, carefully, so not even a shred of macerated flesh jellied in mayonnaise could stick. Dropped the meat and bread into the trash barrel, and tried not to show how much he wanted to hurl.

THEY'D said half an hour for refuel, but two hours later he was still on the ground. The crew was puttering around the landing gear. The sirens turned out to be ambulances, headed for a helicopter pad at the far end of the strip. Not long after, bedraggled men began straggling through the terminal. Their feet dragged. Their eyes, empty. Some were barefoot. Their clothes were stained and torn. The word spread. Shipwrecked sailors, from a sunken sub tender. Some of the marines went over to share a cigarette, candy, see if they needed money.

An hour later Hector and Troy were sitting outside the terminal, nursing yet another Mountain Dew. The sun was sinking toward a flaring horizon burning with red smoke. Troy bounced to his feet as the lieutenant walked past. "Good afternoon, sir," he drawled, snapping off a picture-perfect salute. Hector got up a second behind and saluted as well, though nowhere near as crisply.

"Sir, my buddy here, you remember Ramos." The lieutenant nodded. "He was wondering, Kwajalein, the Corps fought here, right? You know the story on that?"

"Yeah, we fought here."

"Well, sir?"

The officer sighed. "It was the Fourth Marine Division. A four-day battle. The Japanese were outnumbered. We killed about five thousand of them. Only fifty were left to surrender. Our own casualties were pretty light."

Whipkey said, in that smacky way he had around officers, "Well, hey, that's good. We got it right, right, sir?"

"That time. But the enemy figured out they couldn't defend on the beaches. So they decided they'd suck us inland, and really draw blood. That's what they did in Peleliu and Guam."

Troy's head bobbed. "Uh-huh. Thanks for the history lesson, sir. That's good Corps gouge, that's for sure."

*   *   *

ANOTHER hour passed. Hector told Troy he was going over to look at the water. The Pacific. A whole different ocean. The gunny had warned them not to go in, even to wade; there were sea snakes and stinging coral. And to double-time back if they heard a recall whistle. Whipkey was talking to another guy from Florida, and told him to go on ahead. So Hector walked over alone.

The light was almost gone. The sea, flat. The heat was stifling. The waves lapped at the broken coral like an overfed cat licking its food. He walked along smiling at the little crabs that scurried away, halting every few inches to lift their claws as if inviting him to box.

A half-familiar shape, just under the surface of the transparent water. He bent and tweezed it up with his nails.

A cartridge, unfired, the same diameter bullet, but longer than the 7.62s they fed the Pig. Corroded green, coated with coral accretion. He rubbed at the verdigris to expose bright brass. Who had dropped it here? Some marine, wading ashore, expecting to be cut in half by a Jap machine gunner?

He still didn't hate the Chinese. Could he make himself kill them? Maybe. If they came over the wire, trying to kill him and his buddies. But was it true, what the protesters back at the gate at Pendleton, and what Shanghai Sue had said? That this war was being fought for corporations, like Farmer Seth?

That he himself was just another carcass on the Line?

Sirens wailed again. He glanced back, then stiffened. The ambulances were turning in to the terminal this time.

WHEN he got back one ambulance was parked near the door closest to the head area. A trauma cart stood near the men's room. When a corpsman came out, got something from it, and went back in, her boots left bloody prints on the tile deck. An NCO stood with arms folded, keeping everyone else out. The lieutenant emerged, glanced around, and beckoned the gunny in with a crooked finger.

"Fuck's going on?" said Pruss, materializing at his side. They looked half in the bag, and smelled of alcohol. Hector wondered where they'd gotten it. He hadn't seen any on sale.

"Don't know. Somebody had an accident, in the head?"

Hector kept looking at a pack someone had left by the entrance to the head. At the name stenciled on it.

Suddenly it connected. He flinched, then went for the door to the restroom. The NCO was turned away, explaining something to an officer. He made a grab at Hector as he brushed by, but he evaded him and slid past. Preoccupied with whatever the officer was asking him, the sergeant let him go.

The stall door was open. The medics were working on the man inside, but from their faces, it wasn't exactly a rush job. The dark blood pooled on the floor tiles said that too.

Hector crouched next to the body, the big, immobile head, searching the fixed eyes for some spark. But Bleckford didn't blink. Or breathe. Or move. The big, soft-looking hands that had helped the rest of the Booger Squad out of the mud back at Basic, that had manhandled their burdens for the weaker members, even when the DI screamed at him to stop, lay open, palm up as if in surrender.

"What happened?" Hector asked the medic, who was stuffing gear back into her bag.

She spared him a glance. "Buddy of yours?"

"Boot camp."

"This." She pointed to a black tube protruding from the side of Bleckford's head.

He peered closer. It was . . . plastic. The lower casing of an issue ballpoint. The tapered point disappeared into Bleckford's dark kinky hair, and blood and matter oozed out around it.

"What . . . how did . . . ?"

"He took the pen apart. Put his head on the toilet." She sounded tired. "Held the pen in position with his left hand, then slammed the lid down with his right. The skull's thin there, in the temple area. It punched right through the bone."

"How did he know to do that?"

"I guess he was no dummy," the medic said. "Or else he got lucky, 'cause he hit the meningeal artery. The question is, why. Say you knew him in boot camp? Was he suicidal there? Moody? Introspective?"

"I don't think so . . . the DI rode him hard, but, but . . . No, Bleckford, he wasn't the smartest dude in the squad, but . . . he was a nice guy."

"Too bad nobody let us know he had problems."

"I didn't know he was even on the plane. I haven't seen him since—"

"Never mind, that wasn't an accusation." The door to the head slammed open. Voices swelled and echoed. She blotted her hands with a gauze pad. "If you're not in his chain of command, better get lost. Don't worry, they'll tell his family it was a training accident."

He wanted to stay, as if that could comfort the big man who'd all but carried him when he'd fallen. But he couldn't. He slid into one of the other stalls until the officers passed, then slipped out again. He stood in the waiting area, looking out at the darkness, at the stars shining so brightly. Stars Bleckford would never see again.

And good God, under starry skies we are lost. . . .

Not too much later, the order came to reboard.

16

28° 36.25′ N, 133° 26.1′ E
180 Miles East of the Ryukyus

A week later, leaning back in his leather chair on *Savo*'s bridge, Dan felt guilty. He should be down in Combat. At his proper battle station, in front of the screens.

But it was hard to leave this. Spread before him, the morning Pacific heaved with the deliberate massive undulations that had greeted Magellan and, long before him, Zheng He. The sky glowed dawning gold, streaked with cirrus stained pink by the incipient sun. The breeze was warm. The old tea clippers had sailed these waters. Russian, Japanese, German, and British fleets; in World War II, the *Kido Butai*, the Imperial Striking Force, and the great Allied task forces of 1944 and 1945.

He fingered the cover of *Neptune's Inferno*. Then laid it aside regretfully.

He had to forget history. And concentrate, now, on making it.

Or at least, on trying to lose as few lives as possible, while accomplishing his near-sacrificial mission.

"Captain? Four hundred miles from Point Epsilon," Fred Enzweiler said. "We'll begin the last refueling at zero-six." Like everyone else on the bridge, the deputy task force commander was in flash gear, gloves, and hood, despite the heat. Goggles were pushed up on his forehead, ready to be pulled down on a second's notice.

Dan glanced at the clipboard. "Execute as planned. But warn everyone again, we have to be sharp. That means EW, sonar, all sensors passive." He rubbed his eyes, squinting as the upper limb of sun popped yellow-hot into view, firing a glare like a high-powered laser.

He'd opened up the formation as they steamed west, smearing it across miles of ocean. In the old days, concentration meant power. Now it invited obliteration. To starboard, hull down on the horizon, rode the massive hulk of *Gambier Bay*. A helicopter was lifting off, on its way to relieve one that, controlling several autonomous vehicles, sanitized their track, sixty miles and more ahead of the speeding prows. Behind the carrier, plodding far back in its smoothed wake, *Almirante Montt*.

One by one, each ship was falling back to top off one last time. Then the tanker would retreat to the protection of the follow-on force. On the far side of the escort carrier, *Hampton Roads*, the other ABM-capable cruiser, guarded their right flank. Even farther out, on each flank and bringing up the rear, their escorts, including the Korean frigates, rolled in the deep, slow swells. Less a formation, really, than a procession of ships steaming independently, each in its quarter of untenanted sea. Linked only by the short-range squirts of line-of-sight UHF and the up-and-back, narrowly directional beams of satcomm.

And somewhere behind them, even more lost in the trackless deep, cruised the carriers.

"Bridge, Combat," the 21MC interrupted his thoughts. The officer of the deck, Chief Van Gogh at the moment, hit the lever twice to say *Go ahead.*

"This is Combat. EW reports multiple jammers—"

"I'll be right down." Dan's boots hit the deck with a double thud. But at the ladderwell he paused.

He didn't want to go down there.

Descending the ladder made him sweat, made his heart pound. He had to get a grip.

But he really, really didn't want to be belowdecks.

A violet-white flame, burning through the air . . .

"Y'okay, Admiral?" The boatswain, hand on his arm.

Dan shook it off. "Yeah. Yeah . . . just dizzy for a second. Must have gotten out of the chair too fast."

"Want me to call—"

"No. I'm fine," he snapped. If you gave in to fear once, the next time it would be a hundred times stronger. If you fed it, it grew mighty. If you faced it down, it shriveled.

Sometimes the mind had to dictate to the gut. Especially since right now his gut was telling him that every yard west put them in more danger. He felt like a fly on a tabletop, creeping beneath a poised swatter.

Taking a deep breath, as if to make a long dive, he jerked the door open and slid down the ladder boots first, gripping the smoothworn handrails tightly to brake his headlong descent.

* * *

TWO decks down the consoles were lit like side chapels. The dim light gave CIC an almost holy feel. The murmurs into phones and headsets might be prayers. The flash hoods, monks' cowls. The flak jackets . . . okay, you didn't see those in most cathedrals. He sighed, sagging into his pouched seat beside the TAO. Nodded to Min Su Hwang, who was set up with his own comm channel to the Korean element. The large-screen displays didn't show much. The whole force was in EMCON, radios and radars off. In listening mode only, as it had been since it headed out of San Diego, picked up the Chilean tanker, and arrowed west.

Into the islandless vacuum of the South Pacific. He forced out a croak. "What have we got, Dave?"

Branscombe muttered, "Maintaining twenty knots. Formation course, 282 degrees. *Hampton Roads* going in to fuel from *Montt*. All units within station. The Hunters report all sonar, electro-optical, ESM sensors operational. Engines and responses in the green. Four SuCAP F-35s stacked ahead.

"EW reports increasing activity from the mainland. R-band rackets. Jamming, from Ferrets. Air search radars. Air-to-air narrow-beam lock-ons."

"Hunters"—also known less gracefully as ASUVs, for anti-submarine unmanned vessels—were autonomous robots. Supposedly the 180-foot, low-observable semisubmersibles had the smarts not just to detect subs, but to maneuver independently to prosecute them. It was good to have something he could push ahead of the formation without putting a crew at risk. A "Ferret" was an electronic warfare aircraft. "Rackets" were jamming.

"The jammers, the rackets. An exercise, Dave?"

"Could be. Unless they know we're coming."

The third possibility, of course, was that the second-phase offensive was beginning early. This seemed unlikely. According to intel, the Chinese A-Day was still two weeks away. But it wasn't good that their target was prepping its defenses. "Log everything. When you have cross bearings, pass locations to Amy Singhe. She's aggregating the target set for our Tomahawk strike."

The rattle of a cup and saucer. Coffee. Dan nodded to Longley absently as the mess attendant set a sausage biscuit and a sticky bun at his elbow.

He took one bite of the bun, set it aside, and leaned over to Branscombe's keyboard, licking the crystalline glaze off his fingers. The earth zoomed back, the sea shrinking, islands and continents crowding in at the corners of the picture. It wasn't real time. Not without radar, or AWACS data, or really any significant input to the GCCS feed. Just the geo plots resident in the humming-warm blades of the ship's computer. Far behind them, Saipan. To the east, the Bonins and Volcano Island. To the south, ocean. To the northwest, the yellow outlines of Kyushu, southernmost of the Japanese home islands.

And directly ahead, the gauntlet Force 76 would have to run: what was now an all-but-Chinese-owned sea.

The top secret addendum to the op order had laid out his path. It had to be rigidly followed: U.S. subs had sanitized his transit lanes in, and would barricade his flanks as he closed. He would thread the Okinawa chain via an unnamed channel between two small islands, Akuseki Shima and Kotakara Jima. These were distant enough from the newly Chinese-occupied airfields in Okinawa that fighters from the carriers, two hundred miles astern, could knock down an attack from that quarter. From there, a straight-line course for three hundred miles would take him to Point Epsilon, one hundred miles off the mainland.

If they reached it, he could finally kill people and blow up stuff.

He pulled down a long swallow of hot coffee. Of course, it would also place him within range of every long- to medium-range defensive system the enemy possessed, from strike aircraft, to cruises, to ship-killer ballistic missiles.

He twisted in his chair to find Wenck a few feet away, looking over the EW operator's shoulder. "Donnie? Chief?"

"Admiral."

"Our super spoofers on *Gambier Bay*. What're you hearing from them?"

A classified module had been loaded aboard before the escort carrier left Seattle. Even Dan wasn't fully privy to what they were capable of. He did know they were searching for the comm links from the Albatross gliders, and beam-jamming them. Which might help slip them past enemy recon . . . "Not a lot." Wenck passed a hand over his hair, which sprang up like wire grass as soon as his palm left it. "Want me to get on UHF, see what's shakin'?"

"Can they intercept you?"

"If some sub has his mast up, he might hear something." The chief looked wary. "They keep telling us not to depend on comms. Sounds to me like they still suspect a penetration."

Dan told him to never mind, then. He sat back, wondering if he'd made the right decision shifting his flag to *Savo*. NAVSHIPS had offered to put a command module aboard the escort carrier. But in the end, he knew the cruiser. Had commanded her in combat. Knew her capabilities, her limitations, her skipper, and her crew.

It was the same decision Admiral Dan Callaghan had made in 1942: to command from his old ship, *San Francisco*, instead of a newer cruiser with radar. He'd paid for that choice with his life, dying in the night action for which *Savo Island* was named.

A mistake, in retrospect . . . but Dan understood. If he had to go into danger again, he wanted to wield a familiar weapon, feel dependable steel under him.

"Admiral? *Hampton Roads* reports fueling complete. Next up, *Sejong the Great*."

He murmured the standard Navy acknowledgment of any piece of information that didn't require further action on his part. "Very well."

HE was awakened in his chair by a sound from his dreams. Or rather, nightmares.

It was the cuing buzzer from the Aegis console.

A glance at his watch told him four hours had passed. An hour to noon, and eighty miles closer to the enemy.

Staurulakis slid into the CO's seat. Slight and wan-visaged, she had the olive-and-black *Savo* shemagh tucked around her neck, the flash hood pulled off pale hair. Settling her headset, she signed in on the weapons control net as she pattered the keyboard. The central screen, the GCCS geo, blanked. A different display came up.

Dan frowned. What the . . . ? Then he realized the callouts were in kanji. The right screen came up from the forward camera almost like a windshield view. The port display looked aft to a slowly rocking line of far-off blue.

The alert buzzer ceased abruptly. "Profile plot, new Meteor," Terranova announced, and Dan tensed. "Meteor" was the proword for a ballistic missile. "Elevation angels fifty . . . angels sixty. Climbing fast! ID as hostile. A big one, too. Huge radar return." She called out lat and long on the launch point. Originating from far inland, nowhere near the coast.

"We need an IPP," Staurulakis said tensely. "ASAP."

"Stand by . . . ALIS is generating."

"Where's this data from?" Dan called to CIC in general. He twisted, searching for the rider from the Missile Defense Agency. "Dr. Soongapurn. Where are we getting this?"

Her fine-boned face looked spectral, orclike, lit blue from below by a tablet computer. "Download from Japanese air defense."

"*Japanese?* I won't ask how."

"Good, because it's unofficial. There may be interruptions, and it's going to lag real time by about twelve seconds. It's coming via nano downlink, handed off to each bird as it orbits from thirty degrees above the horizon to thirty degrees from its local sunset."

Dan nodded; the Japanese, though publicly cooperating with Zhang, were passing him information under the table. The air picture extended from South Korea, to the Asian mainland, to Miyako Jima in the south. It showed a boil of high-altitude contacts off the Shanghai coast. Planes and RPVs were leaving the Okinawa airfields, but they seemed to be heading south and north, not toward him. More activity showed over Taiwan, in the mountains: attack helicopters. Everything looked quiet in Korea, where the Chinese were digesting one of the world's most vibrant economies . . . but highlighted in red, and jerking toward him in one-second increments, was a tented symbol. The missile they'd just detected, no doubt.

"Can we get an IPP?" Staurlakis asked again, voice sharp.

"Not yet. It's still climbing, Skipper." The Terror sounded calm. "Can't predict impact until it enters ballistic phase."

Dan caught his breath, suddenly fearing the worst. "Run its bearing out," he told Staurulakis.

The screen zoomed back. A green line pulsed. It was curved, but that was an artifact of the geo plot. There was Guam . . . Hawaii. "Keep zooming out," he muttered, and the California coast came into view. Only from memory, of course—their feed didn't reach nearly that far.

The extended track passed south of Hawaii. South of San Diego, of any continental U.S. city. Halfway around the world, the pulsing line met the coast of South America in the middle of Argentina.

Which of course it couldn't be aimed at, but it relieved his worst worry: that it was targeted at Seattle or LA.

"First-stage burnout. Separation," Donnie Wenck said from the console.

"I concur," murmured Soongapurn.

Dan said sharply, "We're not radiating?"

"Hell no, Skipper. I mean, Admiral. Just reading two tracks now, one descending, the other still showing an acceleration vector."

A cool hand on his. Staurulakis's. "Admiral? It might be better if you let me handle this."

He ground his teeth. Whatever this was, it wasn't aimed at the task group. Might pass more or less over them as they steamed west, but it was going too fast, and far too high, to have anything to do with them.

So what was it?

He shook it off, and clicked to the task group voice command net. Though it was short-range and scrambled, he used it as little as possible, but with his ships as far flung as they were, he had no choice now. "Monitor, this is Barbarian. Over." "Monitor" was *Hampton Roads*, his other ABM cruiser, on the far flank of the formation.

The squeal of a synced transmission. *"Monitor, over."*

"We're picking up a launch from the mainland, extended track south of Hawaii. Weapons tight. I say again, weapons tight."

"Monitor. Roger, out."

"Pass to Fleet?" Staurulakis murmured.

Dan twisted, searching for dark eyes, short black hair. "Dr. Soongapurn?"

"They may not have it," the scientist called from the EW console.

"To Fleet, absolutely, Cheryl. Flash. Voice HF—no—sorry. Satcomm Navy Red. But describe the track, so they don't think this is a strike on Pearl or CONUS."

"Initial IPP," Terranova called. "Impact point is south of Hawaii and north of Kiribati."

"Put it on the screen." But even as he said it a shimmering oval appeared, generated from the data downloaded from the hurtling nanosatellites, relayed from the distant radars on Kyushu. Wenck called, "Total flight distance: four thousand five hundred nautical miles."

Dan wondered why he was being told this, then realized: With that range, if its launch bearing had been pivoted counterclockwise, it could hit Honolulu. Farther to the left, and that quivering IPP would have lain over downtown Los Angeles.

He beckoned Soongapurn to him, then led her to the dark blue curtain to Sonar. Lowered his voice. "All right, Doctor. What's this mean?"

Her brows puckered. "Not sure. It's a heavy ICBM. Most likely, one of the DF-41s Zhang sprang on us last year."

"Multiple guided reentry vehicles. Miniaturized thermonuclears. Like our Peacekeeper, or the Russian SS-20. So, what? He's showing us the goods?"

"Either a demonstration of capability, or an overt threat."

"Or both," Dan said.

"Or both." She nodded. "Correct."

He paced back and forth, scratching his nose, then digging fingers into the ache in his neck. Zhang Zurong had already crossed the nuclear threshold with a ten-megaton detonation that had wiped out the USS *Franklin D. Roosevelt* battle group. Six ships, and almost ten thousand sailors and air personnel. So far, the U.S. hadn't returned the favor. But the longer Washington waited, the more Zhang might assume there wouldn't be a riposte.

It was more dangerous than the Cuban Missile Crisis. He just hoped that, as in that long-ago face-off, back-channel contacts were ongoing. If either side made a misstep, they could be over the brink into a massive exchange on each other's homelands.

He shivered, and not from the chill of CIC.

AT the command desk, Cheryl was studying the same screen. Thinking not about the missile, which she'd dismissed once its IPP was clarified, but about the shrinking distance to the Ryukyus and the contacts that had left the airfields there a few minutes earlier. The string of islands led from Kyushu south to Okinawa. The airfields there had hosted American air power for the better part of a century.

Now they were part of a new, expanding empire. *An ancient people regaining our former stature*, their leader had said. But more like a new tyranny, casting its shadow over fresh subjects.

She went to the covered LAN and called up imagery downloaded before they left San Diego. Those airfields—Yokota, Atsugi, Kadena—hadn't been handed over whole. The Air Force had set fuel bunkers aflame, blown up buildings, and extracted every flyable aircraft before demo squads planted C-4 and thermite on the rest. But destroying tens of thousands of feet of concrete runway wasn't possible. The overheads showed fighters, attack jets, and transports on the various ramps, and bulldozers constructing revetments. Also a fat blimp: an aerostat-mounted search radar.

She called up the enemy-capabilities annex of the Recoil op order. She'd already done this days earlier, but with a few dead seconds, wanted to make sure she wasn't missing anything. Most worrisome was a new stealth-shaped attack aircraft. Even if Aegis was active, they might find it hard to detect until it could launch the supersonic ship-killers that had already cost *Savo* her once-graceful bow.

The command net, in her headphones. A South American accent. *"This is* Almirante Montt. *Fueling is complete. Request permission to depart as planned."*

Singhe, on watch as staff duty officer: *"Roger, Steady Rider. This is Barbarian. Proceed on duty assigned."*

"This is Steady Rider. Roger. Out."

The op plan mentioned feints and other attacks to divert attention from the raid, including a land offensive by the Vietnamese, but gave few specifics. There were more details about the strike on the airfields that was supposed to get them through the strait. Just about . . . she checked her watch . . . half an hour ago, an Ohio-class ballistic missile submarine hundreds of miles to the south had fired a full hull load of 154 Tomahawks, mixed cratering and antipersonnel munitions. Attack submarines closer in would also be launching. Long-range strategic bombers would arrive shortly after the missiles.

The EW console operator called, "Kadena ceased transmission."

"Very well . . . Admiral, did you hear that? The aerostat radar shut down."

"Got it," Lenson said from his chair a few feet away. He looked intent on his own screen, though. Probably on chat with Fleet. Great, let him handle Higher.

"Yakota search radar off the air too."

"Very well." She glanced at Lenson again. His face was grim in the light from the screen. He was typing, lips pursed.

She hoped he wouldn't take them past the point of no return. The way he damn near had in the Taiwan Strait last winter, following the Koreans into the very jaws of hell.

He was a puzzle. She'd worked for him as XO, but could never say she knew exactly what was going on in his head. She'd certainly never dare play poker with him. You had to watch for a long time, close up, before you caught clues. He seldom mentioned his wife or his daughter, though Cheryl had met them both. The only hint she'd ever gotten that he thought about them had been when she moved into his at-sea cabin, and found the picture of Blair. Which she'd immediately shredded; something like that didn't need to circulate. And he had some sort of love-hate relationship with the new CNO . . . though it was hard to figure out whether it helped his career. Wearing the Medal of Honor didn't guarantee promotion. But it probably hadn't hurt, either.

He was hard to pin down operationally, too. Oh, he knew tactics and equipment. Maybe better than anyone else she'd ever met—individual experts, such as the chiefs, aside. Occasionally, as in the Strait of Hormuz the year before, he'd left her breathless with an unexpected play. But at other times he seemed overly cautious. Like when he'd abandoned a torpedoed, sinking German tanker.

Admittedly, they were all judgment calls in the end. A commander worked with inadequate information. Electronic clues, fragmentary reports, undependable intel; guesses at the enemy's forces, vulnerabilities, and intent. Still, she'd been relieved when he'd left. Though grateful for whatever strings he'd pulled that had left her (really too junior for the billet) as skipper.

But here he was back again. Taking them into harm's way once more.

"Captain?" It was Zotcher, the Sonar chief.

She lifted an earphone. "What have you got?"

"Pinging. Not sure what it is. Bearing about one-eight-zero."

At the same moment, the EW operator called, "Low-energy transmission, bearing one-eight-five. Correlates with HF data burst."

She frowned, hunching into the headphones. "What exactly have you got? Range?"

The operator said on the circuit, *"No range yet. Tracking to develop. Seems to be stationary, though."*

A submarine, poking a mast up to make a sighting report? But subs didn't ping active. Not if they knew what was good for them. And the ASUVs, scouting ahead of the main body, hadn't reported anything. She clicked to the air net and vectored Red Hawk out, telling the controller to keep him low. "This is the captain. If Wilker spots a 'scope, he's cleared to drop."

"Clear to drop, aye."

"What the hell is it?" the admiral was asking her. "The super-EWs on *Gambier* are picking it up too. Getting cross bearings. What is it?"

"Don't know, sir. A goblin, up for a squirt?"

"Pinging on us? Unlikely."

"One pulse, to make sure there's no one above him as he comes up?"

"That's peacetime SOP, Cher. They wouldn't do that out here."

She said, "Unless the diving officer forgot. And is getting a new asshole ripped about now."

Lenson looked away, expression displeased. At her language, or her reasoning? He'd never much appreciated being contradicted. He also seemed to expect more of the female officers, as far as deportment went.

She dismissed this as Zotcher reappeared at her elbow. "Steady ping, Skipper. Every fifteen seconds. Still dead in the water, and near-surface. TMA shows him about twenty thousand yards off."

She scratched between her fingers so hard that when she took her hand away the nails were stained with blood. What the fuck *was* this? And why hadn't their submarines and Hunters, scrubbing the advance track, picked it up? "Air control, CO, range twenty thousand from own ship, any joy?"

"Red Hawk reports orbiting that point, no joy, no contact . . . uh, wait one . . . something in the water."

"What? Confirm: He knows he's cleared to drop. ASAP, on initial detection." She switched to the air circuit to hear Strafer Wilker drawling, *"Not a snorkel. Not a radar mast. Going in low. Stand by on flares . . . some kind of fucking buoy. Painted blue. Why I couldn't see it until I got right down on the fucking deck."*

Beside her Lenson said, "It's a picket."

"What?"

"The Japanese, in World War II, used fishing smacks with binoculars and radios. This is the same thing. An early-warning line, couple hundred miles out from the coast."

"So we're detected."

"'Fraid so." He kneaded the back of his neck. "But so far no one seems to be headed our way."

She thought about mentioning the small contacts that had departed Kadena, then vanished from the radar. But they hadn't been headed east. "So . . . steady as she goes?"

"Couldn't have said it better." He eyed Enzweiler. "Can't *Gambier Bay* crank it up any faster?"

"Twenty-two's all they say they can make."

"Okay . . . but let's get their fighters off the deck. I'd feel better with more air cover."

Cheryl got up and took a turn around the space, patting shoulders and putting in a word of encouragement to each operator. They looked anxious, but not scared. Well, they'd all been in tight spots before.

She'd just finished thinking this when the EW operator said, "EW reports: Aircraft altimeters at two-six-zero. Correlates with attack aircraft."

Two-six-zero was just about the bearing to Okinawa. She glanced at

Lenson, but his head was down again. "Admiral? They know we're here. Permission to radiate?"

He cocked his head, obviously pondering her question, but still studying the screen. He glanced up at the display, over the half-moon glasses he used now for reading or close work. Then back down, clicking the Transmit button on his throat mike. He was speaking to the air group commander on *Gambier Bay.*

She clicked to the Aegis net. "Get the SPY warmed up."

"*Yes ma'am.*" Terranova, very calm. "*Fifteen seconds to full operate.*"

"Don't radiate just yet."

"*Copy, ma'am.*"

She covered the throat mike. Lenson was still head down in whatever it was. He didn't need Higher's permission to go active, did he? "Sir, we need to get some microwaves out there," she told him. "Find out what's bearing down on us."

"Come left to two-eight-zero first and push up to flank speed. Open the carrier a little more. Then go active."

Seconds later data bloomed on the screens, a rush of information that left her almost dizzy. The SPY-1 reached out over four hundred miles, and as the radars from *Kristensen, McClung, Sejong,* and *Zembiec* came up too Cheryl was suddenly hovering over the western Pacific and East China Sea like an avenging Valkyrie. The outlines of Kyushu, Okinawa, and the Chinese coast populated with contacts, each called out with altitude, speed, direction, and aircraft type. Second by second the picture clarified. Yellow—meaning unidentified—contacts swiftly turned blue or red, friendly or enemy. The weapons net came alive, assigning targets.

And there they were. Small, low to the water, but after taking off heading north or south, they'd hooked back in. Cued to the approaching flotilla, possibly by the automated buoy line. "Two attacks developing, Admiral," she warned.

"I see 'em."

"Permission to—"

The air control circuit droned, "*Weapons free. All stations Horde, weapons free on incoming bandits. —Wait one—*"

She gripped the button on her throat mike as what was happening became clear.

More contacts were blooming, behind and above the incoming attackers.

Blue inverted carets. Friendly air.

F-18s and F-35s from the carriers, which steamed hundreds of miles behind TF 76, but were covering them when it counted.

Lenson, on the command net. "Horde, this is Barbarian. Weapons free for leakers. But exercise caution against blue on blue."

Vibration caterpillared through the steel cradling them as the cruiser reached flank speed. *Savo* leaned like a locomotive on a badly bedded track. Cheryl had noticed a shorter righting arm since two more Phalanx mounts and additional chaff mortars had been added. But she had to concentrate on the immediate threat. "Aegis to self-defense mode."

Terranova rogered. *Savo* would fight herself from now on, assisted by the team only if a threat seemed misclassified.

Though she'd been in self-defense mode before. Last fall, when the supersonic leaker had blown off her bow . . .

On the screen red and blue carets merged. Red contacts, taken from behind and above with air-to-air missiles, winked out. She resisted the temptation to eavesdrop, to see if she could make out Eddie's voice. The task force's own aircraft—not really interceptors, but still with air-to-air missiles—were held close in, low, to intercept anyone who got through.

The EW operator announced, "Vampire, vampire, vampire. Incoming missile bearing zero-four-four. Seeker correlates C-801."

After that, she was sucked down into the battle.

LATE that evening Dan finally hoisted himself from the command desk. His back and neck were a painful mass of knots. And it wasn't over yet.

In fact, the fight had only begun.

They'd made it into the East China Sea. Task Force 76—absent, now, *Gambier Bay*, which he'd detached to fall back toward the carriers, along with the lower-capability Korean frigates—had threaded the gap between Akuseki Shima and Kotakara Jima as dusk fell. He'd stayed on high side chat and the command net, attention riveted to the displays, all afternoon and into darkness. They'd fought off three separate air and missile attacks. But most of the bandits had fallen not to his own weapons, but to fighters from the carriers, which had closed to increase sortie rate. None of his ships had been hit yet, though they'd expended ordnance at a fantastic rate. But it hadn't been one-sided. They'd lost one of the autonomous Hunters to an enemy 801. U.S. aircraft, too, had suffered losses.

Including those from *Vinson*. He reread the clipboarded message just handed to him. The radioman stood an arm's length away. "I didn't . . . didn't know who to bring it to, sir."

"You did right." He sighed and read it again, feeling lead settle in his heart.

"Addressed to the skipper. But I didn't want to take it to her—"

"No, you did right. I'll tell her." He glanced around the space, but didn't see Cheryl. "Where's the CO?" he asked Branscombe, who was occupying the TAO seat.

"She said, up to the bridge. Get a breath of air."

"Take over, Fred. I'm going to the bridge," Dan told Enzweiler. As the deputy slid in, he sighed again. Finished the half cup of cold coffee at his elbow, and checked the displays one last time. No immediate threat, though air activity was building again over the mainland. They'd lost surprise, but he'd never expected to have it, once they got this far. He blew out, forcing himself to walk to the door, and undogged it.

Three ladders up to the bridge, his stiff joints gradually loosening with activity. He wondered how he was going to say this. Or if he even should. The TF was going in for the kill now. Closing the mainland for the final strike. To survive, they'd all have to work smoothly as a freshly greased winch. Ollie Uskavitch was a good officer, but he was in no way qualified to step into the CO's shoes. Not in a situation like this.

But even as he contemplated delay, he knew he couldn't keep it from her.

She deserved the truth.

Everyone deserved that. And in person, from a fellow human being.

The pilothouse was inky save for the dim glow of pilot lamps, the eerie electroluminescence of screens dimmed to near invisibility. He stood motionless, letting his eyes adapt. Then felt his way past the helmsman to the CO's chair. In the dark, reaching, he touched something yielding. Her coveralled leg. "Cheryl?"

A startled gasp in the dark. "Oh—Dan. What is it?"

He took another deep breath, gripping the clipboard. Let her read it, or just say the words? He didn't want to do either. Fuck this war. Fuck all war.

He said reluctantly, "I'm afraid I have some bad news."

17

The White House

I 'LL get the door, ma'am."

"Thanks." Swinging her legs out, Blair scanned the lot. Usually solid with freshly waxed black cars, it was occupied now by uniformed troops, military vehicles, and a truck-mounted missile battery. But the white canvas awning was still flanked by plantings in heavy concrete pots. Marigolds, it looked like, and poppies red as spattered blood. The blooms looked like they were enjoying spring.

She'd driven over from the Pentagon with the Joint Chiefs J3, Operations, General Absalom Lipsey, and an aide. As the just-confirmed deputy undersecretary for strategy, plans, and forces, she'd been getting up to speed with him for the last few days.

Inside the staff entrance a deep-blue-carpeted lobby was hung with framed art. Mostly battle scenes, aircraft and ships flaming, all smoke and death. *Not inappropriate*, she thought. Vases of roses, lilies, and birds of paradise stood on a side table. The air smelled of electricity, perfume, something dusty-sweet, like talcum powder, and coffee. A vacuuming janitor edged aside for them as she followed Lipsey's short-legged bounce.

At the Roosevelt Room they were joined by Dr. Szerenci. The national security adviser's squint was a raptor's. Two agents in dark suits flanked him. "Edward," she murmured.

"Congratulations, Blair. The previous incumbent . . . let's just say, he was not of your intellectual caliber. General Lipsey, good to see you again. Dr. Glancey, General Vincenzo, Dr. Hui will join us shortly. Let's go in."

The Cabinet Room was smaller than one might expect. Freshly vacuumed, by the pristine nap of the carpet. Fresh yellow notepads.

Sharpened pencils. She'd made sure her notebook was charged. As the attendees took seats, Szerenci fiddled with a video player. "Had this sent over," he muttered. "A voice-over translation . . . you'll find transcripts at your places."

"What's on our plate, Doctor?" The chairman of the Joint Chiefs had come in, with Randall Faulcon, a three-star she knew. Vincenzo, in Army greens, pulled out a chair beside Blair as colonels with notebooks took seats against the wall.

"General, good morning. For those who don't know him, the gentleman with General Vincenzo is General Randall Faulcon, deputy commander, Pacific Command."

Faulcon nodded. His cheekbones were hard, almost fleshless, and he looked more deeply tired than anyone else in a room of tired people. He was also the only one in battle dress. Szerenci went on, "Your ears only, but there's going to be a strategy conference in the Pacific—I can't tell you where—a week from now. The heads of state or defense ministers of Australia, India, Indonesia, Vietnam, and the government-in-exile for Taiwan. The president's asked me to staff our options. General Vincenzo will be going. Blair, the SecDef may want you there too. Okay, here we go."

A heavy, spectacled face appeared on the screen. Its lips writhed in staccato Chinese. "Denson, can you understand that?" Szerenci asked Denson Hui, who'd just come in.

The head of the Missile Defense Agency looked as if he got that question too often. "My parents were Cantonese. What he's speaking's as foreign to me as it is to you, Ed."

The torrent of Standard Hanyu decreased in volume. The translation began, a cool high female voice contrasting oddly with the angry male face that spoke. The premier was saying, "I promise those who plunged the world into war that if Shanghai is attacked, Seattle will be next.

"If there is still doubt, our most recent test of what the West knows as the DF-41, launched in central China and impacting southeast of Hawaii, should put all minds at rest. We possess the capacity to destroy every major city in the United States."

He raised a finger, glaring into the camera. "Not only that: our missiles are now so accurate, we can destroy the ability of the Americans to strike back.

"The greatest nation on earth will emerge victorious from this conflict. There are more of us, and we are inured to suffering. America's insults have gone too far. As a great leader once said in the midst of a war that threatened the life of his nation: We will not take one step back."

The premier glanced at his notes. His tone changed; he seemed to be trying to smile. "Our friends stand by us. The Associated Powers present a united front to the aggressors. In addition, those nations which, realizing their past errors, have decided to help inaugurate a new era in Asia are benefiting from our forbearance.

"I refer to the Republic of the Philippines, the new People's Republic of South Korea, and the People's Republic of Nepal and Northern India. Together with the Islamic Republic of Iran, the Democratic People's Republic of Korea, the Islamic Republic of Pakistan, and the People's Republic of Miandan, we will develop the vast resources of the seas and lands of Asia and the Pacific for the benefit of all peaceful peoples.

"Our welcome also extends to the State of Japan. The negotiations now going on will not only end hostilities between these two great nations, but recognize the sovereignty of the Chinese people over those islands called by the Japanese the Senkakus, but whose rightful name is now restored: the Diaoyu Islands."

Zhang swerved aside at this point into a lengthy discussion of the chain of sovereignty on the islands in question. Szerenci, grunting something inaudible, fast-forwarded until he came to the next section he wanted. Zhang lifted a finger, shaking it; the detached female voice translated again.

"This agreement means eternal peace with Japan. However, our forces will have to remain at the former foreign air bases, to assure compliance with new conditions and defend against American attacks. In exchange, the People's Empire promises to respect and defend the territorial boundaries of our new friend and associate."

"This isn't good," Lipsey muttered, across from Blair.

Zhang drank slowly from a glass of water, then set it aside. When he resumed, his tone was deeper. "A further warning to those who contemplate aggression. Behind us now stands the noble population of Russia, with immense armed force and a second nuclear deterrent. That great country too has suffered from U.S. and European hegemonic aggression, on the other side of Eurasia. This, too, in the words of an American president, will not stand."

Szerenci held up a clicker, and the screen froze with Zhang's open mouth a toothy O. The national security adviser said, "He goes on for another hour and a half. But that's enough for the flavor. And did you catch where he quoted Stalin? 'Not one step back.' He's speaking before the

People's Congress, by the way. Which he's just finished purging—probably why the standing ovation at the end lasts for a full thirty minutes."

General Vincenzo said, "First question in my mind: Is his threat credible? About taking out our second-strike capability."

Szerenci lifted an eyebrow. "We should have taken action years ago. If we don't hold escalation dominance, everything changes. We have to either fight wars of attrition, against enemies that don't value life as we do, or surrender, in one way or another.

"Therefore—and I've said this before—our goal in this conflict has to be to eliminate Chinese nuclear capabilities."

"That would take an invasion," Vincenzo said quietly. "You're not seriously proposing that, I hope."

"Too soon to debate." Szerenci let that hang, then added, "We once had ten thousand warheads on delivery vehicles. Right now, we have fewer than fifteen hundred. We scrapped the multi-warhead Peacekeepers. Our ground-based deterrent consists of four hundred Minuteman IIIs, split among Warren, in Wyoming, Malmstrom, in Montana, and Minot, in North Dakota.

"Minuteman used to carry three warheads, of a third of a megaton each. We took two off for START, leaving one for each delivery vehicle. But we kept the front-end platform and the old bulkhead. Right now, we've got a crash program going to reload with all three warheads. But we have to upgrade the software, swap out the mountings, update the support equipment. It will take three months to restore them to the triple-warhead configuration."

"But how vulnerable are they?" Blair asked.

Szerenci nodded to Hui. "Denson, want to take that?"

The missile defense director looked grim. "We've run thousands of simulations on a first strike against our ground-housed forces. Accuracy's the critical variable. If they can field a guidance package good enough to land a terminal vehicle in a hundred-meter circle, they can destroy any silo. Hardened or not."

"And can they?" Vincenzo asked quietly.

Hui looked down. "Based on their penetration of our contractors over the years . . . and what they got from Los Alamos . . . they probably can."

Blair said, "What about our interceptors?"

Vincenzo said, "We have thirty in Alaska and fifteen at Vandenberg. With up to ten MIRVs for each DF-41, and probably steerable decoys, too . . . you see the problem."

"The antimissile laser?" the J3 asked. "The airborne system?"

"It has possibilities. Lockheed's on it. But it's not there yet."

They stared at one another across the polished table. Until Szerenci sighed. "As I said, I warned everyone about this. Didn't I, Blair?"

"You did," she admitted. "Though I think you were a little too ready to—"

"So now," the national security adviser interrupted, "our heaviest weapons are vulnerable. Our bomber leg has lost its advance bases, and NSA's telling me the Russians are shipping their most advanced antiair systems to Beijing. So we may have to rule out strategic bombing as well.

"This leaves our sea-based deterrent. Fortunately, we repositioned it to the far north and south of the equator. Destruction of the main wolf pack in the Pacific, and mopping up the remainder, means our subs are once again secure.

He leaned back. "I only hope that's enough to deter a first strike. If it isn't, we'll be counting our dead in tens of millions."

Blair lifted a pencil. "You were more confident last year, Doctor. As I recall, your exact words were 'Now could be better than later.' You called it an opportunity, not a disaster."

Szerenci looked only mildly interested. "War contains many surprises, Blair."

"Not good enough. Deterrence is supposed to persuade a potential adversary to forgo attack, based on his perception of the benefits of various courses of action, compared to the costs and consequences."

Szerenci waved it away. "Adversary decision making isn't just a matter of mathematics. I admit, I'm sometimes seduced by the quantitatives. And, yes, I've made mistakes too.

"But moves are also influenced by strategic culture, the idiosyncrasies of decision mechanisms, and leadership styles. Zhang's proven to be more of a gambler than anyone expected. Especially since his wounding during the terrorist attack at Mumbai, which he seems to blame on us somehow.

"At any rate . . . I'm not interested in revisiting what could have been done to forestall this. That's a matter for the historians. Right now, we have to outline our options." He looked at the so-far-silent Glancey, at the far end of the table. "The good news is, we have an expert on war termination with us. Professor?"

Glancey didn't meet their gazes. "Unfortunately, there's no road map for war termination between nuclear powers. It's never happened before.

"Our original plan called for depleting their forces in the China Seas, then blockade. The Allies are self-sufficient in food, and we have adequate energy supplies. Beijing has to import both. We estimated exhaustion of oil and grains in three months, followed by rationing, inflation, and food riots, forcing the regime to deal.

"We already have reports of spot food shortages. And there also seems to be some sort of disease outbreak in Western China. But three factors are vitiating a blockade strategy. First, their last-minute stockpiling, trading U.S. debt for grain and feedstocks. Second, Iran and Russia's involvement, in supplying oil, liquefied natural gas, and weapons. Finally, the Chinese are extracting huge quantities of foodstuffs from their allies—mainly rice from northern Burma, what Zhang calls Miandan.

"They're hurting us, too. Financial networks are in ruins. Banks are history. Repeated failures of the power grid are hurting war production. We moved Joint Intelligence to the Cloud, and lost it in the Cloudburst—"

"We know all that," Vincenzo snapped, leaving off doodling. "How do we end this?"

The professor grimaced. "I see two routes to the conference table."

"Which are?"

"Make peace, on the best terms we can, or escalate."

"Escalate to what?" Blair said. "Ed says we've lost dominance. When you don't have that, what's left is total war."

Glancey said, "But if you squeeze this guy too tight, he'll escalate back. Are we ready to lose San Francisco? Seattle? Or the Trident base at Bangor?"

"We can escalate horizontally," said the deputy PaCom, Faulcon.

"Where?" The J3 lifted both palms. "He's beaten us in Korea and Okinawa. Outfought the Japanese in the Senkakus. Crushed the Taiwanese. Fought the Indians to a standstill, and is probably going to roll over the Vietnamese next."

Faulcon said, "First, raise some hell in his backyard. A coup in Alma-Ata, or a revolt of the Uighurs or Tibetans. Then press inward around the periphery, with assaults as close together as possible. Strike where his supply lines are longest and his forces weakest."

"Let's briefly discuss Dr. Glancey's first option," Szerenci interrupted. "I won't advocate it, but I have to present it to the president. In view of the resistance our carrier groups are encountering, as they execute Operation Recoil. We could call off the raid on Ningbo. Sideline the invasion of It-bayat. Then put out feelers through Moscow. Or, better, Tokyo. Thoughts?"

Vincenzo said, "That's a decision for the theater commander."

"No, it's the commander in chief's prerogative," Szerenci said. He glanced at Blair. "What's the feeling on the Hill? You're still tight with Senator Talmadge, right?"

She said evenly, "I won't carry tales between the Hill and the executive, Ed."

"We can't fight without Congress voting the funds, Blair."

"They won't buy a surrender. But neither will they vote funds without a strategy for something that looks like victory," she told him. "So far, I haven't heard one. And just grinding China down isn't going to work while Zhang carries those missiles in his back pocket."

"What's our desired end state?" Glancey asked. "Knowing that might help."

"Regime change," Szerenci said. "Renunciation of nuclear weapons. And freeing of Taiwan, Korea, and the other seized territories."

"Too ambitious," Blair said. "Again, you're talking total war to achieve that."

They glared at each other across the table. Until the deputy said, "What do Zhang's comments about Russia mean? Are they going to intervene?"

"We can't respond if they attack Ukraine or Lithuania," Vincenzo said. "All our forces are deployed, either in the Mideast or the Pacific. Europe will be on its own for at least a year, until the new divisions and new factories come online."

General Lipsey, the J3, said, "There's speculation from State that Russia's really not all that eager to support Zhang. It's as if he's holding something over them. Some kind of threat, or blackmail, that keeps them supplying oil, food, and weapons."

"What about the theater nuclear option?" Vincenzo said, gaze on his doodling.

Szerenci nodded. "PaCom can recommend using special weapons. But employing them requires presidential release authority." He glanced at Faulcon. "Yangerhans hasn't asked for them so far. Does he now?"

"No," said the deputy. "But he'd like to reserve their use. He requested that, as you remember, if we ended up with significant forces trapped in Pusan."

The national security adviser said, "Let's go to the second option. General Faulcon describes this as horizontal escalation, but it's the classic way a combatant with command of the sea reduces one with interior lines of communication. He mentioned raising strife in Zhang's backyard. Much of China is lightly populated, hard to police, and contains restive minorities. I understand Ops and Plans has been working on this."

Lipsey nodded to an aide, and a slide went up. It showed red arrows in four positions around China. "Dr. Szerenci is right in describing this as classic strategy. It's Grant at Richmond, Eisenhower invading the Ruhr. Our next step, assuming Mandible and Recoil succeed, will not only attempt to foment unrest in western China, but coordinate attacks in Nepal, across the Vietnamese border into Yunnan, and naval operations in the South China Sea."

But Vincenzo was shaking his head, pushing back from the table. "We don't have the forces to support simultaneous attacks. Not for another year. And the Indians aren't ready to take the offensive yet. Yet. If ever."

Blair lifted her pencil again. "General Shucheng is still resisting in the mountains of Taiwan. And the Second Marine Division will be free after Itbayat is taken."

"*If* it's taken," Vincenzo snorted. "It's too soon for a general offensive. Strategically *and* logistically. No offense, Abe, but I've been hearing some crazy things out of the work groups at J3. Taking over part of the front in Vietnam. Invading Hainan. Landing at Hong Kong, for God's sake! When all we have is the 25th, in Hawaii, the Second Infantry, and elements of the Ninth. And nine brigade combat teams, two combat aviation brigades, and thirteen multifunctional brigades.

"Against a Chinese army of over two hundred divisions? We land, they cut us off, and we face another massive defeat. That's what I'll tell the president."

"So what *do* we do?" Blair asked him.

"Wait. Build up. Shape the battlefield," he told her. "Meanwhile, let the Navy and Air Force carry the ball."

Szerenci looked from one to the next. Finally he nodded, and began gathering his papers. "All right, good meeting. The decision will be up to the president, of course. In consultation with the other heads of state. But we have clear options. One, sue for peace. Two, escalate vertically. Three, escalate horizontally."

Blair frowned. "I just wish we had a better idea how we tie this thing off."

Just for a microsecond, Szerenci looked agonized. Then bland again. "I agree, Madam Undersecretary. Dr. Glancey, we could use further study on that by your working group.

"I will add one thing. If the president decides to continue the war, I will warn Beijing that if the continental U.S. is attacked, or if nuclear weapons are used again on our forces, we will destroy a Chinese city."

Blair started to speak, but couldn't find words.

He stacked notes in his briefcase, nodded to them all, and rose to leave.

He hesitated, though, and gestured for her to join him in the corridor. Once the door closed he murmured, "Your visit to Seattle. How'd it go? With, what are they calling it—Big Eagle?"

She halted dead. He wasn't supposed to know that. No one outside Special Projects was. If there was an Ultra secret in this war, it was Battle Eagle. "Uh . . ."

"Is it online yet?"

"I'm not cleared to comment, Ed. Not to anyone."

"The attacks are getting more serious. Jade Emperor is learning. Put the screws to them, Blair. For all our sakes."

He turned, and headed down the hall. Leaving behind an uneasy silence, a sense, at least as Blair felt it, that nothing, really, had been decided.

That made her nervous. Given Szerenci's reputation for brinkmanship, and Zhang's lack of restraint.

Put the two of them together and the gates of hell could open.

Back by the conference room, she nabbed the chief of staff. "General Vincenzo?"

"Madam Undersecretary."

"I don't like the idea of drifting. Our economy is bleeding too. We only have one operating refinery left. Gasoline's at eighteen-fifty a gallon. And you know about the peace movements. From both the left and the right. If we don't seize the initiative—conventionally, I mean—the enemy will. Or the voters will despair, and then we're really lost."

Vincenzo bared his teeth. "We aren't *drifting*," he snapped. "If we take the offensive too soon, we'll get kicked back into the sea. Remember how long it took to build up for Normandy?"

"But do we have that luxury this time? I see delay as problematic at best. Lethal at worst."

The general handed his briefcase to one of the colonels, nodded, a near-contemptuous jerk of the head, and turned on his heel.

Leaving her in the hall contemplating one of the paintings, full of smoke, and flames, and bombs falling on a helpless city.

IV

OPERATION RECOIL

18

Western Xinjiang

STUMBLING out of a deep defile, Teddy, Fierros, and Major Trinh halted as if of one accord.

With goatskins lashed over the remains of their prison rags with smoke-dried sinew, they gawked down on a flat green plain like demons encountering Heaven.

The valleys they'd followed, hoping the way led down, had instead bewitched them into a labyrinth of profound ravines and blasted gulches shadowed even in daylight by great mountains. With the final remnants of strength, they'd toiled to the crests of knife-sharp ridges to gauge how the land ran. Only to survey endless miles of the same gravelly, deserted Mars-scape. And looming evermore at their right shoulders, the snow-covered, frowning Tien Shan.

The Celestial Mountains.

Somehow while they'd wandered spring had come. Fierros squinted up at the sun, then back at the snowcapped peaks that still towered, distant as ever.

"So, is this Tajikistan?" Teddy asked him.

The airman wagged his head. "We gotta be close."

"Close ain't gonna cut it, Ragger. One step this side of the border, we're recaptured murderers. The other side, free heroes. We've got to find out where we are."

The airman covered his face with his hands. "I don't have a map. Anyway, we can't go any farther."

Teddy looked at Trinh. The now-fully-blind Vietnamese was a ghost animating scraps of hide and rag. A shriveled mummy, crouched trembling over a stick. Teddy figured he himself probably looked just as bad, with the useless, dragging limb. No. Fierros was right. They were done.

"All right." He sighed. "Time to see what the fat lady's gonna sing."

THE trail meandered down into a valley. After some time it joined another, which jogged for miles beside a creeklet that chuckled noisily over rounded sparkling stones bright as jewels. The snow-fed water was so crisp and cold that when he knelt to drink it made his teeth ache in their sockets.

They'd followed it for a couple of hours when from behind echoed a snorting, a dry padding, the jingle and squeak of harnesses and hooves. They flinched and stood aside.

The leader rode a white pony with a long shaggy mane. Dark-faced, mustached, he wore a turban and a black wool scarf pulled over his face. A long wood-stocked rifle, so old Teddy didn't recognize the make, was slung over his shoulder, and a curved knife was stuck into his belt. Teddy and Fierros returned his nod. Behind the horseman a long string of camels set each padded foot delicately as ballerinas on the rocky, slanted path. The camels eyed the strangers distrustfully from heavily lashed lids, craning their necks for balance as they lurched and swayed downward. Huge bundles and pallets, some nearly as large as the animals' bodies, were lashed on their backs. From the way they puffed and grunted, the weight must have been enormous.

A shout; Teddy caught a glimpse of another horseman on the heights behind them. Yet a third came galloping up from the rear of what seemed to be an endless caravan of the staggering, burdened camels.

Trinh grasped his shoulder. "What is it?" he quavered.

"A caravan, Major. Camels. Guys on horses."

"Look like fucking bandits," Fierros muttered.

"Yeah, but they're probably just traders. Bundles of cloth and trade-good type stuff on those camels. Let's tail on at the end of this bunch," Teddy asided.

"Yeah, but who are they?"

"Who cares? We won't stick out near as much if we ride into town with the circus."

Another rider pelted past, kicking up dirt. Trinh yelled in Russian, trying to flag him down and ask where they were. "*Priv'yet, droog! G'dye my? V' kakoi strane eto?*" The man barely glanced at them, then urged his pony on.

* * *

THE dogs came out half a mile from the village. Snapping, whining curs. They avoided the caravan, but not the three trailing it on foot. Swinging sticks drove them back. The kids arrived next, running circles around them. The boys looked Han, which made Teddy's heart sink. Herds of small, filthy-assed sheep grazed around the village, with many lambs among them. He kept dragging his leg along, cutting a groove in the dirt, gouging through shoots of fresh tender grass.

"We need a cover story," Trinh muttered. "In case this is still China."

Fierros hissed, "It's not gonna hold water, Nguyen. Pretty goddamn obvious what we are, if you ask me."

"It's still going to take time to report us. So what are we? Stick to the Russian story?"

Teddy murmured, "As good as we're gonna get, I think."

The kids circled again, screaming, then pelted back toward the village. Which looked bigger now. A party of men were unloading the camels, watering them, leading them to a corral. This seemed to be a caravanserai, if that was the word. A stopover. Maybe a good place for travelers without papers. Unfortunately, they didn't have any money, either. The sole thing they possessed of any value was the empty AK. Still, though they got glances, no one seemed interested. They trudged through the unloading and feeding area, past a shallow pond where livestock were sucking up muddy water, and into the outskirts of the rather shabby town.

"We gotta figure out where the fuck we are," Fierros hissed.

"Ix-nay on the goddam English-ay, Ragger. Just fucking nix on it, okay?"

Trinh, feeling his way with his stick, asked if they saw anyone who looked like a shopkeeper. Teddy scouted a couple of alleys. Flashing back, as he saw dangling sheep carcasses, to Afghanistan.

A leader's recon, with the Aussie SAS. Bazaar day in a village. Butchered sheep there too, with the severed heads set in front of them. He remembered a long, nicked bayonet with a wooden handle and a hooked quillon that he'd only much later realized must have been for a Martini-Henry. Strong fucking tea, and the harsh burn of the big oval 800 Motrins they called SEAL candy . . . Maybe he could try his Arabic here. And, just like in Afghanistan, these alleys were lined with blankets covered with twisted, dusty roots, sheepskin coats, rugs, brass trivets and pothooks and lathe-turned cups.

At last an old guy smiled and beckoned him nearer. Teddy made a *wait a minute* gesture, went back for Trinh, and led him over, while Fierros squatted and studied the inside of his eyelids on the far side of the alley.

He could follow a good deal of the Russian, though from time to time the conversation veered into some other language. Maybe Trinh knew more Mandarin than he'd been letting on. Finally Trinh called them over. *"Eto maoi drooz'ya,"* he said. "Teodor Fyodorovich, Leonid Andreyevich, this is Gospodin Reyhan."

"As salaam-aleikum," Teddy said, giving him the old head, lips, heart salutation. The old guy beamed, and bowed from where he sat.

Trinh said, still in Russian, "Well, you're a hit. But he says we're still in Xinjiang. About a hundred kilometers from the Tajik border."

Teddy tried to keep his face from falling. *"Bozhe moi.* We need to get home. What's the best way west from here?"

The old man shrugged, spilling a mix of the other language so fast that Trinh motioned for him to slow down. Reyhan gestured for them to sit. He pointed to a rolled-up carpet and turned to a brazier behind him, and before long they were eating pilaf with little pieces of lamb out of soft blue plastic bowls with their fingers, and drinking that great tea Teddy remembered. He'd never had anything as delicious.

When the old man got up and left with the empty bowls, Trinh leaned in. Murmured, "He says—I think—that he can have someone lead us to the border."

"We can't pay. Did you tell him that?"

"I said we'll give his grandson our rifle when we get there. He seemed surprised we had one."

"Hooyah. What else? You were talking a long time."

"Well, he had a lot to say. He thinks we're Muslim, since you gave him that greeting. Anyway, he says this side of the town is 'us.' The other side is 'Han.' He told me to come back after dark, but to stay away from the other side today."

"Specifically today?" said Teddy, but just then the old man came back. He crashed into a table, and Teddy realized the old guy was as blind at Trinh. He thrust a disk of heavy-looking bread into Trinh's hands, and spoke again, gesticulating, as the Viet hoisted himself from the rug with his stick.

Trinh beckoned them toward the alley. "He says we must leave now. Come back after dark, and be ready to walk. Oh, and we should leave the *avtomat* here. It is a wonder we got this far into town with it. If the *militsy* see us with it, we will be arrested."

They exchanged uneasy glances, but at last left it wedged into an upper beam of the shop and covered with thatch.

In the alley they tore at the bread, still ravenous, wolfing big chunks as they walked. Teddy kept careful track of the turns. They had to find their way back in the dark. He glanced at the sun. Maybe three hours until sundown. Then they'd be on their way. Over the border, to freedom. He munched bread, stomach rumbling. Could it be possible? That they'd make it out of here after all?

They came out onto a larger, paved street, and he stopped dead.

Troops were spilling out of trucks. Jumping down, faces set, holding not worn AKs like the camp guards but the current-issue bullpups. Every fire team had what looked like a squad automatic weapon too. Instead of combat green these guys wore black uniforms, black ballistic gear, black helmets with smoked face shields that erased their features. Strapped to their backs were truncheons and black shields bearing Chinese characters and, oddly, the English word POLICE.

"What's this—the riot squad?" Fierros muttered, shrinking back toward a fruit stand. Too late. When Teddy wheeled, other troops behind them were sweeping forward, shields and truncheons deployed, flushing protesting shopkeepers out of their stores, burka'd women from their shopping, forcing drivers out of their trucks and riders off their donkeys. Peremptory shouts, muffled by the face shields, echoed in the street.

Pushed and jostled, the escapees had no choice but to start walking along with the crowd. The men around them muttered angrily in Uighur as from a side street came the growl of a diesel. Teddy's heart sank further.

A vehicle resembling a truck, but more ominous, beetle-black, topped with water cannon and fronted with a steel dozer blade, rumbled out. Its huge tires squealed on the asphalt as it took position behind them. Two Han peered down through armored glass from its cab. Speakers atop the urban control vehicle began blasting out . . . music. A jangly, happy tune that didn't seem to light up the tense, frightened faces around him. Those he could see; the women had drawn their veils even more closely.

They had to get out of wherever this cattle drive was pushing them. But when he tried to fight his way out, dragging Trinh, who had a death grip on his jacket, the townies shoved back, cursing him. "Knock it off, Teddy," Fierros hissed. "Those troops are looking our way. Pull your fucking hood down."

"We got to get out of this roundup. They check IDs up ahead, we're toast." But he subsided. If he attracted attention, they were toast too.

A central square opened. Other gay jangly tunes floated from the streets leading in. Bright scarlet banners fluttered from lampposts, from metal standards. From the facades fronting the square huge posters of a square-faced Chinese stared out. In some pictures, he looked stern. In others he smiled, or held out his arms to children, who approached him holding up garlands, faces rapt in adulation.

Driven by troops and trucks, the crowds were slowly herded in. Around the square hundreds of folding tables were set up as if for a county fair, with more food than Teddy had seen in a long time: brightly colored oranges and lemons, stacks of the flat bread, vegetables, piles of green and yellow melons and cucumbers, sacks of rice and grain, arrays of brightly labeled cans. Suspiciously well-groomed young peasants stood behind the displays, evenly spaced, at attention.

Teddy's band and the Uighur townfolk found themselves in what seemed to be the native section, close to an empty central area set off with portable metal fencing. They stood there for upwards of an hour, while the music played on. Then a woman at the far end of the square made an interminable speech in a language he couldn't follow. The people around him could, though, and didn't seem to like it. They murmured and scuffed their feet and spat, but glanced at the lines of troops and did nothing more.

Meanwhile, a TV crew drove a van in and began setting up not far from where Teddy and Trinh and Fierros still stood, it having been made clear by the troops that squatting or sitting during the speeches was discouraged, on pain of being truncheoned and hauled off.

At last she concluded and the crowd stirred. The television crew, too, perked up. They donned comm phones and manned cameras, panning to cover the cleared space the portable fencing enclosed.

A troupe of dancers emerged from some backstage area Teddy hadn't noticed, down a path the crowd opened for them: tall, pretty, round-faced girls with long black braids, all in the same long scarlet tunics over close-fitting scarlet pants. The crowd, suddenly enthusiastic, cheered and whistled and slapped their thighs as the girls posed for a tableau, then broke all at once into a dervish dance.

The other loudspeakers muted as only one tune came up, mad, whirling, wild, the music of the sun and wind on the open steppe. The braids flew as the girls spun on white high heels, skirts flying up over those long red-silk-covered legs, smiling vivaciously.

Obie was as entranced as everyone around him. When the first pickup came barreling in from a side street, only when one of the Uighurs grabbed him and pulled him down did he look that way.

To catch a confused impression of black flags, spray-painted slogans, and men with black scarves over their faces pointing AKs from the truck beds. Then a confused melange of sight and sound. Trinh shouting in his ear. The *poppoppop* of fire rattling off the buildings. Arms flinging smoking objects. The screech of tires, and a sustained, horrific scream- ing interspersed with thuds as one of the pickups, swerving into the sec- tion reserved for the Han spectators, plowed through human beings one after the other, like a bowling ball through a row of pins.

With heavy, concussive cracks, whatever the guys in the pickups were throwing began going off. The air quaked. Teddy fought free of the hands pulling him down, and stood just as he realized he shouldn't have.

A rattling of bolts came from the troops behind them. He glanced back to see they'd discarded shields and truncheons, and were aiming rifles. He grabbed the also-standing Trinh, and pulled him down as the first volley of full-automatic 5.8mm crackled out over their heads. Trinh grunted and flinched as he went down. Somehow the troupe had disappeared, whisked away. The troops' fire followed the careening trucks, but was knocking down civilians in the shrieking, stampeding crowd as well. The panicked mob rushed the carefully arranged pro- duce displays, upsetting the tables and smashing windows in their desperation to escape the escalating carnage in the confined square, which was rapidly filling with smoke.

Teddy and Fierros and Trinh kept hugging the blood-spattered as- phalt. Someone was shouting commands. The riot troops quick-stepped forward, paused to fire again, then advanced once more. Teddy laced his fingers over his skull and lay very still as heavy black boots marched over him. He tensed for a bayonet-thrust or a shot, but it didn't come. When the soldiers were past he low-crawled to Fierros, who was lying with hands clenched over his head. "Ragger," he shouted.

"Here . . ."

"Nguyen. *Nguyen!*"

But the splatter behind the Viet's head told him the Major had dropped a split second too late. Caught one of the rounds the troops were firing over them, as Teddy had pulled him down. He lay with head cocked, little Ho beard mashed into the glistening asphalt, a puzzled expression on his seamed face. His skull leaked a gray-and-red gruel.

"Nguyen," Teddy said again, hand on the old Viet's birdlike shoulder. Patting it, one last time.

Then, a few yards away, he spotted the rifle.

One dropped, obviously, by the wounded trooper who blinked dazedly at him, lying beside it. Teddy crawled over. Grabbed the rifle, and racked the charging handle as a renewed crackle of fire swept the square.

He glanced at Trinh once more. Then dropped to a knee, grunting as his dead leg all but buckled, and tried to get a sight picture. The optic was queerly perched, too high, too far back on the carry handle. His thumb groped for a safety.

He panned across a bloody, heaped massacre. The pickups were on the far side of the square. One lay wrecked and burning, but the others were still rolling, black flags fluttering, weaving this way and that as they ran down fleeing figures. They'd thrown all their bombs, apparently, but AK fire still popped.

On this side, the government forces were still firing hard. Only not at the attackers, but into the remains of the crowd, trapped between them and the buildings, execution-style. Bodies littered the pavement. Screams and moans filled the air. The four-power scope pulled in an old man's arms raised in plea, a woman's openmouthed scream as she shielded a child. He stared. He'd seen ugly scenes before, but never an SS-style massacre of civilians by troops.

The optic found a soldier speaking into a radio. The crosshairs settled on the back of his helmet. Not more than a hundred yards. Teddy's finger curled. A two-stage let-off. The recoil rocked him back only slightly. Effective straight-line design. It looked weird, but he liked this rifle. His sight picture came back down perfectly, but the trooper wasn't there. He was crumpled to the pavement.

Teddy swept the sight left, then right. Picked out another noncom and fired again. Now if he could only find whoever was giving them orders—

A hand clutched his shoulder. "Oberg. Fuck're you doing?"

"Taking down baddies. They're enemy. Remember?"

"We got three seconds to get out of here before they figure out you're sniping them."

"We aren't getting out, Ragger. There's another rifle over there. Grab it and let's go down shooting."

But the black-clad soldiers had caught on. They were scattering, taking cover. Abandoning their execution-style fusillade, but turning on him. The first shots cracked around them. Bullets whacked and hummed off the pavement.

Teddy flicked the selector to full auto and hosed them down. The return fire slackened, but picked up again as his magazine went dry. And out of the street behind the troops a huge silhouette lumbered, snorted, shouldered its way forward. One of the beetle-black riot trucks, its bulldozer blade raised threateningly.

Teddy rolled for the cover of the TV van, but someone was clutching his leg. The wounded trooper whose rifle he'd grabbed. Teddy buttclubbed the guy until he felt like letting go, and ripped his mag pouch off. Reloaded, he fired out another magazine, ducking out for short bursts. From the other side, Fierros was fumbling at his rifle, but not seeming to understand how to operate it. The volume of incoming kept building. And somebody had a light machine gun. It began ripping chunks out of the van every time he ducked out.

"Where's the Major?" Fierros yelled.

"Dead," Teddy yelled back. "He took one in the head. Sorry."

Obie didn't like having to leave Trinh. It was part of the creed. Never leave your buddy, dead, wounded, or alive. Okay, strictly speaking the Viet wasn't a Team guy. But they'd trekked a long way together. Been through a shitload of hurt.

Anyhow, it didn't seem like he'd have to worry about it much longer. He rolled behind a wheel—the steel in wheels and axles was effective cover—and fired slowly and deliberately, aiming carefully each time. But the truck kept rumbling forward. He put several shots into the windshield, but doubted any of the light bullets made it through that armored glass.

The snarl of other motors behind them jerked his head around. The pickups, flags fluttering, had completed their circuit of the square. The oncoming grilles were smeared with blood and melon pulp. Lean sinewy men with black scarves over their faces braced Kalashnikovs on their hips, firing toward the riot troops. Wildly, without aiming. Though the way the truck bucked and skidded meant they wouldn't have put many bullets into their enemies anyway. Teddy locked gazes with the lead driver, whose scarf was pulled down. Swarthy, black-bearded, his eyes were blasted wide with either drugs or excitement or both as he steered with his right hand and fired a pistol out the window with his left.

A second later the fighters in back grabbed for handholds as the pickup braked, skidded sideways, and rocked crazily to a halt. The driver leaned out and beckoned angrily with the pistol. He had a white streak in his black mustache. Teddy gaped. Then, suddenly, understood.

"Lay down some fire, goddamn it!" he yelled at Fierros. He stood, leveled the rifle, and blasted out the rest of his magazine, walking the crosshairs across the sparkling of muzzle flashes that faced them. The noise was terrific. Every rifle in the square seemed to be on full auto, and a gray smoke eddied over the corpses. His own shots were underlain by a prolonged clatter from the AKs in the truck. When his bolt clicked back empty he burst from behind the van, limping as fast as he could while bullets cracked and snapped around him, nipping at his goatskins. Hands reached down from the pickup. He grunted painfully as he was hauled upward, tumbled over the side, and thrown into the bed like a sack of oats, onto hundreds of spent cartridges, his rifle clutched to his chest. "Ragger," he shouted hoarsely. "Ragger! *Come on!*"

He lay looking up as the pickup jolted forward, bullets *clunk-clunk-clunking* into the sides; as lean, bearded, hostile young faces stared down at him; as the black flags, hand-daubed with what he saw now were verses from the Koran, snapped furiously above them. He rolled up to his knees, pumping the empty rifle over his head. *"Allahu akbar!"* he yelled, grinning as fiercely as they, and they shouted it in return, gesticulating, cursing, firing raggedly back at their enemies as the truck accelerated away, bullets crackling overhead.

19

The East China Sea

M ISSILE eighteen away . . . nineteen away . . ."
At the strike console, Lieutenant Singhe was announcing
each Tomahawk's departure with the grim satisfaction of a professional
executioner.

In Combat, again, still. The dampers had been closed for half an hour
now, but the nitrogenous bitterness of solid-fuel boosters still seeped in.
Air-conditioning had been secured during the launch, and the temperature was climbing.

Dan rubbed his face. Eighteen hours in the saddle. A little while ago
he'd been weary unto death. But the tablets the chief corpsman had
brought up were doing the job. He felt reenergized, spun up, as if he'd
downed eighteen cups of coffee, one after another.

"Twenty away." Eleven seconds . . . "Missile twenty-one, away—"

A weird jubilation kept threatening, a euphoria he had to keep tamping
down. He'd doubted they'd reach their launch point. Now they were here,
a bare hundred miles off Shanghai, and with each minute Task Force 76's
magazines were emptying. American Tomahawks. Korean Hyunmoo-III
land attack rounds. Blazing light blanked the cameras. Cottony smoke
billowed in monitors. Flaming stars lofted, shed boosters, steadied on
their courses, and dwindled, trailing a bourbon haze. Toward radar sites,
comm and command nodes, antiaircraft batteries, airfields, ammunition
dumps.

One look at Cheryl Staurulakis sobered him. Drawn tight, with purple stains under her eyes, she stared with red-rimmed but dry eyes up
at the displays.

When he'd given her the news the night before, in the cramped ruby-lit navigation space behind *Savo*'s pilothouse, she'd squinted up for several seconds before turning away.

"Did you understand what I said, Cheryl?"

"I do understand, Admiral. Thanks for telling me personally."

He'd scratched his chin, unsure how to proceed. Finally decided to offer a smidgen of hope. "They don't give any details about his loss. There's still a possibility he ejected."

"Then they'd carry him as MIA, wouldn't they?"

He'd spread his hands. "I . . . probably, but . . ."

When she'd swung back, there in the tight little space walled with ticking instruments and blue-backed H.O. pubs, her blue eyes were blazing. "They just threw them into those cockpits, Dan. That was his fourth time ever in an F-35."

"I didn't know—"

"They cut the training cycle to a week. Stuck them in a new aircraft and said, 'Go take on the whole Chinese air force.'" She picked up a clothbound ledger. Her hands shook; in the red light the irritated patches on her skin looked black. She stared at the book as if contemplating throwing it across the space, or perhaps at him. Then, after a few seconds, set it aside.

"I'm sorry, Cheryl. I wish we didn't have to lose people. Especially guys like Eddie. If you want to—need some time off, Fred can take over your chair. Or Bart—"

She didn't meet his gaze. "We're going to take more attacks. Enzweiler doesn't know the combat system. Bart's dependable, but he doesn't think fast. I need to be on deck."

He hesitated, unsure again what to do, to say. Words seemed so inadequate. At last he stepped forward and took her in his arms. She braced against his chest, tensely as a torqued-tight wire rope. Her arms were folded, hugging not him, but herself.

"I've got to take care of the ship," she muttered. "Got to forget this. Until later."

Now she sat beside him at the command table, eyes still dry, moving only occasionally to keyboard a command or murmur into a circuit.

"Round twenty-four away . . . rounds complete," Amy Singhe sang out. Why the fuck did she sound so triumphant?

"Secure from strike stations," Staurulakis said into her throat mike. "Admiral, strike package complete. Returning from Strike Condition to Condition One ABM at this time."

"Very well." Dan blew out as the displays winked and changed, the rightmost screen turning amber.

Operation Recoil had begun. Seven other ships and submarines had launched waves of stealth-modified Tomahawks as well. EW reported heavy jamming and spoofing. The SPY-1 picture, linked with radars from *Kristensen, McClung, Hampton Roads, Sejong, Zembiec,* and the reconnaissance drones that patrolled fifty miles out from the task force, occasionally blurred, froze, stalled. But then regenerated as the Aegis team hunched over their consoles, communicating in low curses. Trying to ignore the glitching, Dan kept his attention on the coast.

They'd stirred up the hornet's nest, all right. A hundred miles ahead, the skies were freckled with contacts.

On the display, the great bay of Hangzhou gouged the coast, a square-cornered indentation, as if a chisel had been hammered into northern China. Shanghai lay north of the bay, Ningbo to the south. On the right of the display, the blue carets of friendly air were marching in, spread across a quarter of the screen.

He contemplated them with awe. Over two hundred attack aircraft, from *Nimitz, Vinson, Reagan, Truman,* and *Stennis,* preceded and accompanied by swarms of smaller UAVs. Combined strikes from five heavy carriers: the heaviest punch the U.S. Navy had thrown at an enemy since World War II. After the UAV swarm and fighters swept enemy interceptors from the sky and suppressed the air defenses, the attack squadrons would unload. JDAMs and laser-guided bombs would obliterate oil refineries, power stations, container piers, oil-storage facilities, munitions dumps, bridges, handling cranes, and any ships that thought being in port meant they were safe.

To the northeast, smaller formations were approaching too, with callouts ranging tens of thousands of feet higher. Air Force bombers, nearing the end of a four-thousand-mile, seven-hour-long flight from Alaska. They'd doglegged across the North Pacific, then down the length of the Sea of Japan. They and the Navy would arrive over their targets simultaneously, bringing fifteen minutes of unadulterated inferno.

When they left, yet another wave of Tomahawks from the thirty destroyers and frigates steaming with the carrier strike force would launch. Scheduled to hit an hour after the main strikes ended, they would decimate firefighters, police, medical personnel, repair crews, and anyone else who exited shelter, dazed and concussed, thinking the attack was over.

By that evening, the Shanghai-Ningbo complex should no longer be able to support an invasion of any size, of anyone.

Closer in, wrapped tightly to his task force, fighters from *Gambier Bay* barriered him against air attacks, though the sortie rate was declining as the jeep carrier fell astern. So far they'd fought off three strikes of increasing intensity. None had broken through the tightly woven shield of fighters, data, and missiles Aegis held over the force. Two had come in from the air, with antiship missiles, and one had been a heavy wave of C-802s from batteries near their intended target, the Ningbo base complex. He'd been able to bat each down separately. The only damage had been loss of the second autonomous ASUV, which had gone silent in the middle of the battle. The final incursion had been by a submarine; but it had been swept off the board by a torpedo salvo from *Montpelier.*

So far, no surface forces had sortied from Hangzhou Bay. Had they been so severely attrited that none were left? Above the airfields, contacts swarmed like disturbed ground wasps. Yet oddly enough . . .

"They're not coming out after us," Staurulakis muttered through cracked pale lips.

"Just those air attacks. Which could have been heavier."

"They must know we're here . . . all the megawatts the radars are putting out."

"Oh, they know." He squinted up at the displays, wondering too.

He felt more exposed by the minute, here in the middle of the East China Sea. Intel doubted the PLA Rocket Force had many medium-range missiles left, after the hundreds they'd expended pounding Taiwan and Okinawa. If they'd managed to build more, or buy them from the Russians or their allies the Pakistanis, TF 76 would be a tempting target. But he had three jobs left: SAR, PIRAZ, and ABM. SAR: to linger as a ditching point for any crippled aircraft. PIRAZ: to "sanitize" the returning attack formations, identifying and shooting down any pursuers who tried to tail them back to the carriers. And ABM: screening those carriers, east of the strike force, from anything launched from the mainland.

Like the missile that had destroyed *Roosevelt.* He keyboarded an order pulling the formation in tight around the cruisers. If Zhang responded to the massive attack on the biggest port in China with another thermonuclear warhead, they'd have to cover the rest of the force.

With a sodden-sounding *whunk*, the vents popped open. The fans spooled up. Once again cool air breathed from the diffusers, fluttering the paper streamers someone had taped there. Chin propped on his knuckles, he sat immobile, gaze nailed to the flickering displays.

*   *   *

OVER the next half hour the blue clouds merged with the darting red fireflies above the offshore islands, then over Ningbo itself. He clicked from circuit to circuit, trying to glean some sense of how the battle was going, but jamming was heavy and transmissions were garbled. Every few seconds he checked the high-side chat. Any orders would come through there, not voice.

Loss and damage reports began arriving. The air controller, shadowing the transmissions among the pilots, reported several S-400 anti-aircraft batteries still active. Each time a U.S. plane blinked off the screen, Dan glanced at Staurulakis. But she just nodded. Keeping her head down, typing, or squinting at the displays.

So far, the plan seemed to be working. TF 76 reached the southernmost limit of his box. He checked with *Kristensen*, the ASW coordinator, then brought the formation around to the reciprocal, headed northeast.

On the leftmost display now—the merged feed from the drones, from the other Aegis-capable ships, and from the carriers, behind them—the leading formations detached from the gaggle over the mainland and headed back out to sea. Some lagged their wingmen. Their callouts read slow and low. On the right-hand display, the narrow low-angle beam of *Savo Island*'s own radar, in ALIS mode, fingered the horizon of northern China. Its amber fanlike spokes clicked across hundreds of miles of jagged mountains. Terranova's round face bent over the radar control console, while the Thai physicist hovered perched on a tall stool. But seconds, then minutes, ticked by without the staccato buzz of the launch warning.

He got up abruptly, too hinky to sit any longer, and paced the length of CIC beam to beam. He glanced back at Staurulakis's bowed spine, wishing he could bring her a little reassurance.

But what could he say, other than that the best and most daring died first? Some comfort that would be.

He stopped at the electronic warfare console, where Donnie Wenck was riding the stack operators. Wenck said that what with the jamming from the ground, and the strike group's own jamming from the air, he'd never seen tactical EW this heavy. "Put it on the speaker," he told the operator.

The pulsating whine was like a hundred planing mills, buzzsaws, table saws, going at once. The chief said, "We're freq-hopping as fast as we can. But they're tracking every radar in the task force, wiping us out. They pitch us a couple low-cross-section incomers, it's gonna get brown and lumpy real fast."

Dan grinned unwillingly at the "brown and lumpy," but just nodded.

Jamming explained the freezing screens, the green snowstorms of corrupted data that sleeted the displays from time to time.

Next he stopped at the radar control console, and watched over Terranova's shoulder. ALIS seemed to be punching through, its concentrated beam flicking back and forth, a windshield wiper scrubbing China clean. He patted the Terror's shoulder. She looked back, one quick blank glance, then returned to her screen.

When he got back to the command desk, Mills cleared his throat. "Admiral. On high-side chat: *Reagan*'s detaching from the strike group. Moving closer, with their screen units."

"Moving *closer*? Why?"

"No reason given. I suspect, to recover some of those damaged aircraft. Maybe to back us up as well."

"We could have used more air cover on the way in," he grumbled. But the closer the carriers edged, the more risk they incurred. Or was that the idea? To test the robustness of the remaining forces? Sucker them into a prepared kill zone?

But no one had mentioned a follow-on action. The plan had been to strike, recover, then retire. Not to hang around, giving the enemy time to generate a counterpunch.

Maybe he should clarify what was going on. At his terminal, he typed:

BARBARIAN: Interrogative movement RRR toward enemy coast.

RRR was *Reagan*. A few seconds elapsed. Then:

ENCAPSULATE: Confirmed.

"Encapsulate" was the strike group commander, hundreds of miles behind him on *Truman*. Okay, maybe his question hadn't been clear. He typed

BARBARIAN: Do you require TF 76 to fall back on you?
ENCAPSULATE: Negative. Maintain station pending recovery all
    strikes. Further orders to follow.

"Okay, that's clear enough," Staurulakis observed.

A harrumph. Enzweiler, a laptop under his arm. "I'm available, Admiral, if you should need a relief."

"I don't . . . well . . . maybe for a couple of minutes. Thanks, Fred." He *could* take a leak. And maybe wash his face. He brought the chief of staff up to speed, making sure Cheryl could hear what he was saying. Then let himself out, to use the little head across the p-way from Radio, thirty feet aft of CIC.

When he returned, Cheryl requested permission to come into the wind to launch Red Hawk. A fighter with a shredded wing had gone sinker en route back to *Truman*. The pilot had pulled the curtain twenty miles west of 76's box. Too close to the coast, but he couldn't leave the guy out there. Especially with Staurulakis's gaze on him. "Okay," he said. "But get Strafer off the deck fast as you can, Cheryl. Then return to formation course."

He crossed to the air combat controller and got *Gambier Bay*'s Su-CAPs vectored out to top cover *Savo*'s helicopter. That left the cruiser uncovered at low to medium altitude, but with the rest of the returning strike passing overhead, he felt fairly secure for the time being.

A fresh cup of coffee steamed at the command desk. He got half down before being distracted by Mills, who wanted to discuss repositioning *Hampton Roads* for better coverage. Dan called Soongapurn and Wenck in to join the discussion. After pulling up various programs, he typed the order on the command net. Shortly thereafter, the other cruiser pulled out to the north.

More agonizingly slow minutes inchwormed past. He glanced at his watch, startled to see it was midnight. Or was it noon? No, midnight. Another pill, from Doc Grissett? No more pills. Or maybe another hydrocodone for his fucking neck. How much longer were they going to leave him flapping out here, parading back and forth like a tin duck in a shooting gallery? You could only push your luck so far.

He slid down in his chair and put his head back. Closed his eyes. Just for a second . . .

A hand on his arm brought him snorting out of a doze. Staurulakis. "Something's developing over Okinawa. Also, air activity over Taiwan."

"Fuck . . . we stayed too long."

"What's that, Admiral?"

"Nothing." He blinked grit from his eyes, checking displays as he sucked down the dregs of the coffee. Ugh, glacier cold. How long had he been out?

Yeah, there it was. Air strikes forming up over the ex–U.S. Air Force base at Kadena. He keyed to the callouts, and got J-8s and J-7s.

"Older fighters," Mills said from the TAO seat, squinting at his screen. "Upgraded to land attack, but older airframes. Sending in the second team?"

"Probably, after we took their strip alert out. We gave them time to recover, and patch up the airfield."

More contacts were blinking into existence over Taiwan. Dan keyed to those callouts, and got a surprise. "These guys out of Taipei—"

"Sukhoi-35s," Staurulakis murmured.

Mills gasped. "You're shitting me," he managed at last.

"That's the ID. Su-35s."

"Russians?"

"Sold to the Chinese. The latest and greatest." Her keyboard rattled; she peered at the screen. "Can carry the Kh-31 antiship missile, or the Chinese version, the YJ-91. Mach 3. Hundred-kilo warhead. Passive anti-radar seekers. If they hit the carriers with those—"

"Get this out to Fleet and PaCom." Dan hunched over his keyboard, alternately eyeing displays and typing. Repositioning *Kristensen* and *McClung*, placing them across the line of attack from Okinawa.

Through a haze of fatigue, the heart-squeeze of dream, a cold logic was focusing his brain.

The blitz on the Okinawa fields had shut them down long enough for him to thread the needle in, but now they were reactivating. Yet the Sukhois were even more threatening. If they were carrying antiradiation missiles, he had a dire choice. Either shut down his radars, go blind, or invite the passive seekers to home on the thousands of kilowatts the SPY-1s on his major units were broadcasting.

Or *was* he the target? Wasn't it more likely USS *Ronald Reagan* and her escorts, closing from the east, were the bull's-eyes these strikes were generating for?

The search-and-rescue controller said over the command circuit, *"Red Hawk inbound. Pilot on board. Fifteen minutes to bingo fuel. Wants to know if we're coming to recovery course."*

Dan traded glances with Staurulakis. Put Strafer between the carrier and the threat? A useless sacrifice. Chaff and flares weren't going to fool anything this advanced. If only *Zembiec* had gotten the lasers they'd promised for so long . . . "Pull him back," he muttered. "Hot refuel on whoever's got a clear deck to the south." He snapped off, to the weapons control circuit.

Forty contacts were closing from Okinawa. And they were nearer; even at a lower speed, they'd hit the task force first. Only five from the southwest, from Taiwan, but faster and far better armed. He decided to let *Sejong* and the two other Korean destroyers take on the larger attack, with *Hampton Roads* and *Savo Island* plucking down some of the leaders at long range. With any luck, they might get the rest to drop early and back away. And maybe the carriers could vector some fighters out, cut down their numbers before they arrived. He typed fast.

BARBARIAN: All units Horde, FLASH FLASH ALERT incoming air strikes de Taiwan, Okinawa.

He toggled direct to Encapsulate, the carrier group leader on *Truman*.

BARBARIAN: Request permission retire as previously planned.

Seconds ticked past. This was taking way too fucking long. The closer he could get 76 to the carriers, the more cover they'd have. And the more effective antimissile coverage he could give them. *Concentrate your forces* . . . Instead, they'd strung them out for three hundred miles, pinched in the middle by an island chain with still-active enemy airfields. He clicked to the SAR circuit again. "We got any more pilots in the drink out here?"

"That's a negative, Admiral. The others, no chute seen, no response to radio queries on the SAR frequency."

Staurulakis was looking at him expectantly. He glanced around. Min Su Hwang, eyebrows lifted. Enzweiler, bland face gone pale. The rest were still focused on their consoles.

Back to the command net. He cleared his throat and typed.

BARBARIAN: All units Horde: Immediate execute: Course 100. Speed 30. Maintain formation.

The new course would take him out of the op area and close the enemy's main targets, the carriers. The red carets jumped forward. "Range on those KH-31s," Dan rasped to Mills.

ENCAPSULATE: Disregaard previous message. Immediately execute: course 0 nine zero. All unit reply.

"What the *fuck*," Stauruakis breathed. She pushed back from the desk. "That takes us back toward Shanghai—"

Dan read it again. "This doesn't sound like Encapsulate."

"Or a native English speaker." Hwang bent over him; the Korean liaison put his finger on the screen. "You've got a misspelling. And a misuse of the plural. Is that channel secure?"

Dan typed,

BARBARIAN: Interrogative last from Encapsulate. Suspect penetration of high-side chat.

More lines popped up the moment he hit Enter:

ENCAPSULATE: Disregeard slander from Barbarian. This is admiral. Obey what I say. Course 0 ninety.

ENCAPSULATE: This comm channel compromised. Go to satcomm navy red for voice orders.

ENCAPSULATE: Disregarde other order. Encapsulate orders false. Continue regard this net. Course 0 ninety immediately execute. All will comply.

Commander Jamail stood at his elbow, notebook screen tilted toward Dan. "Launch range on KH-31, from the intel: seventy nautical miles."

Dan rulered on his own terminal, and got a little over a hundred miles to the slower northern gaggle. Aegis was tracking the leaders, bogeys Papa through Tango. The system had designated them to *Hampton Roads* and *McClung*. Dan clicked to the control circuit and asked for *Kristensen* vice the other cruiser. "We have to maintain ABM mode. Keep scanning for ballistics," he explained to Cheryl, who flicked her gaze his way and lifted her shoulders a millimeter.

He plucked the red phone off its socket, hoping whoever had hacked the fleet's satellite-downlinked secret chat hadn't gotten to their voice comms as well. The circuit beeped and synced, and he put the new course out. His units answered, but the voice (not Jung's) answering from *Sejong the Great* sounded doubtful. Dan handed Hwang the handset and asked the liaison to explain it in Korean.

He still didn't hear any clearance from Strike for his turnaround. But they weren't objecting, either.

Wenck, from radar control: "Range to strike Alfa: eighty miles. To strike Bravo: two hundred thirty."

Lenson snapped, "We got it, Donnie. No need for voice announcements."

"Sorry, Admiral."

"Stand by to take tracks 1531, 1532, 1533, 1522 with Standard enhanced range."

A deafening buzz racketed. Heads snapped around. The Aegis operations specialist announced, "Cuing from AWACS. Profile plot, Meteor Alfa. Elevation forty thousand . . . fifty thousand . . . moderate climb out. Identified as hostile TBM. ID as hostile. Launch point . . . near Gwangju, South Korea. No impact point yet."

Shit, he hadn't even known there was an AWACS up. Before he could react Soongapurn called, "Slow climbout, that's liquid-fueled. Single stage, medium range. Looks like a Nodong."

"North Korean," Mills supplied, punching a pub from the ref shelf. "But they fired from South Korea—"

"It's road mobile," Soongapurn supplied, behind them now. "On transporters. They trucked them south once the armistice was signed."

Dan felt nothing. Just the icy detachment that seemed to take him when he got past fatigue, and past fear, into life-or-death mode. A place he didn't like, and had hoped never to inhabit again. Yet here he was.

The buzzer went off again. "Second launch," Terranova announced. Then a third racketed into the cold air. And a fourth.

The Chinese might be fresh out of medium-range ballistics, but their allies weren't. They'd trundled them down to the end of the peninsula, to help Zhang secure the sea lanes. And further threaten Japan, no doubt . . . Dan wrenched his attention back to the command net. The false strike group commander was still trying to steer them westward. No one was buying it, though, and most of the stations had signed off that chat room.

Staurulakis murmured, "Meteors Alfa through Delta acquired. Assigning Alfa and Delta to *Hampton Roads*. We'll take Bravo and Charlie."

"Manage it, Cheryl. I'm going to try to . . ."

But he couldn't think of anything more to do.

He'd turned the formation around. Without authorization, but he'd generated the best defensive screen he could manage, given the numbers and the threat. Everything else was delegated.

"Meteor Alfa, point of aim generated."

"Roll FIS to green?" Mills asked Staurulakis. The Firing Integrity switch wasn't really a safety, but it ended up being used that way.

"FIS to green." She unlooped the chain from around her neck and inserted the key. With the other hand, she depressed the 21MC lever.

"Bridge, CO. Pass 'Circle William' throughout the ship. Launch-warning bell forward and aft." She flicked up the red cover over the Fire Auth switch. ALIS had been computing intercept parabolas since initial detection. She clicked the switch over. Now the system would react as programmed, triggering at the moment kill probability peaked.

Four missiles shimmered on the screen, aimed right at the task group. A down-the-throat shot. Dan opened his mouth, then closed it again. Terranova and Soongapurn were already calling out the litany of engagement.

The deckplates rattled as, one after another, six SM-Xs exited their cells in blasts of flame. On the screen half a dozen blue carets hurtled outward. Picking up the initial guide beam, as far as he could tell. With three interceptors assigned to each descending warhead between the two cruisers, they should stand a decent chance. Of course, the price differential was about six to one, advantage Pyongyang . . . but that wasn't his worry. He leaned back, kneading his neck as he watched the air strikes continue to close on him.

Then he noticed something.

The strike out of Kadena *wasn't* heading for him.

Or rather, it *had* been, but had just altered course. On the display, its extended track was clicking around counterclockwise.

"Strike Alfa altered course to the east," the TAO said, leaning across.

"I'm catching that, Matt." Dan squinted up, getting a bad feeling. "Yep. They're headed for the carriers now."

"Concur. Crossing engagement? Whittle their numbers down, at least."

"How far to their ordnance release point?"

Staurulakis answered. "Ten miles if they're launching on us. Forty-some if they're targeting *Reagan*. I passed a heads-up."

"Got an acknowledgment?"

She nodded, pressing headphones to her temples. "Gaggle Bravo's altering too," Mills said. "Also toward the carrier."

More unwelcome news . . . when he ratcheted his rulers the ranges looked bad. On their new headings, both strike groups would shortly be opening his task force. His antiair Standards were fast, but not all that much faster than a modern fighter on balls-to-the-wall afterburner. An overtaking engagement both shortened their effective range and dropped the probability of kill.

The carriers had already fought off two attacks. They were still trying to recover aircraft; couldn't launch new fighters, or at any rate, not many. The COs of their destroyers had to be watching their weapons inventory displays with the same sinking feeling he had himself.

On the other hand, TF 76 was churning back toward them.

On this hand, on the other . . . Maybe the real question was, how did the strike leaders, riding with the lead elements of those hurtling J-8s, J-9s, and Sukhois, know where the carriers were? Since their mayfly-delicate drones had been swept from the sky?

He had his hand over the socketed handset when the red light lit. The speaker above his head beeped and synced. *"Barbarian, this is Encapsulate."*

He pressed the phone into the crook of his shoulder, pressing the Sync button with his cheekbone as he worked the keyboard with both hands. "Barbarian. Over."

"Dan, this is Encapsulate actual. Have to ask something hard of you. Gangbusters. I say again, Gangbusters. Over."

He couldn't help gulping, but kept his tone flat. "This is Barbarian. Copy, Gangbusters. Standing by."

Cheryl was staring at him, aghast. The others were too. "No," someone muttered. "Not us." But Donnie Wenck was grinning like a madman. Interlacing his fingers, twisting them this way and that, like a concert pianist warming up. Then placing them delicately on the radar control keyboard.

"Going dark of the moon in thirty seconds. Good luck, and thanks."

"Barbarian, roger, out," Dan said. Wishing, as soon as he clicked off, he'd said something more memorable for his last recorded words. Something they could chisel into his tablet in Memorial Hall. How noble and sweet it was to die for . . . no, that wouldn't fly. This wouldn't be noble, or sweet.

Just fucking necessary.

"Dan?" Cheryl, looking concerned. Or scared. "What did he say? Was it, *emulate*?"

He muttered past the handset, "Yeah. Stand by to squawk flattop."

She blinked at him. Then clicked to the EW circuit, and spoke into it in a low, stern voice, as if giving an order that might be disobeyed.

Dan gripped the edge of the command desk. Trying to deny, fight off, the image that kept shooting through his mind.

A lavender beam of fire. From one side of the compartment to the other.

Shearing off heads, necks, upper arms. Leaving charred trunks and flying flame.

The EW operator called, "*Truman* and *Reagan* off the air. No radar. No comms."

Staurulakis rubbed her mouth. For the first time, she looked as if she'd forgotten about her husband's death. "Okay, we're—squawking flattop. Emulating the carrier."

He nodded.

Radars. Other emitters. Even fake comms with the carrier air patrol, prerecorded and broadcast on the proper frequencies.

In the darkness that covered the deep, by the invisible emanations by which war guided itself in the twenty-first century, *Savo Island* looked just like the carrier now.

Five minutes later, both groups of enemy aircraft changed course again.

Back toward Task Force 76.

20

SCRATCHING the cracks between her fingers, Cheryl Staurulakis peered up at the display. Calculating their chances.

Yet her gaze kept being drawn back to the weapons inventory screen. Only three ABM rounds left. Enough for a reengagement, if these failed, but no more.

She leaned back, scratching harder. Until she felt the warm ooze of blood.

She stared down at it. Had Eddie had time to bleed? Wounded in the cockpit of his bright new fighter? Or had he died instantly, stunned and shredded? A tissue from the packet she kept in the drawer blotted the flow. But bright red spots bled through. . . .

Carriers had no business this near the coast. Whoever had ordered them to close the now-alerted defenses was taking a hell of a risk. She'd passed the warning, but *Truman* and *Vinson* would still be maneuvering to recover their returning aircraft. They had their own destroyer screen, but she didn't know how their inventories were holding up. Glancing at the display, she guesstimated the distance to the carriers. Not yet near enough for *Savo* to cover them.

When the Gangbusters order came in, she tensed as Lenson rogered. When he signed off it took him two tries to resocket the handset.

"Did I hear 'Gangbusters'?" she murmured. "Did you say *'emulate'*?"

"Yeah. Stand by to squawk flattop."

She started to protest. Then realized there was no way she could.

That was a cruiser's reason for being, after all. Why *Savo* and her sisters had been designed, equipped, manned, tested, against this very moment.

Protect the higher-value unit.

Still she muttered, so low no one other than Mills could have overheard, "Dan. There can't—you couldn't light up—"

Lenson looked as if he were being torn in two. "Someone *else*? I can't sacrifice *Sejong*. Not politically possible. *Savo*'s, um, the oldest unit out here. And you're nearly out of ABM rounds." His gaze slid off hers. "I'm sorry."

She sat frozen for a second. Both horrified and ashamed. Then, forcing her fingers to function, clicked to the EW circuit. "CO."

"EW, aye."

She blinked at the bloody fingerprints she left on the selector switch. "Make all preparations to squawk Gangbusters. I say again, Gangbusters."

For a second no answer came. Then the voice at the far end repeated the command, acknowledging.

Beside her Mills was typing, transferring command of *Savo*'s in-flight SMs. The missiles got updates, refining their guidance second by second. *Hampton Roads* would have to handle that now, until the third stage popped the nose cone, exposing the seeker.

The EW operator called, *"Truman* and *Reagan* off the air. No radar. No comms." Then a moment later, over the IC circuit. "Radiating Gangbusters—*now*."

The radar picture jittered, faded, changed. Of course: they couldn't both emulate the carrier's radar and gain the optimal picture the SPY-1s provided. Which meant not only that they were attracting the hornets, but that the warheads plunging downward toward them could not be refired on if their first salvo missed. She rubbed her mouth, then remembered: *the blood.* When she pressed her sleeve to her face the material came away blotched red. "Okay, we're—squawking flattop."

The steel around her seemed to snap into focus, in a way it hadn't since Lenson had given her the news last night. She squeezed Mills's arm. "Can you think of anything else we should be doing?"

He evaluated the displays. "We've been at GQ for over twenty hours, Captain. If we aren't ready by now . . . Just get set to let everything fly, I guess. I'll tell the Army guys aft to spin up the Stingers. And we should probably come bow-on to Group Alfa. If they have 802s, they're gonna slide in low, all together."

She leaned past him. "Admiral, should we pull everyone in tighter? Interlock fires?"

He seemed torn. Probably still fearing a nuke. But the two dozen–plus aircraft bearing down were a more immediate danger. "Probably not a bad idea," he said at last, picked up the red phone, and started assigning new stations.

Which they had only minutes to slip into . . . *Savo* heeled as she came to the new course. Cheryl took a deep breath. What was the worst that could happen? That she'd be with Eddie tonight?

No. There were worse things than that. Such as getting her whole crew killed. "Let's get some Standards out there," she told Mills. "Take down the leaders. Maybe that'll give the others second thoughts."

The deckplates tremored. White smoke billowed on the cameras. Over the next minutes eight enhanced-range Standards bolted from their cells, reoriented, and streaked off to the north, leaving contrails that glowed phosphorescent in the dark. *Savo*'s combat system transferred control to *Kristensen*. She noted the time. Still an hour before dawn. The networked picture showed the other task force units launching as well. The system deconflicted them automatically, ensuring no more than two weapons were assigned to each target.

"Stand by for intercept, Meteor Bravo," Soongapurn called. Reminding her that they still had North Korean ballistic warheads burning down toward them. Two for *Savo*, two for *Hampton Roads*.

Cheryl put her hand on Lenson's sleeve. "Dan. Sir. Can I secure Gangbusters? We're standing by for intercept."

He hesitated, squinting at the displays. Then nodded. "Both gaggles are guiding on us now. Back to ABM mode."

The rightmost screen blinked, changed, zoomed.

On a hot, brilliantly white dot, glowing violently in the far infrared. As the warhead plunged through the upper atmosphere, it grew both its infrared signature and an ionization trail. The electrically charged plume actually generated a more pronounced radar return than the metal at its heart. The pulsating brackets of the system lock-on displayed more jerkiness than she liked. The display abruptly lurched from it to another burning white dot, making her stiffen. But then it snapped back. ALIS was switching its attention between the two incoming terminal bodies assigned to *Savo*. The other pair, Cheryl would just have to take on faith that the other cruiser was handling.

She gripped her desk, ignoring the sticky bloodstains she must be leaving. A chill harrowed her back. Watching the bullet aimed at you, as it came in . . . waiting for it to hit . . .

"Intercept, Meteor Bravo . . . *now*," called the Terror.

The brackets jerked, slewing off, tumbling through space. They swerved up, down, left, right, before locking once more.

Cheryl squinted up at the vibrating slushy image. Instead of a single pip, tumescent with ionization, the screen showed three separate returns. Each dimmed, then rebrightened, but at different rates, like uncoordinated strobes.

The brightening and dimming was a deformed body tumbling through space. Varying its radar cross section. Disintegrating, under the massive g-forces of hypersonic reentry.

"Meteor Bravo, breakup," Terranova called. "Shifting to Meteor Charlie."

The screen jerked and zoomed back, hunted, then drilled back in as the brackets snagged the second warhead. The trail of this comet, the nimbus of superheated, radar-reflecting ionosphere, was larger than that of the first. A heavier payload? Or just a stouter airframe, holding together better?

The air controller called, *"Hampton Roads* reports hard kill, Meteor Alfa."

Terranova yelled over his words, "Stand by for intercept, Meteor Charlie . . . *now."*

This time the lock-on stuck tight. A bloom of return coruscated silently onscreen. Flame? Gas? The new kinetic-kill heads carried no explosives. Sheer velocity drove their destructive power. But something odd was happening. . . . "What's that look like to you, Doctor?" she called to Soongapurn.

The MDA physicist was frowning. "I'm not certain . . . looks like some damage, but . . ."

"Stand by for second round intercept—"

The falling comet stayed rock steady. "Miss," someone breathed.

Okay, a miss, but she'd targeted three homers against each incomer. One had yet to hit. The ionizing blur kept growing. The picture pulled back to encompass its swelling bloom. Deep in its center, like a shrunken star after a supernova, the warhead itself glowed. *One thousand, two thousand* . . . as she reached eleven, the picture rocked again.

"Fuck," someone murmured.

A momentary bloom, with fragments hurtling off like sparkling fireflies. But the main body still pulsed slowly. Rotating, but still in one piece.

Soongapurn: "Meteor Charlie, still on trajectory. Call that as a hit on the airframe, maybe, not the warhead."

A line came up on chat.

MONITOR: Meteor Delta, two-round salvo, no apparent effect.

"Shit . . . they missed too. Are these things fucking *armored*? Give me camera, bearing zero-one-five true," she muttered to Mills. The TAO grabbed the joystick, and the rightmost display slewed, rolled up, down, steadied.

A spear of flame appeared, descending from the azimuth. On the far horizon, grayed now with the first taste of dawn, a black silhouette. She'd lost her bearings. Wasn't sure, in that half second, which ship it was.

A tremendous flash blanked the camera. Then, seconds later another, even brighter, even closer. When they faded, leaving drifting afterimages, the bridge talker called, "Lookouts report two explosions on the horizon. Bearing two-eight-zero relative."

Beside her Lenson said tightly into the red phone, "This is Barbarian. All units Horde, report damage. Report ionization effects. Check background radiation and report readings. Over."

A rumbling boom reached them. A low-frequency vibration waned, then waxed again. The vibrations tuning-forked away along the resonating length of the hull girder, dwelled, grew faint, and died away.

She exchanged glances with a stricken-looking Lenson. He murmured, "Do you call those as nukes?"

Mills leaned over. "Maybe some kind of partial detonation?"

"I don't think so," she said. "Not *two* partial detonations." She hit the 21MC. "OOD, CO. Anything from the PDR-65?" The radioactivity detection, indication, and computation system, installed on every warship's bridge.

"CO, bridge. Nothing yet. Continuing to monitor."

She checked the wind gauge. Five knots, from the west. If there was a radioactive plume, they'd get it. "Turn on the water washdown?" she mused to Mills.

"We'd degrade our sensors," he said. "We start spraying salt water, we'll blind ourselves."

"All right, good point. Hold off until we have a beep from the 65. Secure from ABM mode. Go to antiair, full automatic."

"Could just be a very heavy conventional payload," Enzweiler put in, behind them.

One by one, the task force reported in. The CIC officer made a tick mark on the call sign board as each rogered up. When the last ship was checked off, Lenson heaved a sigh, as if he'd been holding his breath. He told the chief of staff to get on Navy Red and report what they knew. "Don't call it as a nuke. Just say, heavy explosion. *McClung* reports light blast effects topside. Otherwise, TF 76, no damage."

Cheryl switched her attention back to the incoming air strike. Which was now only forty miles distant, with thirty-eight contacts. The enhanced-range Standards had marched outward toward the leaders during the minutes the Nodongs had consumed in their descents, their respective destructions or survivals, and their detonations. Other blue symbols, many more, marked weapons from the Korean units, *McClung*, and *Kristensen*, following *Savo*'s initial salvo. She hoped Aegis was deconflicting properly. Seconds ticked by as the markers marched toward the incoming strike.

"Vampire, vampire, vampire," the EW operator called. "Multiple vampires, bearing one-six-zero to one-seven-five degrees true. X-band seekers. Correlate with C-802s. *Many* vampires."

"They're dropping early," Mills muttered.

The lead aircraft began turning away. A few of those following did too. As they wheeled away, the display populated with smaller contacts, as if each had spawned copies of itself.

But *Savo*'s Standards were loose among them. The callouts blinked, spinning downward and upward, documenting radical course and altitude changes. Last-minute maneuvers, by pilots desperately trying to evade their oncoming fates.

Maybe Eddie's last seconds had been like that. . . .

"Three bogeys, headed for the deck."

"Intercept . . . intercept."

"CIC, bridge: still nothing on the PDR-65."

Contacts turned, banked, milled about the screen. Some winked out for good.

But the red carets of the incoming antiship missiles jumped ahead second by second, closing on *Kristensen*, *Hampton Roads*, *Sejong*, and *Savo*. Dozens of them, scores. Too many, really, to count.

"Deploy chaff and rubber duckies," Cheryl put out over Weps Control. "Phalanx, 20mm, Stingers, action starboard. —EW, spoof these guys, jam 'em, get 'em off our ass! We're depending on you."

"On it," Chief Wenck called.

Above them dull thuds thumped like bass drums as the chaff mortars began to go off, flinging hot-burning infrared flares and millions of strips of aluminum foil into the dawning air.

DAN pushed back from the command desk. His coveralls were wringing wet and icy cold. Cold doom chilled his bones, too. Not from what they'd just evaded, screaming down from the heavens. Nor from what was incoming.

But from the fatal numbers that flickered on the inventory screen.

Savo's magazines were emptying. Each incoming antiship missile required at least two rounds to have a decent chance of knocking it down. Those that penetrated, and that Wenck failed to fox electronically, would be met by five-inch VT rounds, last-minute Stingers, then drumfire from the CIWS.

But there were too many incomers. He'd given up after counting thirty. Aegis had been designed to counter mass attacks, but any defense could be overwhelmed.

"Bird eleven away . . . bird twelve away . . ."

"*McClung* reports all Standards expended—"

Fragments of speech. Bursts of transmissions. But only a sidebar, now, to the automatic responses of their digital nervous system. Directed and coordinated by millions of lines of code, Task Force 76 fought now as an immense robot. A hundred-thousand-ton Terminator, flung across sixty miles of sea.

"Vampire bearing one-six-four, take with guns."

Slam.

Slam.

Dust drifted from the overhead, sparkling in the heating, unventilated air. The five-inch guns, aft and forward, were quickly joined by the bass roar of the Phalanxes, then the rapid cracks of the 25mms.

In the flight deck camera, bright points, low to the sea. One grew, but without changing its bearing. A shaft of fire darted out at it, followed by two more as it bored in. Stingers, fired from atop the hangar. Then streams of tracers reached out. The heavy loud *BRRRR* of the Phalanxes tremored the ship.

An explosion. Out of it, tumbling end over end, blunt wings. A flash of flames, blossoming into smears of flying fire. But still something black was coming directly at the camera, rotating rapidly, like old newsreels of shot-down Zeros crashing into carriers. He tensed, gripping his helmet.

The camera went blank. The Phalanxes cut off abruptly. The superstructure shook to a heavy impact, resounding like a struck bell. Lights flickered. The displays faltered, went blank; then lit again, repopulating. A rising whine came from somewhere. A motor, spinning out of control? Then he realized it was a scream.

"Damage report," Cheryl was saying urgently into the 21MC. "Bridge, I need damage reports."

"*Missile hit aft, starboard side, vicinity frame 200,*" the 1MC announced. "*Repair three provide. Damage reports to the bridge.*"

"CIC, bridge. Aft lookout reports hit to upper part of the hangar area. Right about where the Stinger guys were."

"Stinger team, come in," Cheryl was saying urgently. "Stinger team, Army, are you on the line?"

"*CO, Damage Control: Fire, heavy damage, starboard boat deck area.*"

"*CO, Air Control: four F-18s launching for SuCAP, heading our way.*"

"At last," Fred Enzweiler murmured. "About fucking time."

The displays flickered again. Dan pulled his attention away, trying to concentrate on the rest of his force. *Zembiec, Sejong the Great,* and *Hampton Roads* had formed one mutually supporting group, a few miles from the second, of *Savo, Kristensen,* and *McClung.* Reports began to come in. *McClung* had been hit hard, with fourteen wounded and no count yet on KIA. *Kristensen* had absorbed two missiles, both striking well aft, wiping off her after five-inch mount and her Harpoon launchers. Both reported they were fighting fires and nearly out of ordnance. *Zembiec, Sejong,* and *Hampton Roads* were still untouched.

But the activation of Gangbusters had done what it was supposed to: attracted the incoming aircraft to *Savo* instead of *Reagan.*

He caught sandalwood and sweat as Amy Singhe bent over him. "They hit us hard," she murmured. Strong fingers dug into the knotted muscle of his shoulders.

He leaned back, closing his eyes, but feeling unreal. Getting a chair massage from a beautiful woman in the middle of a battle? Not exactly PC, but hell, bring it on. "We screened the carrier."

"You pulled the strike onto us instead? That's what we just did?"

He shrugged her hands off. It felt great, but Staurulakis was eyeing them. And he had to agree. A massage before imminent death was one thing . . . but now that it looked as if they might pull through, it was definitely inappropriate. At the same moment, Mills leaned over. "We're getting some kind of near-sea return from bearing 215 degrees."

Dan pulled a sleeve across his forehead. "What kind of return? Range?"

"Sixty miles. Intermittent. Nothing from EW on that bearing."

"Strike Bravo's still a hundred and thirty miles out," Staurulakis put in.

Dan eyed the display. "Nothing on Aegis."

"It's not sure it's a contact yet."

"Got a speed? A course?"

"Too intermittent." As if guessing what he'd ask next, Mills said, "Commander Jamail said range on the KH-31s was seventy miles."

"So they couldn't have launched yet? The SU-35s, Gaggle Bravo?" But as soon as he asked it, he knew he couldn't depend on the intel alone. "We have to assume there's something there. —Fred, get us reoriented. The three damaged units haul out to the north. *Zembiec, Sejong, Hampton Roads,* move up to the south."

But the callouts were coming up now. In red.

With each update from the SPY-1, they jumped ahead in giant strides.

"Twenty miles and closing fast," Mills breathed. "Christ, they're coming in hypersonic!"

Blue carets winked on from *Zembiec* and *Hampton Roads.* The last defensive missiles clicked outward, but more slowly than the incoming weapons were traveling. Within seconds, Dan could see they weren't going to reach them in time.

"Go EMCON silent?" Mills asked urgently. "Shut down Dan?"

They looked to him, but he nodded to Staurulakis. "Ask your CO."

Cheryl bit her lip. "We shut down, we lose targeting. The gun radar. Phalanx. And jamming. No. We stay up."

From the EW console: "Vampire, vampire! X-band seekers. Correlates with KH-31 seeker head."

"Fire chaff—"

Mills said quietly, "Tubes are empty, ma'am. Never reloaded. Too much fire and smoke topside. If those things are infrared guided, they'll home on us just by those fires."

She reached for the 21MC. Pushed the DC Central button. "Water washdown," she snapped. "Shipwide. Right now."

The 1MC announced, *"All hands retire within the skin of the ship. Set Circle William throughout the ship. Initiate water washdown."* In the one remaining topside camera, a nimbus of fog burst out along the side as dozens of sprinklers activated.

The topside washdown was designed to sluice away fallout, but maybe she could reduce their infrared signature. Blend the ship with the sea around her.

What the hell. It was all she had left.

A terrific shock whipped the deck from beneath her, knocking down everyone on his feet, jerking and whiplashing those buckled into chairs.

Something snapped in her arm where she'd been leaning on it, and her head glanced off the desktop as it came up to meet her skull. A white flash. A bewilderment.

Then another jolt, even harder, whipping the deck up and then down in an undulation like shaking out a carpet. Only this one was steel, beamed with heavy stringers. She grabbed at the arm of her chair, which bucked like a mechanical bull. A console operator staggered back, pawing at a mask of blood under his flash hood.

The whole ship groaned, crying out, as the twin Phalanxes aft fired *BRRR BRRR BRRRRRRRR.*

Slam.

SLAM. More echoing detonations whipcracked them. The air seethed with dust. Papers fluttered. Screens went dark. Lights burst, and shards of glass pinged off consoles and tabletops. A scorching stink like worn-out brake pads filled the air. The 1MC said something, or started to, in the boatswain's excited voice, before it cut off.

The consoles went dark. The large-screen displays blanked. The fans in the consoles descended the scale. With a chatter of relays, the yellow battery-powered battle lanterns mounted in the corners came on, firing dim cones of tallow light through choking, smoky air, outlining staggering figures tugging on EEBDs and gas masks.

Gritting her teeth, Cheryl set her left arm—which felt like it was broken—in her lap, and with the other hand clicked to the sound-powered circuit. A babble of voices. Finally Chief McMottie's growl quieted them. *"For Christ's sake, pipe the fuck down! Damage reports!"*

All four hits had been to starboard, more or less spaced along the side. Only one seemed to be a penetration near the waterline, but that, unfortunately, was fairly far aft, which placed it somewhere in Auxiliary Machinery Room #2, #1 main switchboard, and Main Engine Room #1. Even worse was McMottie saying both engine-control consoles had tripped off. She pressed Transmit. "Chief, CO. Can you get them back online?"

"Can't tell yet, ma'am. Hell of a shock when that last one hit."

"These are the same panels that went down before?"

"Back when the tsunami wave slammed us in the Indian Ocean, yes, ma'am. It's the grounding on the panels. We tried to get it fixed when we were in the yard, but they always said too hard, take too long." A pause, as he shouted to someone else. *"Uh, can I get back to you? I got to work this—"*

"We need those engines, ASAP. Is Mr. Danenhower down there with you?"

"No shit, ma'am. Working it. CHENG's in DC Central, I think." He clicked off.

Lenson wanted an update. She couldn't give him much, just that they'd lost main engines and power to both shafts, and all the gas turbine generators. "When can you get them back?" he asked. "We need power. I can't manage this formation without comms, without radar. You can't defend yourself either."

She unzipped the top of her coveralls and tucked her arm in, gasping at the pain. She bit back an angry reply. "Bart and the master chief are working it, Admiral."

Relays chattered, and the battle lanterns went off. Then came back on again. Flashlights flickered from the consoles. Frightened voices rose, before a shouted order silenced them.

The smoke got thicker, the air hotter. Clicking from circuit to circuit, she tried to raise the pilothouse. But no one answered. Had one of the hits taken them out? "I'm going up to the bridge," she said, pulling her gas mask out of the carrier. "Until we get power back, I can't do a thing from down here."

Lenson raised a hand as if to stop her, then dropped it. She crossed to the watertight door and set her palm to it. Warm, but not hot. She undogged it and jerked it open. Smoke flooded in. She pushed her shemagh back, set the mask to her face, sucked in rubber-smelling air to hold it there, snapped the spider around her ponytail with her good hand, and tested it. Tight. She stepped through, into a smoky murk probed with flashlight beams, and dogged the door firmly behind her.

TWO decks down and far aft, a diminutive strawberry blonde in scrubs positioned herself on a wire-basket Stokes litter. Two smoke-stained repair party team members in dripping-wet oversuits stood gripping the other side.

"He got a name?" the older man beside Duncanna Ryan said.

"No tags, no name tag," one of the HTs rasped, coughing. "But he's an Army guy, from the Stinger battery. They say he was trying to heave one of his rounds overboard when it cooked off."

"Hold his head. Goddamn it, think about the spine! Ready. One, two, three," the chief corpsman, Grissett, said, and they grunted together as they shifted the flaccid bundle on the litter onto the operating table set up in the center of sick bay. The new hospitalman seaman, Kimura, swung out stainless steel overhead lamps from their stowage against the bulkhead. One lamp tinkled as it swayed, broken with the shock of the explosions. Two others clicked on, illuminating what lay beneath with the brightness of noon.

The body was a wrecked horror, torn apart, then roasted. It seemed impossible, but he was still breathing, panting as if after a hard run. Grissett bent to listen to heart and lungs. "Respiratory distress. Impending failure. Ryan, get the IV in. Kimura, get his clothes off. If they're unconscious, the first intervention is to intubate. Watch how I'm doing this!"

Forcing numb hands into motion, she slid in an IV, then hung a plasma bag. The other corpsman seized heavy cast shears and began cutting off bloody clothing, torn, scorched flash gear, half-melted nylon webbing. "Done with us?" one of the HTs said, a heavyset, muscular woman.

"We got him," Grissett murmured. "How many more are there?"

"A lot," said the woman. "Mainly burns. They're screamin' up there. Can't you hear 'em?"

"Well, bring us the next one. —Dunkie, what have we got?"

Steeling herself, she peeled back a torn sleeve.

Under the shredded, bloody cloth, the arm was gone.

Though not all of it. Some unimaginable force had stripped all the flesh away. The bone beneath gleamed white and pink. It smelled like freshly cooked pork. She swallowed, trying not to barf.

"Good thing he had his flak jacket on. Check the other side," Grissett muttered. "Shit, look at that bleeding. We're gonna need a central line, some O neg blood. Lactated Ringers."

When Kimura cut through the other sleeve, Ryan swayed and had to grip the table. The other arm was gone too. Just a macerated stump, and more flesh flayed off down to bone.

Grissett murmured, "Traumatic amputation of both upper extremities. Massive hemorrhage. Pupils equal. Heart rate regular and fast. This guy needs a surgeon, but we're all he's got. You kids ready?"

Duncanna made herself nod, but this was the first time she'd seen an injury like this.

Muffled voices approached again, out in the passageway. A thud made her flinch. But it wasn't another rocket hit. Just a litter-corner whacking the steel jamb of the sick bay. When she stepped to the door and glanced out, her lips tightened. The stretcher bearers weren't bringing them in. They'd just laid the wounded end to end down the narrow corridor, leaving only enough space to walk. Four, five . . . no, six men and women lay moaning and bleeding on the terrazzo. Plus silent ones who lay perfectly still . . . "We're gonna need help down here, Chief," she said. "We got molto wounded. Maybe some dead."

"Get out there in the passageway, Dunkie. Airway, breathing, circulation. Don't fixate on the visible injuries; remember to palpate for internal injury. Try to stop the bleeding when you can. Tourniquets are nice, but they're not limb-salvage devices. We don't have a vascular surgeon, so I'm gonna have to amputate. Kim and I'll treat, you morphine and triage."

"Me? I'm not qualified to—"

"Yeah, you. Pick out our next one. Man up, Dunkie, it's up to us to save them."

She grabbed a fistful of syrettes from the open can and went from litter to litter, icy inside. Bending to lift a bandage that exposed pink-and-gray intestine, to turn a head whose breath bubbled blood through a gashed throat, to inspect chemical burns, flash burns on exposed skin, take mental status and vitals so she knew who could wait and who needed to see Grissett right now.

She'd drilled it, yeah. But this wasn't moulage, the fake plastic wounds they'd trained on. Each body had its own smell, its own glistening, fluid-pulsing horror. Blood, urine, meningeal fluid, and water slicked the deck. The corridor stank of phosphorus, propellant, feces, and burnt bacon. She tightened tourniquets, cleared airways, took pulses, injected succinylcholine so they didn't fight the tube, set up drips, sealed gaping chest wounds with adhesive-edged bandages, injected morphine and lidocaine and norepinephrine, traced letters and the time of administration on pallid foreheads. Hands groped for the leg of her coveralls, clutched, weakened, fell away. One of the limp bodies began convulsing, boots drumming on the deck, then turned its head and died.

More casualties arrived. Their stertorous breathing and hoarse, hacking coughs echoed in the passageway. She dragged oxygen bottles out. Most cases of severe smoke inhalation ended up on the vent. Better sooner than later, due to edema.

"Help me," someone murmured. "Tell my wife . . ."

As Grissett shouted for the next casualty, a heavyset black man staggered around the corner and fell to his knees. He too was in Army camo. His face hung in charred rags, showing bone beneath. Fluid dripped from this ruin, staining the front of his uniform. He knelt there for several seconds, watching her with eyes that wept blood, then struggled up and grabbed the other end of the litter she was trying to drag.

"You're wounded," she muttered, straining under the weight.

"Not bad as some. I got medic training. Washed out, but I remember. I'll give you a hand."

"You're burned. Your face—"

"Let's get these guys taken care of first."

"Jeez, that would be great. Just let me get a bandage on you. . . . Can you do the vitals? That would really help. And bag that guy over there? There's body bags in the med locker. What's your name? What do I call you?" She couldn't read his name tag for all the blood.

"Custis, babe. Jus' Custis."

IN a vestibule off the helo hangar, Bart Danenhower checked his mask. He peered through the circular porthole, but couldn't see the sea. Only eddying smoke. Flames crackled, and something let go with an echoing boom. He picked up a portable fire extinguisher, touched the door gingerly with the back of his other hand, then pulled his glove back on and undogged it.

When he stepped out the wind was at his back. The sea, twenty feet down, was coated with yellow powder and a rainbow slick of fuel. Flames darted and smoked along the swells, but hadn't yet caught over much of the spill. Maybe the wind was driving the fire back. *Savo* was rolling slightly, but otherwise lay dead in the water. He searched the horizon for help, but it rocked empty, empty, empty.

Both engines off the line, #1 switchboard gone, #1 gas turbine generator wrecked, something wrong with the emergency switchboard . . . *Savo*'s former chief engineer swung to look forward.

Flames racked the starboard side, but he couldn't see much. Just smoke, wreckage, flames, bent metal, pieces of aluminum, and here and there, bodies.

One was on fire a few steps away, hanging over the edge of a pit blasted out of the main deck. He pulled the pin and aimed the extinguisher. A frosty cone of carbon dioxide blasted out, instantly quenching the flames. He waved it over the body, then knelt to drag the recumbent form up onto the deck. When he turned it over, though, he might as well not have bothered. The upper chest and throat were hollowed away as if by some huge, sharp-bladed ice-cream scoop.

Forms in metallic-looking oversuits emerged from the smoke, rolled the corpse into a litter, glancing at him through curved faceplates, and trudged off again, vanishing.

Getting to his feet again, Danenhower leaned out over the lifelines, inspecting the hull. The floating yellow powder was moving. Water was sucking into the side. He could feel the incline already. They were heeling at least five degrees.

He unholstered his Hydra, then pushed his mask up. The first breath filled his lungs with reeking fumes. "Damage Control, Danenhower."

"Go, Commander."

"I'm out here looking at a four-foot hole at the waterline, frame 220. Major fires from here forward at least to the boat deck and quarterdeck area. RHIB's gone. Multiple superstructure penetrations. Blast damage. Frag damage. Where the hell are the hose teams? All I see is casualty recovery."

"Lost firemain pressure. No point exposing hose teams until we get that back. We're preparing to counterflood, to fight this list."

"I wouldn't do that until you get power back. Every ton you take on is gonna give you more free surface. Number three GTG's undamaged, right? All the way aft? I'd get that—"

"We're working it, sir. Gotta go. DC out."

The jaygee's voice was succeeded by another. *"N5, you there?"*

He choked back a retch. Without the mask, the smoke was getting to him. "Here," Danenhower said, coughing.

It was Enzweiler, the chief of staff. *"That you, Bart? Where are you? We need you to coordinate damage reports from the task force."*

"We don't control this fire, this flooding, we're gonna all be in the water." He clicked off and turned back to the hangar.

Four figures in flame-retardant suits were gathered just inside the doorway. In the reflective suits and heavy gloves, they looked like robots from an old Flash Gordon serial. One carried an axe. Another stood beside a hose reel.

No water pressure? He stared around.

He seized the heavy stainless nozzle from the reel and began unspooling the thick red rubber hose. The flight deck foam system didn't depend on the firemain. Designed to fight aircraft fires, it tapped pre-pressurized tanks in the hangar. "Tail on to this," he shouted, then doubled over, wheezing.

When he straightened they were ranged behind him. He pulled the mask down again, but still couldn't stop coughing as he bulled his way through the door once more.

Outside was even heavier smoke, the radiant glare of growing flame. His throat felt seared. Through the speaking diaphragm in the mask he choked, "Let's get some foam in there." He pointed to the flames at their feet, an inferno that was starting to roar in earnest. "That's a fuel fire down there. We're gonna flood that compartment with foam. Got it? But be careful, watch your footing, for fuck's sake don't fall in."

Without speaking again—his throat was too raw now, and the howl of the flames blotted out all sound—he signaled them to follow, ignoring the call note from the radio hooked to his belt.

DAN stood tiptoe on the bridge wing, peering aft. The whole starboard side was on fire, from the waterline up to the 04 level. The smoke had been white for the first few seconds, but was turning black now as the fuel floating alongside caught. It blew toward him, making his already-damaged bronchial tubes constrict. There were oblong holes in the steel splinter shield, as if they'd caught a load of square buckshot. Beside him "Ammo," the lookout, stared at a body floating facedown in the burning water. Then jerked his gaze up again, scanning the horizon with binoculars.

The Mark I eyeball, about his only operational sensor left, gave him a blue sky airbrushed with lavender contrails. A blazing Pacific dawn, with the sun a thumb's-width above a glowing sea of molten brass. And his only remaining operable weapons system was the 7.62 machine gun a little farther aft on the wing. Did those distant contrails, glowing lilac in the rising sun, mean another wave of supersonics were on their way? If so, *Savo* was finished.

At least four missiles had connected already. Two had hit high, obliterating the top of the hangar, the Stinger mount, one of the Phalanxes, the after stack and intakes, and maybe a third of the ship's thirty-eight antennas. Another had struck at about main deck level. The last had punched through at the waterline, according to what the phone talker had just reported. Casualties were still being tallied, but at least a dozen were stacked up in sick bay.

Tearing his eyes from the sky, he ducked back in, holding his helmet secure with one hand, and dogged the door behind him. The air inside was nearly as smoky as out. Van Gogh was shouting into the IC circuit, trying to raise After Steering. "Rudder's jammed full left, Admiral," he yelled as Dan brushed past. The helmsman was crouched behind his console, low to the deck. No doubt to breathe as little of the foul air as possible, pending the return of steering control and propulsion.

Staurulakis was speaking urgently into the sound-powered handset at the CO's chair, where he'd passed so many hours. . . . One arm was tucked into a sling—apparently she'd broken it—and both hands were streaked with blood. Cut? There was enough torn metal around. He unholstered his Hydra. "Fred? Can you hear me?"

"You're faint, but I hear you, Admiral."

"Any comms with the task force?"

"Uh, that's a negative, sir. Tried the backups, but no joy. Probably out of touch until we get ship's power back."

He lowered the heavy little radio, feeling helpless. His job as task force commander was to fight his force as long as he could, and when he couldn't, to extract as many of his units as possible.

But without comms he couldn't do squat, other than worry. Were the carriers safe? Were his other ships damaged, burning, sinking, too?

He hated to admit it. And he didn't want to. But there was only one thing left to do.

There were precedents.

In 1813. Oliver Hazard Perry, engaging the British on Lake Erie. With a flagship so damaged it could no longer fight, Commodore Perry had shifted his flag. He'd rowed across a mile of shot-torn water to the still-undamaged *Niagara*. Now commanding *Niagara* as well as the squadron, Perry had taken the fresh brig through the British line and won the battle.

"Cheryl. How's the arm?"

"Greenstick fracture. Apparently I'll live."

"Good. How long till we have comms back?"

"Not getting a solid on that, Admiral." She lifted a liter bottle of water and drank off half. He held out a hand and she passed it over. "Right now . . . well, you know the ship as well as I do."

Dan rubbed his mouth. Ticos had no emergency generators, just the three main gas turbine generators. All three were online in Condition One, in case of a casualty. Backup power now would have to be manually switched to alternate power at the panels. Some vital circuits were on automatic bus transfer—vital lighting, some comms—but not high-current-demand circuits like the radars. But with all three GTGs offline, *Savo* was dark until one could be restarted, either remotely, or locally with the remaining high-pressure air . . . since bleed air wasn't available for restarting while the GTMs were offline too.

She blinked at something past his shoulder. "Trouble is, one hit took out the power panel. Three dead, three more injured in Main One. We're routing casualty power, but it's not going to happen fast. And we've got a main space fire. Halon and CO_2 dumps have been manually tripped. And flooding, and all our fire pumps are electrical . . ." She blinked again, this time meeting his gaze. "We're out of the battle, Admiral. If I could hoist a white flag, I'd be thinking about it."

"Anybody in visual range? Somebody we can signal, who can see our smoke at least?"

The phone talker yelled, "OOD! Radio reports emergency transmitter is up. *McClung* answers on 2182 kilohertz distress frequency."

"Thank God," Dan said, looking around. "Where's Bart? We need reports. We need whoever's still got propulsion to stand by those who've lost power."

But no one seemed to know. He removed his helmet and scratched his head. It was good they had distress connectivity, if they kept taking water and couldn't get ahead of the flames, or couldn't get power back. But he couldn't suck data, and issue commands, through a straw that narrow. He had to either transfer command, or . . .

"Red Hawk 202 reports on deck *Sejong*, awaiting orders," the talker said.

"Good. Can we patch them to . . . no, we can't. No power." He paced the bridge port to starboard, glancing out each time he turned. The haze was still thickening. The fires were eating deeper into *Savo*'s guts. He coughed into his fist, then spat a dark wad into a bucket in the corner. Shit, he had to make a fucking decision. The rest of the task force could be under attack right now, somewhere else under this tranquil blue dawn.

Say he turned over command, since he couldn't exercise it himself. But to whom? The only other flag officer out here was Min Jun Jung. He couldn't turn over U.S. forces to a Korean, could he?

The truth was, he didn't want to hand off the task force. Not just yet, and not to Jung. He couldn't shake the memory of how, in the Taiwan Strait, the Korean had galloped straight for the guns, and almost taken them all to their doom. Dan had had to yank hard on the reins, and even then, the other admiral had nearly gotten away from him.

What if Jung decided to immolate Task Force 76 on the pyre of killing Chinese, or of his ambition, or of his desire to relive the exploits of some medieval admiral who'd defeated a fleet many times the size of his own? No. The guy was just too aggressive.

Well then, could he turn it over to the next senior captain, Tom Wescott on *Hampton Roads*? No. That would be a slap in the face Jung would never forgive.

Or was all this just Daniel V. Lenson, admiral for a day, rationalizing keeping command for himself? "Fuck," he mumbled, and caught a glance from the helmsman. Everywhere he turned, it was Catch-22. But he had to *do something*.

"Red Hawk 202 calling again. Requesting orders," the phone talker said.

Dan seized the seaman's shoulder, shouting above the growing roar of the fire aft. "Tell him . . . is that Wilker? . . . tell him, return to home plate. For personnel transfer to *Hampton Roads*."

Cheryl jerked her head up, almost rotating it like an owl to look back at him. "I'm shifting my flag," he told her. "Bring 202 back in. Get the two—no, the three worst-wounded back to the flight deck."

"You're leaving?"

"Shifting my flag. I can't fight from here."

"You're leaving us, Admiral?" Van Gogh said, as if he couldn't believe what he was hearing.

Dan turned away, suddenly furious. He wasn't only responsible for *Savo*, but for the rest of the force too. Without sensors and comms, a task force commander was as useless as a rifleman without cartridges. "Going below, to get ready," he snapped to Staurulakis. Then turned away, crossed to the door, and slid down the ladder, gripping the worn-smooth handrails to brake his descent.

Was that a disgruntled murmur behind him, as the door sealed? The inner voice that always questioned him formed it into words, though he probably hadn't really heard them.

The big hero put us on the bull's-eye. Now, when it gets too hot, he's jumping ship.

FIFTEEN minutes later, on the flight deck. *Savo* was still without propulsion, though Staurulakis's parting report said McMottie hoped to get #2B turbine and the port shaft in operation, and the #3 generator was being manual-started with bleed air. The rudder was still jammed, though. He'd promised to send help as soon as he figured out who was nearest. The ship had swung, slowly, the sail area of her forward superstructure catching the wind. Now she rode stern to the west, and morning shadows reached across the flight deck. The midships area was still on fire. A huge tower of black smoke leaned to the west, heading for Japan.

Dan gazed into an azure sea with a two-foot chop. *Savo* was down by the stern. Sinking, unless they could get power to the pumps. He remembered a day in the Persian Gulf, when a ship had slipped away under him, and finally gone down. Leaving two hundred men in the water, abandoned . . .

He shook the memory off, squinting up as 202 descended. The down-blast from its rotors lashed spray off a ruffled sea. Strafer Wilker, the pilot, had done a slow orbit, checking out the damage, before lining up for his approach. He flared out, hovered, hanging there. Then dropped, planting the tires on the worn nonskid with a squeak and a thump.

First out on the flight deck were the casualty team, toting litters. Dunkie Ryan trotted alongside, holding up an IV bag. These perhaps might be saved with CAT scans and trauma surgery. With a hot refuel on *Hampton Roads*, Wilker could hopscotch east to the carriers, which had surgeons and operating rooms.

"Min Su, we ready?" Dan yelled to the reedy officer beside him. Hwang nodded. Others had offered to go too. Ron Gault, his self-appointed body-guard. Captain Enzweiler. He'd refused them with a curt shake of the head. Just him, the ROKN liaison, and the wounded. The Korean clutched his briefcase and a carry bag.

Dan's own baggage was even lighter. His notebook, and the clothes on his back. The damage-control leader had halted him in the passage-way when he'd tried to reach his cabin. It had been in the blast area from one of the missiles. Thank God he'd been in CIC when the warheads blew through. More serious, though, was that the unit commander's cabin was just forward of SPY Radar Room #3, where all signal processing took place. If that had been wiped out too, *Savo* would have been sidelined for months.

The last litter vanished inside the helo, and the LSO beckoned. Bending into the rotor blast, the two senior officers trotted toward the air-craft. Hwang climbed in ahead of Lenson. Dan accepted a cranial and an inflatable vest from the crewman, and hauled himself up and in as the door/boarding steps rose to seal and lock behind him.

The litters covered the bare aluminum deck. A crewman was attach-ing IV bags to the overhead. Mute in the engine noise, he pointed Dan and Hwang to fold-down seats behind the cockpit. Strafer and the copi-lot, a rangy smart-ass named "Storm" Differey, waved. Wilker pointed up, hoisted his eyebrows. Dan nodded. *Go*, he mouthed back.

The engine rose to a whining thunder. Red Hawk lifted, fast.

Dan leaned forward and twirled his finger. Wilker nodded, and the aircraft banked away to the right. Dan struggled against the seat belt to peer down through a small, only partially transparent window. From here the cruiser looked hollowed out as a rotten tooth. Her whole mid-ships smoked and flamed. A slick of guttering fuel surrounded her like blood spilling from a mortal wound. The floating corpse he'd glimpsed from the bridge was nowhere in sight.

He pressed his fist to his mouth, fighting nausea. Not just at the damage, but at having to leave her. It felt like deserting a dying child. Like . . . *fleeing.* Had that been contempt, in the carefully noncommital expressions of the flight deck crew? They couldn't really think that, could they? Not if he came back for them. Not if he kept fighting, just from a different ship.

Wilker pointed . . . northeast? . . . and Dan nodded, sitting back. He buried his face in his hands, trying to muffle a choked, agonized sob, maybe more of a muted scream, as Hwang, beside him, looked away.

The helo leveled and dropped. They sped over the azure sea perhaps two hundred feet up. Dan blotted his eyes and tried to straighten. His neck was pure agony, and his throat kept threatening to close. He glanced around for oxygen, just in case, but saw only the slim cylinder of a bail-out bottle clamped to the bulkhead.

Hwang bent to his ear. Shouted, "What is your intention now, Admiral?"

"Shift flag to *Hampton Roads.* Get someone alongside *Savo*, either put those fires out or take the crew aboard. Then get the hell out of Dodge."

The Korean looked puzzled at the reference to Dodge, but he sat back. Dan wanted to ask how much farther to the other cruiser, but forced himself to relax too. They'd be there soon enough.

The helicopter swayed. Probably hitting an air current.

Then suddenly yawed violently, flinging them against the webbing. The litters slid scraping across the deck. Several bangs or thuds went off in quick succession. The sea wheeled up until they were looking straight down on it through the side window. No, not just a thermal. Dan grabbed for a handhold, but missed. Then the bank reversed, hauling over hard to the right. The litters halted their slide, reversed it, and cascaded toward him. Someone screamed as the IV lines went taut, then tore free to dangle, gleaming needles dancing on plastic tubing.

Through the frosted window he glimpsed a loop of white smoke in the air. He couldn't see where it had come from, only the exhaust trail drawn against blue. A bright point of pure fire, describing a double-looped figure rather like a π.

The point of fire emerged from the last descending stroke near the water. Then rose again. Pointing, now, up at them.

A terrific bang and flash overhead deafened and blinded him. For a few seconds, whirling and falling in a jumbled, chaotic blur, he howled mindlessly, arms flung wide, but finding nothing to grip. Then another heavy shock jolted the fuselage.

Dazed, he found himself upside down, being rocked violently while hanging from the web restraints. The seat seemed to have collapsed around his ass. The ringing in his ears subsided, to the absence of engine noise. The silence swelled, then burst like a bubble.

He registered the chuckle and gurgle of water pouring in, and thumps and thrashings from the cockpit. He pried reluctant eyes open to dim light and a jumble of patients on litters dumped facedown. One of the wounded, conscious, was staring right at him. Even as Dan blinked, water surged to cover the man's mouth, nose, hair. He struggled as a bloody froth rose, bubbles bursting on the still-rising water.

Dan scrabbled across his own waist, looking for the release. The straps fell away, and so did he, dropping out of the collapsed seat frame headfirst into a tumble of water and bodies on the overhead of the upside-down cabin. He rolled to his feet, legs splashing in knee-deep water, and tried to right the upended litters. Jammed together, they refused to budge, even when he braced his boots and yanked.

Okay, maybe he couldn't help these men. Even if he could get them out, they were too badly wounded to swim. That left Hwang . . . Wilker . . . the flight crewman . . . Differey.

The window through which he'd glimpsed whatever had hit them bulged inward and split, releasing a gelid flood of sea. Water was flooding in from forward, too. The fuselage angled down, surging the sea to his waist. He wheeled in the near dark, and staggered back as Hwang fell out of his seat, nearly into Dan's arms. They both lost their footing and collapsed back into the water.

Darkness, bubbles, his flailing hands hitting things floating about . . .

He came back up choking and spitting, to an even darker interior. Were they fucking sinking already? In the dunker egress training at Miramar, they'd been told that though most helicopters inverted after crashing, they'd have at least a few seconds before an SH-60 lost enough air to submerge. He could still hear the instructor's voice. *Locate a point of reference. Wait for violent motion to stop. Don't inflate your vest until you've egressed the aircraft.*

They were inverted, check. But already nose down, and water was pouring in fast through the shattered windows and windscreen. Both pilots sat slumped, helmeted heads lolling. Hwang was shouting something in Korean. Dan pointed to the pilots and splashed aft, groping for the crewman. His boots found something soft. He hauled it to the surface. Hwang's fucking luggage. He dropped it and groped again, plunging his face into the cold sea. Caught cloth, and dragged it up.

The crewman's head lolled. Puckered holes showed where something had penetrated one temple. Dan shook him, but got no response. His fingers, exploring the wound, came away pink with diluted blood.

The water was at his chin. Rising faster than ever. One more quick suck of breath, and it was over his head.

Underwater. Wavery blue light. A long, gangly form, silhouetted from behind. Hwang was kicking at the exit door. It resisted, then toppled open slowly. The liaison started to pull himself out, then turned back and reached in for something. A black object, with a strap.

Planting his boots in a yielding mass, hauling the limp weight of the crewman behind him, Dan pushed them both toward the light. But when he tried to lift his foot again, he couldn't. His boot had plunged through the metal mesh of a litter. He tried to shake it free, then twist it out, but it wouldn't move. And the litter, and what was on it, were too heavy to drag.

Discard it, then . . . jackknifing at the waist, he pulled the velcro tab loose and unzipped one boot, then the other. Finally free, he tried for the door again.

But he was out of breath now. The blue light seemed dimmer. Pressure leaned on his eardrums. The copter was sinking faster. He swallowed to buy a few more seconds and swam upward, lips reaching for an airspace to breathe from. But his skull *boonged* into aluminum without encountering one.

Everything was going black when his scrabbling fingers recognized a slim cylinder. He jerked it from its mounting. A regulator dangled on a stub of hose. He twisted the knurled knob and jammed the mouthpiece of the emergency escape bottle between his teeth. Cleared it, and tried a breath.

With air he immediately felt calmer, much more in control. Inhaling deeply, he hauled himself toward the blue light. Grabbing the sides of the door, he looked up.

A silvery mirror heaved far above. Golden rays searched down, playing over the tail boom, a ragged stump of shredded rotor. The turbine hung loose, stripped of sheathing, blasted nearly free of the airframe.

Then he halted, uncertain. A micro bottle like this wouldn't hold much. Enough for nine or ten breaths.

But maybe he had enough time to get someone else out.

Inside the fuselage once again, he pushed and twisted like a moray in a coral head through the narrow opening leading into the cockpit.

Both pilots were still strapped in, slumped as if knocked unconscious. Curved chunks of the shattered canopy lay in their laps. The water was above their heads, around which blue-black tendrils of blood curled. Dan yanked at their restraints, then felt for the releases. A clack echoed through the water and Differey floated up. Dan shoved him toward the gap where the canopy had been, but the copilot snagged on some kind of comm wire. It took several more seconds to locate where it plugged in and disconnect it. He grabbed the lanyard on Differey's life jacket and yanked it. The CO_2 cartridge popped and he braced his back and kicked him through the windshield with both feet as the vest began inflating.

He got his hands on Wilker next. He was feeling around the pilot's upper chest for the release, his own torso twisted awkwardly in the constricted space, when he realized each succeeding breath was coming harder.

The bailout was running empty. Time to bail, if he wanted to make it to the surface himself. Back to the exit door, or out through the windshield? Floating bodies one way. Jagged Perspex to snag on and hang him up, the other.

Wilker opened his eyes suddenly. Blood seeped from his nose and cuts on his face. One hand groped up, across his vest. The other locked into Lenson's, gripping it with enormous force.

Dan saw what was wrong. The instrument panel had buckled onto Wilker's legs, pinning him.

A sudden vertigo, a slippage around them. The glimmering surface receded and dimmed. The wrecked, inverted fuselage was rolling over again as it sank away. Dizzied, disoriented, Dan could no longer tell which way led up. He fought grimly with the pilot's webbing. But it wouldn't release. Wilker was struggling too, one hand clawing at his vest, the other trying, now, to push Dan away.

Colors flashed at the edge of his vision. Blackness flooded in behind them.

A lavender beam of light.

A double-looped π of smoke, scribed with incredible beauty against blue sea.

His newborn daughter's blue-eyed gaze, meeting his for the first time.

He was walking beneath a shaded arbor. White flowers decorated it, hearted with bright yellow, and lush green waxy-looking leaves among which fat bees slowly buzzed. The pavement was of small, richly patterned tile in complex geometric designs of carmine and jade and cream. The path ahead led to a turning, where the arbor's shadow lay deeper, the bees' buzzing louder, the scent of the white flowers with their golden hearts overpoweringly stronger. With each step he neared that turning. But he couldn't see what lay past it.

Still struggling with the belt, pinned into the slowly rotating fuselage, he sank away helplessly into the black void of the sea.

21

The Philippine Sea

IN the darkness, noise. The stenches of fuel and seawater and close-cramped bodies, diarrhea and vomit and bilgewater. Sweat and bean-farts and sea-stink. Wet metal weeps overhead. The clink and scrape of equipment. The deafening roar of engines. Vibration, through the thin metal that surrounds them. The rush and clatter of spray. Beneath it all, the ragged breathing of burdened men and women.

The sickening, endless heave of a massive object in an ocean swell.

Night. Hector Ramos hunches crammed in the hull of an amphibious assault vehicle, an amtrac, elbow to elbow with twenty-four other marines. They've been here for seven hours now, boarding after a heavy evening meal as the machine squatted in the well of an air-cushion landing craft. The plan was to launch at midnight. But something delayed that, then delayed it again. Now they have to shit, to piss, but there's nowhere to go and no room even to move.

"It can't be long to sunrise," someone mutters.

A tide of grumbling rises. "What's taking so fucking long?"

"We're gonna be hitting the beach at fucking daylight."

"They gotta know we're coming," Troy Whipkey mutters, spooned next to Hector.

There's barely room to inflate their lungs. The red interior light flickers as gear sways on the bulkheads. Someone nearby retches again. "They gotta see us on radar," Troy adds. "This is gonna be a fucking slaughter."

Hector's afraid he's right. But no point complaining. There's no way not to go now, so he's eager to get it over with. To find out what he's made of, what going to war is like.

He tries not to think of the chickens, how they suddenly went quiet as they were pulled through the hole in the wall.

Hector wears baggy digital-printed trop camo utilities, with a laser ID tape and heavy boots. His old-style dog tag is backed by a hastily modified pet chip under the skin of his neck. He wears no watch, carries no radio, since his helmet will tell him the time and link him to the intraplatoon net. He wears knee and elbow pads and black tactical gloves and heavy body armor with reactive inserts.

The new lightweight integrated combat helmet has night vision and a BattleGlass interface in the goggles that feeds him data and ranges wherever he looks. Hector hugs the M240 machine gun with laser optic and a hundred rounds of linked 7.62. His secondary weapon is a pistol in a leg holster. He carries a rigger belt, notebook, pen, gas mask, and a folding multitool. On his plate carrier he has thirty more rounds of pistol ammunition, a fragmentation grenade, water-purification tablets, a compass, an LED flashlight, a green chemlight, a midazolam/atropine autoinjector, and earplugs. In the assault pack is an issue Camelbak with a hose clipped to his shoulder strap, two hundred more rounds of linked 7.62, the machine-gun-cleaning kit, a 500-ml intravenous bag with starter kit, two MREs, a poncho and liner, another undershirt, spare batteries, a pistol-cleaning kit, the personal hygiene kit the Marines refer to as "snivel gear," and a pair of heavy leather gloves.

In his main pack he carries half a modular sleeping bag, two undershirts, two pair of socks, a knit cap, two more canteens of water, two more MREs, and a sleeping pad. Also one 60mm mortar round, a combat lifesaving kit, and range cards for the Pig.

Hector wonders how far he'll be able to hump 135 pounds of clothing, gear, weapons, food, water, and ammo when he weighs only 148 pounds. The marines have heard about powered metal exoskeletons. But they've never seen one, and even if they exist, the Corps will be the last to get them. The beast they're riding in, that they're powering along three feet above the water in, was built forty years before. It creaks and shrieks around them as its metal skin flexes.

It's only thin aluminum, after all.

THE brigade had been held aboard ship for weeks at sea. The officers and SNCOs went to sand-table rehearsals, but the grunts just got rumors. Until two days before, when they gathered in the hangar bay for a mass briefing by the colonel.

The operation was named Mandible.

Their target was an island.

("Duh," Troy had whispered.)

The island's code name was Lifeline.

When the graphic went up, Hector leaned forward, trying to peer around the guy in front of him for a better look. It stretched southwest to northeast, shaped like a long turd. It didn't look that big, but even smaller islands lay off to the east and north.

The colonel turned the brief over to a major. She said, "The Navy is carrying out attacks at two other points, starting now. And we have a submarine blockade between Lifeline and the enemy coast. So we don't expect major reinforcements for the enemy, by either sea or air. The battlefield is isolated; he'll have to fight with what he has. We'll have the advantage of surprise and numbers.

"On the other hand, this is an over-the-horizon assault, with multiple repeat sorties by Osprey, helo, and LCAC to get the first echelon ashore. Since shipping will have to stand off, due to area-denial missiles, this will slow the buildup and place heavier demands on the lead assault elements.

"We'll get to the enemy order of battle in a moment. But I wanted to discuss the geography first, because we've discovered difficulties that may not have been appreciated when we were assigned this mission."

An aerial photo, looking down onto an undulating green carpet fringed with black rock. "Lifeline is eighteen kilometers long and roughly five kilometers wide. It is dominated by two volcanoes, Riposet, in the southeast, and Karaboban, to the north. Both are long extinct. Riposet, at a two-hundred-seventy-meter elevation, dominates the island and the airfield. Whoever holds it, holds the island."

"Our first two objectives," the colonel put in, "are the airfield and the commanding height to the south. We have a cruel and determined enemy. Cruel—judging from his conduct in Korea. Determined—he will not surrender easily. In China, defeated generals are shot.

"But Marines have always accomplished the mission. I have no doubt you'll make me proud."

He nodded to the major. She picked up, "Now, enemy forces. Based on all-source intelligence, we estimate Lifeline is occupied by approximately four thousand Chinese."

The marines stirred. Hector didn't like that number either. There were only about two thousand men and women in the whole Second Regiment. Weren't you supposed to land with more guys than you had opposing you?

As if sensing their unease, she said, "But most of the occupiers are not fighting troops. Many are construction crews and civilian contractors, resurfacing and extending the airfield for the next phase of their offensive. Taking it won't just screw up their plans, it'll position us for our next step.

"In two days, at an H-hour of 0400 local, following preparatory strikes by Tomahawk, UAV, Marine and Navy air, and naval gunfire support, Nine MEB will carry out a two-pronged attack. The Ospreys will vertical-envelop at LZ Mallet, which I am indicating with the pointer."

The major hesitated. "It was difficult to select a landing point for the element conducting the frontal assault. The coastline is formed by steep cliffs. Rocky. Precipitous. There are only four places at all suitable, only one is on the eastern coast, and it has no beach suitable for LCACs. Actually, there aren't any 'beaches,' in the sense of a shallowing hydrography shading up into a gradually climbing coastal terrain.

"To be honest, it took us a long time to figure out the best way to get you in, aside from a pure vertical assault, which wouldn't give us a rapid enough buildup or the logistic foothold needed for resupply."

"Then how the fuck *are* we getting ashore?" Whipkey muttered, fidgeting like an eight-year-old.

"Shut up, Troy, and listen," Hector hissed.

The briefer clicked a laser pointer. "First Battalion, Second Regiment, will land on Red Beach Two. Here." The red dot pulsated, but Hector didn't see anything like a beach.

"AAVs, tanks, and vehicles will debark at the foot of an eroded cliff. The incline is about forty degrees. Rough going, but we believe the armor can negotiate the grade. Once the beachhead's secure, the logistics combat element will sculpt a ramp with dozers. The rubble will form a base for a pontoon causeway, where resupply will come in starting at D plus one.

"Until that happens, though, we'll have to hold against any counterattack with organic assets, supplemented by drone resupply. The good news is, we'll have continuous air support from the MAG and the UAV folks. Fifty Stinger teams, antidrone squads, and Navy top cover will further protect us.

"Terrain inland is undulating, with open areas interspersed with scrub jungle in the lower elevations. You will encounter small lakes and watercourses. The former administrating country advises most of the inhabitants have left. For ROE purposes, consider the entire island as a free-fire zone. Of course, try to avoid damage to hospitals and churches, unless they're being used as firing positions.

"Once ashore, push toward the airfield in accordance with the phase lines shown and link up at LZ Mallet. We should have local-area GPS coverage, but it's probably better to depend on your compass and map. Push forward as rapidly as you can. Don't give the enemy time to organize. Second Battalion, landing south of us, will take Mount Riposet. Note this shallow ravine; it will serve as a boundary line. Three-Two will be held in reserve.

"When you make contact, don't halt. Call in supporting fire, then close with and destroy the enemy. Don't get ahead of the phase lines. Your prep fires will be going in ahead of you. But don't fall behind, either. Once fire lifts, the enemy's going to have his head back up again."

The colonel interrupted again. "Let me emphasize that: When counterattacks occur, call in support and attrite the enemy."

His audience stirred, glancing at one another. Hector felt uneasy. If anything went wrong, they'd be stranded ashore without resupply, maybe without tanks.

The major wound up with the repeated assurance that the carriers would have their backs. But most of the marines still looked skeptical.

When she was done, Weapons Platoon went to a corner of the cavernous well deck. They settled between one of the LCACs and the canvas-shrouded bulk of a tank. Hector nodded to the other M240 gunners. He caught Orietta's grin from the mortar section, Pruss beside her. They'd all be hitting the beach with the first wave, apparently.

Lieutenant Smalls's usual procedure was for him to call in the three section leaders and the platoon sergeant, Hern, and let them pass the gouge on to the troops. But apparently he wanted them all together for this. "We haven't been together long," Smalls started. "Especially our new joins. But you heard what the colonel said. If these guys counterattack, you know where you die. In place, behind your weapon. Taking as many of them with you as you can."

And they'd all nodded soberly. Accepting it.

It would be up to them.

NOW, in the hammering well of the LCAC, deep in the belly of the amphibious tractor, "Five minutes" comes back passed mouth to mouth. Hector tries to wriggle, to stretch cramping muscles. But after so long he isn't sure he can get up, much less muscle up close to his body weight.

A strange, prolonged groan. A lurch, as if they've hit something. He grips the Pig as if it can save him. A distant thud. Then another, heavier, closer. If a shell hits them now, no way they're getting out. The "L-cack" floats above the water, driven on a cushion of air, but if it loses power they'll be trapped. . . .

"Stand by," Sergeant Hern snarls, ducking to yell back to them. The AAV's diesel clatters to life with a jolt and a roar. Whipkey and Ramos stiffen as above them a hatch cracks partway. An emergency exit, though every one knows only a few will be able to make it out.

Through it they glimpse fog, and gray light. Slanting gray sky. Spray spatters. Marines bend, heaving into the corners. A tide of vomit slides to and fro on the deck.

The thudding becomes a drumbeat, then a howl as if the world itself is being destroyed. Black smoke stains the sky. Aircraft scream over. Jets, and the crosslike shapes of Ospreys.

Terror squeezes his heart. Hector pants.

The marines crouch as hell gapes a mile ahead. Hector can only catch shattered glimpses. Volcanoes of flame throw boulders free to leap and crash down into the surf. Earth erupts, a russet belch of gritty soil scrambled by high explosive and laced with hot steel. Shells roar overhead, detonating with deafening blasts that walk circles of concussion across the water. Farther inland, even heavier explosions shake the sky. They can't see for the fog, but something up there is unloading destruction on the enemy.

For which they curse and pray, torn between terror and gratitude. Hector, helmet lowered, embracing the Pig, can't pray. Can't even think, in the pandemoniac din. Only two words tower in his mind. Last words he will die without saying, if he dies today.

Mandible.

Lifeline.

The iron stink of torn earth and explosive reaches them on the wind.

SOMEHOW a gap. Like the flicker of a strobe, and

HE'S ashore. Panting, smeared with red dirt, so somewhere in there he must have fallen or been knocked down. His Glasses have gone blank. His radio hisses empty in his earbud. He looks back down the slope, to where the LCAC . . .

Where the LCAC . . .

To where the LCAC lies beached and on fire, canted to one side like

Godzilla used it to wipe his ass, then stomped on it. Huge pieces lie smoking, scattered on the rocks. Two amtracs also lie torn open and burning soundlessly. Silent explosions lift tons of white water a few hundred feet out to sea. Huddled bundles in graytan digital camo lie among them, or surge in the surf. A damaged cargo-robo whirs and bobs in circles until it finally topples, slides down into the surf, thrashes briefly, and subsides beneath the waves.

Only Hector doesn't remember. . . .

His helmet rocks to a blow and his brainpan echoes. It's Sergeant Hern, yelling into his face. Soundlessly. Hector blinks. Only after several seconds do the sounds abruptly assemble into words. Accompanied, now, by the zip and crack of incoming. *Lots* of incoming. Instinctively, he crouches.

". . . and get set up. Hear me? Haul ass! Two hundred meters to the left and set up."

A second face. Whipkey, tugging at his other arm. "Ramos. The fuck, man?—He got concussed, Sergeant. When the cack got hit. Had to drag him out."

"Get him on his feet. Move him out. We got to get off this fucking beach."

Nearer the crest the NCOs and officers, huddled in a cleft of rock, are talking on radios and assigning sectors of fire. Hector, toiling heavily past them, sees through a blankness that beyond that lies a bare hilltop, with very little cover and dirt spurting up continually as it's raked. He feels naked. "Supposed to do this in the fucking amtrac," he mutters. "What the fuck?"

"Forget the track, dude," Whipkey pants, shoving him. "They had us boresighted the second we hit the sand. We were lucky to get out alive. Lots didn't."

Hern leads them out at a scramble, bent double, riflemen in support, and they rush in short sprints from dip to dip, panting under their loads, until they reach a rise on the left flank. Mortars start howling in as they run. The ground shakes. Earth patters over them. Jagged steel sings and whines. Air bursts. There's nowhere to hide. They fall, digging their fingers into the ground, then leap up and sprint again. By some miracle, only one rifleman gets hit. They shout for a corpsman, and resume buddy-rushing once they see him on his way.

The sergeant sets them in overlooking a jungled valley with gray fog eddying up from tangled vegetation. There's a little cover here, at least, stunted scrub trees studded with bare boulders. Their primary field of fire is to the left oblique with a secondary dead ahead. Hern yells, "Make sure you don't fire on any First Battalion guys. They'll be coming up on the far side of the valley." Hector realizes this is the "ravine" mentioned in the briefing, the line between battalions. But where are the Ospreys, the guys coming in vertical assault? He starts to ask Whipkey, then decides he wouldn't know either.

A huge explosion goes off in the air a hundred yards away, thumping deep in his lungs and kicking up the dirt in a huge circle below it. Besides, they have more pressing issues. Like getting dug in before one of those shells, or rockets, turns them into pulled pork.

Hector and Troy dig madly with entrenching tools. The soil's reddish, gritty, not sand, but lighter. Their blades grate on fist-sized pumice rocks. He's never seen anything like this stuff. As they dig it turns to powder and they start coughing. They throw up a hasty position, then spade in the Pig's bipod legs. Roll in, and glass their front.

But he can't see. The fucking fog covers everything. It eddies up from the trees below and hangs opaque and motionless. Still, he pings laser ranges, and Troy sketches a card. Fifteen minutes later a Javelin team arrives on their left, then a rifle squad digs in between them, accompanied by an antidrone gunner. With each arrival Hector feels reassured. They have a perimeter now. But where's the armor? He hasn't seen a single piece come off the beach. He hasn't seen any enemy yet, either, but keeps searching the fog, swinging the 240's muzzle, finger on the trigger. Now and again rain slashes down, hard, chilly, obliterating the last remnants of sight. His helmet radio tells him, *"Hold fire, claymores are going out."* He clicks and rogers, but never sees movement. Either they're really good, or visibility is shit.

The roar of engines behind them . . . the second wave of cacks is coming in. They'll have to thread in, avoiding the wrecks. With a queer-sounding *pop* his radio goes off, then comes back on. "What happened back there?" he mutters to Whipkey. "To the cack?"

"Fuck if I know. Just, we were there, waiting for the ramp to go down, and there's this terrific bang and the whole side opens up. We're spinning around, starting to go down . . . somebody hit the ramp button, though, and they drove the amtracs out. You don't remember?"

"I don't remember dick until Hern grabbed me at the top of the cliff."

"No shit . . . Well, we hit the beach, then there's this terrific whang and the track shudders and stops. The driver's just . . . gone. He's like, paste. We get out but then it's like total clusterfuck. Major incoming. We're trying to rush, but guys are going down. Then I look back and you're laying there. A lot of rocks and shit were flying around." Whipkey bends in. "Shit yeah, you got a hell of a dent here. Can see the ripped Kevlar. Probably woulda tooken your fucken head off, without that brain bucket. Sure you're okay?"

"I think so. Kind of got a headache, though—"

"Ops, this is Whiskey actual, report Alfa Charlie Echo," says Hector's radio. The lieutenant, asking for an ammo, casualties, equipment report.

He peers out again over the sights. "This is Six, six hundred rounds, no casualties, operational. Visibility limited by fog, two hundred meters, no enemy observed. Over."

"Whiskey actual, out. —Ah, wait one . . . Stand by . . . stand by to move out. Follow AAVs, one-zero-five magnetic. Threat direction, left flank. Acknowledge."

"Fuck," Whipkey mutters. "We just got this fucken position dug." But he's already packing and slinging, getting ready to move.

Hector checks his compass and frowns. "Hey, something's fucked . . . am I wrong? That's gonna take us down into that jungle."

"No it won't. You're reading it wrong. We're just gonna skate by it." Whipkey sighs, and Hector looks to see him squatting in their hole with his trou down. "Takin' a dump while I can," he mutters. "Recommend you do the same." He pulls up his pants, slings his rucks, the heavy bag with the extra barrel, and climbs out.

The thick crack of a heavy bullet shivers the air, showering them both with friable red dirt as the earth erupts between them. *"Fuck,"* Whipkey hisses, dropping prone. "That was some big-caliber shit. See where that came from?"

Hector swings the barrel. His finger tightens. A long burst, return fire? He peers through the optic, but sees nothing. No smoke, no motion, no vapor. Though a faint *pop* arrives a second after the bullet. *The bullet travels twice the speed of the sound.* A long shot, which was why they'd missed. Should he fire? At last he doesn't. He keys, "Whiskey, OP Six, sniper fire from across the ravine."

"Roger. All hands, maintain cover. Don't move out just yet. Resupply's on the way. Out."

He hasn't fired Round One yet, but already they're being resupplied? Maybe he won't have to worry about ammo. They keep their heads down, sensing a distant gaze on them. Drink some water, and check the Pig.

A low motor-whine, a discreet *beep* behind them. Whipkey pokes a shaving mirror up. "One a the mules. Water and ammo."

Hector nods. "Stay low."

"Know it, dude."

But the assistant gunner's only halfway to the cart, low-crawling, using every bush and fold of ground, when the robot beeps again. The wheels spin. It backs away. "Here, boy," Whipkey calls. "What choo doing? Get the fuck back here!"

But the wheels are spinning in opposite directions, fighting each other. The cart backs, then rolls forward. Halts. Then, abruptly, whips in a circle, nearly tipping over, the ammo boxes and water cans atop it jolting and clattering.

It bolts forward, narrowly missing Whipkey as he buries his head under his hands, and tears past Ramos, pitching down the slope. It accelerates, individually powered wheels whining madly, heading downhill. Toward the enemy line.

"*Ammo cart's gone rogue,*" someone says on the net. "*Deserting.*"

"*Bastards cyberjacked it.*"

"*Six, take it out. Copy? Take it out.*"

Hector can't believe it. Fire on their own ammo resupply? Their own water, when his mouth is parched? But orders are orders. He's lining up the sights when the cart suddenly explodes, disassembling in a cone of dirt and black smoke. "Aw fuck," Whipkey mutters. "Now we got to worry about fucken mines, too."

Hector eases his finger off the trigger and sets the safety. He smacks dry lips. "*Hijo de puta,*" he mutters. "I coulda used that water."

A snarl of engines grows from beachward. Huge hulks strain to climb, lumbering up, then tipping down as they crest. "At last, some fucking armor," Whipkey yells.

At the same moment trails of fire streak down from the sky. They search here and there across the ravine from Hector and Troy, who freeze, crouched, as the earth gouts in crimson flashes, as jungle and trees are hurtled skyward, turned over, fall, and are hurtled skyward again. Pulverized amid flashes of lightning. A paler cone of fire streaks skyward from amid the maelstrom, but falters, falls back. The thunder goes on and on before gradually subsiding amid flashes and heavy booms that echo away amid the hills.

"*OPs, move out and follow behind AAVs,*" the net says.

Wheezing under their burdens, they trot after the behemoths, sucking diesel fumes. The Javelin team's out on the flank. An attack helicopter flashes overhead, cants, unleashes streams of fire. The rockets impact on the far side of a hill, and black smoke rises along with a faint popping. Hector's headache throbs behind his eyes. The fog and drizzle are growing heavier. Is that thump and hum from helicopters, or inside his head? The AAV dips and slews, treads flinging dirt as it hits soft patches. They're headed down, skirting the ravine. He puffs and blows, trying to keep up. Some of the infantrymen are riding on the armor, forbidden in training, but apparently okay now. The Javelin team drops and sets up, sighting on something in the distance. A nonthreat, it seems, because seconds later they're up and jogging forward again.

"Jeez, I can't go much farther," Whipkey wheezes.

"We got to keep up, Troy."

For some reason Hector keeps thinking of the Line. Of Farmer Seth . . . He looks back to see Whipkey surreptitiously letting a mortar round slip to the ground. "That's five pounds less," he mutters.

"You aren't ditching *our* ammo?"

"Think I'm stupid? I'll drop chow before seven-six-two."

Hector's about to snap something back when he notices he's walking on a smoothly paved road of bloody flesh. Something massive has rolled over the bodies, smashing them into a glistening paste that merges almost imperceptibly with the red soil. If not for the smell, he might not even have noticed. That was what made him recall the factory. The smells of fresh meat, ground-up flesh, drying blood, and crushed intestines. Arms and legs lie to the side, some charred, others with jagged pinkish-white bone sticking out. A head, facedown, still packaged in its helmet as if for shipping.

Then a nearly whole body, in dark woodland camo. The midsection's scattered across the grass, but the upper body and legs are still there. The pale face looks serene. At first Hector thinks she's a girl. Then realizes, no, just a smooth-faced, fine-featured boy. No older than he is, probably, but built smaller. A strange-looking rifle lies near an open hand.

"Get moving, keep moving," rasps in his headset. Hector flinches. Lifts his boots carefully, trying not to step where it glistens. The melted fat, that's what'll be slippery. Just like when a vat of it spills, on the Line.

THE amtrac's burning, popping like firecrackers as the ammo cooks off. He and Whipkey lie prone, tucked under one of its busted tracks, hastily setting up the Pig.

"Gunners, get some fire out there," crackles in his ears. Another M240

opens up to their right, and balls of white fire arch out. Tracers! "Must be all he's got left," Whipkey yells. "Losing that mule fucked us bad."

"How we fixed?"

"Getting short, Heck. Only two more belts."

He charges the gun and bends to the optics. They're cracked and smeared with dirt. He flips them out of the way and goes to irons. Figures move ahead, surge at the crest, sink down. "Four hundred meters," Whipkey mutters. Hector sets the sight and snugs the butt into his shoulder. The Pig hammers his shoulder, pushing him back. But he's braced, boots digging into the dirt, and he walks the rounds in short bursts, *die, motherfucker, die,* picking up the rhythm of their rushes and putting bursts where they'll be, not where they were. Distant figures reel and drop, stagger or just fall. Brass spews. Links tinkle. The blast, confined under the hull of the wrecked tank, is deafening. The gas, choking.

A flame leaves the low hills ahead and darts faster than they can track it somewhere to their right. A heavy, ground-quaking explosion.

The gun to their right falls silent.

With a growl of diesels, another track pulls up next to them. The turret rotates, and the .50-cal and the forty mike mike began clamoring, searching for the enemy. The noise is beyond deafening.

The Pig's barrel starts to glow. Whipkey slaps his shoulder and reaches in for the handle. Wrestles it off, sets it aside to cool, replaces it, slaps his shoulder again. "Last belt," he howls into Hector's ear.

"Look in my ruck."

"We fired all that, Heck-tor. You're blankin' again."

The flame darts faster than his eye can follow. It slams into the already-burning hulk above them. The metal shakes and sheer white fire surrounds them for a tenth of a second, blinding, deafening. After the blast, the darkness again.

THEY'RE riding one of the robot carts, the auto turned off so the enemy can't hijack it. A lance corporal's steering with the joystick. Troy and Hector are slumped in the back, the Pig between them. The wheels grind in plowed-up soil where something big's gone off. They bump over wreckage. Between the slanted, battered tubes of abandoned, broken mortars. The fertilizer stink of explosive. Another crater, a gigundous one. Something must have hit an ammo dump. His empty gaze wanders among wrecked equipment, overturned, smoking boxes, piles of empty packing tubes, bodies.

One is helmetless, dark hair unraveled. Olive skin and a hawklike nose. One leg lies several yards away. He slides off the cart, disregarding Whipkey's shout, and limps over. Takes a knee beside her. Touches her face.

"Orietta," he whispers. She's cold. Bled out. Pruss lies not far away. Also dead.

HE blinks, crouched in an emplacement he doesn't recognize, looking over gunsights. He shakes his head, scrapes dirty nails over his eyes. Vertigo reels the world. He hasn't dug this position. But there's his entrenching tool, smeared with red dirt—

"Y'okay?" Whipkey snaps down the feed tray. "Loaded. Go hot."

Without conscious thought Hector hauls on the charging handle, tests the traverse, wiggles the bipod feet to dig them in. "Where the fuck are we?" he whispers.

"You're starting to worry me, dude. Look behind you," Whipkey mutters.

When he cranes around, they're dug in at the end of an airstrip so long it seems to stretch out forever. The fog has lifted some, and it isn't raining, though it looks like it might again. But the fog's been replaced by choking black smoke. Broken vehicles and crashed aircraft burn along the strip. Corpses lie around them. They wear woodland camo and Marine digital. Marines crouch with pointed rifles around a gaggle of prisoners and wounded on the far side of the tarmac. Gunfire crackles to the west, and heavier explosions boom out. The battle's moved on. An MV-22 Osprey burns fiercely three hundred meters distant. As he stares, an amtrac noses up and begins shoving it off the strip.

"We're there? We took the field?"

"Where the fuck you been? We dug in three times. Fired over four hundred rounds."

Hector inspects his hands. They're black with dirt and powder. His fingernails are broken. But they've taken the objective. He pounds the Pig, overtaken by joy. He's alive!

Then he remembers Orietta, and Pruss, and the torn bodies lolling in the surf. The joy fades. He looks at his hands again. "Where are my fucking gloves?"

"I don't know where your fucken gloves are!"

In his helmet comms. *"Six, Whiskey actual, report."*

He swings the 240 across his sector. "This is Six . . . nothing to report."

"Stay alert. UAV reports activity to southwest of the strip."

He rogers, suddenly sobered again. *Stay alert for counterattacks.* "Southwest will be out to our left oblique," Whipkey says, pointing. Hector orients and searches, pressing the laser button for ranges when he can pick out a landmark, but doesn't see anything. The Glasses give him nothing. Either they aren't working, or he isn't getting data over the link. Once again, the lieutenant's put them on a slope looking down. About three hundred yards, above scrub deepening to jungle. A motion to his right; he traverses; is taking up slack in the trigger when digital MAR-PAT registers. A dude's dragging a spool of springy concertina. It unfolds as it unrolls across their front, expanding into a barrier a yard high laced with hundreds of razor teeth to grip and slash, but mainly to pin an attacker in the kill zone.

"This is Whiskey actual. Listen up. Word is, they're using our chips to target."

"What the *fuck*," Whipkey murmurs.

"Apparently they can read location off them. Listen carefully. You have to remove each other's chips." The squawk of a transmission; a hiss; a break. *"Then destroy them in the following manner; either insert into your barrels and fire a round, or heat with your MRE heaters until red hot. Copy?"*

The section leaders roger up doubtfully. Hector and Troy eye each other, and Whipkey grimaces. "I hope they figured this right."

"What do you mean?"

"The chips. They're supposed to identify us to our own targeters, too." But he unsheathes his KA-BAR and peels down his uniform collar. Pinches up the hard little kernel of the chip. And looks away, biting his lip as Hector inserts the tip of the knife, works it under, and pops it out. Then it's his turn. A field dressing with anticoagulant stops the bleeding. They jack a round into the Pig, drop both chips down the barrel, and fire them at the enemy.

Suddenly he's incredibly thirsty. Hector fumbles out a canteen and drinks half. He checks his other canteen and finds it's already drunk dry, though he doesn't remember doing it. His head aches as if someone is driving a log splitter through his brain. "We got claymores out?" he mutters. "How much 7.62?"

Whipkey says they do, and have two hundred rounds left. Somehow they've fired almost all their load and more, though he doesn't remember doing so. He's blacking out, apparently. Maybe he should find a corpsman. No . . . he's still manning the gun. As long as he can do that, he owes it to the platoon to stay in the line.

*   *   *

THEY occupy that position all that afternoon. They're exhausted, but there's no time to sleep. Taking turns manning the Pig, they deepen the fighting hole, then extend it in a semicircle and sculpt platforms. They bolt their MREs cold, keeping watch. Whipkey jogs to the still-smoking wreck of the Osprey and drags back a fiberglass panel. With the excavated dirt piled on it, then a poncho over the raw earth, it provides some overhead cover. A Humvee comes by. They kick off two cans of linked and a case of grenades. The sergeant walks the line. Hern says they can take half-hour naps, one at a time, but to stand to at dusk. "Expect a counterattack after dark," he advises.

"Can't the air break that up for us?" Whipkey asks. "Or the drones?"

"They laid down most of their load in prep fires. And a lot of our UAV assets got 'jacked. We can't depend on our computers. Or even our radios. They're fucking with us. We're trying to figure it out."

Hector says, "Uh, Sergeant, is there a corpsman around?"

Hern eyes him. "There a problem?"

"Ramos got a brain rattle," Whipkey says. "Been blinking on and off since we hit the beach."

"I can stay on the line," Hector says. "I'm okay."

"I'll send Doc over soon as I see him. Get your chips out?"

They bare their necks for inspection, and the NCO leaves. Whipkey breaks out the ammo boxes, but pauses. "Hey. Shit!"

"What?"

"Look at this crap. What is this?" He holds up a belt. Instead of brass cartridges, they're gray. Gray steel, linked not with metal but with some kind of plastic. "Fuck's this shit? Fuck's this writing? What the fuck, over!"

Hector grabs it anxiously. "It looks like 7.62. Isn't it 7.62?"

"Looks like, but what the fuck!"

"Lay it in the tray." He cycles five rounds through. All five feed and eject. The plastic links fall out the bottom just like steel links.

But he still doesn't trust it.

HE tries to get his head down but can't close his eyes. Too wired. Images. Pink paste. Vats of blood. Detached heads. The shudder of chickens being electrocuted. Instead he cleans the Pig. He feels better when it's finally clean and lubed. So much better that he cleans it all over again.

At dusk they stand to. But nothing happens other than flares, or something, that light up the sky now and then to the north. Somebody's getting his shit hammered there, that's for sure. But it's far away. He decides not to worry about it.

Worry about their front. About whether the funky ammo will feed if they get hit.

An hour after dark comms go down. Suddenly, no warning, with the dull *pop* they've heard before. Only this time they stay down. Half an hour later a runner jogs along the perimeter. Hissing, "Stand to. Stand to. Motion to the front."

"Fuck they think we been doing?" Whipkey mutters sourly. But he flips down his NVGs. Clicks them on and off. "Fuck. Gotta op check these things too. Yours work?"

Hector slides his down and turns them on. But instead of the familiar seething green all he gets is black. "Nada."

"Whatever fried our comms got them, too."

He pats the Pig. No matter what, the Pig will keep them safe. He loosens his pistol in its holster too. Not much, but a last resort.

Distant chugs echo. "Fuck," Whipkey mutters, and they dive for the bottom of the dugout.

The earth rocks. The detonations walk up and down the line as if the enemy knows exactly where they are. A near miss shovels dirt over them and sucks the air out of their lungs. Hector lies with eyes and asshole squeezed tight, praying for it to be over. Then not praying, just enduring. His arms are wrapped around the assistant gunner. Another near hit blows the overhead cover down, burying them. Fumes choke him. He screams and claws at the dirt until he gets just enough airspace to breathe. Starts to dig out, then stops. Let the earth cover him. Let it bury him. Until this is over.

The detonations go on and on. Far from waning, they're succeeded by deeper, more violent ones. The sides of the hole quake, battering them. Someone's moaning, barking in his ear. He can't tell if it's himself or Whipkey. There no longer seems to be any difference.

FLARES trickle down, shedding a glaring unearthly illumination that makes the shadows all the darker. Beneath the lurid light the ground's pocked with bomb craters, shell craters, still smoking. Between them figures creep. They drop into cover and vanish, while others pop up and rush forward. Drones buzz overhead, their own or the enemy's Hector doesn't know. A steady wink of fire gutters from Chinese guns, and trails of fire from RPGs or something like the marines' Javelins flash toward and over the battalion's line, succeeded by hollow explosions. Something deep red flickers back and forth, over there, in the night.

Hector hunches his shoulders, sets the sights by feel, and squeezes the trigger.

The Pig fires five rounds, *bam bam bam bam bam*, and jams. Hector drags the operating handle back, ejects the bad round, and recharges. Fires eleven more rounds before it jams again.

The deep red flickers. It reaches out, searching among the craters.

He's fumbling at the action, trying to clear it, but the cartridge is jammed in hard, caught on the bolt face, when a deep carmine brilliance bursts, fragments, echoes and resounds all around him. It smears cobwebs over his vision. His whole brain turns red.

"*Laser!*" Whipkey screams, and claws at his face. He keeps screaming, staggering up.

"*Get down!*" Hector shouts, grabbing for him, shielding his eyes with his other hand. But bullets crack, whiplashing across the hill, and then something buzzes overhead, whining in, dreadfully close.

It cuts off suddenly and Whipkey screams again, a choked-off burst of animal terror. Ramos catches the flicker of a muzzle flash, frames it in the sight, and fires, fires, fires until the gun halts again, jammed once more.

When he looks back his assistant gunner lies half in, half out of the caved-in fighting hole, chin back at an unnatural angle. In the light of the falling flares a scarlet well pulses at his throat, in which is wedged something small and black, with stiff stubby wings. His open eyes stare up at the stars.

HE'S lying in the open, on his side, hugging the Pig. Somehow he knows he's out of ammo. Something heavy weighs down his right hand. When he lifts it the flare-light shows him his pistol, smeared with blood.

HE'S in a hole with three other marines. A rifle in his hands. No idea where it came from. Where's the Pig? He has to find it. But right now he's slapping in magazines, firing them out. The others are firing too, as fast as they can. One is Lieutenant Smalls. Face contorted, snarling, he's firing his pistol two-handed, double-tapping Chinese after Chinese. The rifle barrels glow and smoke in the darkness. They're not built to fire burst after burst, mag after mag. But the shadows keep coming. One ducks, straightens, flings out an arm. Smalls yells "Grenade" in a strange hoarse voice. He dives to the ground just before the explosion, and his body jumps, humps up, as Hector fires a burst over him into the grenadier.

HE'S hammering at something in the darkness. Without looking, he knows it's the Pig. Hammering its butt down again and again. Grunting. With rhythmic force. Then a flashlight illuminates the thing he's flailing at. A face. A mashed-in, concave mass of blood and bone now. But still breathing. Bubbles burst and slide. It's still trying to get up.

"Stand back," Hern orders. Hector sledgehammers twice more, slowing, exhausted, and finally obeys, staggering to his feet.

The flat final report of Hern's rifle.

RUNNING. Staggering. Figures in front of him, fitfully illuminated by explosion-flashes.

The wreck of a mule. Hundreds of cartridges lie scattered across the dirt. Brass ones, he notes dully. The driver blown into shreds of meat where he's been perforated from above. Strips of flesh hanging.

AN interminable night. A night that never ends. That never will end, in the memories of those who survive it.

DAWN. Somehow, they're overlooking the water. Dimly he understands they've crossed the island's waist during the night. Fought their way here, to a new sea. Crouched in a shallow fighting hole, he's obsessively, compulsively cleaning the Pig. Scrubbing burnt carbon off the bolt. Lubricating it. Reassembling it. No idea where the gun came from; at some point during the night there it was again, after he thought he'd lost it. Inexplicable. Or maybe it's someone else's. And maybe it doesn't matter.

The waves walk out of the fog, shattering on the red sand.

The dawn is old silver. Mist seethes above the surf.

An unfamiliar sergeant walks along, straightening the line. A net bag of liter bottles hangs off his shoulder. Two young women trail him, belts of cartridges draped around their shoulders like golden shawls. He tosses down a water bottle. Hector catches it in midair, tears the cap off, fastens his mouth to it greedily, and beckons for another. The sergeant tosses him a second liter. "Tail on to him," the NCO tells one of the marines with him, the black woman. Then, to Hector, "A ship went down out there. Some of 'em might try to make it to shore. Gunner, your new assistant. Private Phelps."

"Aye aye, Sergeant. Oorah, Phelps."

"Oorah," the woman mutters.

"Ammo's on its way. Keep an eye to seaward. Phelps, get this hole dug deeper."

Hector nods, fastened again to his bottle like a baby to a nipple. The private eyes him, then unsheathes an entrenching tool. The sand caves in nearly as fast as she shovels it out. But she keeps working, piling it up in front of them.

Faintly, out of the sea-mist, voices are shouting. Many voices, raised in what sounds like pleading.

Hector drains the first bottle and flips it over his shoulder. Eyes the second, but doesn't open it. He sets up the Pig and slaps in a belt. "The King fucks the Queen," he mutters.

"What?" says the private. She stops digging, looks at Ramos. Then at the sea, then back at the blood-caked, dirt-smeared, crazily mumbling gunner.

"M'name's Sheeda," she says tentatively.

"Safety on 'F,'" Hector says. "Bolt to the rear."

"What?"

"Double link at the open end. Free of dirt and corrosion."

The shouting from seaward is growing louder. The private resumes digging, faster now.

"The sear holds the bolt open," Hector mutters. He slots the charging handle back and flips up the cover assembly. Ensures the feed tray, receiver assembly, and chamber are clear. He slaps it down and pulls the cocking handle again. Where's Troy? Oh yeah. Troy's dead. Orietta. Pruss, too. Smalls. Hern. All dead.

"Gun one, Condition One, ready to fire," he slurs.

She frowns. "What?"

"Now listen up. We only got the one barrel. You're gonna pour that water on it, once I start firing, got that? Pour it on. Don't matter if it gets in the action. It'll cook out. But you got to keep that barrel cool. Hear me?"

She nods, looking scared. He swings the muzzle this way and that, making sure the bipod's dug in. Should be on a tripod in a fixed position like this. Somewhere, during the night, the optic has disappeared too. Doesn't matter. "Fucking optics gonna go south on you," he mutters. "Learn the fucking irons. Fuck the Queen."

"Huh?" Phelps looks concerned. Then shrugs as she slides into the hole next to him. "Whatever."

He barely notices. Out in the mist, dim figures are taking shape. They wade forward through the uneasy surf. They call out, voices plaintive, hands in the air. They stagger like zombies as they advance. Only a few carry weapons.

"Open fire," someone yells.

The Pig jackhammers his shoulder as other guns along the beach open up too. He traverses, picking out clusters. Geysers of white spray burst up. Those few who still carry weapons throw them away, raise their hands too. They cry out, pleading, but he keeps firing. Under the impacts they wilt, spin, drop, sink back into the sea. The water turns red beneath the silver mist. Screams reach them. The other guns fall silent. Someone grabs his shoulder, but he shakes it off and keeps firing.

"Cease fire. Cease fire," comes down the line. A few rifle shots crack out, then they too cease.

But Hector Ramos keeps firing. Traversing. Firing again, as a few belated figures coalesce from the sea-mist, staggering, wounded, some with only one hand stiffly raised.

"What are you doing?" Phelps screams into his ear. "They're surrendering. Cease fire. Stop!"

But he fires that belt out and reaches for the next. She grabs his wrists to keep him from loading it.

Then others are standing above them. The sergeant who assigned her. An officer. Hector whispers something to the ghosts around him. "What did you say?" the woman screams over the ringing in his ears.

"You got to learn," he mutters.

"What?"

"Learn to hate. Learn to kill. Bring your buddies back. Make sense of it later."

"He's fucking lost it," the officer says. "Get him out of there. Phelps, take the gun."

Someone helps him out of the fighting hole. He sways, head bent, hands to his face. Mind echoing. Lightning in his head. He tears off his helmet and throws it into the surf. Where the bodies bob and wash. So many. Where did they all come from? But before he can ask, the hands lead him away.

22

Xinjiang

S O here they were, back in the mountains after all. The mujahideen, or whoever they were, the guys who'd raided the marketplace, had blindfolded Teddy and Fierros after getting out of town. Taken their rifles. And covered them with heavy sacks of sand. Then rode for jolting miles, upgrade. The road surface had changed from asphalt to what sounded like crush and run, then gravel, and finally ungraded rock. Jolting from side to side, the pickup had climbed the last few kilometers with motor straining.

Ordered out, the two captives, or hostages, or whatever they were now, had had their blindfolds checked and tightened. But—and Oberg had taken this as a good sign—no one had yet offered to tie their hands. Instead, someone had thrust a piece of bread into them. He'd gnawed it hungrily. Thick fried dough, sweetened with honey and garnished with nuts. It had to be what angels ate in heaven.

"*Hao*," he grunted. *Nice.* Then, in an undertone, "Fierros. *Ni zai ma?*"

"*Horosho'.*"

Oh yeah. Right. They were supposed to be Russians hunters. Or at least ethnic Russian Tajiks.

Teddy was rethinking that now. That had been in case they ended up in official Chinese hands. Maybe Russian wasn't the right way to play it with these guys. Or even Tajik.

Of course, that depended on exactly who their captors were.

They climbed a rocky path for what felt like hours. The air grew cool. Evening, or they were really gaining altitude. Maybe both. He grew weak, dizzy. He could hear the airman's harsh breathing ahead, making heavy weather of it too, but didn't dare ask for a break. They might get a permanent rest. With a bullet to the head.

THE entrance to the cave was so low they had to crawl in on hands and knees. Straightening, Teddy grunted as rough hands jerked the blindfold off, taking some of his hair with it. Suppressing a yelp, he blinked into the guttering orange light of torches.

The cave went back into darkness. Bats twittered and squeaked far above. Down here camping gear, camp beds, and tables of rough wood were scattered across water-eroded limestone.

To his left spilled a tumbled mass of masonry and statuary. Dozens of ancient Buddhas lay toppled and shattered, their heads scarred and gouged into facelessness. The rock itself had been carved, obviously centuries before, into a haunting, eye-seducing frieze of . . . Dancers? Gods? Demons? Whatever they once had been, their images had been hammered apart in a lynch-mob ecstasy of destruction. When he looked down, his feet were shuffling through a crushed mass of ancient parchments, trodden in with centuries of bat excrement.

Ahead, in the direction they were being shoved, the same black banners as had flown from the pickups were draped behind a stone lectern that looked as if it had stood in the same place for at least a thousand years. A book lay open on it, with a Kalashnikov propped against one side. Teddy was pretty sure the book wasn't *The Lord of the Rings*.

He turned his attention to the men shepherding them forward, senses sharpened by the knowledge that in the next few minutes he would live or die depending on what his captors decided. The men were all young, and all black-bearded, or trying hard to grow beards and mustaches. Bandy-legged, but with the suggestion they were going to be husky lads. They had the flattish features and darker coloring of the crowd that had oohed and aahed watching the red-clad dancers, not the look of the more slightly built, lighter-complexioned security troops.

Actually, they reminded him of the guys on the caravan ponies. So, obviously, these were the Uighur bandits-slash-terrorists he'd heard about back at the Team briefings. How long ago that seemed. . . .

The Central Asian states had been fighting Islamic insurgencies long before 9/11. Spilling over China's western borders, the rebels were giving Beijing a hard time too. The local version of the al-Qaeda and Taliban he'd fought, himself, in Afghanistan.

The terror attack in town squared with that. It suddenly registered that the old merchant had known about it too. He'd warned them not to be in the Han part of town that day.

Teddy was still mulling all this when they shoved him to his knees in front of the lectern. Their captors settled on blankets and began chatting in low voices. One kept working the bolt on his AK, and complaining in a whine. Jerking the bolt, and flipping cartridges out. Making a wagging motion with his hand, as if the rifle wasn't ejecting right.

Now, to the side of the stone lectern, Teddy noted a large curved sword. Fierros cleared his throat. Breathed, so low Teddy could barely hear him, "Who *are* these dudes?"

He must be getting nervous. Well, Teddy was too. That was a hell of a mean-ass sword, and it looked well used. The tripod-mounted videocam next to it didn't look promising either.

Well, at least Trinh had missed this. A bullet in the brain was better, any day, than a twitchy amateur executioner with a dull blade and bad aim.

Fierros whispered, "Al-Qaeda? ISIS?"

Teddy pitched his answer so low he could barely hear himself. "Islamics. Not sure what brand. Better let me do the talking."

"We're not still Russians, are we?"

"No, that wouldn't be smart. Like I said, let me talk."

One of their escorts said something in the language he didn't know—not Han, probably Uighur—and slammed his shoulder with a rifle butt. The message was clear: *You guys, shut the fuck up.* Which he did, trying to sit back in a way that hurt his leg as little as possible.

Not too long after, three men came in carrying AKMs. They set them against the cave wall and eased themselves down on the blankets. They looked terribly tired and two were wounded, to judge from the bloody bandages and the wincing as they adjusted their crossed legs. Teddy recognized the one in the center. The driver of the pickup, the guy who'd gestured him aboard with the pistol. The one with the half-white mustache. The handgun was stuck into his belt now, one of the old high-velocity Tokarevs that made you deaf shooting them, but that penetrated helmets and body armor. Not a bad choice for a gunfight, actually. The guy pulled down the book, and Teddy nodded. He'd seen this before, with the Abu Sayyaf in the Philippines. On the operation to steal the rocket torpedo, with Commander Lenson's TAG team.

It was a drumhead court. The kind that really only pronounced one sentence, and finished up with somebody's noggin bouncing on the floor.

The Uighurs conferred among themselves, glaring at the captives. Teddy kept glancing at the guy who was fiddling with his rifle and complaining. Finally he reached over and took it out of his hands.

Before they could react he had the magazine out, chamber cleared, and top cover off. He flipped the rifle upside down and shook the piston assembly out onto the blanket. Just as he'd figured, a handful of crud fell out with it. Somehow, probably by dropping it, the guy had gotten sand inside the gas port holes, clogging the piston inside the tube. Which meant it stopped feeding. Yeah, that happened, even with Kalashes. But it was super easy to fix. He stripped the grit off the piston with his sleeve, blew the tube clear, and squinted through the barrel to make sure it was clear too. He reassembled the weapon, worked the action, and laid it back down in front of the rebel.

Who looked with astonishment from him to the judges. Who were also staring, no longer whispering among themselves.

After a few seconds they cleared their throats and seemed to regain some self-possession. The questioning began with the guy on Teddy's left, in Han Chinese. He wanted to know who they were and why they'd been firing at the police. Or at least, Teddy assumed that was what he meant by *jingcha*.

He'd been doing some thinking about this even before Fierros surfaced the issue, but held up a hand while he formulated his answer. Trying to project confidence. Dignity. Finally he said haltingly, in his prison Chinese, *"Women shi mengyou. Wo shi meigyo ren."*

We are allies. I am an American.

The judges gaped, lifting their eyebrows. White 'Stache looked especially doubtful. He shot some rapid Han Teddy only partially caught. He leaned to Fierros. "Ragger, did you catch that?"

"Something about . . . how we got here? How we came to Xinjiang, I think."

The judge on the right put his oar in, jabbing a finger threateningly. *"Zhe shi shui de ne? Ta shi meiguo?"*

"I think he wants to know if I'm American too. These guys have a way different accent than the guards."

"Well, goddamn it, answer him."

Bit by bit, fumbling with a language neither was overfamiliar with, they managed to get across that they were both both fighters, prisoners, captured in the great war raging far to the east and south. They had escaped from the prison camp, and fled over the mountains. "If war still on, we are on same side. We, and you, all brave fighters." Or at least, that was what Teddy hoped he was saying.

The center guy cocked his head. He seemed to have as much trouble following what they were trying to say as they had putting it out. Their interlocutors conferred in mutters. Then one said something that Teddy made as, "What camp?"

"Camp 576."

Impressed looks. "That is a hard place. Much sickness. They mine the rock that rots the bones. No one escapes from there."

"We did," Obie told him. "But we were five in number when we started." He explained about Maggie and Vu and Trinh: one giving his life on the live wire, to help them escape; one lost in the mountains; the third shot by the Chinese in town.

The judges nodded, apparently reassured by the high loss rate. White Mustache pressed, "You are American. Army? Air Force?"

Teddy had thought about this. He figured guys like this, out in the hinterlands, might know what U.S. Navy SEALs were. Then again, they might not. There were three initials, though, that pretty much everybody in the world recognized.

"Colonel Fierros here is with the United States Air Force. I'm with the CIA," he told them.

The effect was everything he'd hoped for. Shock, recoil, outrage; then heated debate. Two of his judges almost came to blows under the torches. But finally Middle Guy shushed them. He pulled the old pistol from his belt and threw it down on the blanket. Pointed at it. Said a word that Teddy figured had to be "disassemble."

Five seconds later it lay field-stripped into barrel, guide, slide, recoil spring, barrel bushing, slide stop pin, magazine, hammer assembly, and frame. He gave it a beat, then reassembled it. Four seconds.

They brought him a clayey gray paste in waxed paper and the sort of junk drawer a geek teenager might accumulate, filled with old batteries, broken radios, scrap wiring, miscellaneous electrical shit. Then sat back and fingered their beards, watching.

Teddy sniffed the plastic—nearly odorless—and figured it for Semtex, or maybe a Chinese rip-off of the Czech explosive. It didn't look recently manufactured, but the binder was still malleable. He rooted around in the junk box and came up with a bent nail. He also found a spring-loaded switch.

His mimed request for a tool produced a pair of battered pliers. Which might work . . .

He bummed a cartridge from the guy whose rifle he'd fixed. Wrenched the bullet out, discarded it and the powder, and packed the case with a teaspoonful of the plastic explosive. He crimped the case by hammering the handle of the pliers with a rock. After straightening the nail, fitting it into the switch, and filing on the switch for a while with another rock so that it held the nail back, he screwed the case into it.

He got up and hobbled on numbed legs across the cave, unraveling a string out of Fierros's disintegrating blanket. He tied that to a broken statue of a dancing god, lashed the other to his improvised device, and tied that to the stone lectern, despite a frown from one of the judges.

Then stood back and, with a bow and a sweeping gesture, invited them to try it: *Be my guest.*

"*Ni neng xíng de,*" said Tokarev Guy. He returned Teddy's bow. *No, you go ahead.*

Teddy put his hands over his ears, hoping he hadn't gotten too generous with the Semtex. Then limped between the stones, catching, as if by accident, his trailing foot on the low-strung string.

The loud crack and flash, the ping of hot steel around the cave, brought shouts and exclamations. Also raucous laughter, as Teddy howled and slapped at his buttocks, which stung like hell. Other fighters ran in from side chambers, weapons at the ready. They got loud explanations in jocular tones, complete with acting out and repeated exclamations of "CIA, CIA."

Teddy made a production out of rubbing his ass and grimacing, but made sure that when he eased himself down again, it was up front, beside his erstwhile judges. He wasn't sure which one was head honcho. But they'd had the same problem in the Philippines. With the Abu Sayyaf, there'd been three guys to play to. A clan chief, a war leader, and also an imam, a religious leader. But he didn't see anybody like either a clan chief or a religious leader here. They all seemed to be fighters, and none over thirty, at a guess.

Which might make it easier. He spread his hands, mustering his Chinese. "*Women shi mengyou,*" he said again, making it slow. "We are allies. The great war. It is still being fought?"

"Oh, yes. America, China . . . Zhang still fights."

"Then we both fight Han. Yes? America on east, Uighur on west. Same enemy. Yes?"

He read mingled agreement and doubt in the murmurs, shakes, and nods. Okay, making progress, but not there yet. He gave Fierros a squint, trying to signal him to quit kneeling in the position of the suppliant, the defendant, and to come over with him, with the council, as it were. After a second squint, the airman got up. His guards looked doubtful, but when none of the judges objected, let him join them. Good, another step forward.

"Let me find out . . . let me . . ." Christ, his rice-bowl pidgin wasn't up to this. "Does anyone here speak English? Russian? How about Arabic?"

The reference to Arabic got dropped gazes. Thought so. Teddy almost grinned.

"Ya gavorit' nim noga Russki," said White Mustache, reluctantly. "I speak little bit Russian."

"Great. *Horosho'. Kak vas zovut?* And I'm calling you . . . what?"

"My war name is Tokarev."

Figured. Teddy hesitated. Go with his real name? Probably a bad idea. His Team name? Maybe an op name . . . But before he could respond, Tokarev was tracing the scars on his face with his finger. *"Vy poluch'te eti boyev'ye kitaiski?* You get these fighting Han? Or in camp?"

That was an easy lie. "Fighting Han."

The Uighur laid a hand on his bad leg. Teddy couldn't help wincing. "And this?"

"Pytali . . . tortured. By Han interrogators." No point telling them where he'd picked up the original injury. In the White Mountains, fighting the Taliban.

Tok translated it for the others, who nodded and stroked their beards. Teddy bowed. They bowed back.

"So, you are CIA agent," Tok said. *"Vy tak stary."*

Teddy inclined his head modestly. Time to get the conversation off them and onto their hosts. He said, "Yes, I am old. But not as old as I probably look right now. Please translate this for your friends. I fight Han because my country is at war with Beijing. Zhang is a tyrant. An aggressor. Please tell me why you fight."

They nodded and milked their beards, and gradually the answers came. "We fight for independent Uighuristan, under rule of true Islam," said one.

The older guy said, at least as Tokarev translated, "No Muslim should live under the rule of infidels. Those who worship Confucius and Marx are not people of the Book."

One of the guards, who'd sidled up to join the discussion, put in: "They have taken our land with arms. The mujid must resist until we are free again."

"We must overthrow Zhang and set up a democracy. Then all can live together in peace, both Han and Uighur. But of course, we were here first."

Yet another said, "Our brothers in Kyrgyzstan, Kazakhstan, and Turkey are of one blood with us here in Xinjiang. We must all be united. Can America help us in this?"

Teddy nodded sagely at each statement, contradictory though they were, patting his own beard too, as if taking it all aboard. Murmuring "Ah" and *"Ponimayu."*

Presently a small figure draped head to toe in black appeared from the shadows. It waited silently until the oldest guy beckoned. Gave peremptory orders. When it returned, accompanied by several others, the women—if that was what the toe-to-head sacks covered—set out plastic trays of rice, naan, and lamb. Not a hell of a lot of any of these, but apparently as close to a feast as the resistance could muster on short notice. Tea arrived too, steam rising from the cups as a trembling hand poured it. The dark eyes behind the *hijab* never rose to meet his. "Looks like we're in," Obie muttered to Fierros, rolling a piece of bread preparatory to digging in.

"No haircut?"

"Not today."

"What was all that about? I only followed parts of it."

"They want to know what we can do for them. I had to make some promises."

"Promises about what?"

"Weapons. Support."

"I thought the idea was to get across the border. Get the fuck out of this fucking country. We're still in fucking China. You know that, right?"

Teddy tested the tea. *Way* too hot. "That's still the idea, Ragger. I'm just playing with a different approach here, okay? Trying to establish friendly relations. Feel out a quid pro quo. Maybe plant the idea, they help us out, we got something to offer too. Okay?"

The airman subsided, reaching for the rice and lamb. Teddy grabbed his left hand just in time.

THREE days later he and Ragger stood under an overhang of rock while the pickup idled not far away, while boys with sticks urged baaing sheep up a plank ramp into the bed. Tok, whose real name was Guldulla, said they had to stay under overhead concealment, and anyone traveling by truck had to remain hidden beneath the sheep while on the road. The Han had drones that watched, and struck from the sky. He and the older rebel, Akhmad, stood a few paces off, letting them say their farewells. The third leader, Nesrullah, had gone over the mountain, into the town on the far side, for supplies.

Teddy doubted that Chinese internal security would have drone coverage out here, in this terrain, but these guys were the local knowledge. They did seem to have an effective lookout system: the shepherds all toted cheap walkie-talkies.

Fierros was dressed like one of the locals. Black embroidered four-cornered hat, long-sleeved black shirt, raggedy pants, cheap Chinese running shoes. With hair all over his face, he might pass. At a distance. If they didn't get stopped.

Oberg was out of the lice-ridden goatskins too. He had his rifle slung over his shoulder, the one he'd taken off the wounded Han back at the square. Tok had given it back to him. "A fighter needs a rifle," he'd said. Teddy had cleaned it, and lubed it properly. They'd been able to give him only five rounds for it, but it would do for now.

Ten paces off, squatting in the shadows, Dandan waited. A shadow herself, in the black cloak that covered her from bare feet to crown. That was her name. Dandan. They'd assigned her to him after he'd made clear he intended to stay. Rather to Fierros's annoyance. Teddy wasn't sure of her status. Slave? Volunteer? Temporary wife? Hostage? As far as the rebels were concerned, women seemed to be on a par with sheep. She didn't seem to be Uighur. He doubted she was even thirteen, though it was hard to tell, and they had no language in common. But she looked old enough for the basic purposes. To cook his naan, and keep him warm at night. Beyond that, he was still too weak to be good for much. Although he had ambitions.

He told the pilot, "Tok says they'll have you over the border tonight. Deliver you to somebody who can get you to the embassy. Couple days and you'll be back in uniform, dude. And they'll be counseling you about that beard."

"You're really not coming," Fierros said, not for the first time. As if he couldn't believe it.

"These guys are pretty hopeless right now. Just small-town bandits. But they could be made into a significant resistance. Cause Zhang some real headaches. Pull maybe as much as a couple divisions out here, if I do this right."

"You don't think we've done enough? You and me?"

"This war's not over." Teddy gripped Fierros's hand again, then wrapped him in a guy hug. They held it, unembarrassed after all the nights spent cuddling in the mountains. "But you gotta get back. Tell them what we got here, and what we need. Primarily comms, to start coordinating. An A-team, if they can spare one. If not, I guess I can run things for a while. But they need weapons—LMGs, rockets, grenades, ammo. Mines, for the roads. All these guys have is worn-out AKs and some construction-grade explosive they stole. Send boots. Food. Medical supplies. Ballistic vests. Gas masks. Water treatment. But mainly, we need comms."

Water and ammo and comms, a voice from his past said in his head. Who had that been? Oh yeah. Old Master Chief "Poochin'" Stroud. *Never have too much ammo*, Stroud had always said. And *Let the fucking officers display the fucking leadership. You just make goddamned sure everything's there when your troops need it, and it all works.*

Fierros stepped back, but kept a hand on Teddy's shoulder. "You really okay, Obie?"

"Yeah—yeah. But hit that ammo button hard, okay? And comms— squirt transmitter, a prick-one-seventeen or the new one, if they can spare one. With lots of batteries, or a solar. There's a lot of resentment here. Akhmad says if he had the weapons, he could put two hundred fighters in the field next week. Anything they can get to us, air drop, even mules over the border, we can build this thing into a real pain in the ass for the fucking Chinks."

"What about you, Teddy?"

"Me?" Since his vision on the mountain—or hallucination, or whatever it had been—he didn't seem to want anything. He, himself, didn't seem to matter so much. If something was going to happen, so be it. Then he remembered the slip of paper he'd prepared. "Oh yeah. Here, I wrote down the measurements. That's in centimeters. If they can make me some kind of a brace for my fucking leg, that would be cool."

"Sure, of course. What else?"

"What else? Oh . . . a thin-blade knife. And maybe a case of beer, if they're really . . . no, that wouldn't go down with the fucking mujes. Can you believe now we're on the same side? Scratch that. The beer, I mean."

The airman scuffed the dry pebbly soil, not meeting his gaze. "I meant personally. You told me about Salena. Your girlfriend? What do you want me to tell her? And that Japanese woman. Your producer, you said?"

"Hanneline." Teddy took a breath, peering out from under the shelf at the distant mountains. The last of the sheep were loaded. The driver was beckoning.

On the far side of those snowcapped peaks, Tajikistan. But not safety. The war seemed to have spread while they'd been prisoners, from what he was able to gather from BBC World Service on the single little radio the rebels had. The whole world seemed to have been dragged in, one by one, while they'd been starving in camp. And it didn't seem as if the Allies were winning.

Salena? She was a distant memory. A scene from a film he'd watched long ago.

Hanneline, his mother's friend, his old agent? He could hardly believe he'd wanted to make movies once. He couldn't even remember the name of the project now. No. That was all gone. Blown away, like the pollen of the poppies, lost on the thin cool wind of the Tien Shan.

You have always done My will.

There was no such thing as choice. There was no such thing as chance.

Teddy Oberg said, "Just tell them that the guy they used to know is dead."

23

Arlington, Virginia

THE house overlooked a creek that ran through a wooded ravine. A brick colonial, with flagstone walks and three bedrooms and a family room in the basement, though Blair and Dan didn't have children, aside from his grown-up daughter. She'd furnished it from the antique shops she liked to stop at when they drove to Maryland to visit her parents. Other pieces were from her family's estate, things her mom and dad had let go when they'd redecorated.

It wasn't as nice a home as she'd grown up in, but it was all they needed. She spent most of her time elsewhere anyway.

"You bad boy," Blair said. "Go on. Eat your food." Jimbo preened under her hand, purring, stretching as if his black-and-white body were made of taffy. She didn't mind talking to the cat when Dan wasn't around. Actually, he did sometimes too.

The teapot began to whistle. She made a peach momotaro. Glanced at the clock while she waited for the sachet to open. Frowned, then realized the power must have gone out again during the night.

In their bedroom, she dressed. A severe blue suit. Dark pumps. Then clattered down the stairs. They wanted her in the Tank at seven.

She was checking her briefcase when she noticed activity on the street in front of the house. Several people had stopped their bicycles, or held their dogs on leashes, just standing there. Watching her house? She frowned, peering through the curtains.

No. They were watching two people who stood beside an official-looking sedan, consulting tablet computers. A short white woman and a Hispanic-looking man. Both were in Navy blue and gold.

Taking a deep breath, she searched around for a chair. "Not this house," she murmured. Then immediately thought: How selfish. Do I really want someone else to get such news?

That's right. Anyone else. Just not me.

When the doorbell chimed she couldn't make herself get up. Her knees didn't feel like they'd hold. Finally she groped to the door, pausing to lean on a side table.

"Mrs. Blair Lenson?" the woman, a lieutenant by the two gold stripes, said, meeting her gaze. In unison, a practiced movement, they both removed their hats.

"Um, well, I'm Blair Titus."

"Wife of Captain Daniel Valentine Lenson?"

She braced a hand on the jamb, feeling, somehow, stronger than she'd have thought she would at such a moment. Or maybe the collapse would come later. "He's an admiral. Not a captain." The next second she thought, Why did I say that? What difference can it possibly make now?

The Hispanic guy nodded soberly. "I'm sure that's being corrected, ma'am. But you are Daniel Lenson's wife?"

"I am." Let it only be a wound, God. Even his legs.

But they called you on the phone to report someone was wounded. They didn't send official notifiers.

The woman said, "Would you like us to come inside?"

"No, I don't—you can tell me whatever it is out here."

The man, a chief, said, "Ma'am, I'm sorry to have to notify you that Captain—Admiral—Lenson has been reported missing in action."

She sealed her mouth with a palm. Said though her fingers, "Missing. What does that mean? Exactly?"

"You understand, we can only give confirmed information," the lieutenant said. "All we know at present is that he was involved in an aircraft crash, in the line of duty. No bodies have been recovered, and the status of survivors, if any, is unknown."

This felt like a dream, but she didn't think it was one. "Um . . . an, a crash. You say. Was he lost at sea? In battle? Is it possible he was captured?"

The woman said, "I'm sorry, Mrs. —Ms. Titus. We really don't have any more information. I wish we did."

The man said, "Is there anyone we can call for you? A friend, or a pastor?"

"No. No, I don't think that's necessary. A crash. Does that mean he's probably dead?" Wait a minute . . . she'd already asked that. Hadn't she? Now she couldn't remember.

The chief said patiently, "We really don't have any more information, ma'am."

After a pause the lieutenant glanced at her tablet, and thumbed something on the screen. "I have secondary next of kin listed as a Nan Lenson, daughter, residing in Seattle. Do you know if that's correct?"

"Yes. His daughter. Seattle." She gripped the jamb, trying not to slide to the floor.

"Would you have a current number for her, ma'am? We don't seem to have up-to-date data on the secondary next of kin."

Hands shaking, she went back to Dan's office and rooted until she came up with what she hoped was his daughter's address. Carried it back out. "Here it is. I'm not sure if this is current, but it's the latest I could find."

"If you'd just sign here, that you've been notified," the lieutenant said, holding out the tablet and a silver stylus. "Also, please check that the contact number we have for you is correct. You'll hear from us again with an update as soon as additional information becomes available. Here's my card, if any further questions occur in the meantime. I sincerely hope the next news you hear is good, ma'am."

The woman took a step back, fitted her cap on. Together, in unison, they saluted. Blair took a deep breath, and tried to smile. "Thank you. You have a hard job."

"We've both lost people. Family, and friends," the woman told her. "That's why we volunteered for casualty notification."

"Well, you've carried it out very professionally. Thank you. Would you like—I have water hot for tea, or coffee—"

"Thank you very much, ma'am," the woman said. The man was already scrutinizing his tablet again, turning away toward the sedan. "But I'm afraid this is only the first stop we have to make today."

SHE went to sit in an upholstered chair in the front room, hands over her face, trying to take it in. Then forced herself up. She couldn't just sit here. Sitting here wasn't doing anyone any good. She went to the foyer and checked herself in the mirror. Pale, but no tears. Good.

She was still due in the Tank.

THE first call came in her car. She almost didn't answer when she saw who it was from. Then, finally, pushed the Talk button on the steering wheel. "Titus."

"Blair? Hu Kuwalay."

Senator Talmadge's senior staffer. "Hu. What can I do for you?"

"I just heard. I'm so sorry."

"I thought there was a news blackout until after they notified the families."

"Uh, Bankey has back-channel. You know that, right? The congressional liaison notified us. The senator wanted me to call right away. Express our condolences."

"He's not dead, Hu. Just missing. So condolences are not in order. Not yet."

"Right, right. Important to keep that in mind."

"Why didn't he call himself?"

"I'm sorry?" Kuwalay said.

"Why didn't Bankey call me? I know he's up. He's always been an early riser. Why didn't he do this?"

"Um, well . . . he's got someone in there with him."

"He doesn't want to speak with me?"

"I'm sure that's not it, Blair."

But from his tone, she knew it was. She and Talmadge had had a set-to three days before, about the funds he'd pledged to reimburse her for her campaign. Since she'd lost, it seemed to be a forgotten promise. Speaking off the record, woman to woman, his aide had let drop that the party's isolationist wing cherished a grudge against her.

"What for?" Blair had asked.

"What for? For joining the other party," Mindy had said, as if it were obvious.

Now Blair said, "Hu, put Bankey on. I know he's there in the office."

"He's not here right now, Blair. I told you that."

She felt her face heat. "No, you said he was busy. So I'm on the other side of the fence now? For joining a wartime coalition government? Think this through clearly, Hu. You know what the national security adviser keeps pushing for? A hard-line strategy. Escalation. Without me pushing back, we could be in an all-out nuclear war."

The staffer said, *"I hear what you're saying. Seriously, I do. But you have to accept the reality, Blair."*

She was pulling off the cloverleaf, under the overpass, up to the Pentagon. "What reality would that be, Hu? Make it fast, I'm on my way in to the Tank."

Kuwalay said, *"The middle of the road is where people get run down, Blair."*

* * *

THE E Ring, Corridor 9. Officially it was the JCS Conference Room, or the Gold Room. When the guard opened the door most of the Chiefs were already gathered around coffee urns and plates of sweet rolls set out on a sideboard. The room was carpeted and curtained in gold and centered with a glass-covered conference table. She wondered why the truly important spaces—the Situation Room, the Oval Office—always seemed too small. The chairs were covered in cordovan leather. Yellow pads and pencils lay precisely squared at each place. Bowls of peppermints and lemon drops were spaced along the table, at a convenient arm's length from each seat.

The chairman, General Ricardo Vincenzo, was already seated, reading a document, halfway down the table. When he noticed her, he pointed to the chair to his right. An honor; usually the SecDef sat there. Obviously he wasn't going to be here today. She nodded to the other generals, to Dr. Hui.

A bearlike form intercepted her. Nick Niles. "I heard about Dan," the CNO rumbled. A huge hand enveloped hers. "I'm very sorry. What have they told you?"

"Not much, Admiral. Just that he's missing, after a crash. Do you know anything more?"

"Apparently he was leaving his ship and the helo went down. Unfortunately, it was in a battle zone. Which complicates the search. But if he's out there, we'll find him."

"Let's get started," the deputy chief called.

The first agenda item was the battle in the East China Sea. A naval captain she didn't know briefed. On the whole, Operation Recoil had proceeded satisfactorily. Transit to the objective had been accomplished without significant loss. Advance force operations to degrade air defenses had gone well. Heavy carrier air and long-range bomber strikes had struck airfields on Okinawa and the mainland Ningbo complex. Preliminary reports estimated a 50 percent reduction in enemy forces. During the intrusion, two enemy submarines were also destroyed, and a total of twenty-one enemy aircraft and dozens of UAVs were shot down. No enemy surface forces had participated in the battle. Four theater ballistic missiles were launched from South Korean territory. Two got through, but inflicted no damage.

"Friendly losses were limited to damage to four ships and a loss of ten aircraft, as follows: six fighter, two strike, two helicopters. Also, significant losses were experienced in drones and autonomous vehicles. Overall, though, lower own-force erosion than was forecast, mainly due to the absence, so far, of a nuclear response, which was predicted by some staff officers."

The briefer paused, but none of the admirals or generals spoke. He went on. "Advance elements are withdrawing under cover of the carrier groups. PaCom recommends recovering damaged units and continuing search-and-rescue efforts, then transiting the combined force southward, after refueling and rearming, to cover continuing action in the northern Philippines."

The Chiefs questioned him closely on details. The captain seemed to have the answers, and after thanking him, Vincenzo let him go. As the door closed he said, "Any necessity for deliberation?"

Shaken heads. Niles glanced at her, then away. She inspected her yellow pad. *DAN DAN DAN* was written on it in increasingly jagged cursive.

"Next agenda item: Mandible," Vincenzo said.

A Marine general briefed on the landings on Itbayat. Blair kept her head down, but registered that fighting was continuing and casualties were heavy. Computers and electronics had been taken down by sector-wide cyberattacks. A lot of dead on the beach. More as the Marines moved inland. Severe losses, too, among the Navy units getting them ashore. She realized that those must be the other calls the casualty team had said they had to make this morning.

"The island's been cut in half," the general said. "But the enemy has regrouped to the north and is counterattacking. All our reserves have been committed," he concluded. "The major shortage is ammunition. Expenditure has been heavier than planned and due to the nature of the beaches and the loss of ship-to-shore transport, resupply is difficult.

"To be blunt, the issue's still in doubt. Additional support from the northern strike group will be greatly welcome."

"Deliberations?" Vincenzo asked again, leaning back.

The Air Force deputy chief of staff: "How soon can the airfield be made operational?"

"We'll staff you an answer on that," the chairman said, scribbling a note, tearing the paper off, and handing it to an aide. "Other comments? All right, then I have a quick update.

"Our global security overwatch has been preempted by responding to China. But the New Caliphate is threatening Israel. Russia's infiltrating Latvia and Belarus, a replay of the destabilization tactics used in Ukraine. NATO and the EU are debating their response, but we can't help. All our forces are either in the Pacific or en route there, except for the advisers left in the Mideast.

"Basically, we're still weak—mobilization is far behind schedule— and we're facing a long, grim war. I presented our options to the heads of state conference in Sydney. The strategy agreed on there is to tighten the encirclement, aid those currently fighting the common enemy, and open two new theaters of war, as well as to stir up internal dissent. That will be a CIA mission, mainly. We'll also be taking steps against Iran.

"In the middle of the conference, we received disheartening news. The Vietnamese lines were penetrated by armored forces. The People's Liberation Army is surging toward Hanoi amid bitter fighting and massive casualties on both sides. We had to offer increased logistic and air support, or risk having Vietnam knocked out of the alliance."

The Air Force deputy said, "They've invited us to establish a forward base at Da Nang. We've identified a bomb wing and initiated forward movement and initial security."

Vincenzo nodded heavily. "All right. Now, I'm going to ask that the room be cleared. Principals only."

"Deputies?" one of the generals asked. The chairman hesitated, then nodded, reluctantly, Blair thought.

When the doors were resealed, Vincenzo turned to her. "All right, Blair. Tell us about Jade Emperor."

She took a breath, composing herself. "We actually know very little. A lot is inference, gleaned from traffic between the mainland and an island outpost.

"The Jade Emperor was a legendary figure in Chinese history. He overthrew an army of evil demons through his wisdom, and became the supreme sovereign of men and gods."

Vincenzo gestured impatiently; she cut to the chase. "'Jade Emperor' is a massively capable artificial intelligence being built in western China. Even in a partially completed state, it can infiltrate and degrade any Internet data packet anywhere in the world. It's behind the brownouts on the West Coast, the nuclear-power-plant scrams, the disruptions in satellite communications, the fires at our refineries, the banking-network takedowns. There are indications it can penetrate our most secure high-side command networks.

"As its capabilities increase—as it *learns*—it will be able not just to degrade, but actually to take control of industrial processes, financial networks, and communications and power nodes."

"Can we bomb it?" someone asked.

"Anything *can* be bombed," the Air Force general said. "The question is, what losses you're willing to take."

Vincenzo said, "Now tell us about Battle Eagle."

Blair nodded. "Battle Eagle began building three years ago, in secret, of course. A DARPA-chartered joint venture of eight software developers, known as Archipelago. Dr. Hui here probably knows more about it than I do, since one of its earliest outputs was a hitherto unsuspected way to degrade North Korean ballistic missile guidance. Denson?"

"I'm constrained by classification," Hui said, a bit stiffly.

"Even in front of the Joint Chiefs?" Vincenzo frowned. "Doctor?"

Hui inclined his head. "All I can say is that the way Ms. Titus describes the enemy AI more or less resembles Battle Eagle as well. The architectures differ. But they're both massive self-programming neural networks, designed to dispute digital infrastructure with peer competitors."

"I'm having difficulty buying this," said Niles, unwrapping a peppermint. He examined it doubtfully, then popped it into his mouth. "Are you serious?"

"Every war brings technologies forward," Blair told him. "Bombing aircraft were a fantasy in 1913. Atomic weapons were science fiction in 1939. Now, instead of teams of human hackers or code breakers, we'll have two massive programs locked in combat in cyberspace. And whichever wins, I'm sorry to say, may determine the course of this war, whatever we do on the ground."

The officers looked disbelieving. A tap came at the door. "Come in. We're done here," Vincenzo called.

The captain who'd given the opening briefing came in. "New developments, General. The Chinese are finally buckling on Itbayat. Marines report accepting surrenders at the company level."

"That's good news," said a National Guard general.

"Also, the Philippines have announced they'll send a force to take over the occupation."

"Oh no they won't," Vincenzo said, flicking his chin. "They handed it over to the fucking Chinese. We paid in blood to get it, and we're keeping it. I'll call State and make that clear. Anything else?"

"Yes, sir," the captain said. "Tokyo has renounced Zhang's cease-fire. Also, they've announced stand-up of a nuclear deterrent, which they will use if China attacks the home islands."

One of the generals whistled, but the captain pressed on. "Along with that, they made a commitment to eject all foreign forces from Okinawa.

And they will support the Allies quote, 'wherever else in Asia they may move against aggression.'"

Blair sat back as the others smiled. Japan had returned to the war. The third-biggest economy in the world, with a skilled if small military. Situated directly astride the sea lanes from China out into the Pacific.

The Pacific, where . . . Dan was still missing. And after a crash . . . not even bodies recovered . . .

She was a widow, it seemed, whether she could bear to acknowledge it or not.

Not that her personal suffering mattered much, in a world at war.

Because that's what it was turning into: A *world* at war.

And a war that looked, increasingly, as if it might go either way.

The Afterimage

THE yellow raft bobbed gently on the blue. Three figures sprawled with heads back, eyes closed, bandages wrapping hands and faces. Seawater sloshed slowly under sagging bodies.

The last drinking water was long gone. The last food, a few dry bars in the raft's survival pouch, had been eaten at the end of the third day.

A gull circled, first curious, then avid, onyx eyes agleam. It descended gradually, tilting this way and that, tee-tertottering on the westerly wind. A cruel beak gaped greedily.

None of the figures moved. Only the raft stirred, tossing uneasily on a gentle chop, under a burning sun.

The gull circled again, a wary eye cocked for competitors. It dipped lower, spreading white wings to land.

The figure in the blue coveralls suddenly twitched. A hand removed a hat. Red swollen eyes blinked. Blackened fingers dug at an itching rime of pus and salt.

Dan Lenson blinked up into the glare of the noon sun as the angry squawk of a frustrated bird drifted down. He panted, rubbing cracked, bleeding lips. Hoisted himself an inch or two, and peered around.

Flat empty sea. He couldn't tell its color, he'd stared at it so long. Only that it glittered like a broken mirror, agonizingly bright by day, then chilled with an inky black stirred with streats of phosphorescence by night.

WILKER'S groping hand at his chest, in the cockpit of the sinking helo, had been for his own bailout bottle, which the pilots carried zipped into their vests. Once he'd gotten that into his mouth, holding his broken jaw closed with one hand, he and Dan had buddy-breathed until they'd extricated the pilot's legs from the crushed-down instrument panel, popped their inflation, and made for the surface.

He and Wilker had bobbed for a time, calling out for other survivors. At last a weak response. Captain Hwang, breaststroking toward them, but with difficulty. His life jacket trailed uninflated. Something seemed to be weighing him down. Dan checked the jacket, but kept bumping something hard. At last, between waves, he'd sputtered, "What's that you're carrying?"

"Notebook."

"You saved your computer?"

"Classified. Must save."

"Let it go, Min Su. It'll drown you."

"I will go down with it . . . if so." His head went under just then, and both Dan and Wilker had to haul him up. The Korean coughed desperately, but muttered, "Must safeguard. At all costs."

Then his eyes had lit suddenly, and he'd raised a dripping arm to point. "Raft!"

They never knew where it had come from. Either deployed automatically by the sinking helicopter, or released, before he'd died, by the crewman. But there it was, riding high and about the most welcome sight they could have imagined, aside from a rescue helo. Unfortunately, it was drifting away from them, driven briskly by the wind.

"You guys wait here," Dan had snapped, and struck out.

The swim had exhausted him, but he'd caught up, finally. Then, after a short rest, climbed in, and paddled back with the little emergency oar. A slick coated the waves, a stink of fuel, bobbing plastic items, paper debris. Hwang pulled himself in, with his computer. They tried to be gentle, but Wilker screamed as they hauled him aboard. "I think they're both broken," he'd gasped.

Feeling the pilot's legs through his flight suit, Dan had to agree. But he couldn't think of a thing to do about it, other than to find the survival kit. Unfortunately, the radio had absorbed a fragment from whatever hit their engine. At about that time, he also realized the raft was softening under them, leaking from multiple holes.

Fortunately, the patch kit was intact.

For the first day, after he'd wrestled Hwang's computer away and thrown it overboard, they'd tried to paddle northeast, along the vector Wilker said he'd been flying to *Hampton Roads*. The breeze made it hard. Each time he lifted the paddle for a rest, it blew the raft's blunt nose off course. And he tired all too quickly. Whether it was from lack of sleep, the shock of the crash, or whatever, he couldn't seem to muster much energy, though he was still alert.

He just wondered how long he could stay that way.

NOT far into the second afternoon, Hwang had gasped out, "Submarine."

Dan had stopped paddling after a spell that had left him so woozy he'd almost lost the paddle. He stared where the Korean was pointing. "I don't see anything."

"Wait until we rise."

The slow Pacific swell lifted them, and he saw it. A low black shape was cutting their way. He frowned, shading his eyes. But submarines didn't transit on the surface. Not in this century. And it didn't seem as large as it ought to be. Also, the shape was wrong—

"It's a hunter," he said. "One of ours. I think."

The autonomous semisubmersible glided silently on. Its course would lead it past, he saw, not directly to them. But there was a bare possibility. . . .

The others saw this too. Bending, they began prying and scooping at the sea with the plastic oars, with bare hands. The raft spun under their uncoordinated efforts, then straightened as they dug in together. It didn't exactly speed over the waves, but they were making way. Dan paddled as hard as he could, aiming by seaman's eye for a point where they might intercept the hunter. Assuming the thing didn't change course. Which, since it was probably headed back to a preset rendezvous, didn't seem likely.

They paddled like demons, until their lungs burned and their hands bled. The slanted side of the conning tower, or whatever you called it on a robot vehicle, barely broke the water. The deck itself was awash. The prow peeled up only the slightest wave, though it had to be doing six or seven knots. He couldn't remember what powered these semisubmersibles, fuel cells or batteries, but it was absolutely silent.

"We're only gonna have one shot at this," he panted. "Hwang, grab that line. Make it up in a bowline."

"A bow—?"

"In a loop. A circle." He eyed the swiftly nearing craft, searching for protrusions. Hitting at any speed, it would just bounce the inflatable aside. Their only chance was to lasso some mooring point or sensor stub, then scramble aboard as the raft was towed along. Once on board, they could probably find some way to get below. The things must have accesses for repair and rearming, and surely there was some way to steer them from inside. This could be their ticket home.

If they could get aboard . . . "*Harder*," he gasped, paddling with all he could muster. "Almost there."

Hwang held up a loop of line. "I see a place to put it."

A vertical jut, halfway back from the bow. Either a sonar receiver or some sort of digital transmission head. "Go for it, Min Su. But don't miss."

Beside him, paddling with one hand, Wilker groaned encouragement.

They covered the last yards with a rush, and now he could hear it, a low hum as the thing powered through the water. A rotating optical sensor atop the pyramidal black fin stopped revolving, swung back, and locked on them.

"Stop," Dan shouted, knowing it was probably silly, that the thing wouldn't respond to voice commands. But he couldn't help it. The others cried out too, waving, shouting.

The unwinking eye of the optical seeker tracked them. He felt a thrill of hope. It had noticed. Whatever intelligence guided it had registered their existence. It would have to take action of some kind. It couldn't just pass them by.

The oculus stayed on them, even as the black craft neared. Suddenly a chill ran up his spine. Something about its unwavering yet passionless gaze implied both recognition, and an inhuman, pitiless dismissal. . . .

"What the fuck," Dan breathed. "No."

The black silhouette was altering.

The stern swung toward them. The chuckle of water increased. It was speeding up, too.

"Avoidance subroutine," Wilker croaked though his shattered mouth.

In a few minutes it was a speck, shrinking away.

SINCE then they'd drifted with the wind. Searching the sky for aircraft, seeing only the distant traceries of high contrails. But none swerved their way. They squinted into the reflected glare until their eyes teared and dazzle played inside their skulls. But never saw a ship.

It was strange no one had vectored a search-and-rescue helo to the crash site. Well, maybe they had more pressing issues.

Now Dan pried crusted, sticky lids open once again, peering at a bank of clouds. The raft jostled uneasily. Thank God they hadn't had to ride this thing, patched and overloaded as it was, through any storms. So far, anyway. That would finish them for sure.

Instead they would die slowly from dehydration. There'd been only two cans of emergency water in the raft, and the desalinization kit hadn't worked beyond a drop or two.

The gull was back, circling lower, evaluating him with head cocked. Hoping to feast on his eyes, no doubt. Hadn't someone in another life raft, another castaway, caught a curious gull, wrung its head off, drunk its blood? He half closed his lids and lay totally still, hand concealed but ready to grab. But the bird just kept circling, and uttering its harsh reproachful cries. Actually, he could understand what it was saying now. It was quite plain. "*Die. Die.*"

"Yeah, soon enough," he muttered through cracked lips. Squinting between salt-swollen lids, he examined a paler patch of sky.

Then hoisted himself, shading his stinging eyes.

A white sky. Which often signaled surf ahead.

He shook the others back into consciousness. They stirred, murmuring, groaning. Then stilled as he pointed to the east.

Over the next hour, as the steady wind scudded them, it came into view. A low island, maybe half a mile long. Ringed by white surf as long swells built, toppled, and broke. They watched silently as a dark mass pushed up out of the sea, becoming beach, palms. Eventually they could make out individual trees.

Dan reached over the side to scoop up water. He grunted as the salt seared into scabbed eyes, burned skin, bleeding lips.

There would be coral under that surf. Sharp-toothed, razor-edged reefs. A hundred to one the raft would capsize going through those breakers, and they'd be torn into sharkbait. Who knew what island this was, or who held it. The three men stared hungrily. None of them spoke.

Shuddering as the surf-line crept nearer, they gripped one another's hands.

The voyages of USS Savo Island *and* Task Force 76, *and the story of the war with China, will continue in David Poyer's* Deep War.

ACKNOWLEDGMENTS

EX nihilo nihil fit. For this novel, I began with the advantage of notes accumulated for previous books about Navy and joint operations, as well as my own experiences at sea and in Central Asia and the Pacific. The following new sources were also helpful.

For details on Apra Harbor: Globalsecurity.org and Tim Gorman of Joint Region Marianas. Procedures for exiting dry dock: Interview with John Vitzthum, *Naval Engineers Journal*, Sept. 2015.

For Marine Corps passages: Specs on M240 are from DM 3-22-68 (italicized material is quotes) and "M240B Machine Gun," USMC website. Mike Pasquini of the Crimson Lion in Wilkes-Barre read the hookah scene. Ramos's equipment description began with "The Modern Warrior's Combat Load: Dismounted Operations in Afghanistan April–May 2003," Task Force Devil, Coalition Task Force 82, Coalition Joint Task Force 180, *US Army Center for Lessons Learned*, combined with USMC input. Info on Itbayat coastline from Pub. 162, *Sailing Directions (Enroute) Philippine Islands*, National Geospatial Intelligence Agency, 2010. USMC structure: MCRP 5-12D, *Organization of Marine Corps Forces*. These chapters were read and commented on by Katie Davis and Peter Gibbons-Neff; many thanks to them and to Drew Davis for introducing us.

About China's "lost territories": Barbara Tuchman, *Stilwell and the American Experience in China 1911–1945*, (New York: Macmillan, 1971), p. 250.

My portrayal of the fictional USS *Hornet* was aided by bull sessions with crew and officers aboard USS *Wasp* (LHD-1), with subsequent availability for specific questions as they arose. Interlocutors included William Tonacchio, Dane Lathroum, Kurt Kastner, Toy Andrews, Mack Nolen,

Joe Towles, Andy Smith, and Todd Lewis. A deep bow to all for unfailing hospitality!

Discussion of Expeditionary Strike Group makeup: Michael Moran, *Modern Military Forces Structures*, Council on Foreign Relations, 2006.

USAF Rapid Capabilities Office: Lara Seligman et al., "As Industry Awaits Bomber Contract, New Details Emerge," *Defense News*, Sept. 5, 2015.

The following sources were valuable as background for tactics, mind-sets, and strategic decisions:

James D. Hornfischer, *Neptune's Inferno: The U.S. Navy at Guadalcanal*, (New York: Bantam Books, 2012).

Lisle A. Rose, *The Ship That Held the Line*, (Annapolis: Naval Insitute Press, 1995).

Joseph H. Alexander, *Storm Landings: Epic Amphibious Battles in the Central Pacific* (Annapolis: Naval Institute Press, 1997).

Wayne P. Hughes, *Fleet Tactics: Theory and Practice* (Annapolis: Naval Institute Press, 1986).

Contending with China issue, *Armed Forces Journal*, Apr. 2008.

Joint Operation Planning, Joint Publication 5-0, Joint Chiefs of Staff, 2011.

David Sears, *The Last Epic Naval Battle: Voices from Leyte Gulf* (Westport, CT: Praeger, 2005).

Dale C. Reilage, "The Imperative to Engage," *US Naval Institute Proceedings*, Apr. 2015.

Hunter Stiles, "1941 Asiatic Fleet Offers Strategic Lessons," *US Naval Institute Proceedings*, Aug. 2016.

The Future Surface Fleet issue, *Naval Institute Proceedings*, Jan. 2014.

David C. Gompert et al., "War with China: Thinking Through the Unthinkable" (Santa Monica: RAND, 2016).

For autonomous ships: IHS Engineering 360's "Unmanned Anti-Submarine Vessel Ready to Set Sail," Feb. 29, 2016.

The discussion of deterrence is from Joint Publication 3-12, "Doctrine for Joint Nuclear Operations" (unclassified).

The discussion of BMD was backgrounded by Jonathan Masters, "Your Pocket Guide to How U.S. Missile Defense Works," Council on Foreign Relations, Aug. 18, 2014. The discussion of the ground-based deterrent is from Robert Spalding and Adam Lowther, "Rethinking the Ground-Based Strategic Deterrent," *Breaking Defense*, Dec. 29,

2014; also, Amy F. Woolf, *U.S. Strategic Nuclear Forces: Background, Developments, and Issues*, Congressional Research Service, March 10, 2016. Also, from an unpublished thesis I did at George Washington University. On the DF-41: "DF-41 (CSS-X-10)," George C. Marshall and Claremont Institutes, *Missile Threat*, Mar. 22, 2016.

For Chinese empoyment of hackers: Katie Williams, "Chinese National Pleads Guilty to DOD Hacking Conspiracy," *The Hill*, Mar. 23, 2016.

For the Army point of view on joint operations: Dennis Steele, "The Hooah Guide to Pacific Land Power," *Army Magazine*, Apr. 2013. Also Nicholson and Trevithick, "The Army's New Role in the Pacific Pivot," *Naval Institute Proceedings*, Oct. 2015.

For Oberg's story, sources about Uighur resistance included Igor Rotar, "The Growing Problem of Uighur Separatism," *China Brief*, vol. 4, issue 8, Jamestown Foundation, accessed Nov. 23, 2015. Also Matthew Oresman and Daniel Steingart, "Radical Islamization in Xinjiang— Lessons from Chechnya?" *CACI Analyst*, July 30, 2003.

For background on helicopter crashes and survival thereof: Mike Hixenbaugh, "Training Gives Helicopter Crews a Shot at Survival," *Norfolk Virginian-Pilot*, Aug. 11, 2014. Also NATO RTO AG-341, *"Specification d'un respirateur de sauvetage pour aeronefs a voilure fixe et a voilure tournante en mission de survol maritime,"* May 2001. For trauma procedures: Dr. Frances Anagnost Williams. For Battle of Lake Erie: "We Have Met the Enemy," *Shipmate*, May–June 2012.

For overall help, recognition is due to Charle Ricci and Stacia Childers of the Eastern Shore Public Library; Matthew Stroup and Corey Barker of the Navy Office of Information, East; Mike Hatfield of Expeditionary Strike Group Three; and James DiAngio, Commander, Naval Surface Forces Atlantic. Deep bows to Mark "Dusty" Durstewitz, James W. Neuman, Bill Doughty, John T. Fusselman, and others (they know who they are), both retired and still on active duty, who put in many hours adding additional perspective. If I inadvertently left anyone out who wanted to be named, apologies!

Let me reemphasize that these sources were consulted for the purposes of *fiction*. The specifics of personalities, tactics, units, and locales are employed as the materials of story, not reportage. Some details have been altered to protect classified capabilities and procedures.

My deepest gratitude goes to George Witte, editor and friend of over three decades, without whom this series would not exist. And Sally

Richardson, Ken Silver, Sara Thwaite, Young Jin Lim, Adam Goldberger, Naia Poyer, and Anya Lichtenstein at St. Martin's/Macmillan. And finally to Lenore Hart, kindest critic, best friend, anchor on lee shores, and my North Star when skies are clear.

As always, all errors and deficiencies are my own.